T0096255

"Czyz creates an exciting thriller ne which challenges the traditional relig ic church, but all Christian sects."

—D. R. M 's

"Often, the best novels are difficult to categorize. Perhaps more often, novels that try to do too many things don't succeed at doing any of them particularly well. Fortunately, every now and then, a novel comes along that is both hard to define, yet exceptional at juggling multiple genres whose sum is even greater than its individual parts. Such a novel is *The Christos Mosaic*, which melds historical fiction with contemporary adventure and produces a compelling mystery that is as educational as it is entertaining."

— US Review of Books

"Vincent Czyz's *The Christos Mosaic* accomplishes the rare trick of having it both ways, delivering a fast-paced, action-packed storyline that challenges the mind rather than epileptically dazzling it with portentous piffle. This novel turns out to be the rare adventure story that rewards the reader's attention by being as diverting as it is rigorously encyclopedic.

—Matt Hanson, *The Arts Fuse*

"*Christos* puts the reader on Istanbul's every street corner—the cafés, bars and apartments—awash in the sights, sounds and even the smells of the city, and the colorful language and mannerisms of its inhabitants ... an impeccably framed thriller that will hopefully spark new discussions and provide insight into the future of Christian thought and study for the new century."

— James Campion, *Aquarian Weekly*

"I can't come up with enough superlatives to express how thoroughly, completely, hugely, immensely I enjoyed reading this novel. It's everything I could have wished for and much more. It must be read by as many people worldwide as possible. I have a gut feeling that it could effect a sea-change in the common understanding of Christianity. It's a masterful synthesis of solid scholarship and adventure."

—the late Paul Palmer, former assistant editor, *American Atheist*

THE CHRISTOS MOSAIC

A NOVEL

VINCENT CZYZ

Blank Slate Press | Saint Louis, MO

Blank Slate Press | Saint Louis, MO 63110
Blank Slate Press is an imprint of Amphorae Publishing Group, LLC
For information, contact info@amphoraepublishing.com
Amphorae Publishing Group | 4168 Hartford Street | Saint Louis, MO 63116

Publisher's Note: This book is a work of the imagination. Names, characters, places, organizations, and incidents either are products of the author's imagination or are used fictitiously. While some of the characters, organizations, and incidents portrayed here can be found in historical accounts, they have been altered and rearranged by the author to suit the strict purposes of storytelling. The book should be read solely as a work of fiction.

www.amphoraepublishing.com
www.blankslatepress.com
www.facebook.com/vincentczyz

Cover and Interior Design by Kristina Blank Makansi
Cover Photography:
Hagia Sofia by Dennis Jarvis from Halifax, Canada (Turkey-3019 - Hagia Sophia
Uploaded by russavia) [CC BY-SA 2.0 (http://creativecommons.org/licenses/
by-sa/2.0)], via Wikimedia Commons
Deesis Mosaic By Edal Anton Lefterov (Own work) [CC BY-SA 3.0 (http://creative-
commons.org/licenses/by-sa/3.0)], via Wikimedia Commons
Set in Adobe Caslon Pro and Felix Tilting
Manufactured in the United States of America

Library of Congress Control Number: 2015950846
ISBN: 9781943075041

I would like to dedicate this novel to my mother,
Louise Jaworski. A devout Catholic, she nonetheless understands
that her relationship with God is not more important than her
relationship with the people in her life.

I would like to dedicate this novel to my mother, Louise Jaworski. A devout Catholic, she nonetheless understands that her relationship with God is not more important than her relationship with the people in her life.

THE
CHRISTOS
MOSAIC

See page 528 for a list of historical figures and a timeline outlining major events from 198 BCE when Judea came under the control of the Seleucids to 120 AD when the Gospel of John begins circulating within the early Christian community.

Our age is retrospective. It builds the sepulchres of the fathers. It writes biographies, histories, and criticism. The foregoing generations beheld God and nature face to face; we, through their eyes. Why should not we also enjoy an original relation to the universe? Why should not we have a poetry and philosophy of insight and not of tradition, and a religion by revelation to us, and not the history of theirs? [...W]hy should we grope among the dry bones of the past, or put the living generation into masquerade out of its faded wardrobe? The sun shines to-day also. There is more wool and flax in the fields. There are new lands, new men, new thoughts. Let us demand our own works and laws and worship.

- Ralph Waldo Emerson, *Nature*

BOOK 1: 1 - 2

CONFEDERATES OF THE DEVIL

Though he was mortal, yet he was of great antiquity, and most fully gifted with every kind of knowledge, so that the mastery of a great many subjects and arts acquired for him the name Trismegistus [Thrice-Great]. He authored books and these in large number, relating to the nature of divine things, in which he avows the majesty of the supreme and only God and mentions Him by those titles which we Christians use—God and the Father.

— Lactantius, *Institutes*

1: 1

TWO WISE MEN

SAINTS LIE. At least as far as Drew was concerned, Saint Augustine had. The question was whether or not his paper presented a convincing argument. Uncharacteristically early for class, he was sitting at one of those minimalist desks that looked more like a chair with a paddle for an arm. His hands were probably as cold as the steel tubing the plywood seat was screwed into. It was the same chill that deadened them before a wrestling match. Today they were getting back their term papers—a hefty fifty percent of their final grades.

December light streamed through a row of tall windows. Drew could see the slate walks of the mall and the wilted lawns flecked with dead leaves. Laaksonen Hall was a nineteenth century brownstone renovated to accommodate classrooms, and from out there, he knew, the windows looked like bronze panels in the late-afternoon sun.

It probably hadn't been a good idea taking on a saint, especially the author of *City of God*, an epic tome written to explain why pagan Rome had stood for nearly a thousand years, but shortly after making Christianity its official religion, had been sacked by the Visigoths, presaging the disintegration of the empire. And then there was Augustine's *Confessions*, a sort of eternally bestselling memoir recounting the saint's spiritual conflicts. Professor de la Croix, as it happened, was particularly fond of Augustine, once remarking that he'd had more influence on Christianity than any writer since the apostle Paul.

Drew used to picture the saint, robed in black, habitually sequestering himself in a stone tower overlooking a shore of North Africa. There, as Drew imagined it, he peered down a corridor of time as if through a telescope, in search of the moment when God's infinite design had first been set in motion. Or, quill in hand, scratched out his meditations by oil lamp in such profound early-morning stillness he could hear the continents drift.

Drew's research, however, had revealed a very different Augustine, a cantankerous old man more interested in spin than truth. One chapter of *Confessions* was titled: "Whatever has been correctly said by the heathen is to be appropriated by Christians." In other words, if philosophers—particularly the Platonists—had said anything that agreed with Christianity, Augustine insisted it was up to Christians to claim it as their own since the pagans had "unlawful possession of it."

While church officials presided over book burnings, enthusiastically consigning to flames works now considered classics of antiquity, Augustine wrote a polemic declaring that "good men undertake wars," particularly when it is necessary "to punish" or to enforce "obedience to God." So much for Christ's call for love and compassion.

Drew's head turned when the door opened, but it was Jesse Fenton. Her skin pale, and her dark hair brutally short, she had a disarming smile and a sky-high IQ. At the fetish level, what Drew found irresistible was an abundance of freckles—forehead to chin and even the top of her chest. She nodded to him without quite smiling. They never saw each other outside of class, but there was a tacit understanding between them that they were the two best students.

Drew glanced down at his notes. As disappointed as he was in Augustine, he wasn't interested in exposing his faults. An English major with a minor in religion, he'd been caffeinated to the point of insomnia by the idea of welding the two disciplines together. While tracing the influence of the occult in Romantic poetry, he'd come across Augustine's critique of the *Corpus Hermeticum*, which, by the Middle Ages, had become a compendium for alchemists. There, in Augustine's argument, was a fabricated accusation; to put it bluntly, he'd lied.

Drew couldn't use Augustine's critique for his English course, but he'd found a place for it in de la Croix's New Testament class. He knew he'd written an A paper—he had a 4.0 within his major—but he was hoping for something extra, some kind of acknowledgment from Professor de la Croix that he'd done first-rate work.

The problem was she couldn't stand him. She made snide remarks when he walked in late. She called on him when she thought he wasn't paying attention, and was delighted when she was right. While he got good grades, there was always a grudging comment on his test or at the end of a paper.

The door opened again—Lisa. A girl so quiet Drew sometimes wondered if she wasn't some kind of nun keeping a vow of silence.

Professor de la Croix came in right behind her, an overstuffed briefcase and a stack of books under her arm. A short woman, she nonetheless did a pretty good job of blocking a doorway. Her gray hair, pulled back in a bun, had a metallic sheen, but a few wiry strays sprang out at random as if to spite her sense of order. And though she had put on a smear of orange lipstick, aside from not quite hitting the mark—something like a child's crayon job—it just didn't look right.

She let the books thump to her desk and appraised the class from behind a pair of glasses that were almost modern. Everything else she wore looked as if it had been rescued from an attic. She pulled their papers out of her briefcase and began handing them out as students trickled in.

"Miss Dent ..."

"Miss Fenton ..."

"Mr. Demko ..."

She called out names and returned papers until she had only one left. "Mr. Korchula ..."

Professor de la Croix fixed her gaze on Drew, but the white glare of the fluorescent lights on her glasses erased her eyes.

Drew's fingertips tingled.

Professor de la Croix slapped the paper on his desk, face down. "A particularly poor piece of scholarship," she muttered.

Drew's stomach lurched, as if he were on an elevator that had suddenly dipped.

Bending down, she whispered hoarsely, "A C- is a *gift*," and then headed up the aisle between desks.

"*C-?*" Drew was surprised by the force of his own voice.

Professor de la Croix turned to glare at him. "If you're going to call Saint Augustine a liar, you'd better back it up."

Faces swiveled toward him.

Drew cleared his throat. "Well, he ... made a false accusation."

Even Jesse looked skeptical. "How do you know?"

"Good question, Miss Fenton." With a twist of a smile, Professor de la Croix answered it: "He doesn't."

Ignoring the professor, Drew looked at Jesse. "Scholars who lived during the Renaissance assumed that the author of the *Corpus Hermeticum* was an Egyptian priest."

Professor de la Croix rolled her eyes. "Hermes Trismegistus, the supposed author, never existed. He was a fiction created by the Gnostics."

Drew conceded with a nod. "Yes, but Hermes was *thought* to have lived at about the same time as Moses—"

"In point of fact," Professor de la Croix interjected, "the *Corpus Hermeticum* was compiled in 100 AD at the earliest and probably closer to 300 AD, well after Christianity had been firmly established."

Drew pushed a wing of dark hair from his eyes. "But Augustine didn't know that. Augustine, like everyone else writing around the fifth century, believed that the *Corpus Hermeticum* was as old as the pyramids. And because Hermes refers to God the *Father* and uses the expression *Son of God*, and because he says God created the world through *a luminous word*, there were a lot of theologians who thought Hermes must have been a prophet who foresaw the coming of Christianity. Augustine denied this of course."

Professor de la Croix waved a hand dismissively. "Augustine saw through the absurdity of this Gnostic heresy."

"Yes, maybe, but according to Augustine, everything Hermes knew about Christianity came from the Devil." Drew flipped through the pages of his paper. "*Hermes presages these things as the Devil's confederate, suppressing evidence of the Christian name ...*" Drew looked up for a response.

"And who is to say he wasn't, Mr. Korchula? Who is to say that is not a valid explanation?"

Drew was too surprised to answer. It had never occurred to him that a college professor might consider the Devil as valid an explanation as an algebra equation or a logical proof. "Umm ... well, there *was* no one named Hermes Trismegistus, and the *Corpus Hermeticum* came *after* Christianity so ... so there was nothing to explain. But when Augustine *thought* Hermes knew about the future, and Augustine couldn't explain how a pagan could be a prophet, he just made something up about conferring with the Devil. He—"

"Oh enough of this rubbish! The Gnostics were plagiarists who, between them, never had an original idea. Nor do you, Mr. Korchula."

Drew was furious. His gaze slid over to Jesse, but she was looking down at her notebook. His best paper, probably in all four years of college, and the professor had just announced to the class it was crap.

"Just who are you to call Saint Augustine a liar? Have you ever written anything worth publishing? Let alone texts that have been studied for a millennium and a half."

"No, but I haven't written any lies lately, either." His voice cracked on *lies*.

"This from a student who can't seem to make it to class on time— *when* he bothers to come."

Drew had missed only three classes. "Christianity," he shot back, "was a little late too, don't you think?"

Professor de la Croix put the back of her hand on her hip and took off her glasses. "What is that supposed to mean?"

Drew's paper was no longer the issue. Neither was his grade. PhD or not, de la Croix was wrong. "Religion is what? About 30,000 years old? If we call those paintings in Lascaux and Alta Mira religious? Assuming a Christian God has been up there all this time, why did He wait 28,000 years to put in an appearance? Isn't it kind of a cruel joke to leave human beings in the dark with all those pagan gods the saints insist were really demons? I mean, those guys painting in caves? Why not give them a little light to work by? Why not give them a ... a goddamn *clue?*"

Her eyes narrowed. "How dare you use profanity in my classroom."

Drew had to hold onto the arm of his desk to keep his hand from shaking. "Yeah, okay, sorry, but you haven't answered my question."

"You are lucky, Mr. Korchula, extremely lucky that I tolerate your presence at all. As to your question, which involves thousands of years that are utterly dark to those of us in modern times, who can possibly know? Who are we, after all, to question the ways of God?"

Drew looked to the other students, but he could tell from their faces he wasn't going to get any support. "I thought this was a university, not Sunday school."

Professor de la Croix slammed a desk with the heel of her hand. "Get out! Out of my class!"

Gathering up his books, Drew glanced at Jesse, hoping she would say something in his defense. All he got was a sympathetic look.

"I will not tolerate that kind of disrespectful back-talk from a student."

As he left the classroom, the professor's words pelting his back, he wasn't sure if the backs of his ears were burning from anger or humiliation.

Let's see what the head of the religion department has to say about your C-.

1: 2

BYZANTIUM

WHENEVER HE CAME ACROSS the word, he instinctively imagined the letters embossed on gold foil. It reminded him of Yeats's gold-enameled bird singing to keep drowsy emperors awake. Of Constantine the Great's bronze lions that—powered by steam—actually roared. Sitting in Professor Wittier's office, it was hard *not* to think of Byzantium; along with the antique desk, a fountain pen in a gleaming holder weighted by a marble base, and bookshelves fitted with glass doors and brass hinges, there were several Byzantine icons—Jesus among them. The Savior's robes, a rich red, looked as though they had been stained by smoke. They contrasted with a gilded background that had lost much of its shimmer. Although gold doesn't tarnish, this was paint webbed by fine cracks. All of the icons looked as though they had been rescued from a fire—the colors sooty, and the parched wood beginning to split along the grain—but the fire was just time, time consuming everything at an imperceptible smolder.

A short man with a receding hairline, Professor Wittier had dressed up the informality of his jeans with a herringbone jacket. He had puffy eyelids that made him seem permanently sleepy and, like his mahogany desk, fit in perfectly with the Old World look of his office.

"Look, Drew, you're a bright kid, but some of your comments, you have to admit, were a little inflammatory." He sighed heavily. "Couldn't you have just said *darn?*"

"I know I shouldn't have said that, but it's one ... little ... word."

"The universe began with a word."

"Yeah, I guess. But my paper has about five thousand of them." Drew's hair was pulled back in a ponytail, and he'd tucked a button-up shirt into a pair of black jeans. "Couldn't we give that a little more attention? I mean, do you think it's C- work? Can't she be brought up in front of a board for being unprofessional...?"

Professor Wittier leaned forward. "Look, Professor de la Croix was angry, she stepped a little over the line. And, no, your paper isn't C- work. You'll get a B+. I'll see to that."

"But—"

"You would have gotten your A if you had just been a little more ... *diplomatic* in the classroom. I hope, at least, that you've learned something from this incident."

Drew smiled bitterly. "I learned that if Professor de la Croix can't attack my work, she'll attack *me*."

Professor Wittier laced his fingers together and lowered his eyebrows. "Drew, let me ask you something. You're an English major ... are you planning to teach?"

"I really don't know. I just ... I enjoy reading." He shrugged.

"Well, chances are with an English major that's exactly what you're going to do at some point or another—teach. Now I'm not saying Professor de la Croix is right, but in a few years, if you're running a classroom, you might have a little more sympathy for her position. Don't forget that, like the rest of our staff, she has put decades of research into her subject. Sometimes, I'll admit ..." He waffled a hand. "Sometimes we're a little too sure of ourselves, that's all."

Drew nodded. This office with its rustle of paper, its air faintly musty with the dust-covered wisdom that lined the shelves, its corners and niches where shadow was a reminder that so much more had been lost beneath the crush of history than could ever be imagined—let alone retrieved—yes, he could spend any number of hours in an office like this. But a classroom...?

"Can I ask you something a little off-topic here, Drew? Your last name is Korchula. Where does that come from?"

"My father's Croatian," Drew answered. "We're named after a town. And my mother's Gypsy." He purposely left out the indefinite article to indicate his mother's ethnicity rather than comment on her personality.

"Quite a mix. I suppose I can see it now."

Drew was dark-skinned enough to make people wonder about his ethnic background. Prominent cheekbones and eyebrows that slashed down at a sharp angle gave his eyes something of the Asian, although his nose and the rest of his face had the straight lines and right angles most people associated with Westerners. He lifted his chin. "Are those icons authentic?"

Professor Wittier glanced back at them. "Ah … they're beautiful, aren't they? Yes, they're genuine. I picked them up at the Grand Bazaar in Istanbul. Even after bargaining to get the price down, I paid quite a bit for them."

Rain tapped against the glass of the office windows.

"You're a senior, aren't you, Drew?" Professor Wittier lifted his graying eyebrows. "One more semester and it's out into the world, right?"

Drew nodded. *Yeah. Out. Then what? Grad school? Peace Corps?* He had no idea.

Professor Wittier stood and skirted the edge of his desk. "So let's just put this whole thing behind us, shall we?"

Drew pushed out of his chair. "Sure."

Wittier gave him a friendly pat on the back as he opened the door and shook his hand. "Keep up the good work, but keep it clean, okay?"

So that's it, Drew thought as he walked down the hall. One of the best papers he'd ever written gets a B+. Pulling on an old pea coat, he slid his hands into the worn pockets and walked out into a cold drizzle. The mall was lined with venerable brownstones half-covered with ivy.

It was only December, but he had begun to worry about May: what was he going to do after graduation? His father kept asking him the same question.

"You don't wanna teach so what the hell kinda work you gonna find? You wanna drive a truck like me with your fancy diploma?" His father was up at four every morning to deliver cold cuts. "You know what BS stands for, right? *Bullshit.* MS? *More shit.* And PhD is just piled higher and deeper." His father would drag on a cigarette. "What you really need, is a *jay oh bee,* so you can pay back those loans."

Drew's father was a practical Slav. He didn't understand the point of an expensive education that couldn't be converted into a job paying a lot more than his.

"And what did you study? Stories that never happened. They call it *lidderacher* like it's important. What the hell is the point if it never happened?"

Drew had never been able to answer his father. He couldn't even appeal to the storytelling tradition of the Gypsies—Drew's mother was the only Gypsy his father liked.

The one rule Drew set for himself when he'd started college was that he enjoy the next four years. And he had. While some students were doing indifference-curve analysis in microeconomics or working out integrals in calculus, he was reading a Greek play or buzzing through a chapter in a Dickens novel. But now that the trees had lost their leaves and the weather had turned cold, the feeling he found himself facing wasn't anxiety; it was dread.

"Hey."

Her voice startled him.

"Deep in thought?" Freckles, disarming smile, and short, dark hair safe under a paisley umbrella, Jesse was looking up at him.

His own hair was beginning to soak through. "Yeah, I guess I was."

"You have your powwow with Wittier?"

"Just now."

"And?"

I got a B+."

"Not bad."

He pulled his head back, a contrived grimace expressing a mixture of disbelief and disgust.

"All right." Raising her eyebrows and pressing her lips together, Jesse nodded. "For *us* a B+ is an unmitigated disaster. But you'll still ace the course."

"That's not the point."

"I think you made your point. And I owe you an apology. I shouldn't have just sat there."

Drew shook his head. "Nah ..." The apology made something in his chest that had been uncomfortably tight go slack.

"I'm not saying I totally agree with you, but Professor de la Croix was wrong to turn it into a personal attack."

"Well, it's done with."

"Yeah, I guess. Just remember, there are more things under heaven and Earth than are dreamt of in your philosophy." She smiled again, and shallow dimples deepened among the freckles. "Horatio."

He nodded appreciatively. "*Hamlet* is Shakespeare's best if you ask me."

This was the first time they'd ever spoken outside of class. It was also the first time their conversation had gone beyond theology, and he was suddenly desperate to spend the drizzly December afternoon with her.

"I don't know about the play, but the line definitely suits you … you're just a little too enamored of logic."

He nodded. "Maybe." For a long second he listened to rain drum lightly on her paisley umbrella. "How about hitting Café Insomnia for a coffee or something?"

The rain came down harder, and the drumming intensified.

"I'd love to, but I'm meeting my boyfriend in about fifteen minutes."

Maybe because it was unexpected, the word *boyfriend* stung almost as much as what Professor de la Croix had said about his paper. A little too quickly he asked, "Another time, maybe?" He knew there wouldn't be.

"I'll see you at the final." She snickered. "Horatio."

He watched her cross the mall wondering what her boyfriend was like.

Long hair hanging down his back like drenched seaweed, Drew started toward the dorm. *Nothing*, he decided, *is as gray as rain on a sidewalk*. Under his breath he said, "Byzantium." And the gray was back-grounded by gold.

BOOK 2: 1 - 7

MARKET OF SECONDHAND BOOKSELLERS

Yale University has announced the discovery of the oldest extant manuscript of the Book of Isaiah. The manuscript was brought to light in the Syrian monastery of St. Mark in Jerusalem. Written on a scroll of parchment dating to the first century BC, it was identified by American scholars conducting research in Jerusalem.

— *The Times*, April 11, 1948

2: 1

ISTANBUL

Ex *ORIENTE LUX. OUT OF THE EAST, LIGHT.* Late afternoon cast a glow on Beyazit Square. That was one of the things Drew loved about Istanbul—the light. Sometimes it seemed almost solid as it slanted down. Other times, like today, it gave the weathered stone of Beyazit Mosque and the other Ottoman buildings a kind of halo. Paved with cobblestones and shaded by ancient trees, the square was dominated by the mosque on its eastern side, and, to the west, the massive stone gateway of Istanbul University. An arch rising to a height of fifty or sixty feet, the gate was flanked by a pair of dwarf towers, crenellated but unimposing.

Pigeons rose in a confusion of flapping wings at his approach.

He had ended up, as Professor Wittier had predicted more than a decade ago, teaching. Nothing that required a PhD, though, just English as a foreign language. He'd scored high enough on the GRE to get in just about anywhere, but he'd never applied to graduate school. He still turned the idea around in his head, like a curio, examining it from different angles, but then he'd gaze out his apartment window at the spectacular view of the Sea of Marmara and the Golden Horn—a finger of the Bosporus Strait that pointed west—and put off the decision. Grad school would be books of critical theory and novels that had to be read in a week, all-nighters and thirty-page term papers. He didn't know if he could bring himself to do it, not when he'd gotten used to a teaching load of only twenty hours a week, to long summers traipsing around the Mediterranean and Europe, to lazy weekends raiding secondhand bookstores and antique shops. One other thing held him in Istanbul: it was easier to be a failure abroad. He didn't run into old friends, and even when he flew back home for a visit, he had the air of an adventurer.

He glanced up at Istanbul University's arch, at the permanently stopped clock in the form of Roman numerals engraved near the top: MCDLIII—1453, the year Constantinople fell to Mehmet the Conqueror. The year Constantinople ceased to be Byzantine, ceased to be Christian, ceased to be the guardian of Rome's legacy. It was also the year the university had been founded. The mosque and the square had been named after Sultan Beyazit II, Mehmet's grandson, who lay entombed in a courtyard garden beside the mosque.

A backpack slung over his shoulder, Drew passed under the far less impressive archway of Sahaflar Charsisi—the Market of Secondhand Booksellers. Canopied by trees and vines that broke sunlight into jigsaw pieces, the secluded courtyard was home to an enclave of chain-smoking dealers whose stalls and shops carried the odd, the obsolete, the sordid, the antique, the counterfeit, the pirated. Generally in English, French, German, Arabic, and of course, Turkish. Booksellers had been congregating here since in the seventeenth century, when they had vacated their stalls in the Grand Bazaar.

The shops were like family mausoleums that had been in use too long; only the more recent arrivals and the most prized editions rated indoor shelving. The rest were heaped up in front, obscuring display windows and clogging doorways. These tended to be out-of-print paperbacks with lurid titles. Those on the bottom—the pages water-stained, the garish covers faded and gritty with soot—would likely turn to compost before they were ever bought. But the sellers, smoking in front of their shops, held onto them. Drew regularly sorted through the teetering stacks and occasionally came upon a hard-to-find gem or a ridiculously underpriced first edition.

The market narrowed to a broad alley as he walked.

One of the shopkeepers, a dwarf, slid off a long-legged stool and grinned. In spite of the balmy weather, Kadir wore jeans cuffed at the hems, sneakers too dirty to be called white, and a black leather vest that sagged with age and with whatever had been stuffed into its half dozen pockets.

"Look who comes! The only donkey I've never seen before with two legs."

"*Ever* seen," Drew corrected.

Kadir's shop sheltered under a lush tangle of vines. Although Drew's Turkish was fluent, Kadir always spoke to him in English—he enjoyed the free lessons.

"So you admit it?" Kadir smirked.

"I admit it's painful listening to your English. And your stall smells like you keep a goat in it."

"At your borning time, you came out from a wrong hole, I think."

Drew shook his head. "When you were *born* …"

Kadir's abrasiveness was a callus the dwarf had grown while making his way through a city in which he faced humiliations foreign to someone of normal stature. He needed a ladder to reach books in his shop that were eye-level for Drew; packs of kids sometimes followed behind him, imitating his side-to-side tilt as he walked; he couldn't see over the dashboard of a car, and because his legs were so short, phonebooks wouldn't help if he wanted to drive. Kadir's features, however, were well-proportioned—no bulbous forehead, no blob of a nose. His nose actually had a certain nobility to it, as if it had been taken from a Greek bust. Admittedly though, his head belonged on a larger body.

"Anything worth my while come in?"

Kadir shrugged. "Are you sure you are capable to read?"

Drew rolled his eyes. "In English, Turkish, *and* Greek. If I couldn't, you'd have gone out of business a long time ago. I mean, who would buy pulp like this?" From one of the leaning stacks outside the shop, Drew picked up a disintegrating paperback. "*Warlords of Mars?* The pages are falling out." He reached for another. "*She Walks by Night?*" Drew read from the cover: "*She climbed a ladder of lovers into the lap of luxury.*"

The dwarf shrugged.

Stepping inside the shop, Drew was surprised to find someone sitting at Kadir's tiny desk.

"Good day." The man nodded to him and smiled. Swarthy, his black hair tightly curled, he looked North African. He wore a skullcap of white wool and a sort of white gown called a *jalabiya*.

"He is Tariq, a friend of me from Cairo. He looks for bargains in Istanbul."

"And I have found these!" Tariq held up stack of thoroughly dilapidated books from the eighteenth or nineteenth century. "The one on top is a prayer book once owned by Sultan Selim III. I know a collector in Cairo who will give a very good price for it. Once it has been restored, of course."

"You see, American infidel?" Kadir said. "This makes more worth than all the books outside added together."

"Is *worth* more ..."

Finishing the tea in his tiny tulip glass, Tariq stood up. "I will be going now, Kadir. We will see each other soon, *inshallah*."

"*Inshallah*."

Tariq nodded affably to Drew.

Half-heartedly, Drew scanned the creased paperbacks and aging hardcovers with their torn dust jackets, but they were all familiar.

"I'm heading out, Kadir." Drew hiked the straps of his knapsack over a shoulder.

"One moment, please." Kadir waddled to the register and came back with a flat box wrapped in brown paper.

"What's that?"

"An old book. Please, for one night, let it stay next to you."

"Why? Don't you lock the place up when you go home?"

"Tariq is the friend of me, but sometimes competitor men are following him. Such men can be know the way to open locks, without keys."

"Black market competition, huh?" Drew thought of the massive iron doors at the arched entrances to the market, which were swung closed and locked every night. "It's not for me, Kadir. Don't you have other friends? A sister somewhere?"

"But in a hundred years they cannot think of you! One night, *dostum*, that's all."

Drew hefted the box, which was flat, wide, and not very heavy. "All right." He slid his knapsack off his shoulder and dropped it between zippered teeth.

"Keep it in a safety place."

Drew put his knapsack back on, wondering what Kadir had given him. Arabic calligraphy Tariq had brought from Egypt? No, it was too heavy for that. An old book written in Coptic? And why had Tariq brought it to Istanbul? Unless he knew a seller here and Kadir was the middleman. The more Drew thought about it, the more he wanted to open the box.

2: 2

MERE INK ON PAPER

DAY HAD FADED to a glow in the west, and the sky over the Golden Horn was a blue deeper than any length of velvet a jeweler might spread to display his diamonds. When had the sky been such a perfect veil between heaven and Earth? Perhaps Tariq only saw it that way because he would soon be a wealthy man. Behind him, the minarets of the New Mosque were lit up as though to attract the faithful. A mere three or four centuries old, the mosque was indeed new compared to the treasures of Egypt.

Istanbul, which had given up the anarchy of the Arab bazaar in exchange for a façade of European enlightenment, was not nearly as noisy or crowded as Cairo. And it was surrounded by water—the Bosporus, the Black Sea, the Sea of Marmara, the Golden Horn. Cairo of course had the Nile—the life-giving Nile—but only the Nile. Here the August wind was neither burning nor ragged with sand. Perhaps, after he found a buyer, he and his family would settle in Istanbul. The scrolls would bring him more than enough money to leave Egypt—perhaps a million US dollars! It was not an unreasonable price. To many people, they were nothing more than ink on paper, but mere words were sometimes enough to ignite wars.

And now Kadir was holding his guarantee of safety.

Tires shrieked and Tariq whipped his head around. Two Turks

jumped out of their cars and began shouting at each other. Roads merged in complicated intersections here because of the bridge spanning the Golden Horn.

"Less traffic than Cairo perhaps," Tariq said to himself, "but drivers are just as impatient."

He leaned on the steel railing of a quay along the Golden Horn, which reflected colored lights from restaurants tucked under the bridge. Peering into the water, dark and sparkling at the same time, he smiled as he waved to fish he could not see.

"Tariq."

He flinched and turned toward a man not more than a meter away. He didn't recognize him. Tariq looked to his left and realized there were two men. Leaning casually on the quay's railing, they had taken up positions on either side of him. One was likely Egyptian, but the other, with his pale skin and red hair, was almost certainly a Westerner. Perhaps American or British.

"How do you know my name?"

"Your name isn't all we know."

The Egyptian spoke to him in Arabic. Tariq straightened up. Had he seen them before?

"We know you did business with Abu Kobisy until his death a few weeks ago."

Yes! He had seen the redheaded one before. In Cairo. "Peace be upon Abu. He was a good man. A fair man." Had they followed him?

"But you haven't been entirely fair to him. Have you?"

"Why do you say this?"

"We know what you took."

Tariq scanned the crowded quay and busy street, calculating his chances of escape. "It's in a safe place. If anything happens to me—"

"If anything happens to you, I guess we'll have to deal with the dwarf."

They knew! Tariq's heart began to pound as though trapped.

One of the men put a hand on his arm, but Tariq jerked it away and sprinted across the quay.

"Wait! Tariq!"

The men took off after him.

"We just want to talk!"

Tariq knocked over a woman, who shouted at him in Turkish.

"*Tariq*! You don't understand!"

Tariq darted into the road, and a taxi skidded to a stop inches from his hip. Legs trembling, *jalabiya* flapping in the breeze, he was unsure which direction to take.

"Tariq!" The Egyptian one would reach him in a few more steps.

Leaping away from his pursuer, he stumbled over the curb of an island separating two roads and staggered into traffic. The rubber of locked wheels screeched as a truck slammed into him, catapulting him into the air.

The men who had given chase watched his body smack against pavement sixty or seventy feet from the truck, roll a few times, and flop to a stop.

A crowd surged into the street and gathered around the fallen man.

Faces turned toward the two men, but they were walking briskly toward Galata Bridge.

2: 3

A THOUSAND PLACES OF MISRULE

GALATA TOWER LOOMED on Drew's right, illuminated for the tourists. Straight as a minaret but stout, almost squat, it had a conical roof that reminded Drew of a witch's hat. He was fond of this quarter with its eroding tenements and cobblestone streets winding up and downhill.

Whenever a cross street broke the wall of buildings on his left, he could see the dark mirror of the Bosporus and the Asian shore dotted with lights.

End of Empire. That's what they should call these neighborhoods of neoclassical buildings that had lost their grandeur and been converted into apartment buildings. He passed cracked marble steps, fluted pilasters stained by coal smoke, huge double doors that creaked on rusty hinges and opened onto dank stairwells.

In Ottoman times Galata had been teeming with sailors from all over the Mediterranean. Like any port town, it had had more than its share of taverns. One seventeenth century Ottoman, writing with the disdain of a Muslim who abstains from alcohol, claimed that Constantinople had "a thousand places of misrule."

Drew had been a little unruly himself that evening. He'd met a few friends at Timur the Lame's, where he'd downed one pint too many. There had been a chorus of protests when he got up to leave, and although he smiled when somebody tugged at him to keep him in his chair, he missed

Yasemin in a way that being around other people only made worse.

Pain was supposed to be like glass in the sea: after a few years, it should be worn smooth. Hard, but no longer sharp. But that hadn't happened. After two years, the divorce hurt as much as it had after two weeks.

A little unsteady on his feet, he walked down the hill in the warm night air.

From somewhere within the labyrinth of dark streets, he heard the cry of a *boza* seller, who sounded not as though he was hawking fermented slush out of a vat-sized bucket, but as though he were calling to a lost child. Or wife.

Christ it was hard sometimes, living in the city where he and Yasemin had met.

Drew turned down his street, hardly more than an alley just below Galata Tower.

Standing in the recess of the doorway across from his building was one of those Turks who probably conducted business by the light of a street lamp—part of the shadow population of the city. A couple of inches shorter than Drew, he was broader and a lot thicker. Shoulders, head, and neck of a bull, all he needed were the horns.

They exchanged glances, and Drew wondered if the guy had decided to roll him. Trying not to look drunk, he kept the Turk in his peripheral vision while he stuck a key in the lock. He yanked hard on the steel door—the goddamn thing was as heavy as the stone lid of a crypt.

The man crossed the street. "*Bey Efendi,* one moment—"

Drew ignored him and let the door swing closed under its own weight. He heard the lock click and went up the staircase. His apartment was at the top, the fourth floor.

Another shout of "*Bey Efendi!*" was muted by the stone walls of the old building. "One moment, please!"

Not tonight, Drew thought. There was a reason, after all, that the first- and second-floor windows in this neighborhood were barred.

Drew let himself into his apartment, closed the door, and turned on a light.

Books were strewn all over the hallway that ran the length of the flat. Had he been ... robbed?

One of the floorboards creaked loudly under Drew's foot. He stopped and listened.

All he heard was his own suppressed breathing. *What the hell am I doing?* He hit the switch to the bedroom light, but nothing happened. A fried bulb?

There was a silent explosion of light, and the floor buckled underneath him—no, his knees had caved in.

Somehow he managed to keep his feet, but a shoulder to his chest knocked him against a wall, and a man shoved past him. He caught a fist in the gut, sank to the floor, and had to fight for his next breath.

The front door opened, and he heard another set of footsteps in the hall.

Damn. He had to suck hard to get air. He'd felt something like this during wrestling matches when he was so tired he just wanted to quit.

Someone was coming up the stairs.

With a grunt and a wince, Drew got to his feet.

Before he was able to close the door—now flung wide open—the Turk he'd seen on the street stepped inside.

"*Iyimisiniz?*" Are you all right?

"Who the hell are you?"

"Zafer. Kadir sent me to keep an eye on you."

"I guess he picked the wrong guy."

"Did they get anything?"

"*I* got something—I got my ass kicked."

"Sorry about that. But I only came a few minutes before you. I rang the bell …" He shrugged. "Why didn't you wait when I called you?"

"Because I'm a little drunk, and you don't look like the kind of guy I should be letting in the building at night."

Zafer smiled. "You prefer men in suits?"

"I prefer not to get cold-cocked when I walk into my own home."

"Cold-cocked?"

"Clocked when I'm not looking."

"Ah, you mean sucker punched."

It wasn't until Zafer's face had eased into a smile again that Drew realized he had a certain crude charm and a square jaw that belonged on a steam shovel—one you could probably break a knuckle on. His curly black hair was short and his forehead tapered a little towards his hairline. No gray. A few creases in the corners of eyes more Asian than Western, he looked to be in his late twenties.

"Your slang's pretty good."

"American movies. Did they find the package?"

Drew glared at him. "What exactly did Kadir give me?"

"*Bilmiyorum.*"

"You don't know? Well, I doubt they got what they were looking for because it's not in my flat." Drew pointed at the ceiling. "It's on the roof."

Drew went out the door again, up another flight of stairs. Zafer followed.

Istanbul was all shadow and glitter below them. Ships, like floating lanterns, moved slowly through the Golden Horn.

Sections of rectangular duct had been stacked against a parapet. Drew reached into one and pulled out the flat package. It looked about the right size for copy paper, maybe a couple hundred sheets. *What the fuck was in here?*

Zafer held out a large hand. "You can give it to me."

"I don't think so."

"It belongs to Kadir."

"Kadir almost got me killed."

Zafer stepped toward Drew. "You shouldn't—"

"Back off or I'll toss this thing as far as I can. Onto some other roof."

"Okay …" Zafer pulled his hand back and held it up as a gesture of submission. "Open it."

Drew tore away the brown paper. The box underneath had no markings. He lifted the top flap and squeezed his hand inside.

Zafer stepped forward to get a closer look.

"I don't believe this."

Zafer shook his head. "Me neither."

2: 4

A TEMPESTUOUS SAGA

WALLED-IN ON ALL SIDES as though they were eunuchs in a harem, dealers were just opening their shops and setting out their wares under a canopy of leafy vines. Several men standing in front of Kadir's shop shook their heads and clicked their tongues. His stall had been broken into. Entire shelves had been cleared, and aging books with weak spines had given up many of their pages. Kadir picked up two weighty volumes, one in each hand, but then despaired about what to do with them and simply held them out.

That was how Drew found him—looking like a strange bird with wings too heavy to flap.

"Yaaaa," Kadir moaned. "Look what has been done with my shop." His arms sank to his sides.

"They did the same thing to my apartment." Drew was standing in the doorway of Kadir's ruined livelihood. "And for what?" He pulled the box Kadir had given him out of his knapsack and turned it over. A faded paperback fell out and slapped the tiny Turkish rug at his feet. "*Bastard Prince of T'orrh?*"

Kadir stepped around Drew. Dappled with sun and splotched with shade, the dwarf looked almost like he was wearing military camouflage. He held up his hands, stubby fingers splayed, and addressed the other dealers in Turkish. "My friends, thank you for your kind wishes, but please … return to your shops. My friend and I will clean up."

Reluctantly, the other dealers retreated.

"*Salak!*" Kadir lowered his black eyebrows. "Some of these men are knowing English."

"So what? All you gave me was …" Drew looked down and read from the cover: "*The tempestuous saga of a man, wrongfully dispossessed, battling to regain the throne of an alien planet.* I thought you gave me a—I don't know—hieroglyphics or something."

"To you I gave nothing. To them I gave an idea of you are given something."

"What did they *think* I had, Kadir? And who are *they?*"

Kadir tapped his head. "If a few amount of people are knowing a secret, the chances are increase that no one will learn this secret."

"Kadir, they were in my *apartment.* I could've been hospitalized. Or killed. I have a right to know why."

Kadir ambled into the shop and took a Turkish newspaper from his desk. He handed it to Drew.

Drew translated a page three headline—*Egyptian Tourist Killed in Traffic Accident.* The photograph didn't show much more than police pushing back a small crowd of onlookers, but the man who'd been killed was identified as Tariq Soufanati. Police had ruled the death an accident, but they were looking for two men who witnesses said had been chasing him just before he'd been hit by a truck. They were believed to be foreigners.

"I'm sorry, Kadir. I didn't know."

"Tariq and I we are like brothers. Why else does he give so much trust to me?" Kadir shook his oversized head, stuck three fingers in a vest pocket, and pulled out a box of Marlboros. From another pocket he fished out an antique lighter. He liked to call the tattered vest—its black leather worn gray where it had suffered the most—his flak jacket, a term he'd picked up from some pulp novel about the Vietnam War. He lit his cigarette and exhaled. "You have nothing. They understand this. It is I who is dangerous now. But they cannot kill me like Tariq."

"Why not?"

"Because of Tariq gave me something they are wanting."

"If you give it back, they won't want to kill you."

"If it is given back, there is nothing for bargaining."

"What exactly did Tariq give you?"

"Are you want to become like Tariq? If you forget about this, they will forget about you."

"C'mon, Kadir. I have to see what Tariq got killed for."

Kadir shook his head. "I am thinking it is a bad idea."

"Then you shouldn't have given me that goddamn package in the first place," Drew hissed. "You *owe* me."

Somebody behind Drew whistled loudly. Drew whirled around.

"What a mess!" Zafer shook his head.

Kadir gestured to Zafer. *"Bana yardim etsene." Why don't you help me out?*

The dwarf and the much larger man stood a piece of shelving shaped like a section of bleachers on end and blocked the shop doorway with it.

"You're going to leave your place like that?" Drew jerked his thumb at the makeshift barricade.

"My friends will be watch." Kadir dropped the cigarette on the ground and crushed it under a sneaker. "I want something more strong for smoking. Let's go *narghile* café. There we are able to talk."

As Drew followed the Turks, he noticed a leather satchel resting against Zafer's hip and realized it probably held what Tariq's killers had been looking for.

2:5

THE SCROLLS

THE *NARGHILE* CAFÉ was tucked inside a sixteenth century courtyard behind a thoroughfare along which the tram rumbled. An untended graveyard—its slim tombstones leaning or fallen—would have spilled out onto the sidewalk were it not for a stone wall pitted with age and streaked with soot. The wall's unglazed windows were gridded by iron bars. Through this Cartesian space they could see a man with a hefty paunch rearranging tables and chairs on a patio behind the tiny cemetery.

Kadir rattled the gate. "Tolga, you son of a whore, let us in! We want to smoke."

"Why don't you fuck off, Kadir? I only serve tourists these days, and they haven't even eaten breakfast yet."

"Here's a tourist." Kadir slapped Drew's thigh. "He asked me to take him to the shittiest *narghile* café in Istanbul. Where else could I bring him?"

Tolga, his wavy, gray hair speckled with black, grinned and unlocked the gate. He bent down so he and Kadir could exchange a kiss on each cheek. When Tolga straightened up, the belly of his shirt puckered around its buttons. He turned to Drew and said, "Welcome."

Judging from his pronunciation, Drew guessed that was the extent of his English. "*Hosh bulduk,*" he replied. *Nice to be here.*

The courtyard proper, a marble fountain at its center, was hidden behind a procession of stone columns supporting a vaulted ceiling made of the wide, flat bricks used by the Byzantines and Ottomans. Stained with age and smoke, the bricks were almost black, while the walls had been plastered smooth and whitewashed.

The three men sat at a low table. The tiny stools—relics of centuries past—were made of twine and wood.

Kadir grinned. "You see? Many years ago, Turks are my size."

Drew's knees were almost up to his chin.

Zafer and Kadir shared a *narghile*, but Drew had one to himself. The glass of his was blue; theirs was green.

Hookah in Arabic, a *narghile* always reminded Drew of a genie's bottle except that its mouth was plugged with a clay stem that ended in a small brass bowl with a brim to catch ashes. Perforated tin foil separated the tobacco from the hot embers Tolga placed on top with a pair of tongs.

"You're lucky. A few are still hot from last night." Tolga was standing under an iron chandelier that hung down from a vault. Although it had once held wax candles in upside-down glass bells, the candles were now electric.

"And a Turkish coffee," Kadir said.

"Right away. At double the usual price, of course, since I don't feel like being open." Tolga winked at Drew.

"This is just what we would expect from a man with no honor."

Drew smiled. The insult would have lost all its zing in English. A man without honor was usually a pimp, and that implied your mother was among the women who worked for you.

Tolga walked off, shaking his head. "Son of a donkey."

Drew inhaled deeply; the *narghile* bubbled. He didn't smoke cigarettes, but the apple tobacco was mild enough that it didn't make him cough. What he exhaled was as white as winter breath. "So, tell me about Tariq."

"Tariq was a … *ne demek*? A runner. This means he is also a thief of graves."

"A grave-robber."

Kadir's dark face emerged from swirling white. "He sells antique things to dealers. Dealers sell to collectors. A collector who is called Abu Kobisy was paying very much money for these things, but one month earlier, he died. After Abu was died, a servant stole a manuscript of Abu.

He gave to Tariq. Tariq brought this scroll to Istanbul."

"A scroll?"

Kadir held up a stubby finger. "Wait, please, for whole story. There is another manuscript. Tariq did not have."

"Another scroll? Who has it?"

"A farmer maybe."

"A farmer? What would a farmer be doing with an ancient manuscript?"

Kadir shook his head. "So little you are knowing, infidel. Sixty years before, an Arab shepherd discovered many scrolls of Dead Sea." Kadir wagged a finger. "You think I am only a seller of antique prayer books and shitty novels? Listen, a Norwegian rich man bought very tiny pieces of Dead Sea Scrolls. Each piece was written with only one letter. For five letters he gave 25,000 US dollars. You see how much valuable these old writings are? Twenty pieces and you are getting 100,000 dollars US." Kadir's eyes widened. "Think of a whole scroll!"

"Jesus."

Zafer inhaled and the *narghile* bubbled.

"You see the why I am studying so much English? I make searches on the Internet. I am reading *New York Times* online. My speaking isn't so well, but I am understand everything."

Drew glanced at Zafer. The stem of the *narghile* poked out of the corner of Zafer's mouth. He drew on the pipe deeply, held his breath for a second, then let a leisurely cloud of white curl toward the ceiling. Zafer's eyes, which looked almost sleepy behind the intermittent smoke, were on Drew.

Drew turned to Kadir. "What did Tariq need you for?"

"In Cairo he couldn't sell the robbed scroll. Cairo is the most big black market in the world for antique things, but in Cairo, everyone is knowing Tariq. Everyone is knowing Abu Kobisy. And there is another problem. This scroll was already sold."

"Sold? What do you mean?"

"Abu made a promise. He would not sell it until he was dead."

"He left it in his will?"

"No. The purchaser did not want his name in Abu's will. Wills are bringing lawyers. Abu was a very rich man, a very big man in Cairo. Abu gave his promise—"

"Ahhh ... now I see. The manuscript was supposed to go to the anonymous buyer after Abu's death, but one of Abu's servants stole it before it could go to the new owner."

Kadir nodded. "*Oyle*."

"So when the scroll wasn't delivered to the anonymous buyer, the buyer sent a couple of goons to find out what happened and get his manuscript."

Tolga returned with Kadir's Turkish coffee in one hand and smoldering coals in a long-handled pot with breathing holes in the other. After placing a tiny coffee cup in front of Kadir, he used a pair of tongs to knock white ash onto the brass *narghile* brims. He then put embers with a healthy orange glow on the tin foil.

"You forgot my water."

"Yes, yes, Kadir, I only have two hands."

"And half a brain."

"Go back to the brothel you were born in and smoke there." Tolga walked off, pretending to be offended.

"So why don't you give this guy his scroll?" Drew asked. "It's his."

"Do you make joke? Are you think Abu bought this scroll in a legal way? Antique things belong to the government of the place where they are found. This is the law everywhere."

"What about those fragments the Norwegian bought?"

"These are just little pieces scholars are not able to use, and they were bought in a legal way." Kadir laughed. "If all collectors added their unlegal manuscripts together, they will have very many more than all the museums."

Drew frowned. "Come on ..."

"Believe me, my friend. The black market is very much bigger than the legal market."

Tolga put down Kadir's water glass. "Okay?"

Kadir sipped his coffee and shooed Tolga away with a fluttering hand.

"Do you know what kind of scroll you have?"

Kadir shrugged. "A Qumran writing."

"One of the *Dead Sea Scrolls*?" Drew's voice went up an octave. "That's ... that's impossible."

"Yes, of course impossible. Tariq is dead because *Bastard Prince of T'orrh* is so valuable book."

"You *have* this scroll?"

Kadir nodded.

"Where?" Drew looked at the leather satchel at Zafer's feet. "You know you have to keep it somewhere dry—very dry."

Kadir rolled his eyes. "Tariq taught me the ways for the keeping of such things many years ago."

"Do you know which scroll you have?"

Kadir shook his head.

Smoke wreathed Zafer's face, clung like fog hugging the ground. When it lifted, the bull-necked Turk was still watching Drew.

"I want to see it." Drew didn't just want to see the scroll, he wanted a say in what happened to it. It was as though his whole unmotivated life he'd been waiting for something to fall into his lap—only it had fallen into Kadir's. Drew had never identified with the van Goghs of the world, the Mozarts, the Hemingways, who went to their graves wrapped in their canvases, sheets of music, pages of writing. For them, there *was* nothing else. Their lives were pure pursuit. The urge Drew felt now wasn't the same—couldn't be—but it was probably next of kin.

Kadir shook his head. "It is in a safety place. Even Zafer doesn't know where."

Drew glanced at Zafer. "Who the hell is he anyway?"

A hint of a smile crept into Zafer's features. "Soldier of fortune."

Drew lifted his chin to indicate the bike-messenger's bag in Zafer's lap. "What's in there?"

"Photographs."

"Of the Dead Sea Scroll?"

"Both scrolls."

Drew took another hit of the apple tobacco, hoping the sweetish smoke would calm him. "Let me see the photos at least." Howard Carter must have felt the same short-circuiting of nerves before diggers broke the seal on King Tut's tomb. Kadir probably had no idea—nor did he care—he was holding something that could rewrite the history of Judaism or even of early Christianity. The possibility was remote—Kadir probably had a copy of a scroll scholars had already studied, translated, and published. But it what if he didn't? What if this was a scroll no one had ever seen before? Or had seen only as fragments? "I *have* to see the photos."

"What for? Can you read languages from antique times?"

"Yes," Drew lied. He had taken a single semester of Ancient Middle

Eastern Languages—not remotely enough to achieve anything like fluency in any of them. And that was better than a decade ago. "I'll tell you what you have."

Looking at Zafer, Kadir tipped his head toward Drew. "Show to him."

Zafer opened the leather bag and took two eight-by-ten photographs out of an envelope.

One photograph looked professionally done. The scroll had been laid out on a surface that was smooth and flat. The source of illumination wasn't apparent, but it could have been daylight: every letter was perfectly defined. The scroll itself was sepia—the color that gathered in the corners of old photographs like chemical twilight. Since there were no fibers visible, Drew assumed it was parchment, not papyrus.

The other photo was a black-and-white haunted by the ghostly blue of unwiped plums. It had been taken by an amateur. The lighting was uneven, and the photographer, who clearly knew nothing about scroll preservation, had used a flash. But the resolution was good enough to make out the letters.

Drew was certain of one thing: the scrolls had been written in either Hebrew or Aramaic. The neat rows didn't have the flow of script. Closer to incisions, the strokes were short and intricate, almost machine-like. Which made sense because Hebrew wasn't originally *written*; it was etched into stone or metal. Not quite as beautiful as the natural calligraphy of Arabic, the writing had a certain gravity to it, as if the words it comprised were meant to impose God's laws on the universe.

Since he wasn't well acquainted with Aramaic or Hebrew, and he assumed Aramaic could be written in Hebrew script, Drew couldn't tell them apart without hitting on a familiar word—and there it was: *sh'mow*, the contraction for *his name* in Hebrew. One of the most common. In Aramaic it would have been *sh'may*.

"It's Hebrew," he announced.

Kadir nodded. "Tariq told me this already. Read more."

"I can't. And since you're showing the photos to me, you don't know anyone who can." Drew puffed on the *narghile*. "But I do."

2: 6

MOST LIKELY TO SUCCEED

DREW STOOD OUTSIDE his apartment building. Four narrow stories, each with a windowed alcove projecting from the façade—a *jumba*. Definitely End of Empire. The ocher paint had faded to an unhealthy pink where it wasn't worn away altogether, and exposed stone had been tarnished by pollution. The marble stairs were missing sizable chunks.

Billowy clouds drifted past the strip of blue sky he could see; the afternoon couldn't have looked less ominous.

Why would they come back now?

He pushed open a wing of the ponderous steel door. In spite of the warm September weather, the breath of the building was cool and damp. He mounted the marble steps, worn with shallow depressions made by countless feet.

At the top of the stairs, he inserted the key into the lock to his apartment and clicked it over. Pushing the door open, he peered into the hall before stepping inside.

His books were on the shelves. The furniture was where he had left it this morning. He poked his head in every room just to make sure.

Convinced he was alone, he sat down on the couch in the parlor. For the first time since he'd moved into the flat, he felt uncomfortable in his own home. Was he under surveillance? Were the men who'd broken in last night professionals or just hired thugs? They had to have been watching Kadir's shop or they would never have known Kadir had given him anything. And they'd followed him home.

He jumped when the phone rang.

Drew lifted the receiver after the third ring. "Hello?"

"Drew? It's your father."

"Hi, Dad." Were they listening to his phone calls? "Isn't it a little early to be calling?"

"Yeah, it's about 6:30. I only gotta do half my route today. I don't leave until seven, seven-thirty. How's it goin'?"

"Everything's good." Well, if they were listening, they'd find out how goddamn ordinary his life was. "How are things in Jersey?"

"Ah, you know, nothin' much changes over here. You start teachin' in a couple a weeks, right?"

"Uh … yeah."

"So you're not thinkin' about comin' back home, maybe getting' a job that pays a little better?"

Drew sighed. *Not again.*

"I don't mean to be a pain in the ass, but you were third in your class—1,200 kids, not some dumpy little school. And captain of the wrestling team. Your brother never went past high school, but he's got a house because he learned a good trade."

His father's biggest fear was that Drew would take after the Gypsy side of the family. "Your mother's brothers?" he would say. "Not a one of 'em can keep a job. They sit around at their little gatherings throwin' handfuls a horseshit at each other and call it storytellin'."

"You graduated sooma cooma whatever from college—"

"Summa cum laude. Yeah, I know. I paid off the loans."

"And what're you doin'? You're not even teachin' lidderacher. You're just teachin' sixth-grade English to foreigners. You gotta be getting bored, cuz you're a lot smarter than that."

How exciting, Drew wanted to ask, is that delivery route of yours after twenty-two years?

"I mean, you're thirty-two, you need some equity. Your brother's two years younger, and he got a three-bedroom in a decent neighborhood."

"Yeah? What am I gonna do with all this equity?" Drew looked out the window. The Princes' Islands were gray humps, a little unreal in the hazy distance. It always seemed a pocket-sized miracle that they reappeared in the Sea of Marmara every morning precisely where, as dusk settled the day before, they'd faded against the horizon. At sunset he watched the Golden Horn run with warm bronze and spilled amber. He smoked his *narghile*, and, in the absence of anything new, re-read Thoreau or Emerson or Whitman, glancing up every now and then to take in how the streaked sky and reflective waters were gradually losing their shimmer. That was the equity he wanted.

"You wanna leave your kids something don'tcha?"

His father's voice, diminished by distance, was reduced to vibrations in a wire.

"*What* kids, Dad? Yasemin and I didn't have any." His thumb went instinctively to his ring finger, but it was like reaching for a bottle that was empty.

"I told you not to marry a foreigner."

"Dad, that had *no-thing*—" Anger stretched the word out of shape. "—*nothing* to do with why we split up."

The failure had been half his and half hers, but he'd been the one who'd left. Three months later he was pleading to be taken back, but she was already seeing someone else. He hadn't known until then emotional pain could be so *physical*. Like a fist had tightened in his stomach, like that same fist had been pushing on his diaphragm. Breathing became a chore. Sometimes it still was.

"Yeah, all right, but you might have a family one a these days, and you can't be savin' too much with what they pay you over there."

Drew rubbed his eyes with a thumb and two fingers. This conversation was doing for him what feet and decades had done for the uneven stairs he'd just come up.

"Look, I don't even have a girlfriend right now, so I don't need a house, I don't need equity, and I don't know if I'm ever going to have kids. Is that the point of life? To make some little Drews I can bitch at until they do what I want?"

"Izzat what I'm doin', bitchin'?"

"That's what it sounds like to me."

"You know what these phone bills cost me? I can bitch at your mother for free."

"You can Skype for free, too." Except that his father wouldn't go near a computer.

"I call because I give a shit what happens to you."

Drew thought about hanging up.

"You know what pisses me off so much? You wanna know? You got brains. Like I never had. You got opportunity like I never had. You think I coulda gone to college even if I had your smarts? Not a chance. Your grandfather had me working since I was seven—*seven years old*! School was for girls, not men, that's what he said."

Drew rolled his eyes. "I know ..."

"You think I like drivin a truck for a livin'? You think I'm in love with the Rat's Ass Meats Company?"

Renzland Meats.

"I couldn't do no better is the sad fuckin' fact. But *you* can. I mean, you coulda done anything you wanted—a lawyer, a doctor, whatever. And whaddid you do? You studied books. Not even *real* books, like history. *Lidderacher*. Horseshit if you ask me."

"I didn't ask you."

"Well I'm tellin' you, you fucked up so far, I don't wanna see you fuck up any worse. I mean why didn't you write articles for a newspaper or somethin'? Don't you like to write?"

"No."

"Yeah, I know, you like to read, but you're not even usin' your degree! And you got ... what? A dollar fifty to your name? Who you gonna support with that?"

"Me!" Drew shouted. "*I'm* the only one I have to support. And maybe you don't like my job, but *you* don't have to do it. And maybe *I* don't even like my job, but it's *my* choice. Thanks for raising me and not running out on Mom, but here's a little reminder for you—you know how many of my friends are cokeheads? Alcoholics? I'm not the best son, maybe, but I'm not the worst either."

"I'm not sayin' you are, I'm just—"

"Look, Dad, we've had this conversation before. Why don't you save yourself that big phone bill you were talking about?"

"You're right. Talking to you is like tryina kick-start a bicycle."

"Well thanks for calling."

"Yeah, g'bye."

"G'bye, Dad."

Drew let the receiver slide into the cradle. At least this time the conversation hadn't ended with the slam of plastic parts.

Padding across the Turkish carpet and down the hall, Drew made a left into the tiny room he used as a study. He plopped down on a padded leather chair that squeaked as it swiveled. He tapped a key on his laptop. The black screen vanished, revealing his e-mail inbox. He scanned the list of senders until he found *Stephen Cutherton.* Stephen had retired from Oxford as head of the theology and religion department. Drew had met him a few years ago at a poetry reading in Istanbul, and they'd taken an immediate liking to one another. Although Stephen lived in London, he had a summer place in southeastern Turkey and made frequent stop-overs in Istanbul. Once in a while, Drew bounced religious queries off him, but Stephen never answered directly. He would reply with a few keywords, leaving Drew to do the research and suss out how the data bits fit together; it was a long-distance game they played.

Yesterday Stephen had sent an e-mail—still unanswered—proposing that they meet for dinner some evening since he would be staying at a friend's flat in Istanbul for the month of September while his friend was traveling around Nepal with his wife.

Stephen would know what to make of Kadir's scrolls.

Opening a desk drawer, Drew took out a stack of term papers he'd saved from college. He glanced at their titles, mentally contextualizing each paper. He realized he hadn't actually produced anything in a long time; he sat around reading instead. He was a species of alchemist who preferred deciphering the moldering notes of long-dead predecessors to conducting his own experiments. His father had never come out and said it, but they both knew Drew's problem. He was lazy. Not at work or in class, but without deadlines or a structured setting, he wasn't likely to finish a project he'd taken on—or even to take it on.

He looked down at the paper he was holding, "The Mechanics of Belief in Fiction and Religion". Even this one, probably his best, had been only marginally original. De la Croix had been more or less right about that.

For five or six years after college, he'd read her articles whenever he came across them. One year he turned up a book she'd authored: *The Gospels as Eyewitness Accounts.* Coincidentally, Stephen had panned it in *The London Times.* When Drew mentioned in an e-mail that she had once been his teacher, Stephen had replied, "What an obtuse, silly, old cow. How she ever found employment is beyond me." Since Drew hadn't seen anything with her name attached to it in years, he assumed she'd retired from the field. Occasionally he did a web search for *Jesse Fenton* but had never come up with a hit. He'd caught Lisa Dent's byline though. The quietest student in de la Croix's class, who was now a professor of religious studies at Stanford, had written an article in the *Biblical Archaeological Review*. Drew had felt a ghostly stabbing pain that was guilt, not envy—guilt because Lisa had made something of herself in her field, and because, despite how vehemently he argued with his father, he knew his father wasn't entirely wrong about what he was doing—or wasn't doing—with his life.

He put the stack of papers back in the drawer and opened up a new document on his laptop. He wondered what his father would say if he knew he was typing a letter resigning his position at Istanbul Technical University.

2: 7

PROFESSOR CUTHERTON

"STEPHEN?"

Drew was at a row of payphones in Taksim, a bustling quarter crowning one of Istanbul's seven hills. The main thoroughfare was Istiklal Avenue, which, while serviced by a relic of a trolley, was all but closed to traffic. Now and again there was the inconvenient car that took the cobblestoned length of Istiklal at the pace of a trotting horse as the driver, tapping the horn, nudged people aside with its bumper.

"Drew! What a pleasure to hear from you. When can I expect you for dinner?"

"I was hoping you had time to see me today. I have something ... well, I guess you could say it's urgent."

"May I ask with regard to what?"

Drew was on a side street just below Istiklal.

"I know how this going to sound, but I have a friend who claims to have a Dead Sea Scroll."

"Have you seen it?"

"Only a photograph. It looks intact."

"Do you know which scroll it is?"

"No idea. All I could figure out is that it's written in Hebrew. There's something else ... photographs of another scroll he claims didn't come from Qumran. In Aramaic, I think. He's not sure where that one is."

"Very tantalizing I must admit, but in all probability, forgeries."

The red-and-white trolley car, a nostalgic reminder of an earlier Istanbul, clanged its bell as it made its way up the avenue.

"They might be, but I'm pretty sure someone was killed over one of them."

There was enough of a pause for Drew to become aware of the sudden change in light as the Sun emerged from behind a mass of drifting clouds.

"Oh my. That *does* change things. You're not in any danger yourself, I hope…?"

"No, I don't think so." He decided to leave out the drubbing he'd taken in his apartment.

"Drew, listen. I've a dinner engagement with a museum director tonight that I'm afraid I simply cannot break. Tomorrow, I'll be meeting with a pair of Greek scholars who are going to give me a guided tour of the Christian mosaics that have been preserved here in Istanbul. I suspect it will be a rather drawn-out affair. But after that, I'm at your disposal. Why don't we say eight o'clock tomorrow evening?"

"Great. Where should we meet you?"

"Here in Taksim, at my friend's flat. Seventeen Oba Sokak."

"I know where it is."

"Now let me understand this correctly: your friend has one of the Dead Sea Scrolls in addition to the photographs?"

"So he says." Drew suddenly realized that someone was standing directly behind him. He cupped the receiver with his hand, and lowered his voice.

"What do you know about the Dead Sea Scrolls?"

"Not much really. Just that they were mostly copies of Old Testament books and records kept by Essenes living near the Dead Sea."

The other phones, from what Drew could see, were also in use, but no one else was waiting; for some reason, the guy had decided to stand behind *him*.

"If you're up for a keyword search before we meet, try Muhammad the Wolf, Roland de Vaux, and John Allegro."

"Muhammad the Wolf?"

"Roland de Vaux and John Allegro."

"Got it."

Drew turned sideways and tried to get a look at the man behind him without being obvious. From what he could tell, the man was wearing a suit and was pale, redheaded, and freckled, which meant he might or might not be Turkish. Some Turks were fair and even freckled.

"It would be rather exciting if your friend really has gotten hold of a Dead Sea Scroll. The scrolls, you see, are primary source material. Unlike virtually every other document we have from antiquity, later scribes did not make biased insertions or deletions—there *were* no later scribes. But I must warn you … what the scrolls have to say about Christianity does not always support Church doctrine."

The man reached into his pocket, and Drew's heart speeded up and his mouth dried out.

"I can live with that." Drew accepted Christ as his savior, even though he was not a regular at church. Turning casually, he got a better look at the man standing behind him but still didn't have a sense of whether or not he might have been one of the men who attacked him in his flat.

"If one makes a habit of prying into these things with an open mind, one will discover a good many things about Christianity that are less than reassuring. Its founder, to take a particularly significant example, did not die on the cross as is supposed."

"You're saying that Jesus of Nazareth wasn't crucified?"

The man behind him stuck a piece of gum in his mouth and went to a phone that had just been freed up, but Drew barely turned his head.

"I'm saying no one who went by the name of Jesus of Nazareth ever walked the Earth."

BOOK 3: 1 - 10

THE FIFTH GOSPEL

It is an undeniable fact today that there is a great deal of diversity among the manuscripts, either because of the carelessness of the scribes or the perverse audacity of their superiors in adulterating the text, or again to the fact that among us are clergy who add or delete as they see fit, deeming themselves correctors.

— Saint Origen, 185–254 AD

3:1

THE DEAD SEA SCROLLS

N O ONE WHO WENT BY THE NAME *of Jesus of Nazareth ever walked the Earth.* Drew was sure the professor had thrown him a curve ball yesterday, that maybe what he'd said was true in some *technical* way, but in some other way it was misleading. He just had no idea *how* it could be true.

With a couple of hours to go before their meet-up, Drew sat down to his computer and got started on the professor's keyword search. Moments later he found himself descending some 1,200 feet below sea level to the lowest point on Earth: the Dead Sea.

Dusty yellow cliffs pocked with caves predominate. Some thirteen miles east of Jerusalem and about a mile from the Dead Sea, the ruins of Qumran sprawl over a small plateau. It was here in one of these caves in 1947 that Muhammad adh-Dhib—Muhammad the Wolf—made one of the great archaeological discoveries of the century: eight or nine large earthenware jars that contained leather rolls swathed in tattered linen.

There was Stephen's first keyword.

The fate of the vast majority of the scrolls in this cave cannot be known with any certainty. Archaeologists who later explored the site believe the cave at one time held as many as forty jars, which suggests that well over a hundred scrolls had been stored there. Only seven from this cave were ever revealed to the public.

"Well," Drew said to himself as he downloaded the article, "maybe Kadir really does have one of the scrolls." He continued to read.

A number made their way to the black markets in Jersualem and Cairo, where they were most likely acquired by private collectors. Eager to stem the clandestine flow of scrolls, Christian clergymen, to whom the Bedouin had brought the scrolls, began excavating the site. The work proceeded by night in order to escape the notice of the British authorities who ruled Palestine.

Cave 4 yielded a hoard of some eight hundred scrolls, albeit mostly in fragments. Father Roland de Vaux, director of the Ecole Biblique et Archeologique, a Dominican school in East Jerusalem, put together an international team to study the recovered material.

De Vaux was the second keyword.

The seven original scrolls found by the Wolf ended up in the hands of Israeli scholars. The Israeli team published the material in their possession relatively quickly. The international team, however, refused not only to publish their scrolls but even to let other researchers look at them. The most eminent scholars in the field were turned away as "unqualified," while graduate students of team members were readily granted access. It took more than half a century for the majority of scroll material to be published.

Drew frowned. The *majority?* Were there fragments that were s*till* unpublished?

The fireworks among the team members began when it was discovered that some of the texts mentioned a "Teacher of Righteousness," considered by the scroll authors to be the Messiah of Old Testament prophecy. "The just shall live by faith," a quote from Habakkuk 2:4 in the Old Testament, almost certainly inspired the following scroll passage:

"...all those who observe the Law in the house of Judah, whom God will deliver from the House of Judgment because of their suffering and because of their faith in the Teacher of Righteousness."

The Teacher, however, was persecuted by two men enigmatically known as the "Liar" and the "Wicked Priest" before he was martyred. The Teacher's followers, Qumran Essenes suffering under Roman oppression, were certain that his death signaled the end of the world.

Since de Vaux, a militant Catholic, and the others on the team of the Ecole Biblique insisted that the scrolls predated Christianity by at least a century, the find was disturbing. One scholar called the Teacher "the exact prototype of Jesus."

Friction developed between John Allegro and the rest of the Ecole's international team.

The third name: John Allegro.

The sole team member who was not a Catholic, he made startling discoveries of his own. "I shouldn't worry about that theological job if I were you," he quipped to a colleague. "By the time I've finished, there won't be any Church left for you to join."

What Allegro had found in his fragments were chiefly phrases once thought to have applied only to Jesus. In a letter to de Vaux he wrote:

As for Jesus as a 'son of God' and 'Messiah' – I don't dispute it for a moment; we now know from Qumran that their Davidic Messiah was reckoned a 'son of God,' 'begotten' of God—but that doesn't prove that he was God Himself. There's no 'contrast' in their terminology at all—the contrast is in its interpretation.

"Huh," Drew said aloud. The Jews, or at least the Qumran sect, apparently had seen David as well as other messianic figures as sons of God. Drew wasn't attached to the idea that Jesus was God's "only begotten son," but he wouldn't have to go far to find people who were.

Allegro was given only a small fraction of the eight hundred scroll fragments to look over, and he expressed his deep misgivings in a letter: "*I am convinced that if something does turn up which affects the Roman Catholic dogma, the world will never see it. De Vaux will scrape the money out of some or other barrel and send the lot to the Vatican to be hidden or destroyed.*"

Where, Drew wondered, was the material Allegro never saw?

Although subsequent scholarship has determined that some of the scrolls do not, as de Vaux originally supposed, predate Christianity, the mystery remains unsolved: who was the Teacher? It could not have been Christ since there is no mention of a crucifixion or a resurrection. Who were the Liar and the Wicked Priest who had persecuted him? The ancient drama continues into our own time.

Drew pulled up a few more articles, which essentially corroborated the first. He had a lot of questions for Stephen, but there were nearly two hours before he and Kadir were supposed to meet the professor.

He closed his laptop and leaned back in his chair.

Next to the computer—he knew it was a bad idea, but he had never been able to bring himself to move it—was a picture of him with Yasemin. Her head thrown back and her mouth pried open by laughter, she had her arms around him. His smile was more subdued, his long hair like a dark stream caught in mid-flow. The picture had been taken in a bar before they'd gotten married. Before they'd started fighting.

It was Thursday. Yasemin and a coterie of colleagues at the publishing house where she worked crowded into the same restaurant in Taksim for dinner and drinks. He could drop in, feign casual indifference, talk her into sitting down with him for a few minutes. After getting her to smile and maybe admit she still missed him, he'd look at his watch, announce that he *had* to go—he couldn't talk about it right now but why not get together on another night when they'd have more time?

Drew snatched his keys off the desk and headed out the door.

3: 2

HORATIO

WHEN DREW LOOKED at his ringless finger, he still didn't really understand what had happened. How little things had gotten so out of hand. Like the Saturday he was reading in the living room and Yasemin was still in bed. Early morning was his favorite time of day, before the city kicked into gear and the streets became noisy. Eighteen-carat light streamed in through a pair of windows, and he'd backed himself against an arm of the couch, knees drawn up, book in hand.

When he heard Yasemin's slippers scuffing the floor in the hall, he closed the book. She was wearing a long T-shirt as a nightgown. She answered his "good morning" with a grunt; she wasn't in a good mood.

Hopping off the couch, he followed her into the kitchen.

Her caramel skin had taken on a morning glow. The crescents under her eyes, which she thought made her look old but he found sexy, were puffy from sleep. He brushed one of her cheeks, the texture of acne scars fascinating to his fingertips. She always turned her face away when he tried to kiss her after she woke up, self-conscious about what cigarettes and a night's incubation had done to her breath, but it never bothered him. Being denied the kiss bothered him.

Finally, with the coffeepot on the stove, she hugged him back and moaned as if she had sunk into a heap of silk pillows.

"Omelette?"

There was nothing prurient about the nipples he saw through her

"Okay." His voice took on the tone of a prosecuting attorney. "How often do you make breakfast? In all the years we've been together, how many? Three? Four?"

She didn't answer.

"What does it take to make the bed? Two, three minutes? Doesn't a little more go into breakfast?"

"I told you. The sink is full. And you're sitting there reading."

"Yazz, I *do* the dishes. I just didn't do them this morning. What *is* this? Why do you have to find problems everywhere you look? Why can't you be like other people who are happy they don't have to go to work on Saturday?"

"Maybe you should find someone else."

"Jesus, how many times do we have to do this? I don't *want* someone else, I just don't want you to be ..."

"Such a bitch?"

He made another gesture of surrender. To say *no* would be a lie. To say *yes* would make things worse. But then he blurted, "Yes! Do you really have to?" Now there was belligerence in his body language, and he stepped close to her. "*Do* you?" He brought his face closer to hers.

She turned her back on him. "Conversation's over."

"What?"

She walked away. "Conversation's over."

"Conversation's *over*?" Blind rage took hold of him. He grabbed a vase and hurled it at the wall. It shattered against the plastered-over brick and sprayed the couch with glass.

Yasemin stormed back into the room. "What did you break?"

"Conversation's over?" he hissed. He brought his fist down on the seat of a chair and to his surprise cracked the wooden panel.

"Baby, *don't* ..."

Drew didn't even hear her any more. "Conversation's over?" He slammed his fist into the chair again. The wood gave with a satisfying snap, and his hand went through.

"Drew! I've had that chair since I was a girl! *Pleeeease*, Baby, please stop."

She wrapped her arms around his chest. "Please, Baby, *please*."

He was still looking over her head for things to smash. That particular Saturday, he'd stopped himself, but there were times when he'd actually shoved her out of the way to continue his rampage. Then, disgusted with himself, he would grab his jacket and run out the door.

Now he was running back. Because in the last two years he'd learned that being miserable without her was worse than being miserable with her, that bullying her with logic until he'd proved his point wasn't as important as keeping the argument from escalating.

Fucking Horatio.

3: 3

AFTER TWO THOUSAND YEARS

HE CRESTED THE HILL that put him in a tiny square encircled by shops and cafes. This was the Tünel end of Istiklal Avenue. His mouth had gone dry, his fingers were like icicles, and there was too much give behind his knees as he walked. Cobblestones under his sneakers, he went through an iron gate that opened into a narrow courtyard. A niche of artificial twilight paved the ocher flagstones, and the courtyard overflowed with potted tropical plants and tables occupied by upscale customers—men wearing shimmery summer suits and heavy rings, women with curving birds' necks and shoulders exposed by light dresses.

He peered through the glass of Asmali restaurant. There she was, standing at the bar with a couple of other editors, her hair as short as ever but streaked blond now. She was wearing a gray skirt and a sleeveless black top that outlined her proportions a little too well. Seeing her look this good without him was like catching an elbow to the gut. Her angular jaw had come from her father. From her mother, cheekbones she rarely bothered to accentuate with makeup. The thick eyebrows, like her jaw, suggested masculinity, but her nose, ever so slightly pert, was purely feminine. So was her mouth. From the neck down, all comparisons to men ended.

His pulse thumped in his ears, and the pit of his stomach felt suddenly drafty as he reached for the brass door handle.

How could she still turn him into a seventeen year old on a first date?

Yasemin's friends spotted him and leaned back a little, their eyes widening as though he were an apparition. Yasemin turned to see what had caught their attention.

"Drew."

A restrained smile, not the one he'd fallen in love with.

"Why didn't you call?"

He shrugged. It was all he could muster in the way of nonchalance. "Nothing planned. I was just headed up Istiklal and thought I'd peek in. Do you have a few minutes?"

Selma and Esra tilted their chins up, looked down their noses at Yasemin, and shooed her with their hands, "*Hadi, hadi* ..."

Selma caught his eye and winked.

"Five minutes, Drew." Yasemin stepped away from the bar.

They sat down at a table for two, its polished marble disk tinted pink.

Waving away a menu, he ordered a beer. "Look, I just ... I really wanted to see you. Just see you. In person."

She was made up today, foundation nearly obliterating her acne scars, mascara blackening eyes shadowed slate blue. Her lips shone with coppery iridescence, and, as though they weren't sensual enough, she'd lined them.

"I don't think that's such a good idea anymore."

"We were married for four years, and we can't get together for a beer once in a while?"

"It always ends badly, Drew." She lit a cigarette. "I don't want to hear anymore about what I did wrong in our marriage. You're the one who walked out."

"I know. Probably the biggest mistake of my life."

"It's over, Drew. I'm not taking you back."

Christ, she knew where to stab him.

"I've thought about it a lot, and if I could go back and do things over, I wouldn't change anything."

"*Nothing*? You wouldn't treat me just a little better? I mean, you don't think your disdain validated every insecurity I ever had? I grew up with a father who made me feel everything I got excited about was basically worthless. Four years of high school wrestling and he went to two matches."

"You told me."

"Well I couldn't take it from you. That ... *scorn*. Not from the person I was closest to. Did you always have to snap at me? Then hit me with a list of my character flaws?"

Her cell phone rang. She put her cigarette in her mouth and dug it out of her purse.

"Alo?"

Within a sentence he knew it was her boyfriend. And then that stunning smile—for *him*—the guy on the phone.

More proof pain isn't fatal.

The waiter brought his beer, and he drank off a third of it in a few gulps.

She kept saying, "I promise ... promise ..." Laughing her deep laugh and trying to hang up, she wasn't able to until she'd said *Soz veriyorum* three more times. *I promise.*

"Who is he these days?"

She put her phone back in her purse. "Why should I tell you? You wouldn't approve."

He glanced over at Selma to let her know that he could find out if he really wanted to. "Why wouldn't I?"

"He's twenty."

If emotions translated to skin color, Drew would have flushed pure rage. He strained his voice until only mild sarcasm trickled through. "Is that what the blond's for, to look younger? Hipper?"

"The blond is for me. Can't I have a change if I want one?"

"Where the hell did you meet a college kid?"

"I knew I shouldn't have told you. He's an intern."

Drew had always thought it would be one of the authors she worked with, not a fucking intern. "He's probably been fantasizing about sleeping with his boss since he was hired. And now he thinks he woke up in heaven. He doesn't even have to wrap it." It hurt him to say it at least as much as it hurt her to hear it, but he was willing to drive the blade in a little deeper as long as she felt it, too.

No doctor had been able to find anything wrong with either of them, but for two years they had tried—vitamins, the six critical days of the month, fertility drugs, artificial insemination—and still, at the end of every month, a bloody wad of bathroom tissue in the little blue pail, sometimes an ugly clot in the toilet. And then the week-long depression. The living room foggy with cigarettes first thing in the morning, the curtains drawn and the lights off, an open bottle of wine on the coffee table.

Her eyes narrowed. "That's why I shouldn't have said anything. I'm glad we're divorced." She stood up. "Don't come here again."

He finished his beer as she walked away. He didn't mind so much that there was someone else. What he couldn't bear was knowing that it was some kid who couldn't possibly appreciate the woman he was with. Who was just in love with the idea of nailing his boss.

The bottom of his mug hit the table hard enough to chip glass and turn heads. He left money on the table and walked out with a nod to Selma and Esra.

He negotiated the maze of tables in the courtyard.

Of course, no one named Jesus of Nazareth had ever walked the earth. After two thousand years nothing had changed for the better. Nothing at all.

3: 4

Q

STEPHEN WAS STAYING in a building very much like the one in which Drew lived—four stories, a *jumba* on each floor, neoclassical flourishes carved into the stone—except that it had been renovated. Painted a shade of terra cotta with burnt sienna trimming and fitted with wrought-iron railings, typical of the better neighborhoods in Taksim.

Drew pressed a button.

"Yes?" The intercom wrapped the professor's voice in tinfoil.

"Drew." He was afraid to say more than his name because his voice, like his legs, was still shaky.

"Just a moment."

A metallic click followed an irritating buzz.

Pulling on one of the steel doors, Drew held it open for Kadir and Zafer.

The professor took Drew's hand in his bony grip, kissed him on both cheeks, and embraced him as if he were a wayward son finally returned home. The white stubble on the old man's jaw felt like wire bristle against Drew's face, but Drew hardly noticed. The professor's smell—musty, like the wood-and-pulp odor of old bookshops—was reassuring. He wanted to cling to Stephen, take in his professorly smell, absorb some of his wisdom, put the emptiness he woke up with every morning behind him.

"Good to see you, Drew."

"You, too." The truth was there was no one he would rather see right now.

As tall as Drew, Stephen was still trim—lean, in fact. His movements were quick, his eyes backlit by a keen intellect, and his hair, now a
uniform white, was surprisingly abundant. Although only slightly wavy
on top, it made tiny curls behind his ears and at the back of his neck—a
touch of unruliness his comb couldn't tame.

"Kadir," Drew said, stepping back, "this is Stephen Cutherton."

"I am glad to be meet you, *Hojam*." Kadir shook the professor's hand.

"Do call me Stephen."

Drew knew that Kadir wouldn't; *hojam* was Turkish for *my teacher*.
And teachers were generally accorded inordinate respect in Islamic
societies.

"And this is Zafer."

"A pleasure." Stephen smiled warmly.

Zafer nodded as he shook the professor's hand. "*Hojam*."

"Well, shall we get down to business—or should I say *up*?" The
professor led the climb up a spiral staircase, pushing open a wooden
door with iron hinges.

Drew followed him in. His hand lingered on the heavy planks as
though the grain concealed the secret of the wood's longevity.

The professor's friend, a journalist, owned the building and had trans-
formed the fourth floor into a study lined with bookshelves and glass
display cases. The room brought to mind a safari hunter's den except
that, instead of animal skins and trophy heads, there were artifacts—a
mask from Bali with fierce eyes and tusks curling past the upper lip, a
fabulously elongated African head carved out of ebony, a huge crucifix
that had been spattered with oil-paint gore.

The wall facing south was almost entirely glass, affording a view of
Taksim's orange-tiled rooftops and, beyond them, the Sea of Marmara.
The Midas touch of the sun's last rays had turned the surface of the water
into a sheet of red-gold fresh from the forge, rough and unfinished. The
balcony overflowed with fronds and tropical leaves.

Drew sank into the couch. Kadir sat between Zafer and him, still
wearing his sagging flak jacket.

"It would be positively indecent not to offer guests tea—especially in
Turkey," Stephen said. "Be so kind as to give me a moment."

He returned with a tarnished copper tray. Glasses, biscuits, and a
traditional Turkish teapot—essentially a double-boiler—were arranged

on the tray's dimpled surface.

"Thank you, *Hojam*."

The professor set down the tulip-shaped glasses in front of his guests and poured tea from the top boiler and diluted it with hot water from the bottom. He handed Drew a glass set in a tiny saucer with scalloped edges.

"Well, I guess we should tell you about Tariq." Drew did most of the talking while Kadir interjected occasionally. This time, Drew included the home invasion.

Zafer said nothing. His hands, which looked like they could swat a horse into obedience, rested against his inner thighs.

"All right then ..." The professor put on a pair of glasses. "Let's have a look at what you've got."

Zafer took a yellow envelope out of the satchel he carried.

Clicking on a lamp next to the chair, the professor slid the photos out of the envelope and held one up to the light. "Excellent photography." He took a pad and pen from the coffee table and put the pad on his lap.

Drew noticed the prominent veins on Stephen's hands as he took notes.

After a few moments silent enough to hear the pen scratching paper, the professor began to read.

"The Wicked Priest who rebelled against ... or perhaps violated God's precepts ... the Wicked Priest who was delivered by God into the hands of his enemies because of the evil committed against the Teacher of Righteousness ..."

The professor looked up. "This seems to be from the Habakkuk Commentary. It is indeed one of the Dead Sea Scrolls. You have the *entire* scroll?"

Kadir, whose feet barely reached the floor even though he was sitting on the edge of the couch, nodded. "Yes, *Hojam*."

He glanced again at the photos. "We have this scroll nearly intact, but, as well-preserved as it is, there are a few missing sections. If your copy is *genuine*, it's ... well I don't deal in antiquities, so I can't estimate a suitable price, but it's worth quite a sum of money I should say." The professor handed the photos back to Zafer who exchanged them for another set.

"Hmm. Quite obviously an amateur took these shots, but ... legible enough." Taking up a magnifying glass that had been lying on the coffee table, Stephen examined the photograph more closely. Then he began to write, occasionally crossing out and starting over.

From where Drew sat, the professor was silhouetted by the sun's afterglow, a few stray hairs burned into translucent amber.

When Professor Cutherton looked up, his mouth opened, but there was no sound. Looking at the photograph again, he shook his head slowly. "Impossible." He glanced at what he had written on the pad on his lap. "It's …" He looked directly at Drew, his blue eyes intense. "If this scroll exists, if it's genuine … I can't even say what it's worth in terms of dollars, but it's worth to scholars is incalculable."

"What is it?" Drew asked.

"The beginning seems to be missing but … here, listen to this, *No one puts fresh wine into old wineskins. To do so would cause the skins to burst, and the wine is lost and so are the skins.* This saying occurs in Luke, Mark, and Matthew." Once again the professor gazed down at the pad in his lap. "But there's no mention of Jesus or any of the disciples. It seems to be merely a list of sayings. Of far greater significance, it's written in Aramaic. The entire New Testament is written in Greek. This—" he held the photograph up and let go an old man's triumphant cackle. "This is an Aramaic version of Q!"

Kadir frowned. "What is Q?"

"My good man, nothing short of the Holy Grail of New Testament scholarship."

3: 5

NAZORAEANS

Kadir's forehead creased.

Stephen and Drew exchanged looks; how were they going to explain Q to a Muslim who hadn't been educated beyond high school?

Kadir seemed to know what they were thinking. "Please tell me what is Q. Why is it important? My friend is dead because of these photographs."

The professor nodded. "The problem, Kadir, is this: there are four gospels in the Bible. Three of them are quite similar—Mark, Matthew, and Luke. But there are still disturbing differences. Mark, for example, makes no mention of the virgin birth, Bethlehem, or Jesus' genealogy. Luke and Mark make no mention of Wise Men or a flight into Egypt. These appear only in Matthew. Furthermore, only Matthew and Mark agree on Jesus' last words. Luke and John recorded something else entirely.

"Now, while there are all sorts of differences and contradictions among the Gospels, many of the sayings and parables are identical— word for word. Which leads us to conclude that, in the case of Matthew and Luke, which share the most sayings and parables, the Gospel writers had access to a collection of quotes attributed to Jesus. This collection of sayings is referred to as the Q document or more commonly, Q. To make matters more confusing still, there is the Gospel of Thomas, which consists of 114 sayings attributed to Jesus but was never accepted by the Church."

"These photographs are a Q document?" Kadir asked.

The professor's sharp chin seemed to tap out an urgent message as he nodded. "Not just Q, Kadir. This appears to be an Aramaic original that was only theorized about by a handful of scholars who believe that Q—not Paul's letters—comprises the earliest Christian material. However old it is, Q is the foundation on which the Gospels were eventually constructed. Although Q was never found, we are fairly certain it existed. An *Aramaic* original, however ... that's something else entirely."

The professor put a hand on one of the photographs. "And this *does* seem to have been written earlier than any of the Gospels. Of course, that's just an intuition. I'm not a paleographer, but the Gospels were all written in Greek—as was the Q document used by Matthew and Luke.

"This scroll *could* be the Aramaic sayings source mentioned by Papias of Hieropolis. Papias claimed that Matthew's Gospel *preserved the sayings of the Lord in Hebraic dialect*. But no one has ever been able to discover such a source. While Matthew may have gotten his hands on an Aramaic version of Q, he must have worked from a Greek translation—the same one Luke later worked from. Otherwise, the verbatim conformity we find in various passages in the two Gospels would not exist."

Drew didn't think *verbatim conformity* would mean all that much to Kadir. "In other words, if Luke and Mark each made their own translation from the Aramaic, there would be differences in the sayings."

The dwarf nodded.

"It's always been assumed that Q was written by followers of Jesus some time *after* the crucifixion. But if this manuscript was written *before* the first century AD, then ..." Cutherton smiled triumphantly.

Drew frowned. "But ... that's impossible. How can Jesus' sayings pre-date him?"

The professor stood and began to pace the room, his footsteps cushioned by a collage of intricately patterned rugs. "If this is a collection of Christ's sayings written *before* he was born, it means the entire New Testament has only tangential contact with history."

"You're saying ... it's fiction?"

"Why not? It's not nearly as fantastic as resurrecting the dead or walking on water." The professor clenched a gnarled fist. "If I *just* had access to this scroll ..." He turned to Kadir. "Do you have *any* idea where it is?"

Kadir shrugged. "Only Tariq could be know."

"Do you understand the significance? We are talking about the single greatest find in New Testament archaeology. Christianity will have to be rewritten if … *if* it's genuine." The word *genuine* seemed to have the effect of a tranquilizer dart shot into the professor's flank. The sharp angles of his lanky body softened, and his arms sank to his sides. "Forgive an old man's wishful thinking. In all probability, it's a forgery."

"Then why is Tariq dead?" Zafer asked.

"Someone at least *believes* it's genuine." Stephen picked up a photograph and reexamined it. "It *could* be a clever forgery. There's simply no way to tell without the manuscript itself. Kadir, are these *all* the photos?"

"Yes, *Hojam*."

The professor eased himself back into his chair, his knees creaking. "I must tell you, I've been waiting for something like this" —he shook the photo so that it flapped in his hand—"my entire career. I've written my fair share of books, but my last—perhaps my best—isn't quite finished. I put forward a meticulous argument that, not only was Christ not divine, but also that there *was* no crucifixion under Pontius Pilate."

"*What?*" Drew said. This was how their phone conversation yesterday had ended.

"Until now I was convinced that he'd lived and been executed in decidedly non-dramatic fashion. It seems I've still more rewriting to do."

Drew was shaking his head. "Nothing I ever read led anywhere near such a conclusion."

"The evidence is sound, Drew, but faith furnishes believers with armor virtually impervious to logic. A scroll like this … only a fool would miss the obvious conclusion." The professor smiled, his teeth gleaming in the lamplight. "Not that there's any shortage of those in the world."

Drew resented Stephen's gloating. Jesus may not have been the actual son of God, but denying he'd ever been crucified was ludicrous. "Are you out to demolish Christianity?"

"No, Drew, blind faith. I have no sympathy for it—from any quarter. What do you think guided those airliners into New York's Twin Towers?"

Drew was so angry he looked away. The deepening evening had turned the southern windows into dark mirrors.

"Like the Gnostics, I consider knowledge to be our best hope, not faith." The professor took a deep breath. "Yesterday I said there was no

Jesus of Nazareth. To put it bluntly, Nazareth did not exist when the Jesus of the Gospels was said to be growing up there."

Drew had *known* it was a goddamn technicality, but he still wasn't convinced. "What makes you so sure?"

The professor shrugged nonchalantly. "There's not a single reference to Nazareth in the Old Testament or the Talmud, which mentions more than *sixty* Galilean towns. Nor does any historian from the period ever mention Nazareth, not even Josephus. Which is most curious because Josephus lists some forty-five cities and villages in Galilee. Perhaps more persuasive is this: Josephus fortified a town not two miles from modern-day Nazareth. Surely if Nazareth had been a city in Josephus's time—and the Gospels refer to it as a city with its own synagogue— Josephus would have noticed it. Especially since he was writing *decades* after Jesus was supposedly executed. Indeed, even if it were only a village he should have mentioned it. What's more, there isn't a single letter in the New Testament, including those of Paul, that mentions Nazareth. Mark, who wrote the earliest Gospel, doesn't either." The professor smirked. "Well, there's Mark 1:9, but careful examination has shown that to be a later insertion into the Gospel."

"Yes, but that doesn't—"

The professor raised his hand. "Nor does the archaeological record substantiate the existence of Nazareth as a city anytime prior to the second century AD. Even the digs of a couple of Franciscan priests who fancied themselves archaeologists could turn up little more than a system of caves used as tombs. Prior to the second century AD, there were a few farms in the area at best."

Drew leveled a finger at the professor. "Then how can you explain why the early Christians were called Nazarenes?"

Stephen smiled. "They weren't. Matthew 2:23 states, *And he came and dwelt in a city called Nazareth that it might be fulfilled what was spoken by the prophets, He shall be called a Nazoraean.* What Matthew actually wrote in Greek is *Nazoraios*—which, in English, is not Nazarene at all but, as I said, Nazoraean. This doesn't link up very well with the Greek for Nazareth, which is *Nazaret.* More to the point, nowhere in the Old Testament is any such prophecy mentioned! Matthew is simply wrong. Even in Hebrew, Nazareth is *Natzrat* or, according to a piece of masonry dug up a few years ago, *Natsrat.* Thus, someone from Nazareth would be referred to as a *Natsrati*. Again, quite distant from *Nazoraios*.

"The prophecy Matthew probably misinterpreted is recounted in Judges 13. An angel informs the wife of Manoah, who is barren, that she will give birth to the savior of Israel: *For behold, you shall conceive, and bear a son; and no razor shall come upon his head for the child shall be a Nazarite unto God from the womb, and he shall begin to deliver Israel out of the hand of the Philistines.* The *nazarite* prophesied, however, was Samson, not Jesus. Notice how many elements of the Gospel narrative are already in place—divine visitation, miraculous birth, a savior figure, and a *nazarite*, which in Greek is *nazir*—there's your Nazarene."

"Okay." Drew nodded curtly. "But no Jesus of Nazareth doesn't mean no Jesus."

"Fair point. But be that as it may, Paul of Tarsus—not Jesus—is the de facto founder of Christianity." Stephen aimed a bony finger in the general direction of the satchel on the couch. "You'll find him mentioned in that scroll of yours."

Drew frowned. "The Essenes wrote about Paul?"

The professor stood up again. "If I were to give you a key-word search. it would be a page long—John the Baptist, James the Just, the Ebionites, Ananus, Damascus, Judas of Galilee, Simon bar Giora, Iscariot, the Sicarii, two thousand pigs, the Clementine *Recognitions*, Serapis, Ezekiel's *Exodus*, Philo of Alexandria, the Therapeutae ... not to mention *The Bacchae* and the Nag Hammadi Library."

Drew's forehead wrinkled. *Two thousand pigs?*

"Here we are, after all, in the city of Constantine, the first Roman emperor to profess himself a Christian." The professor spread his arms as if to encompass centuries of history. "It was Constantine who presided over the debate that divided Christianity for centuries: was Christ mere man or the Son of God? And it was here in Asia Minor that the Council of Nicaea voted to make Jesus God."

The professor waved a hand. "It's all in my manuscript. I'll be happy to give you a copy on disc. I should at least, however, tell you what the scrolls had to say about Paul. It makes clear why he was the actual founder of Christianity."

As though punctuating the professor's last sentence, the lights went out.

3: 6

PRIDE WARS

YASEMIN STOOD OUTSIDE smoking a cigarette in the chalky light that made it through the front window of a café. She was uncomfortable meeting Mehmet at Asmali Restaurant because no one they worked with knew they were dating.

Dropping her cigarette on a cobblestone, she crushed it under a boot heel.

She was still unnerved by the way Drew had shown up at Asmali—and she was still bitter about the divorce. It didn't matter that he had begged her to take him back. By that time she had already suffered through three humiliating months, and in spite of the fact that she had kept her ring on, everyone knew her husband had left her. No matter how politely they smiled at her, she was a woman who couldn't keep her husband.

She would never forgive Drew for those first three months of separation. She would never forgive him for breaking his wedding vows. For the string of men she had dated—men who had seen nothing in her but a bed-warmer. She tried to explain to Drew that this was one of the ways Turkey was different from the West, that being a divorced woman in Turkey was shameful. Every time she said she was divorced, she felt like she was admitting she had once been a prostitute. And that was how most of the men she had dated had treated her, as though without one of them on her arm, that's what dressing up in boots and a skirt made her: a whore.

If Drew showed up now, she'd slap him.

It had begun in an almost a fairytale way. They used to laugh about the chain of coincidences that had brought them both to the same restaurant, on the same night, at the same time. "And if you didn't speak English," Drew had said, "that would have been the end of it."

It had all felt like it was *supposed* to happen—not through the Internet or a friend or even a co-worker but almost as though the city itself had arranged for it, as though the criss-crossing streets made up an enormous chess board and had sat them at tables right next to each other. Just to see what would happen.

The attraction had been sudden and inexplicable. It wasn't that Drew was all that good looking; it was his laugh, his five mispronounced words of Turkish, his ridiculous American jokes, his long hair falling around his face before he raked it back with his fingers, the way he looked at her and at nothing else the whole time they sat together, the way he *listened* to her, as though he couldn't hear anything else.

There had been no kiss on that first night, and later, walking down Istiklal Avenue, they had joked, "And this is where for the first time we did *not* kiss ..." But they had hugged. Being in his arms for the first time had made her feel as though a good breeze might lift her off the cobblestones.

On her way home things she'd noticed a thousand times before—a sky as glittery as glass dust, the Moon sinking behind the stanchions of one of the two bridges spanning the Bosporus, the wind shivering the boughs of trees—none of it would ever be the same.

The memories, too, were as glittery as glass dust.

It was over now, and she was too bitter to consider marrying again. Marriage was something you did once, something that lasted forever. She had loved him as much as she could love a man, and it hadn't worked. He'd made her suffer for that love—why shouldn't he suffer too?

Maybe what Drew had said was true, that whenever he upset her, accidentally or not, she punished him. By refusing to so much as look at him—let alone speak to him. No good morning, no *Hi, I'm home*, nothing. For days. But if, say, a girlfriend called, her voice would have its natural bounce, she'd laugh easily, and no one listening in would have any idea she was in the least upset.

"You realize you're doing that to hurt me, don't you?"

She would look up from the phone she'd just hung up, vaguely aware she'd gone out of her way to be friendly during her conversation, but it never really occurred to her that it was more than reminding Drew of what he was missing.

"I really can't take that—not talking to me, sleeping on the couch, walking around here with a face like you can't stand me, but you're stuck in the same prison cell."

She didn't answer.

"I lose my temper sometimes, I know. But this is cold. It's spiteful and calculating."

She would walk away, smiling inwardly. She had won.

Mehmet, leaning forward to kiss her, startled her.

"Cut it out, Mehmet. We're still in Turkey."

"Who's going to see?"

"Everyone in the café. Where are we going?"

"Your place?" He smiled impishly.

She raised an eyebrow as a reprimand. "I'm a little upset. I want a drink."

"Why? What happened?"

"Drew came by Asmali today. He got angry and broke a glass."

Mehmet's face changed. "Why do you still talk to him?"

"Because I was married to him for four years, and I spent six years of my life with him, and when you're a little older, you'll understand."

"I should have a talk with him."

She studied Mehmet. He wasn't much taller than she was. He had curly black hair, dark skin like hers, and a sweet smile. But Drew was a grown man. Mehmet was a boy. "Don't take this the wrong way, Mehmet, but I don't think that's a good idea."

"Why not?"

"What are you going to say to him?"

"I'll tell him to leave you alone."

"First of all, I can do that myself. Second, he'll tell you to piss off."

"Then I'll have to introduce him to some of my Turkish friends."

Yasemin glared at him. "*Mehmet.* You and your friends are *not* going to attack my ex-husband. If you're such a *maganda*, you fight him yourself. But then don't tell me I didn't warn you."

"So now you think I can't protect you?"

"Protect me? From what?"

"You said he has a temper. You told me he used to break furniture when you had arguments. He broke a glass tonight."

"Not really. He chipped the bottom."

"I don't want you around him."

"Mehmet, don't turn into a typical Turkish man. Don't tell me what I can or can't do."

Mehmet punched himself in the jaw, crossed his eyes, and his knees wobbled like a cartoon boxer about to fall.

She burst out laughing. "That's the Mehmet I like going out with."

They hooked elbows and walked up Istiklal Avenue.

They hadn't decided where they were going, but she was glad to be moving. What if she ran into Drew now? Drew was never good with pride wars—that's what he called it when they were too angry to speak to each other. And if he saw her with Mehmet, he would lose again.

3: 7

THE ESSENES

DREW GAZED OUT OVER the Sea of Marmara. Its dark breadth, intimated by the glint of moonlight, was studded by the twinkle of scattered ships.

"Power outages are common enough in Istanbul," Stephen said, "but there's always the possibility this isn't one of them." He pointed. "The lights in the buildings across the way are still on."

Zafer stood up. "I think we have a problem." He went out on the balcony, a silhouette outlined by the lemony brightness of the tall windows across the street.

Drew imagined the crack of a rifle, Zafer's stocky frame tightly wound with muscle crumpling to the flagstones.

After peering over both ends of the balcony, Zafer closed the glass door behind him and pulled the curtains. "We're the only ones without power."

Professor Cutherton looked at Kadir. "Are either of you armed?"

Zafer nodded.

"Well then, I suggest you and I go downstairs and have a look at the circuit breakers."

Zafer reached into the satchel and took out a pistol. The black automatic gleamed darkly in the frail light.

Christ, Drew thought to himself, *what have I gotten myself into?* He had to hold onto his knees to keep his hands from shaking. *What have I gotten* Stephen *into?*

"There are a few decorative candles around here—"

The professor sounded entirely matter of fact. *He's not sweating this ...*

"I have something more better." Kadir pulled a penlight out of his flak jacket. Zafer clicked it on, the illumination startling.

"Outstanding." The professor looked at Zafer. "Shall we?"

Look at him, Drew thought, *at seventy-something. Do not go gentle into that good night? Stephen was going into it like a flaming brand. And here I am, thirty-two, with half his conviction and half his guts.*

"Should we call the police?" Drew kept imagining the pistol in Zafer's hand going off.

"And tell them what? Our electricity is out?" Zafer asked. "That an Egyptian tourist is dead because he was putting stolen scrolls on the black market? That we have what the men who killed him are looking for?"

"Never mind."

The two men descended the stairs, the professor leading the way with the flashlight.

Drew and Kadir listened.

For a few moments, there was only the sound of their breathing.

Abruptly, the lights went on.

It was another fifteen minutes or so before the Drew heard footsteps coming up the stairs.

"Nothing," the professor said. "We checked every door, every window, every room, every closet."

After putting the pistol back in the satchel, Zafer sat back down on the couch.

The professor picked up the photographs, his pad, and the magnifying glass and resumed translating.

The three other men watched in silence. Occasionally, Drew sipped tepid tea.

Stephen looked up from his pad. "It's nearly identical to Q1, the earliest version of Q. All that's missing, as far as I can tell, are proper names. Kadir, is there any chance you might leave these photographs with me this evening?"

"*Hojam*, it is not a good idea for me."

"Yes, I suspected as much. Would you allow me to photocopy them? There's a machine downstairs."

Kadir glanced at Zafer.

The larger man shrugged.

Kadir nodded. "Okay, *Hojam*."

"Right. Give me a moment ..."

Zafer, shouldering the satchel, accompanied the professor downstairs.

Drew heard a click, like something had been turned off. He looked at Kadir, but the dwarf seemed not to have noticed.

When the professor returned, he looked grave, as though he were bearing the head of John the Baptist instead of evidence that might rewrite Christianity's origins.

"I'm sure I'll be awake half the night looking these over, but they're meaningless if the scroll is a forgery. Kadir, isn't there *some*one who knew ... even the smallest thing about this scroll? Where it was found for example."

"Who can be know, *Hojam*? The man who found this scroll too is dead maybe."

The professor nodded slowly, as if his head had turned into iron.

"What about ..." Drew began. "You said something about Paul and the Dead Sea Scrolls."

Stephen sighed and dropped into the chair beside the coffee table. His vigor gone, he flicked a gnarled finger at Kadir. "If you're going to understand what you've got hold of, it's important for you to understand the world it came from." He leaned to the edge of his chair. "While there is no shortage of controversy over this idea, the Qumran Essenes may have had close ties to the early Christian community. John the Baptist was quite probably a former Essene, and Jesus himself shows not a few Essene traits.

"But you have to bear in mind one exceptionally important fact when looking over the Dead Sea Scrolls: the Essenes built a few mysteries of their own into them. The scrolls were written during a period of Roman oppression, and the Essenes feared they might one day fall into Roman hands. Thus, for example, the word *Babylon* in the Dead Sea Scrolls actually refers to Rome. The *Kittim*, who, in the Old Testament, are the Babylonians, are now the Romans. This way, were the Romans to discover these writings, their translators would assure them they were reading about history long past."

"The Book of Revelation does the same thing, doesn't it?" Drew asked.

The professor nodded. "Yes. There are no actual names in Revelation—or the Dead Sea Scrolls. Who was the Teacher of Righteousness? Who was the Wicked Priest? The Liar? We have no choice but to interpret.

"By the time of Jesus' birth, you see, the Jews had long been an occupied people—the Persians, the Greeks in 332 BC, the Greco-Syrians, and then, in 63 BC, the Romans. The Jews could do very little without consulting their Roman overseers. Among the Jews themselves, there were four principle groups vying for power—the Pharisees, the Sadducees, the Zealots, and the Essenes.

"The Pharisees concerned themselves with keeping the Law of Moses and with the ethical ramifications of the Law. They were directly opposed by the Sadducees, whom they outnumbered. Moreover, the Pharisees had the support of the people, who considered the Sadducees a snobbish elite. So, while the high priest of the Temple was always a Sadducee, the Sadducees often gave in to the demands of the Pharisees because the public would not have tolerated them otherwise.

"The Essenes, on the other hand, were outsiders. Although they emphatically maintained that they were 'zealous for the Law', they performed a different ritual of purification for their sacrifices and so were barred from the Temple. According to Josephus, without whose writings we would be utterly lost, they observed the Sabbath with such rigor that they refused even to defecate on the Lord's Day!"

Kadir looked at Drew. "Defecate?"

"*Shit*," Drew answered.

Kadir nodded sagely. "Very pure men."

"And the Zealots believed they had been called by God to take up the sword against the Romans and reclaim the land for Yahweh?" Drew asked.

"More or less, yes," the professor agreed. "Now, there is one other important point regarding the Essenes: they expected two messiahs. One would be descended of the line of David; one would be descended of Moses's brother, Aaron. One would be a king who would lead the Jews in battle and the other a priest who would guide them spiritually. So you had the line of David and the line of Zadok—Zadok being an heir of Aaron. The Essenes insisted the high priest of the Temple be chosen only from among Zadokites."

Drew glanced down at Kadir. He was actually listening.

"The problem here is that the Sadducees always furnished the High Priests, but they were not Zadokites. The Sadducees were therefore a source of continual outrage to the Essenes. Moreover, since the Sadducees cooperated with Rome, the Essenes looked on them as traitors.

"What the common Christian does not understand is how many messiahs came and went in ancient Palestine. *Messiah*, in fact, was the accepted term for a king centuries before the Christian era. It simply designates the *anointed one*, of God of course, and Jewish kings were all ceremonially anointed with oil. David was a legitimate messiah as was Solomon.

"Nor do most Christians bother to discover how many Jews were crucified by the Romans. At the turn of the first century, for example, Judas of Galilee led a revolt. It was eventually put down—but not until Herod's palace in Jericho had been left a smoldering ruin and some two thousand Jews crucified. Two *thousand*. Jesus' punishment and suffering, however unfortunate, were far from unique.

"Of greater significance is the fact that Christ is not, strictly speaking, Jewish." The professor turned to Drew. "You should know this. He is the last in a long line of dying-and-rising gods."

"You mean the Mystery cults ..."

Stephen nodded. "The authors of the Gospels and Church historians *had* to make Jesus unique. They *had* to make him more than a mere messiah ... quite a few had already come and gone, you see. They had to make him *divine*. The Son of God. Hence the various miracles—most of which had been performed by pagan cult figures centuries earlier." His hands drifted back into his lap.

"I seemed to have got sidetracked. And despite the fact that I have a gift for sustained monologue, I think I'll save this lecture for another time. I'm *retired* after all." The professor shook his head. "Anyway, it hardly matters. In the end people believe exactly what they want to believe."

Stephen looked exhausted as he pushed off his thighs and stood up with an exaggerated groan. "Kadir, you've a business to run, and, if I must admit it, I want to be alone with my photocopies ..."

Drew heard the same clicking he'd heard earlier. Vaguely he wondered what it had been as he and Stephen exchanged handshakes and a kiss on each cheek.

"Kadir," the professor said, "I expect to hear from you soon."

"Inshallah."

"Zafer, I'm not a fan of firearms, but under the circumstances, I suppose some sort of protection is warranted."

"Don't worry, *Hojam*. I've had extensive training."

"Well, there's some reassurance in that."

The street was empty except for a fruit-seller on the corner who'd parked his cart under a streetlamp.

Zafer pointed at Kadir and then at Drew: "A glass of *raki?*"

Kadir nodded. *"Evet."*

Drew shook his head. "I think I'll head home." He looked at Kadir. "You going to call Tariq's friends?"

Kadir shook his head. "Turkish Airlines."

"Turkish airlines?"

"These things are not done by the phone. We must go Cairo."

3: 8

THE SAVIOR

DREW'S CELL PHONE RANG just as he reached the end of Istiklal Avenue. He stopped in a tiny plaza coldly lit by the neon of the shops around it. Glancing down at the name and number displayed, he frowned and answered. "Stephen…?"

"Drew. This scroll …"

It sounded as though the professor's voice was trembling … or was it the connection?

"You think it's a forgery?"

"No. Just the opposite. This is the first time I've ever seen solid proof that there may have been no actual man on whom the Gospels are based."

"But that's—that's *impossible*. There are records. I mean, Tacitus…"

"Drew, you know as well as I do that Christ is not a proper name—"

"Here's what I know—it's from the Greek, *christos*, which is how the Gospel authors translated *messiah*, or *the anointed one*. In other words, *christened*."

"All well and good. Now listen. Jesus' given name would have been Yeshua—Joshua in English. Do you know its meaning?"

"No." Directly across from Drew was Kaffeehaus, a German café with an enormous front window. Through it, he watched a woman with a cigarette between her fingers lean toward the man across from her.

"*Yeshua* translates to *savior*. Now, in the Gospel of Thomas, the 114 sayings are attributed to Jesus, and throughout the gospel various apostles—often identified by name—ask him questions. But in Kadir's scroll there are no names. There is only what is essentially the passive tense ... 'when asked' or 'he was asked'."

"When *who* was asked?

"That's what I'm trying to tell you. It's simply *the savior*. Paul was the first to mention Jesus, but Paul may have meant *the savior, the anointed one* as general terms—Jesus Christ, or as he sometimes wrote, Christ Jesus. Don't you see? They were *interchangeable*. They were not proper names."

Drew wanted to be in Kaffeehaus with that woman who was smoking across from her boyfriend, who probably had nothing more pressing on her mind than a witty reply to whatever he was saying.

"Drew, when the Gospels originally circulated, they were anonymous—no signatures. Everything was written in capital letters, and there was virtually no punctuation."

Drew was beginning to understand. "So *the Savior, the Anointed One* could have been translated into Greek as *Iesous Christos*. And later scribes, assuming it was a proper name, wrote Jesus Christ."

"Exactly. This scroll uses the same style as Mark."

"What do you mean?"

"Throughout his Gospel he writes not Jesus but *the* Jesus."

"What?"

"*The* savior, obviously. I told you, it was a title. You never bothered to read the Gospels in the original Greek?"

"I never learned Koine Greek." Drew glanced at the dark sky above the Golden Horn, at the cafés and restaurants, at the passersby on their way to other parts of the city. Nothing had changed, and yet, because of the voice on the other end of the phone, everything had changed.

"Never mind that. Just remember, Drew, history repeats. And it does so on every scale, in a fractal sort of fashion."

"Fractal?"

"I've no longer any doubt that Jesus is *never* mentioned outside the New Testament."

"Oh really?" Drew couldn't keep the sarcasm out of his voice. "Let me quote Tacitus for you: *Christus, the founder of the Christians, had undergone the death penalty in the reign of Tiberius, by sentence of the procurator Pontius Pilate ...*"

"I'm quite sure that's a late addition to Tacitus's text, but let's say it's not. Tacitus was writing some eighty years after Christ was supposedly crucified. He was *not* a contemporary. More importantly, he never records the name *Jesus* but merely Latinizes *Christos* slightly. A *title*, not a name."

Drew pressed the phone harder up against his ear. "You're saying no one … no one recorded a proper name?"

"*No one.* If anything, Tacitus recorded a rumor. Had he taken the name from official documents, you can be sure that Pontius Pilate would not have recorded crucifying the Messiah of the Jews! It would not have been the general *Christos* but the specific *Jesus* or *Yeshua.* The name *Jesus*, however, is nowhere to be found outside of the New Testament and Josephus, and the passage in Josephus is clearly a forgery."

"Sounds kinda flimsy to me, Stephen." Drew's tone bordered on rude.

"Does it? Tacitus refers to Pilate as *procurator* of Judea, but that's incorrect. He was *prefect* of Judea. If Tacitus had gotten his information from Roman records, he would have known that. In fact, there isn't a single historian writing in the first century AD who mentions Jesus or the Christ. Nor do Pliny the Elder, Philo of Alexandria, Justus of Tiberias, Seneca, Lucan, Plutarch, or Pausanias—some of whom were contemporaries of Jesus. And these are only the better-known authors of the period."

"Stephen, I might be able to accept that there was no resurrection—"

"You have something harder to accept, Drew. If you really want to follow where this leads, you'll discover that virtually everything you were taught about Jesus is a lie. He was not born in Bethlehem. He was not raised in Nazareth. There was no Sermon on the Mount. There were no miracles. He was not crucified under Pontius Pilate, he was not the Savior, and he did not rise from the dead—"

"I'm sorry, Stephen, I just can't." Drew was almost too angry to listen anymore.

"Do you want to side with the truth or a comfortable illusion?"

"Christ is not an illusion!"

A woman walking past glanced at him.

"Christ existed," Drew asserted in a muted voice. "Maybe he didn't start out divine, but God raised Him up, and God works through Him now. He brought a message of peace and compassion, of non-violence—"

"The message, Drew! The message is what's important! Why are you clinging to the messenger? That was Paul's mistake. Didn't I say earlier tonight that the Essenes expected *two* messiahs, one a king and one a priest? Look at the name that has come down to us through history: Christ is Greek for *messiah*, a king descended of David; Jesus is Latinized Hebrew for *savior*, a priest descended from Aaron and Zadok."

There was a ringing in Drew's ears that he thought came from his cell phone. Until he realized that it was in both ears.

"There *was* a Savior, Drew, but it was not Jesus. Look again at Paul's letters. In 2 Corinthians 11:3, he accuses the apostles of preaching *another Jesus*. Doesn't that seem strange? Now read it—"

There was a pause.

"Drew, there's someone here."

"What?"

"Someone's in the house."

The phone either fell or was dropped, and Drew heard a door slam. He recalled the aged lumber barring the way to the study.

"Drew ... they're here."

"Who?"

"The men who killed Tariq I imagine. Listen—"

There was pounding on a door.

"Stephen, you have to *get out* of there."

"Drew, I'm on the fourth floor. There's nowhere to go. Now *listen* ... try substituting *savior* for *Jesus* in Paul's letter. He's accusing the apostles of preaching *another savior*. Now it makes sense! They couldn't agree on who the Savior was! Paul must have been The Liar in the Qumran scrolls—he *must* have been!"

The pounding grew louder.

"Stephen. Tell them you *know* where the scroll is. That's what they want. Tell them you can lead them to it—anything! I'll get Kadir and Zafer—"

Drew heard the sound of old, solid wood cracking.

"*Listen*, Drew. I can't explain it now, it's too complicated, but the scroll has a signature. None of the Gospels is signed, but this document most definitely *is*."

"*Who*? Who signed it?"

"The name would mean nothing to you. What you must remember is that Jesus was not the Savior, not the one recognized by the Essenes or the early Christians, but there *was* a Savior."

"Who was he?"

The line went dead.

3: 9

HISTORY REPEATS

KADIR'S PHONE RANG for the sixth time ... the seventh....
"Come on, *answer.*"

Drew was already trotting up Istiklal, dodging pedestrians and trying not to collide with couples who seemed to dawdle specifically to get in his way. His pony-tail slapped against his back as cobblestones bruised his feet through his sneakers. Sweat filmed his forehead.

"Pick up, Kadir!" Why was he just letting it ring?

"What is it, American infidel?" His voice was almost drowned out by music and loud conversations.

"Where are you?"

"At whorehouse."

"What?"

"We drink *raki.* Where you are thinking?"

"The men who killed Tariq ... I think they found the professor."

"Gerchekten?"

"Yes, really! You and Zafer have to get back there—*now!*"

"Don't call police!" he shouted. *"Anliyormusun?* We are closer than police. In two minutes, we are there!"

"Call me when you—"

Kadir had already hung up.

Drew bumped into a man who had started suddenly across Istiklal. Sweat shook free from his face. *"Pardon."* He held up a hand apologetically but didn't stop. The tram, which was nowhere to be seen, never moved much faster than Drew was going now, and there were no taxis up the avenue. Turning off Istiklal, Drew took the sloping backstreets down through Jukurjuma and came up back, slowing to a stop in front of the building he'd left less than an hour ago. The night air felt like a damp cloth pressed against his sweaty face.

The phone in his hand came noisily to life. "Kadir?"

"Drew, you must come. You must see."

"Is he all right?"

"You must come."

Drew tugged on the steel door, but it was locked. *How did* they *get in...?* "I'm here!" he shouted into the phone.

The buzzer went off and the lock clicked open.

Taking the stairs two at a time, Drew hauled himself up by the railing.

On the fourth floor he saw what he knew he would see. The lock had been broken off the door. Fresh wood—blond rather than tawny—had been exposed. Splinters littered the floor.

Kneeling beside the professor, Zafer looked at Drew and shook his head.

"It *can't* be."

"It is Allah's will," Kadir said.

"No one could have saved him." Zafer pointed to the professor's body. The gray shirt had turned crimson, and a bloodstain was spreading on the carpet like a dark ocean overflowing an oversized map. "Four shots to the chest. He was probably dead by the time he hit the floor."

Although Drew's vision had begun to blur, some part of him still refused to believe the evidence. "They couldn't have ... *couldn't* ..." He sniffed hard and swallowed a salty lump.

One of the professor's eyes was half closed, the other almost completely open. For some reason, this made Drew cry harder. The human body had been exposed for what it was: an organic machine. Stephen, whose bristly cheek he had kissed not an hour ago, was dead.

As though Zafer had read his mind, he brushed the professor's eyelids closed with an open hand.

"What are we going to do with him?" Drew's lower lip trembled.

"They've taken everything," Zafer said. "The computer on the third floor is gone—not the monitor or the printer, the tower. And the professor's laptop. All that's left is the bag. They ransacked the bedroom and knocked over a few things up here to make it look like a robbery. Even his pockets are empty."

Drew barely heard him. Gaze sinking, he saw that the professor's left hand had cramped into a claw. He was suddenly furious. He pushed Zafer aside, distantly surprised even in his rage at how solid the Turk was. Drew grabbed the professor's clawed hand. It was warm, still pliable. He straightened the fingers out and held them. Tears burned his eyes. Never did he believe less that anyone had ever been raised from the dead—not Lazarus, not Tabitha, not Christ himself. Dead was dead. It was unholy. Something irreplaceable was gone. He didn't know if it was chemical or spirit, but it was absolute, utterly beyond retrieval or comprehension. Whatever it was that had responded to the name *Stephen* had fled.

Drew stood and wiped his eyes on a shirtsleeve. "How did they find him?"

Zafer shook his head. "I don't know."

Drew looked at Kadir. "What about your cell phone? They have your number, don't they?"

"*Ne?*"

"They probably stopped at your shop, Kadir. You didn't even know who they were. They took a business card maybe—do you remember anyone taking a card recently? A foreigner? Maybe two of them?"

Kadir scratched the stubble on his chin. "This is possible."

"If they have your cell number and the right equipment, maybe they can use the GPS to track you." He looked at Zafer. "Can't they?"

"If the phone is on ..."

Kadir took his phone out of his vest and shut it off.

"There's an easier way," Zafer said. "Every phone has a signature—that's how the cell recognizes it. If they get the signature, they can listen in on the conversation. They don't need to track the signal with GPS." He shook his head. "But only governments have access to that kind of technology."

"That's who you are, right?" Drew asked. "*MIT*. Turkish CIA."

"Not MIT," Zafer said. "Special forces. And not anymore."

"Dishonorable discharge?"

"Something like that."

"But you know something about how they operate."

He nodded.

"So how did they find us?"

Zafer shrugged. "Maybe when they ransacked your place they found something. Where else would you go with an ancient manuscript?"

"If they find that scroll before we do," Drew said, "we're done."

Zafer lifted an eyebrow and smirked. "Maybe, maybe not."

"They're not after the Dead Sea Scroll. It's the other one they want. If they find it, they won't need your photos, Kadir. Remember what Stephen said? You can't be sure if it's forged or genuine from a photo. Once they find that scroll, they'll just send somebody to shut us up. Because we know there's a thread—and if someone pulls hard enough, centuries of Church dogma start to unravel."

He glared at Zafer. "I don't care if you're James Bond. You have to sleep some time. Do you want to spend the rest of your life wondering in which restaurant, in which bar, on which street someone is going to put you in the crosshairs, or poison your drink? Do you have family? Can you keep them safe? This isn't some rich businessman we're dealing with. This is much bigger. This goes way back. More than a thousand years maybe."

"How you are knowing this?" Kadir asked.

"History repeats, Stephen said. I know who killed him. And Tariq."

3: 10

KANKARDESH

ZAFER WALKED A FEW METERS from Timur the Lame, which was tucked into one of Taksim's narrow backstreets, and took out his cell phone. Neon stained the cobbles red and blue. Inside, Kadir was trying to pry out of Drew what he knew about who had killed Tariq and the professor. The American, however, had suddenly turned solemn and was unwilling to talk. About anything.

Zafer dialed the number of his *kankardesh*, his *blood brother*. He and Gökhan had met in the Army. After serving together in operations along the Iraqi border, Gökhan was accepted to MIT while Zafer opted for special forces. A few years later, during the second Persian Gulf War, an incident with an American soldier had ended Zafer's military career.

"Kankardeshim! N'aber?"

"Fine, fine. And you?"

"Same old MIT, same old me. What can I do for you?"

Zafer glanced up at a couple hugging each other by the waist as they walked. They disappeared inside Timur's.

"There's a mess your boys will have clean up on Oba Sokak, number 17. A murder. Stephen Cutherton, a British national. It was made to look like a robbery, but it wasn't. That much I know. See what you else you can come up with."

"A British citizen?"

"Yes. He has a flat in Antakya. Can you lock it down?"

"Tonight?"

"Unless you can do it sooner."

"Anything else? I think you're out of wishes."

"He has a house somewhere in London. See if you can get British intelligence to lock it down. The guy was a well-known professor of religion. Shouldn't be hard to find an address. He's probably in the phone book."

"Tonight, huh? You'll have to give me something to feed the Brits."

"Tell them you think religious fundamentalists are involved, probably terrorists. That ought to get them to put down their teacups."

"Is that all you've got?"

"I'll have more for you in a few days, but I think this is big—very big. If I play this the right way, I think you guys might consider hiring me. We'll see what happens after Cairo."

"Cairo? You have a passport?"

"Three."

"I mean, a *valid* passport."

"Three."

"You're amazing."

"After the dust settles, I may be more amazing than you think."

BOOK 4: 1 - 8

THE EBIONITES

The main charge against the Ebionites, as Hippolytus tells us ("Philos," vii, 34) is that they, like all the earliest "heretics," denied the later doctrine of the miraculous physical virgin-birth of Jesus. They lived according to the Jewish customs, claiming that they were justified "according to the Law." They further declared, so says Hippolytus, that Jesus had been so justified by his practice of the Law; it was for this cause that they called him "the Anointed (Christ) of God and Jesus; for none of the other prophets had fulfilled the Law." They further declared "that they themselves could, by doing the same, become Christs; for, they said, that he (Jesus) was a man like all men."

— GRS Mead

4: 1

ASHES

DREW HARDLY SAID A WORD during the first hour of the brief flight to Cairo. He spent most of it among rustling pages and an assortment of books, underlining sentences, making notes, and muttering to himself.

Now he was staring out the window at a massive cloud formation that looked like a billowy island. He still couldn't believe Stephen was dead. For three consecutive nights he'd slept only a handful of hours. Two of those nights in a cheap hotel in Sirkeji—Zafer's idea. When Drew had complained, Zafer had said. "Do you want to wake up with these guys standing over you?"

Drew shook his head numbly.

"And another thing, get me eight photos. Passport size."

"What for?"

"Just do it."

Drew's cramped airline seat, along with the peculiar smell of airline upholstery and carpeting, was nauseating. When he closed his eyes, he saw the blood-soaked shirt. The bony fingers of one hand curled like the talons of an enormous bird. The eyes as lusterless as costume jewelry beneath lids unevenly open. Why the hell hadn't Zafer closed them before he'd gotten there?

The morning after Stephen had been murdered, Drew had found his way to the roof of their Sirkeji hotel before sun-up. As though being just a little closer to the sky made a difference. As though he could press himself against Atlas's burden—no, Atlas had shouldered the Earth, so who was propping up the heavens? He scanned the dark sky over the Sea of Marmara, but no god had been sufficiently moved by Stephen's death to reach down, gather up his lanky shape, and place it among the constellations.

He missed Stephen's voice almost as much as the man himself. It wasn't the sound of it so much as the tenor, its bearing as it conveyed Stephen's impeccable word choice. Exquisitely rational. Even reconstituted from an e-mail, his voice expressed something that was quintessentially *Stephen*. It was the voice of Jung's Wise Old Man. Whether commuting on the bus or feeling the weight of another night without Yasemin in his Istanbul flat, Drew had often turned to that voice. The professor had become like the familiar silhouette of a mountain looming in the distance. No matter where Drew went, it was there, a marker from which he could always orient himself.

The last time he'd visited Stephen at his summer house in Antakya—ancient Antioch—they'd spent the evening on the rooftop terrace. The flagstones held the leftover heat of the day, and there had been the blood-warm gleam of wine. Jasmine wound around a trellis overhead scented the sultry breeze. From there they had an inspiring view of the valley.

"I don't miss my youth any more than, I imagine, this city misses its own." Stephen was gazing toward an uneven horizon of hills. "Of course, I can't say I wouldn't be pleased no end if this old body of mine were somewhat more like yours." He glanced over at Drew. "The ancient Greeks were right, you know. The body is as beautiful and sacred as anything that might be called intellect or soul—assuming the latter actually exists."

"Seems to me one isn't much good without the other."

"Well said, Drew, well said. But I'll tell you this also: these visits, from you and a few of my old students, are what keep me from feeling as though I've mishandled my life. Yes, of course, I'm still involved in my work. I publish the occasional article or review, but I also experience a certain vicarious living. What I am driving at, I suppose, is that I ... I see myself reflected in small ways in all of you, and I can't say that I regret never having had children of my own."

He started to say something else, something that Drew instinctively felt he'd kept to himself for a long time, but he turned away and gazed off at the hills.

"The Gnostics, you know, would not have much cared for this view."

Stephen had changed the subject.

"Their concept of the visible universe … they saw it as the opposite of a ghost more or less … a rather poor material copy of a perfect realm of pure spirit."

Drew shrugged. "Platonism revisited. Just like Christianity."

"Yes, but with such elaborate and rather poetic departures." Stephen swirled the wine in his glass to stir up its bouquet. "What I particularly like about the Gnostics is that they believed in a *spiritual* resurrection of Christ, not a *physical* one."

Smiling, Drew shook his head. This was their perennial bone of contention. Drew was a believer while the professor was an atheist.

"To the Gnostics, all doctrines—be they pagan, Christian, or Jewish—were merely approaches to truth. But the truth itself, they insisted, was beyond words or even symbols."

Drew shrugged. "It makes sense if Gnosticism evolved out of the Greek Mystery religions. Didn't initiates in the Mysteries eventually learn that the myths and stories about their gods were allegories and metaphors?"

The professor grinned. "Studying literature isn't so far from studying religion."

So Drew had often said.

And now he was supposed to believe that Jesus Himself was a *metaphor*. He was supposed to wipe heart and mind clean of the Jesus he'd grown up with, the teacher, father, brother he'd come to believe in. As though his heart and mind were a couple of blackboards he carried around inside him. But even on blackboards, the ghost of erased letters remained. What was he supposed to do with the … could he call it love? The love he'd projected toward heaven when he'd felt the presence of a Jesus who cared about him—*him*, Drew Korchula? Had he been setting human warmth loose in a vacuum? The same as the ancient Greeks and Sumerians and Hopi and Dogon and all the rest who had imposed shapes on the constellations? Jesus had been Drew's comfort when there had been no one else. The voice inside him when there was no other voice—not even the professor's. All knowing, all forgiving, ever patient, ever tolerant. How was he supposed to give that up?

Maybe he didn't have to. Maybe all he had to do was find out who, if Stephen was right, the real Savior had been.

Christ, he said to himself without meaning to invoke the Savior. *Hadn't giving up Yasemin two years ago been enough?* Drew closed his eyes and massaged his brow.

If the professor had enjoyed picking through the charred remnants of pagan beliefs, Drew had a penchant—like constantly sticking a tongue in the bloody gap left by a pulled tooth—for rooting around in painful memories.

The morning after Stephen had been killed, he'd gone through photocopies of the letters he'd written to Yasemin. One he found particularly painful and, true to his peculiar brand of masochism, he'd reread it not once, but twice.

He let his head rest against the window. Sunlight reflecting off the fluffy clouds beneath made him squint. Closing his eyes, he saw luminous red. Blood did that, he knew. And it seemed he was sinking into a lake of it.

4: 2

A MILLENNIA-OLD COVER-UP

DREW STIRRED AND RUBBED an eye with the heel of his hand. His face was numb where it had been pressed against the window.

Kadir elbowed him in the ribs. "The man stewardess is looking to you when he passes this way. I think he is wanting a long-hair boyfriend."

Drew's tray table was still covered with papers and books.

Kadir glanced around at the other passengers though he couldn't take in much since he couldn't see over the seat in front of him. Lowering his voice to a whisper, he asked, "What about Tariq? You said ..." He gestured with a hand instead of completing the sentence.

The night of Stephen's murder, Drew had said he knew who had killed both the professor and Tariq. But when they'd gone to Timur the Lame's for a drink, he'd put off Kadir by telling him that he didn't have specific names. "Give me a couple of days," he'd said. Now, he supposed, he had to give Kadir something more solid.

"The uh ... the last phone call from the professor, he was trying to tell me ... I'm not sure exactly what, but he insisted that there's no historical documentation of Jesus' existence."

Kadir looked confused.

Drew lifted a pair of books and shuffled through some of the pages. "The main source of history for Palestine in the first century is Josephus, who'd been a Jewish Zealot before he went over to the Romans."

"A Zealot killed Tariq?"

"Do you remember that Stephen said the Essenes wanted to cleanse the land of Romans and install a high priest who was of the same blood-line as Aaron? A Zadokite?"

"*Tamam*, okay."

"So did the Zealots. When Josephus and his band were defeated by the Roman general Vespasian, Josephus surrendered, insisting that Vespasian himself was the Messiah. He predicted Vespasian would be the next emperor of Rome and swore loyalty him."

"*Eh*-eh?"

So what? was about right, Drew thought.

"Josephus is the only historian who wrote more than a sentence about Jesus, but *look* at what he supposedly wrote." Drew handed a photocopy to Kadir.

About this time lived Jesus, a wise man, if indeed one ought to call him a man. For he was the achiever of extraordinary deeds and a teacher of those who accept the truth gladly. He won over many Jews and many of the Greeks. He was the Messiah. When he was indicted by the principal men among us and Pilate condemned him to be crucified, those who had come to love him originally did not cease to do so; for he appeared to them on the third day restored to life, as the prophets of the Deity had foretold these and countless other marvelous things about him.

"*Chok sachma.*" Kadir held the paper out to Drew, but Zafer took it from him.

"Exactly—pure nonsense."

"If Josephus was being a Zealot Jew, then he does not believe Jesus was the Messiah."

"Exactly. Since he lived in Vespasian's house, it's hardly likely he'd call a man the Romans executed as an enemy of Rome the Messiah. The passage isn't in Josephus's writing style and it doesn't fit in the rest of the narrative. This is an interpolation, something added to the original text by a Christian scribe.

"What's worse, the oldest copy of Josephus is from the *tenth century*, about nine-hundred years after it was written. The first Church historians, looking at earlier copies, never mention this passage—it couldn't have been there. No one noticed it until the *fourth* century."

While Drew had no doubt this argument held up, it was almost like patting himself on the back for correctly diagnosing himself with cancer.

He didn't want to believe Stephen, but he desperately wanted to know the truth. Had Christians, along with the rest of the world, been duped for two thousand years?

Zafer handed the page back to Drew.

There was an announcement first in Turkish then in English: "The plane will be landing in a few minutes. Please return your seat to an upright position ..."

Drew's ears popped as the plane descended. Glancing out the window, all he could see was desert.

"*Eh*-eh? Josephus is the one who killed Tariq?"

Drew shook his head. "Christians added Jesus to Josephus's history. Scribes must have been involved, and there must have been men who gave the scribes orders. I wouldn't be surprised if some of these men eventually formed a kind of shadow organization within the Church. If their organization is still around, then a Q document older than Jesus is a threat to them. And to the Church. If they have the Vatican's backing—"

Zafer finished his sentence. "They're well-financed and well-equipped."

"So the interpolators of hundreds of years before are Tariq's enemies?"

"Yes."

The stewardess checked their seatbelts. The three men smiled at her in unison.

After she was gone, Kadir whispered hoarsely, "I am not caring about Jesus. If he lived or not, he is dead now. I am caring about Kadir."

Zafer patted the dwarf on the shoulder. "That's the problem, Kadir. We're looking at a new breed of Zealots."

Drew nodded.

Kadir looked first at Zafer then at Drew. "I am thinking you two have pumpkins instead of heads. Just some false writings in an old book. This is unrelated to assassinators."

"Listen, Kadir, there's more. Mark was the first and simplest of the Gospels. It doesn't mention the virgin birth, Joseph, or Bethlehem. The oldest copies of Mark's Gospel *all* end at chapter 16, verse 8, where several women are terrified to discover Jesus' tomb is empty. The new ending, which is now standard, shows Jesus alive again. Someone *added* those eleven verses to make Mark more like the other Gospels."

Kadir shrugged.

"Okay ... here's one more for you: Matthew and Luke both had access to Q, but no copy of it has ever been found. Except for the one Tariq photographed, and that one isn't in Greek. Why do you think that is?"

Kadir shrugged. "My sister lost her virginness after she is married. No one ever found that either."

"Did anyone look for it?"

"Defol git."

Piss off yourself, Drew wanted to say. Instead, looked over Kadir's head at Zafer. "I wish I could talk to Stephen. I wish I had at least written down what he said that night ..."

Kadir reached into a pocket of his flak jacket and pulled out a micro-cassette recorder. He hit a button and Drew heard the professor's voice, far away and metallic. "I'm *retired* after all. I've given you nearly two dozen keywords tonight. Put the pieces together for yourself ..."

Click.

For a second Drew couldn't talk. Taking the recorder out of Kadir's hand, he looked at it as though he were a primitive who believed Kadir's little machine had captured Stephen's soul.

"*That's* the clicking sound I heard that night. You sneaky little bastard. Who even uses microcassettes anymore?"

"If my phone is closed, still I can record."

"Why the hell didn't you say something?"

There was a jolt and a bounce as the plane touched down.

"*Eh*-eh. I say it now."

4: 3

CAIRO

LEAVING THE AIR-CONDITIONED arrivals hall of Cairo International Airport was like walking into a wall of heat. Drew had to squint even with sunglasses on. Decorative palm trees waved in the hot breeze. A granite obelisk incised with hieroglyphics—an enormous compass needle pointing skyward—rose from the parking lot. Drew remembered it from his first visit to Cairo a couple of years earlier.

A taxi driver accosted Drew, insisting, in English, that there was no bus to the city's center and that "feefty Egybtian pounds ees good brice."

Zafer snarled at him in Arabic. The cabbie shrank back and disappeared in search of more gullible customers.

"Drivers here have to pay a fee to get inside the airport," Zafer explained, "so they charge a lot more than the ones outside the gate."

Arabic, Turkish, and English. Drew wondered what else Zafer had up his sleeve.

They crossed the parking lot, each carrying a single piece of luggage.

The taxis lined-up outside the fence were black with white quarter-panels, generally Fiats that looked as though they'd logged most of their miles in war-time Beirut.

Ignoring the shouts of other drivers, Zafer picked out an old man with a white skullcap and a gaunt face.

The Egyptian smiled and motioned them toward his car; he was missing several narrow, brown teeth. His skin, the color of Turkish coffee, contrasted sharply with the skullcap and the silver stubble on his chin.

He and Zafer spoke briefly—bargaining?—before nodding amiably. The fare turned out to be twenty-five Egyptian pounds, about five dollars.

The taxi's black interior smelled like the abandoned cars Drew had played in as a child—a musty odor browned at the edges by countless afternoons in the sun. Amazingly, the air-conditioning worked, although the draft it created was noticeably dusty, and like the rest of the car, it rattled incessantly.

On the way to the airport's exit, Drew saw a traffic sign that almost made him laugh out loud: *You are going in a wrong way.* The warning had been written below the Arabic.

The freeway into Cairo was hemmed in by apartment blocks twenty or twenty-five stories high and sidewalks lined with trees. Every so often, a spectacular mosque would dramatically part the high-rise monotony. While mosques in both Cairo and Istanbul consisted primarily of domes and minarets, there was no mistaking one for the other. The façades of the Egyptian mosques were far more ornate and, with their emphasis on arabesque designs, more suggestive of the Oriental. Turkish mosques tended more toward what Drew thought of as solid, Greek lines.

An enormous statue of Ramses II towered over traffic from an island of palm trees and lush tropical plants that divided the freeway.

As they edged into Cairo's car-clogged downtown, the city took on a more European look. Neoclassical architecture prevailed: fluted pilasters, balconies with wrought-iron railings, floral flourishes carved into the stone. The buildings, however, were not the four or five narrow stories fitted for Istanbul streets—many hardly wider than alleys—but upwards of eight floors with enough breadth they looked somewhat squat. Crumbling cornices, fading paint, and exposed stone stained the color of mourning, these relics of European colonialism stood along wide avenues cluttered by overpasses.

The city itself was not, as was commonly assumed, ancient. Founded at the end of the first millennium by the Islamic conquerors of Egypt, it was hardly more than a thousand years old. The pharaohs' capital had been farther south, in Memphis, and until the twentieth century the pyramids had belonged to the desert. The suburbs of Cairo, however, spreading like an absurdly slow tsunami, now lapped at their feet.

The Samar Palace Hotel, where Zafer had booked rooms, stood in an alley blocked off to cars. Zafer considered this a selling point. "Nobody can pull up to the door," he said looking both ways. The odd thing about the hotel was that it didn't occupy the whole building; it only took up the third and fourth floors.

The building's lobby, as dark as a cave, led to a spacious staircase with granite steps wound around an elevator shaft. All wood and glass with a few tarnished brass fittings, the elevator could barely fit the three of them. Drew made sure he was in front of the doors. If the lights went out, he'd panic in such a small space, but with the way out visible and inches away, he felt nothing but a slight uptick in nervousness.

They stepped out on the third floor where they were greeted by a manager with a limp and a cheerful grin.

"Welcome to Egypt!" He held out his arms like he was going to grab them up in a group hug.

The room to which he led them had a stunningly high ceiling equipped with a fan, plastered walls in need of a fresh coat of paint, and a set of glass doors that opened onto a narrow balcony but no window. There were two beds, a small desk, and a hardwood floor whose finish had been stripped off by years of foot traffic.

The manager said something to Zafer in Arabic and handed him two sets of keys. Then he limped off.

Zafer closed the door.

Drew held his hand out to Kadir. "Gimme that recorder."

The dwarf pulled it out of a pocket of his flak jacket and handed it over.

While the Turks unpacked, Drew sat down at the desk and listened to the professor's disembodied voice. He wrote the list of keywords twice: once in his notebook and a second time on a page that he tore out and stuck in a pocket. He marked about half the keywords in the notebook NFI—*no fucking idea*. Then there were those he knew, and those he *thought* he knew but was unsure about how they related to Jesus. He marked the latter CU: *connection unknown*.

- *John the Baptist – Prophet who baptized Jesus shortly before his own death.*
- *James the Just – Brother of Jesus (CU—other than the obvious)*
- *The Ebionites - NFI*
- *Ananus – Vaguely familiar (CU)*

- *Damascus – City in Syria. Paul had his vision on the way there. (CU)*
- *Judas of Galilee – Zealot who rebelled against Rome (CU)*
- *Simon bar Giora – NFI*
- *Iscariot – Last name of the apostle Judas (CU)*
- *The Sicarii – NFI*
- *2,000 pigs – NFI*
- *Clementine Recognitions – NFI*
- *Serapis – Egyptian god? (CU)*
- *Ezekiel's Exodus – NFI*
- *Philo of Alexandria – Hellenized Jew, prolific religious commentator. (CU)*
- *The Therapeutae – NFI*
- *The Bacchae – Play by Euripides. (CU)*
- *Nag Hammadi Library – Collection of Gnostic Christian gospels. (CU)*

"We all stay in the same room," Zafer announced, "and we switch hotels every night."

Drew looked up. "Why?"

"People see you come and go enough, they remember when someone asks."

Drew nodded. Zafer had already made him get rid of his old cell phone. Looking at the two beds, he wondered who was sleeping with whom.

"When we leave the hotel, we leave together," Zafer said. "This way neither one of you gets snatched."

Kadir scowled at Drew. "If you become kidnapped, I don't give away the scroll for you."

"I don't give a scroll about you, either."

"Look, that's the point," Zafer said. "If we're together, that won't happen. Right now we need some clothes. After that I'll call a dealer who knew Abu and Tariq. Maybe he knows where Tariq got these photographs."

Drew looked at Kadir. "You told the professor Tariq was the only one who knew anything about the photos."

"*Eh*-eh? If the dealer knows nothing, I said the truth. If he is knowing something, I said a lie."

4: 4

KHAN AL-KHALILI

CAIRO'S LARGEST MARKETPLACE, Khan Al-Khalili, was something like the Grand Bazaar in Istanbul except that it was mostly outside and even more chaotic. Tourists, merchants, boys carrying trays of tea in their hands or long pallets stacked with round loaves of bread on their heads all fought for position in dusty, often-unpaved streets. With some of these narrow byways, a car was not an option. Sellers had set up their tables so that even pedestrians had to pick their way through.

They were stuck behind a man in a turban who was pushing a cart with wooden wheels. The cart was topped by a wood-fed oven with a tall pipe. The man, who was having difficulty maneuvering around tables piled with wares, was selling roasted yams.

And then there were the flies. Smaller, faster than the ones Drew was used to. They were everywhere. You could wave them away, but they'd settle right back on you—generally around your eyes and mouth, drawn to the moisture.

Khan Al-Khalili reminded Drew of an amusement park ride called the Tilt-a-Whirl, where everything blurred as you were spun around and then came into focus as the ride slowed down for a second or two only to speed up and turn the world into smears of light and color again.

Every stall was covered from ceiling to floor with meticulously arranged merchandise: a rainbow waterfall of fabrics, a profusion of leather bags, an Impressionist assortment of fruits, an array of ground spices—like multi-colored sand—in open sacks. The merchants patrolled their shop fronts with long broomsticks tipped with metal prongs, which they used to unhitch goods suspended overhead.

At one of the clothes stalls, Zafer did all of the talking while Drew and Kadir pretended they understood. Zafer bargained hard, making sellers knit their eyebrows, spread their arms, and whine as though some catastrophe had befallen them. They would start at one hundred Egyptian pounds and Zafer would counter with five. He reminded them he wasn't a tourist, and if they couldn't meet his prices, he knew sellers who could.

It took about ten minutes for him to buy three *keffiyehs*—the head-dress made famous by Yasser Arafat—and three *jalabiyas*, the gown-like garment Tariq had been wearing.

Drew looked at the clothes dubiously, swatting half-heartedly at a small cloud of flies.

"The best thing about these *jalabiyas*," Zafer said, "is you can put them on right over your regular clothes."

Drew still couldn't see himself in one of those get-ups.

Zafer's hand shot out, snatched at the air, and clenched into a fist.

Drew shook his head. "You missed."

Zafer opened his fist. The mangled body of a fly rested in a palm crease.

"How the hell do you do that? I can only catch them if they land."

"Training."

"The Turkish army trained you to catch flies?"

Zafer scowled. "How do you catch a fly after it lands?"

"I sweep my hand a few inches above it because I know it's going to take off when my hand gets near it."

"Right. If the fly doesn't move, you miss. If it's a sleepy fly, a slow fly, a starved fly, you might still miss because you expect it to react quickly. Same thing in the air. The fly is faster than I am so I have to guess. Come on." He beckoned with a hand. "Time for our phone call."

"I guess we have to assume that this, uh … dealer's phone is tapped and that his shop is being watched?" Drew asked.

Zafer nodded. "If they could follow Tariq to Istanbul, then they know he worked for Nabil. I'm going to tell Nabil that I have a family heirloom to sell. He'll know from my accent that I'm not from Cairo. That won't matter once we meet face to face."

"Won't he ask you to come to the shop?" Drew asked.

Zafer shook his head. "A coffeehouse, maybe his apartment. Those are the usual places for this kind of business. I'll insist on the coffeehouse."

Drew listened to the conversation, catching a few words—*tijaret, muhtemel*—that were the same in Arabic as in Turkish.

Zafer hung up the phone looking pleased. "Nine o'clock, Aswan Coffeehouse. In the Islamic Quarter."

The Islamic Quarter was no more or less Islamic than the rest of the city, but it was home to the oldest mosques in Cairo.

Zafer grinned at Drew. "Can't wait to suit you up."

4: 5

NABIL

THE LONG LIGHT of the Egyptian evening had mostly flattened into shadow when they entered the Islamic Quarter, a labyrinth of alleys, narrow streets, gloomy workshops, and tightly packed houses. Reminiscent of Istanbul, the architecture favored *jumbas* (much shallower, they were called *gambas*) and slim balconies. The motif was no surprise given that the Ottomans had ruled Egypt for nearly three hundred years. One *gamba,* its wood exquisitely carved, was crowned with the last of the Sun's dusty gold.

Overhead, clotheslines crisscrossed strips of fading blue.

European influences all but disappeared. Minarets rose in tiers marked off by sculpted balconies. Slender columns flanked windows and keyhole-shaped niches in the minarets. These restored pillars of Islam towered over rutted streets canyoned by crumbling walls, piled with rubble. Drew wondered if it hadn't been the North African light itself that had eroded Cairo and its monuments.

The taxi dropped them off far enough from the coffeehouse that they still had a ten-minute walk; anyone following them would have to go on foot.

The oldest part of the city, the Islamic Quarter was an inscrutable maze to Drew, but Zafer seemed to know exactly where he was going. Men wearing *jalabiyas* and cheap rubber sandals, turbans and *keffiyehs,* brushed past them.

Tiny Suzuki pick-ups, which looked to Drew like oversized toys, squeezed through the streets, occasionally getting caught behind a load-ed-down donkey or a horse pulling a cart.

The *gambas* that weren't shuttered were covered with latticework—*mashrubiyya*—that allowed women to see the street below without being seen. With such forced intimacy, it was no wonder the Orient was enamored of the veil, the screen, the curtain.

Aswan Coffeehouse was in one of the better maintained areas of the Islamic Quarter. Its entire front opened onto a cobbled alley crowded with tables and chairs. Inside, walnut-stained wainscoting trimmed mustard-yellow walls. The high ceiling was hung with lethargic fans and Islamic chandeliers—clusters of lamps with glass panels or tarnished brass with perforations that cut the light into star and moon shapes. Archways with tiny pillars marked the open boundaries between rooms. At least half the patrons puffed languidly on *narghiles*, and in spite of the open front, the mellow light inside was hazy with smoke.

A waiter guided them to a small table that was simply a wrought-iron stand with a copper disc riveted to it.

Although Drew felt absurdly conspicuous in a silk suit—a tasteful pearl gray—he had to look the part of a wealthy Turkish American. Both armpits lubricated with sweat, he was amazed that so many Egyptians could walk around in Western clothes in this heat.

Zafer asked to see the owner, and a moment later a short Egyptian with a potbelly and a red vest embroidered in gold thread appeared. Zafer explained that he was meeting Nabil and asked if he would direct the dealer to their table.

The owner lifted his chin toward the front of the coffeehouse. "He is here now."

Nabil was in Western clothes, too—pleated trousers, a worn jacket, a cell phone clipped to his belt. His curly hair was gray at the edges, like charcoal turning to ash. Creased by sun and age, his face was the color of foamless cappuccino.

The three of them stood up and greeted the obviously bewildered dealer. When Zafer introduced himself and Kadir, a look of recognition rearranged Nabil's features.

"Tariq's friends," he said in English. "From Istanbul." The Egyptian's eyes were never still, darting around the room, checking and rechecking.

"And an American purchaser." Kadir looked up at Drew.

"We wanted to talk to you because Tariq ... left a few loose ends."

Nabil nodded sagely. "You are aware that Tariq was double-dealing?" He turned to Kadir. "Please excuse me if I speak openly. Tariq was a good man. He was more clever than most, but he came from a village. He was not educated. He was only a runner, and runners do not leave Egypt to do business. They supply dealers."

While Nabil's English was good, his *P* came out like a *B* and his *TH* sounded more or less like *S*, which meant "that" sounded more like "sat."

"Three years ago, Tariq made a very lucky find. He sold it to a buyer of his own—a tourist or perhaps another dealer who paid a very good price. From this he got the idea he could become a dealer himself. He left his village and moved his family to Cairo. He bought a small car, rather old. He bought a cell phone. He dreamed of owning a shop and retiring in another country. Cairo's air is the worst in the world."

The waiter brought four cups of Turkish coffee served not in cups, but in tiny water glasses. The conversation paused while the waiter unloaded his tray.

Nabil sipped from his glass. "Tariq got ahead of himself. Over the years, he somehow made contact with some of our customers. He began to go to them in secret, promising better prices."

Nabil, Drew noticed, was wearing a gold ring on each hand. Which was odd because Muslim men are forbidden to wear gold. While Turks often flouted the proscriptions on alcohol, they generally observed this one. And Egyptians tended to be a good deal more conservative than Turks. Women covered their hair, and quite a few were veiled in black with nothing but their eyes visible.

"It may be that one of these contacts got him killed." Nabil shook his head sadly. "It may be that it was an accident as the police say. But there was a scroll ..."

"Abu's scroll," Kadir said. "This is the why he came to Istanbul."

"Ah, so the rumor is true." The darting bird eyes that seemed attuned to movements as insignificant as the twitch of an insect's wing settled on Kadir. "What happened to it?"

Kadir shrugged. "Tariq was too much clever. No one can find it now."

Zafer waved away flies. "A professor from England was also killed. Shot to death."

"A British professor? Why?"

"Because there's another scroll, more valuable than the one stolen after Abu died."

Nabil shook his head. "Even in the black market two deaths is … what's the word? Unsettling." The expression on his face changed. "Why did you pretend you wanted to sell a family heirloom?"

"Your phone might be tapped."

"I see."

A waiter passed and Drew felt the heat of the coals he was carrying.

"Do you know anything about the other scroll?" Zafer sipped Turkish coffee and glanced at Drew.

Drew reached into the breast pocket of his jacket. He took out a wad of bills held neatly by a silver clip, counted out $1,000, and put the money on the table.

Nabil glanced at each of them, his quick eyes glittering, sensing that while Drew had the money, Zafer was conducting the bargaining. He tucked the wad away.

"If you can give us any information—something we can use to locate the scroll, there will be a finder's fee. Say, five percent?"

Nabil's eyes closed slowly, and he nodded.

"Do you have any idea who has the other scroll?"

"Unfortunately, no. Runners never reveal their sources. If they did, dealers would steal them. And runners who talk about where a dealer has acquired his goods …" He shrugged. "There is a kind of brotherhood in this business. He who betrays one, betrays all. That is why Tariq could not sell the scroll in Cairo. Abu was a very great customer."

Zafer nodded. "Has anyone else come to you about the scrolls?"

Nabil sighed. "Yes."

"Who?"

"As I said, we don't reveal the names of buyers or sellers. It would make for very bad business."

And they're probably offering a lot more money, Drew thought.

Nabil reached for his coffee. He tipped back the glass, and a gold ring glinted. "Tariq was not a bad man. He merely wanted to be successful. He left a wife and three children. I was among the first to visit them when we received the news." Nabil stood up. "Please excuse me. My wife is waiting."

"Of course."

"Stay as long as you like as my guests. I will settle the bill tomorrow."

He was barely out of earshot when Drew held up his cup. "Four very expensive coffees. Kind of watery to boot." Luckily, the thousand dollars he'd just shelled out wasn't *his* money. All Zafer had asked him to pay was his own airfare.

"And now they know we're here." Zafer was following one or another of the flies zigzagging over their table.

"What do you mean?"

"Nabil is probably on his cell phone right now." Zafer's hand shot out. When he opened his fist, a bit of black dropped to the floor. He turned to Drew. "You think he told us the truth? There isn't a businessman alive who enjoys competition. Nabil's giving Tariq's wife guilt money. As for our competition … they got here first. And promised Nabil at least what we just paid, maybe more, to contact them as soon as we made contact with him. It doesn't matter to Nabil who finds the scroll first. As long as he gets a cut."

"So that's it? They're onto us already?"

Zafer nodded. "Probably, but we had no choice."

"Where are we supposed to go now? Back to Istanbul?"

"*Salak,*" Kadir said. "We go to see the Tariq's wife."

"Stay as long as you like he said." Zafer smirked. "He wants us to be relaxed."

"I guess we should go then before whoever he calls gets here."

"Exactly." Zafer was already on his feet. Shouldering the satchel with the photos, he stepped into the alley and began negotiating the obstacle course of tables and chairs.

After a couple of turns, they were on a narrow street lit by a streetlamp riveted to the stone wall of a building. Like a camera flash, the lamp created as much angular shadow as cold illumination. Patches of cobblestones attested that the street had once been paved, but it was now mostly dirt, the color of which gave Drew the impression that a drizzle of unrefined petroleum had recently fallen. As they neared the corner—a continuation of the same street at a right angle rather than an intersection—someone began shouting in Arabic.

The three men stopped and looked back.

An Egyptian, dressed in *keffiyeh* and *jalabiya,* waved a hand over his head as he ran. Another, the size of a freight car, lumbered behind him.

Drew glanced at Zafer. "What's he saying?"

"He has a message from Nabil."

"Don't turn around."

The voice, which came from behind them, was familiar. Apparently, Nabil had decided to deliver his message in person

4: 6

DEBT COLLECTION

CURSING HIMSELF UNDER HIS BREATH, Zafer kept his back to Nabil.

"Hands behind your head."

Elbows out, Zafer laced his fingers together on the back of his head. The muzzle of the pistol was pressed between his shoulder blades.

"I have been waiting for you." Nabil spoke in English. "So have they. The story about a family heirloom was believable, and you speak fluent Arabic, but it is not Egyptian Arabic. You think I am stupid? You think I don't know the midget has the Habakkuk Scroll? He is going to be my guest in Egypt. You are going to fly back to Istanbul with your American friend and bring back the scroll. You don't even know its worth, do you? Don't worry. You'll be paid. One hundred thousand dollars each. I am not a thief."

Zafer said nothing.

"You two! Get on your knees!"

A massive hand thumped against Drew's shoulder; he glanced imploringly at Zafer.

As if cued, the Turk twisted his torso violently, and his left arm came down in a sweeping movement until his hand caught hold of Nabil's wrist.

Drew gasped as a forearm locked across his throat. He expected to hear the pistol go off, but he didn't have time to be afraid of getting shot;

he couldn't breathe. His body reacted without him—his left arm shot up under the Egyptian's armpit, his right leg swung back, and he squirmed out of the larger man's grasp. But he hadn't put enough space between him and Nabil's gorilla. The Egyptian plowed into him and—*goddamn dress shoes*—Drew lost some of his footing. He fought not to be thrown to the ground, his vision suddenly made of cards someone was shuffling.

He shut his eyes.

He was in tight now where he could feel shifts in the other man's center of gravity, where he'd be able to intuit how to offset what he was going to do. He slipped deftly to one side, and Nabil's goon lost his balance. Straightening up so he was almost chest to chest with him, Drew snaked an arm around the thick waist, over-hooked an arm, and paused for a second. The Egyptian threw all of his weight forward and tried to lock up a bear hug. The momentum was what Drew needed. Stepping to one side and pinning the over-hooked arm with his own, he threw the Egyptian over his hip. The man's feet were suddenly where his head had been. Drew bent at the knees and lowered his weight to accelerate his descent. He landed with a wicked thud. He lay gasping, the wind knocked out of him.

Drew knew exactly how he felt. A Russian he'd faced in a freestyle tournament had taught him that throw—the hard way. Drew whirled around to see what had happened to Kadir.

The dwarf and the other Egyptian were on the ground. Kadir had latched onto his legs—he must have cannonballed in and tackled him—but Nabil's man was holding his upper body up with one arm and whacking Kadir's shoulder with the other.

Drew grabbed the stick and twisted it away from him. Adrenalin flooding his veins, he brought the stick down in a swift backhand. The Egyptian raised a forearm but turned his head away at the same time, and Drew cracked him behind an ear. The man went so limp Drew thought he was dead.

The goon Drew had hip-tossed had rolled to his side and was trying to get to his hands and knees.

Zafer shouted something in Arabic, and the Egyptian stopped moving.

Face-down, Nabil started to moan. Zafer had his pistol in one hand, and with the other, held Nabil's arm in a lock that involved using his knee as a fulcrum. From a wrestler's perspective, the hold was impressive. Also highly illegal.

The moan turned into a scream.

"You're a Christian, aren't you?" Zafer asked.

"Yes!"

Drew should have known: the gold rings.

"Who else is looking for the scrolls?"

"The Ecole Biblique. Two men."

"The Ecole Biblique?" Drew remembered the name—a Dominican school based in Jerusalem. Father Roland de Vaux, the man primarily responsible for refusing other scholars access to the Dead Sea Scrolls, had operated from there. It made perfect sense: Q was far more threatening than any Dead Sea Scroll.

"Names," Zafer said.

"In my wallet." Nabil grunted. "Their cards."

"Kadir. Get his wallet. *Chabuk ol.* Drew, keep an eye on the other one."

Kadir took out the wallet and began searching through it.

Drew stood over the guy he'd dropped, the night stick still in his hand. The situation seemed all the more surreal to him because he was dressed as though he were on his way to a wedding. Glancing up, he saw a boy gazing down from a balcony.

"What do they look like?" Zafer asked.

Nabil's cheek was pressed against the dirt. "One is blond. Very short hair. Blue eyes. Tall. The other ... small. Black hair. Dark eyes. He looks like a businessman. Thirty. Thirty-five."

"*Buldum.*" Kadir held up two cards.

"Good. Take back our money too," Zafer said. He asked Nabil, "How much is the scroll worth?"

Nabil didn't answer.

Zafer torqued his arm until the dealer screamed.

"Four million dollars." He was panting heavily. Maybe five."

"Oh-*ha!*" Kadir gasped.

Two Egyptians rounded the same corner from which Nabil must have come. They stopped but didn't seem to know what to do.

Zafer spoke to them sharply in Arabic.

"Kadir, hold up the money and drop the wallet," he said in Turkish.

The wallet hit the dirt with a slap.

The boy on the balcony joined in the conversation, speaking excitedly and pointing at the fallen men.

The one Drew had clubbed was stirring. Drew tried to hide the stick behind an arm.

"*Hadi, gidelim,*" Zafer said. *Let's go.* He bent down close to Nabil's ear. "If you try to follow us, I'll kill you. With your own pistol."

As they left, the two new arrivals helped Nabil to his feet.

"The kid backed us up, didn't he?" Drew asked.

"Yeah."

"What did you tell them?"

"I said Nabil owed me money."

4: 7

EPITAPH

THE TAXI TOOK THEM over the Nile, which was plied by miniature, floating carnivals—party boats throwing off light and blaring music. Zamalek, an island in the river, was an upscale quarter with a large population of Europeans and Americans. The basement bar Zafer took them to was one of the few drinking establishments in Cairo that wasn't attached to a hotel. The walls paneled with oak, the tables and chairs burnished to a shine, and the huge mirror in a gilded baroque frame were all meant to evoke Europe.

At least, Drew thought, *I'm not particularly overdressed.*

"*Ya*, my shoulder tries to kill me," Kadir moaned.

He and Drew sat down at a table with a copper ashtray in its center, like a single dull eye.

Zafer went to the bar and brought back half-liter bottles of beer. The three men were arranged like the apexes of an equilateral triangle super-imposed on the round table.

"You're crazy you know that?" Drew sipped his beer. "Nabil had a *gun* in your back."

Zafer grinned. "Nothing better for an unarmed man than a shooter who feels secure with the barrel of his weapon pressed against you."

"*Why?*"

"Because average reaction time is about a quarter of a second—a little faster for women. Anyone—I mean *any*one—can knock the gun away before the shooter can fire. The problem is, most people don't know what to do after that. I do."

"I noticed."

Zafer lifted his chin. "You had me a little worried when that cave bear grabbed you."

Moves Drew hadn't used in years had lain intact somewhere in his body, like train tracks beneath asphalt. "You could've ended that a lot sooner," Drew accused.

"I wanted to watch." Zafer smirked and reached over and slapped Drew on the back with a heavy hand. "You did all right. Didn't even fuck up the suit."

Kadir held up his bottle. "Better than Turkish beer."

Zafer reached into a jacket pocket. "And now we know something about who we're dealing with. We know they're French. We know their home base." He snapped two cards down on the table. One for Raymond Duvall, one for Jean Saint-Savoy. *Special Acquisitions, Ecole Biblique* had been written under their names. The address in Jerusalem, office phone, and fax number were the same; only the cell phone numbers were different.

"You surprised me, too." Drew jabbed a finger at Kadir. "You're tougher than I thought."

Kadir grunted. "His head kills him worse than my shoulder kills me I think."

"I whacked 'im good, trust me."

"*Dostum!*" *My friend.* Kadir lifted his glass. "*Sherefe!*" *To honor!*

"*Sherefe.*" Zafer and Drew clinked their glasses against his.

"So how did you guys meet?" Drew asked.

"I am friend to this bastard for long time." Kadir slapped Zafer's shoulder. "Since the days of high school."

"My family is from Urfa," Zafer said. "Kadir and I were neighbors after we moved to Istanbul."

"Urfa? Not too many Turks there. I guess that's why your Arabic is so good. How did you get into MIT?"

"I told you ... not MIT, Special Forces. But I did have about six months training in Army intelligence before I got kicked out. Speaking of intelligence, here's an update: the professor's house in London was wiped clean. A friend of mine who *does* work for MIT looked into it. It was precise, not like the mess in Istanbul. The professor's computer was still there, but there were no files on the hard drive. No flash discs lying around either."

"What about his flat in Antakya?"

Zafer lit a cigarette. "Untouched from the looks of it, but no discs, no manuscript pages."

"*Inanmiyorum!*" Kadir slid off his chair but wasn't any taller. "This man I know." He looked across the bar toward a far corner. "He is a runner, like Tariq. Maybe we can make some business." Kadir beckoned to Zafer with his head. "You come, too."

Zafer rolled his eyes as he pushed back his chair. "He has a scroll worth five million dollars and he wants to make another hundred lira. Hold onto our seats, will you?"

Drew nodded and glanced around the bar without really seeing it.

He'd been a tourist on his last trip to Egypt and seen a dozen or so dead pharaohs in the museum. Thutmoses IV, whose name sounded like a lung ailment, had been one of the best-preserved. His face was unwrapped, the black skin exposed for the crowd filing past his glass coffin. Nose slightly hooked, lips pressed grimly together, hair still clung to the scalp in wisps. Judging by Thutmoses, the face of immortality was neither youthful nor cherubic; it was shrunken, skeletal, and nearly as inhuman as the pocket of void over which the parchment-dry skin had been stretched.

If the pharaohs were to be remembered by their mummies, pyramids, and tombs, Stephen would be remembered by his articles and books. And his students.

Zafer pulled out a chair and sat back down. "The Egyptian's English is worse than Kadir's, but they can manage without me."

Drew nodded.

"You look depressed all of the sudden. What happened?"

Stephen's death had left Drew feeling as though his liver and heart and lungs had been removed and dumped into canopic jars. "Thinking about Stephen."

Zafer nodded. "But the professor—"

"Yeah, I know. He'd want us to go after Q. Which is probably a forgery. Which means he died for nothing."

"We don't know that." Zafer lifted his chin. "What about you? Kadir says all 'ex-patriotics' are running from something."

Drew smirked. "My father, I guess. My mother doesn't get me, but she's okay with that. My old man is a hard-assed Slav, and he just keeps hammering at me like ... like I'm a piece of clay, and if he pounds long enough, I'll come out the right shape."

Zafer grinned. "Sounds like a Turkish father."

"The war in Iraq made everything worse. He was all for it. I accused him of being uneducated and naïve. He accused me of being an unpatriotic dupe playing into the hands of terrorists." Drew took a swig of beer. Kadir was right; it wasn't bad. "How could my father be so ... so ignorant?"

Zafer shrugged. "People believe what they want to believe. Just like the professor said. And you have to remember your father comes from another generation. No college, right?"

"No."

"You have to make ..." At a loss for a word, Zafer gestured with a hand.

"Allowances?"

"Allowances."

"You're probably right." He drank from the bottle, held the fizz in his puffed-out cheeks for a second, and swallowed.

"The war's what got me in trouble," Zafer said. "I was in Baghdad right after the city fell. A joint operation with the Americans. You have no idea ... *no* idea what went on over there."

"What happened?"

Zafer shrugged. "Saw something I wasn't supposed to. A couple of executions in a bombed-out building. The Ministry of Education to be exact. You know who your guys killed? Not soldiers or terrorists or Ba'athists. Intellectuals. The kind of men who could have rebuilt the museums and libraries."

"And?"

"The American still had his pistol in his hand, and the bodies were at his feet. I had a rifle in mine. We were like ... like a couple of predators that had never seen each other before. A bear and a lion, maybe. Unsure what the other was capable of. We locked eyes trying to figure out who was going to do what."

"*And...?*"

"I think my body reacted. His arm moved, a millimeter maybe. Maybe less. I took him out."

Drew grunted. "Damn."

Zafer nodded. "I had a lot of explaining to do. The Americans wanted my head, but they couldn't afford to alienate the Turks. The bombing runs on Iraq take off from the American base near Adana. But I was done." He rubbed his hands together as though wiping chalk off them. "Out of the military."

"Better than prison."

"True."

"You know, since the professor died, the littlest thing can bring me to tears. I just want to … I want to hear him *say* something again. Anything. I want to give the old bastard a hug. You know what he smelled like? Like one of those secondhand bookshops where the pages are falling out of the books. It was a good smell … I don't know, grandfatherly." Drew put out a hand toward Zafer, but couldn't find anything to take hold of, so he made a fist over the table instead. "Why am I like this? Why do I feel like my father died?"

Zafer finished the beer in his glass. "Because he did."

4: 8

TRUE CHRISTIANS

THE TAXI DROPPED THEM about a half mile from their hotel. Zafer motioned for them to take a side street while he kept an eye on passing traffic. After he was satisfied nothing was out of the ordinary, he followed, walking on the balls of his feet as if he had too much energy to be flatfooted.

Drew felt a bit dazed. Not from a couple of beers, but because Zafer had slapped him awake. Stephen hadn't been his father, but a visit from Drew was generally an occasion to open a bottle of wine rather than deliver a lecture on how to live his life. Far from criticizing Drew's interests *ad nauseum*, Stephen had shared them. He'd even accepted Drew's … all right, *laziness*. Stephen hadn't been his father; he'd been the father Drew had always *wanted*.

When they turned up the familiar alley of their hotel, Zafer was in front, his jacket stretched tight across his shoulders. One hand rested protectively on the satchel at his side.

The three of them crowded in the glass-and-wood elevator and took it to the third floor. Zafer went to the reception counter to pick up the key. A couple of steps behind, Drew saw Zafer's back tense right through his jacket. He barely had time to register the two Egyptians in the lobby who stood up—one in a suit, the other in a priest's black robe—and the absence of the hotel manager. Zafer lunged at the one in the suit with a punch, but the man parried with a forearm.

"Please—!" The priest put both of his hands out.

Drew didn't watch how Zafer followed up. Dropping his body to waist level, he shot forward looking for a basic double-leg take-down. The priest collapsed. Besides being surprisingly light, the priest offered no resistance whatsoever. Drew felt like he'd taken out a scarecrow.

"Please! We just want to talk." Lying on his back, the priest held his hands open, his forehead a wrinkled map of worry lines. "Please!"

Zafer and the Egyptian in the suit were locked in a kind of martial ballet, with Zafer offering all of the offense and his opponent backing up and countering deftly. It was mesmerizing. Both moved with startling speed and fluidity, both seemed aware of nothing outside their own contest, and, except for a few moments of indecisive grappling and a leg sweep at Zafer's ankle that made him stumble into a coffee table, it seemed to have been choreographed.

Zafer suddenly stopped and let his hands fall to his sides. "You're just countering."

The Egyptian in the suit smiled, although he hadn't relaxed his defensive stance. "We only want to talk."

Zafer glanced back and saw Drew sitting on the priest.

Kadir, for the first time since Drew had met him, had nothing to say.

"Yes, we want to talk." The priest kept his open hands in front of him.

The hotel manager, who had come down the stairs by this time, looked horrified.

Drew let the priest up and offered a lame smile.

The Egyptian in the suit put a hand on Zafer's uneasy shoulder and looked at the manager. "We trained together in the army. We never could decide who was better!"

The manager, who seemed half-relieved, limped behind the counter.

Getting up, Drew noticed the priest had a peculiar smell to him—not at all unpleasant, just … foreign. Not quite sweet, but a scent that reminded Drew of incense.

Zafer took advantage of the Egyptian's vulnerable stance and frisked his upper body. All he came up with was a cell phone.

"We don't carry weapons." He held out a hand. "Nathan, by the way."

His accent, Drew noticed, was American. Probably East Coast.

The Turk pressed the back of his hand against the man's crotch, inside his thighs, around his waist and even his socks. Finally he took the offered hand. "Nice to meet you. Zafer."

"I am Father Hawass," the priest said. "We are Ebionites. Violence in any form is unacceptable to us."

"Ebionites?" One of the professor's keywords had dropped into his hands.

"True Christians." Father Hawass raised his chin slightly. "Our church is founded not on the teaching of the apostate Paul, but on those of Jesus, Our Savior, and James the Just, the brother of the Lord."

"*Paul* was a heretic?"

None of this meant anything to Zafer. He frisked the priest, too.

BOOK 5: 1 - 13

THE SICARII

The Knights of Malta have a convoluted history going back to the time of the first crusade in 1099, but it was Leo XIII who in 1834 allowed the Knights to establish their headquarters in Rome. The American branch was founded in 1927. In 1941 Francis Cardinal Spellman was the "Grand Protector" of the order, and quite a few American knights are linked to the unsuccessful attempt to stage what amounted to a fascist coup in this country that was designed to put General Smedley Butler in power. Butler, however, blew the whistle and implicated a number of Maltese Knights including John Farrell, then the president of US Steel, and Joseph P. Grace. After the war, Spellman worked with then-bishop Montini who was undersecretary of state at the Vatican, in running the "Vatican ratlines," which provided phony passports, shelter, money and transport for war criminals heading out of Europe.

— Conrad Goeringer

5:1

BLESS THOSE WHO CURSE YOU

THE TWO BEDS IN THE HOTEL room became sagging couches facing one another. The fan on the high ceiling squeaked as it turned, while a slender air-conditioner, fitted onto the wall, hummed.

Father Hawass's hands trembled slightly from the encounter in the lobby, but the depths of his brown eyes were undisturbed, like water in a well. He exuded a kind of cleanliness, as though he shied from meat and kept his surprisingly white teeth in good health by chewing palm fronds.

Nathan, perpetually on the verge of a smile, gave the impression that he was in his own home, and they were all old friends. His curly hair, pure black, he had what Drew thought of as classical North African features: full lips, rounded cheekbones, a straight nose with generous nostrils that seemed capable of scenting urgency. The incipient smile was neither sardonic nor ironic but a genuine effusion of good will. He was one of those people whom, if he were hitchhiking, people wouldn't hesitate to pick up.

Father Hawass, with a few strands of gray winding through his hair, was probably in his mid forties. Slightly built, his dark-skinned face floating above the black in which he was shrouded, he seemed to have grasped some mystery that everyone else was still trying to work out with rulers and telescopes and equations.

"We're very small," Nathan explained. "We only have a few churches but we have members all over the world."

"And an Ebionite is … what exactly?" Drew asked.

"We are followers of the true Church, which was led by James the Just after the death of Jesus," Father Hawass said. "We recognize Jesus as our Savior, but we do not believe that he was the Son of God. Rather, he was the Messiah only after his baptism by John. His birth was natural and Mary was a woman like any other."

"We also don't believe, as James the Just did not believe, that Jewish Law can be discarded," Nathan added.

"Jews for Jesus?" Drew asked.

Nathan's smile filled out with large, straight teeth. "Not quite. We accept the Old Testament, but of the four gospels we accept only Matthew."

Father Hawass quoted: "*Bless those who curse you. Pray for your enemies. Love those who hate you. Give to everyone who asks of you, and do not refuse them.*"

"And you reject Paul?"

The priest nodded. "We reject Paul for the same reason James the Just rejected him: for trying to make Jesus into God. James was the true leader of the early Church after the death of Jesus—not Paul, not Peter."

"The irony," Nathan continued, "is that Paul insisted that Jewish Law could be abandoned, that through faith in Jesus Christ alone you could be saved, yet he never mentioned a single miracle."

Drew's first instinct was to contradict Nathan, but rummaging through what he could recall of Paul's letters, he couldn't come up with anything.

"We reject Paul and we reject violence even in self-defense," Father Hawass insisted. "'*To him who strikes you on the one cheek, offer the other also.*'"

"What about your own gospel, Matthew?" Drew asked. "Doesn't Jesus say, '*Do not think that I came to bring peace on Earth. I did not come to bring peace but a sword*'?"

Nathan lifted a cautionary finger. "If you look at Jesus' arrest in Gethsemane, also in Matthew, Christ says, '*Put your sword in its place, for all who take the sword will perish by the sword.*'"

"All right," Drew conceded, "but there's also Luke, where Jesus says, '*He who does not have a sword, let him sell his garments and buy one.*'"

"We reject Luke," Father Hawass reminded him.

"Find a passage in any of the Gospels that shows Jesus with a weapon of any kind." Nathan shook his head. "You won't."

"So you are Ebionites," Kadir said. "Good for you. I am Turk. I am wanting to know who killed my friend Tariq."

And Drew still wanted to know how exactly this obscure sect was connected with questions of Jesus' existence.

The Ebionites exchanged glances.

Every trace of Nathan's smirk disappeared. "I killed Tariq."

5: 2

THE ECOLE BIBLIQUE

THE HOTEL ROOM had the smoke-blurred atmosphere of a *narghile* café. Kadir, Nathan, and Zafer had all lit cigarettes. Even Drew had pulled out a small cigar. He watched the drifting gray arabesques as they lengthened and uncoiled, making tenuous shadows on the wall. In the swirls just above the lamp, Drew thought he saw, for a second or two, a pair of wings slowly spreading out until they were scattered by currents from the air conditioner.

"It was an accident." Nathan dragged on his cigarette, held his breath for a second as if considering what to say next, and then let go a stream of bluish smoke. "We just wanted to talk to him, but he ran—"

"Who is we?" Zafer asked.

"Another Ebionite. We're the only two who … do this sort of thing. In fact, we sort of founded our two-man team to keep an eye on the Sicarii."

Drew recognized another of Stephen's keywords. "Who are the Sicarii?"

Nathan's sigh was full of smoke and regret. "I'll have to start from the beginning." He looked at Kadir. "The scroll you have is ours."

"*Ne?*"

"Abu had already promised it to our monastery. Although he'd been raised as a Coptic Christian, toward the end of his life, Abu became sympathetic to our church. Mainly because of Hatija, his second wife."

Zafer cocked his head. "Abu's wife is one of you?"

Nathan nodded. "Hatija didn't get him to formally convert, but she persuaded him to bequeath the Habakkuk Commentary to our monastery. But after he died, the scroll disappeared. A household servant named Ahmed went missing, too. We think Tariq met him during his dealings with Abu. No doubt he planned to show up after the scroll was sold looking for his share."

"No police?" Zafer asked.

Nathan shook his head. "The scroll was acquired illegally. It belongs to Israel. It *has* to. It's one of the Qumran scrolls."

He and Zafer exhaled smoke at the same time.

"Hatija was able to give us Tariq's name but not much else. My partner and I became something like private detectives for her. I actually *was* a detective for a while—"

"Where?" Drew cut in.

"Jersey City."

"*Jersey City?* I grew up in Lyndhurst." It should have a been a fact like any other—where Nathan was from—but his Jersey roots, along with his East Coast accent and American mannerisms, inclined Drew to trust him.

"Right down the road." Nathan smiled. "There's a big Coptic community in Jersey City. In fact, the Coptic Church is sort of our big brother. They don't agree with our beliefs, but since we're such peace nuts—and so poor—they let us have an office in one of their buildings."

"Wait a minute …" Drew pointed accusingly at Nathan with his cigar. "If you're an Ebionite, how could you be a detective? Didn't you have to carry a gun?"

"I resigned from the department after I became an Ebionite."

Drew tapped his cigar, and half an inch of gray dropped into a shallow tin ashtray. "A Copt cop?"

Nathan nodded. "Something like that. We've got a little more money now because Hatija is generous. Unfortunately, Abu's sons got most of his estate. Hatija is much younger than Abu was, and they didn't have any children together. Every time I get on a plane, she foots the bill. My partner, Josh, is a Brit. We managed to follow Tariq to Istanbul, but in the process lost him for about a day—the day he must've gone to see you." He lifted his chin in Kadir's direction. "We didn't know your name

then. We only knew a dwarf was involved as a dealer of some kind."
Nathan leaned forward and mashed his cigarette into the tin ashtray as
though it had done something wrong and then let go a final plume of
smoke. "We bluffed Tariq. We said, 'We'll just have to talk to the dwarf.'
He panicked, ran out into traffic and …" Nathan shrugged.

"So you are not the destroyers of my shop?" Kadir flicked ashes into
an empty cigarette box that he held in his hand since he couldn't reach
the ashtray on the night table.

Nathan shook his head. "We didn't even know where your shop was."

"And you guys didn't rip apart my apartment and knock me around
on the way out?"

"That was the Sicarii. They're also the ones who killed Professor
Cutherton."

Drew was confused. He'd assumed the Sicarii were somehow related
to ancient Palestine.

"Usually, the Congregation for the Doctrine of the Faith tries
to destroy a scholar's reputation," Father Hawass said. "Or they use
blackmail to keep information from getting out."

Drew frowned. "The Congregation for what?"

Nathan ignored the question. "But sometimes there are unexplained
deaths. Two years ago a young scholar who claimed he could prove that
Christ couldn't have been crucified under Pontius Pilate was found dead
in his apartment in England. Gunshot wound to the head. Oddly, he
didn't leave a suicide note and supposedly burned all of his research
before allegedly killing himself."

Father Hawass wagged a brown finger. "They are not so different
from the Sicarii of old."

"The Sicarii of old?" Drew asked.

"The first Sicarii were Jewish Zealots who resisted the Roman occupation," the priest explained. "*Sica* is a knife with a curved blade. This was
their favored weapon. They were assassins who were happy to die so long
as they killed their targets."

Now it makes sense, Drew thought.

"We think," Nathan continued, "they murdered the professor and then
tried to make it look like it happened during the course of a robbery."

"So that's our new breed of Zealots." Drew nodded. "But whom do
they work for?"

Zafer dropped the smoldering butt of his cigarette into the box Kadir was holding.

"The history of the Catholic Church is a chronicle of their struggle for power," Father Hawass said. His shoulders narrow, he looked small next to Nathan, but his dignified air commanded another kind of respect. Maybe it had been faith shining down on him rather than the Egyptian sun that had turned his skin an earthy brown. "At the end of the nineteenth century, there were many Catholic scholars who found it difficult to believe Jesus was the Son of God. The more they investigated biblical history, the more they found it contradicted Church doctrine."

Drew exhaled a stream of smoke in the general direction of the ceiling, adding to the cloud hanging over their heads.

"In 1902," Nathan said, "the pope created the Pontifical Biblical Commission to make sure any archaeological evidence Church scholars turned up didn't contradict the 'authority of the scriptures' or, as they put it, the 'right interpretation' of the scriptures.

"About a decade earlier the Ecole Biblique had been founded."

"Raymond and Jean," Drew said.

Nathan nodded. "They're the modern Sicarii."

"Christian," Drew interjected, "not Jewish."

Nathan nodded again. "Around 1955 Father Roland de Vaux became director of the Ecole Biblique."

Drew remembered his name. He was the scholar who'd stonewalled everyone on the Dead Sea Scrolls.

"Beginning with de Vaux, every director of the Ecole has been a member of the Pontifical Biblical Commission—officially listed as a 'consultant.' They founded a magazine called *Revue Biblique*, edited by de Vaux.

"When the Dead Sea Scrolls were discovered, the Ecole did everything they could to date the scrolls to a period well before Christianity."

"Why?" Drew asked.

"Isn't it obvious?" Nathan looked at him skeptically. "The scrolls never mention Jesus."

Drew sat on the edge of the bed dumbfounded. Yes, it *was* obvious.

"De Vaux used the review to push his interpretation of the scrolls while denying other scholars access," Nathan went on. "We'll never know how much of the material disappeared into a black hole in the

Vatican. We do know that the Ecole Biblique approached Abu about the Habakkuk Scroll and apparently offered a fantastic sum for it. But Abu denied having it."

"I don't know anything about Church history," Zafer said, "but there's something about you two that doesn't add up. You said you didn't know where Kadir's shop was when you got to Istanbul. So how did you find us in Cairo?"

Father Hawass crossed himself. "Professor Cutherton—may God bless him—was an Ebionite."

5: 3

ANCIENT ENMITY

NATHAN LOOKED AT FATHER HAWASS disapprovingly. His nostrils seemed to quiver slightly as though something unpleasant had worked its way into the air of the room. Nathan turned to Drew. "Professor Cutherton was an atheist."

"I *know*," Drew snapped.

"But he did have Ebionite sympathies. Non-violence, he believed, was a good cause no matter what name you gave it. We contacted him as soon as we found out the Habakkuk Scroll had disappeared. We were hoping he might hear something."

"And he told you we'd been to see him?" Drew asked.

Father Hawass nodded.

"Why didn't he just tell us the scroll belonged to you?"

Zafer put a hand on Kadir's shoulder. "Our pal here was an unknown variable. If the professor had pointed out the scroll belonged to the Ebionites, Kadir might have disappeared with it."

"Yes," Kadir said. "Unless someone is giving to me five thousand dollars for a letter."

The Ebionites exchanged dismayed glances.

"It was much smarter to have the professor play along with us," Zafer said. "This way he could keep an eye on the scroll and keep them up-to-date."

Nathan nodded. "Exactly."

Drew sighed. "It's starting to make sense. One of the last things Stephen said to me was that Paul must have been the Liar mentioned in the Dead Sea Scrolls, which is the Ebionite interpretation."

"Yes." Father Hawass agreed.

"And the Wicked Priest?"

"Ananus, of course."

"Ananus?" Keyword number three.

"Ananus the Younger was high priest in 62 AD. He was the enemy of the Teacher of Righteousness. He was also the enemy of the Ebionites."

"Now I remember. Ananus the Younger was responsible for—"

"The Wicked Priest persecuted the Teacher tirelessly," Father Hawass continued. "In the end, the Teacher was killed."

"James the Just." Drew pointed a finger. "Ananus had him stoned to death."

"Yes. In the year 62."

"Are you saying that the Essenes who wrote the Dead Sea Scrolls are, in fact, the early Christian Church?"

Father Hawass shook his head. "No, but many Essenes revered Jesus. Why should they not? Jesus borrowed many Essene teachings."

Stephen had said something similar the night he was murdered.

"After Jesus' death," the priest said, "the Essenes put all of their faith in James the Just."

Nathan picked up the narrative. "*Moreh ha-Zedek* is the term used in the Scrolls for the Teacher of Righteousness. *Ya'akov Zaddik* is Aramaic for James the Just."

"I'm sure," Drew said, "quite a few leaders were referred to that way."

"Only James and Jesus," Nathan said. "We know the Teacher is not Jesus because the Teacher's death doesn't conform at all to Jesus', but there are quite a few similarities to the way James died. It was James."

"There is also the account of Saint Hegesippus," Father Hawass said, "an Ebionite of the second century."

"Hegesippus was an Ebionite?" Drew had heard of him only as a Church historian.

Father Hawass nodded. "Saint Hegesippus tells us that James was *holy from the womb* and a high priest permitted to enter the Holy of Holies in the Temple. He drank no wine, ate no meat, and no razor ever touched his head. So often was he was found on his knees beseeching forgiveness for the people, that his knees grew hard like a camel's. Because of unsurpassable piety, he was called the Righteous."

Odd that James's holiness was legendary, yet he hadn't been one of the twelve apostles.

"The scrolls say that the Liar seduces some members of the Qumran community into breaking the law—Jewish Law. This is presented in Acts of the Apostles as the conflict between Paul and James."

"That's *right*." Drew shifted his weight on the bed. "Paul wanted to dispense with Jewish Law to make it easier to convert the gentiles. His strategy was to be a Jew to the Jews, a Gentile to the Gentiles."

"In the scrolls, the Essenes who followed Paul were called Seekers-After-Smooth-Ways." Father Hawass explained. "The Essenes, you see, were very strict about ritual purities."

"Ya, we know," Kadir said. "On the day of Sabbath they are not shitting."

Drew looked at Kadir as if he were a brother he didn't want to admit being related to.

Father Hawass's face remained unperturbed. "The Essenes constantly refer to themselves as zealous for the Law. Obviously, they could not abide Paul."

"So Paul was the Liar, and James was the Teacher of Righteousness?"

Nathan put out his cigarette. "The Habakkuk Scroll, you have to understand, is an interpretation of earlier scripture. Pick up your Bible and you'll find a book called Habakkuk. Habakkuk was a minor prophet who lived when Babylon—not Rome—was the threat. But because the Jews who lived centuries later were desperate to overthrow the Romans, they tried to apply what ancient authors had said to their own times.

"Habakkuk's most famous quote in the Bible—actually, he is quoting God—is *But the just shall survive by faith*. Centuries later, the author of the Habakkuk Scroll, who was an Essene, got a hold of this and wrote: *Interpreted, this concerns all those who observe the Law in the House of Judah whom God will deliver from the House of Judgment because of their suffering and because of their faith in the Teacher of Righteousness*."

"You see?" Father Hawass interrupted. "They believed the Teacher was the Messiah."

"In Romans," Nathan continued, "Paul turns this into *the righteousness of God is through faith in Jesus Christ to all and on all who believe. He* completely ignores observing the Law in the House of Judah. In a direct challenge to James, Paul also says a man is not made righteous by good works but by faith."

Nathan held out his hand as if to say, *There it is.* "This is the whole of Pauline Christianity, elevating faith above everything else. It was his own brand of Christianity. *'Even if an angel from heaven preaches any other gospel to you other than what I have preached',* Paul says, *'let the angel be accursed'.*"

"James," Father Hawass added, "was rebuking Paul when he wrote, *'For whosoever shall keep the whole Law and yet offend in one point, he is guilty of all'.*"

Drew shook his head. "Let me get this straight. After Jesus died, there was a power vacuum ... and Paul and James were fighting for control of the early Church?"

"Not exactly. There was a clash of ideologies," Father Hawass corrected, "which spilled over into their biblical letters."

"Right," Drew picked up, "with Paul saying Jewish Law could be discarded as long as you had faith, while James insisted faith wasn't enough, that you had to prove your faith by adhering to the Law ..."

"And by doing good works," Nathan added.

"And if Paul and his followers ignored the dietary restrictions, circumcision, and the other prescribed rituals of Jewish Law—" Drew paused to write in his notebook,"—then it makes sense that the Dead Sea Scrolls refer to them as Seekers-After-Smooth-Ways."

"*Exactly.*" Nathan laced the fingers of his hands together and rested his forearms on his thighs. "There's one other thing. The Habakkuk Scroll says the Liar flouted the Law in the midst of the whole congregation. This is what happens toward the end of Acts when Paul is accused of blasphemy for shunning Jewish Law."

Drew let the pen drop from his fingers. It slapped softly against his open notebook. Putting his forehead in a palm, he tried to think. Stephen could have made sense of these frayed strands of theology and history: Paul's heresy, James's adherence to the Law, the Essenes—who were also the Keepers of the New Covenant, and the Ebionites, who claimed to be the only true Christians.

Eyes closed, fingertips digging into his scalp, Drew wanted to pray, to ask for guidance. For a moment, the dark behind his eyes seemed equal to that expanse of black which, for millennia, astronomers had been searching for signs of a maker.

"Drew? You all right?"

It was Zafer's voice, but it seemed to come from a long way off. Drew lifted his head. "Paul … Paul derailed the Christianity of the early Church by making the messenger more important than the message. Is that what you're saying?"

Nathan stabbed at Drew with a finger. "Yes!"

"But you believe in the resurrection," Drew asked, "don't you?"

Father Hawass leaned forward slightly. "Jesus was raised by God the Father. He did not raise himself."

Which was more or less what Drew had always believed.

"All right!" Zafer pushed off the edge of the bed, stood up, and clapped his hands together. "You passed the interview."

Father Hawass seemed startled out of a trance.

"All we have to do now is check your references."

"And the scroll?"

"We're not going to settle that tonight. It's not even in Egypt. But we'll need a way to contact you when we're back in Istanbul."

Nathan sighed and, standing up, reached in his back pocket for his wallet. He took out a white card and handed it to Zafer.

Zafer glanced at the name in red lettering: *Nathan Zarqal.* There was a Jersey City address, the usual phone number, fax, e-mail, and cell phone. After tucking it in his shirt pocket, he shook Father Hawass's hand. When he reached for Nathan's hand, he gripped it firmly, then suddenly jerked him forward and tried to put his arm in some kind of hold.

Drew jumped off the mattress, but Nathan, as though he'd been expecting something like this, shifted his weight, blocked Zafer's other hand, and the two grappled for a couple of seconds, each trying to gain an advantage.

Zafer started to smile. "You're good, really good. Jujitsu?"

"Aiki jujitsu, aikido, judo. I've studied in different schools since I was about twelve." He grinned. "You're not bad either."

As the two men left, Kadir closed the door behind them. "A lot of history, ya. I am not able to understand all."

"Neither am I," Drew admitted.

Zafer raked his short black curls with his fingers. "The shit's getting deeper."

"I wonder," Drew said, "what the Sicarii are like."

Zafer smiled. "You just met two of them."

5: 4

EVERLASTING FOOL

ZAFER'S EYES FLUTTERED OPEN. Without looking at his watch, he knew it was early. He always woke up early. Lying motionless in bed, he listened. It was an old habit.

He heard nothing but the hum of the air conditioner.

Something was wrong. He sat up and scanned the room. Kadir was asleep on the floor with a blanket under him.

Drew's bed was empty.

The bathroom door was open and the light was off.

"*Hay Allah,*" Zafer hissed.

Last night they'd changed rooms, a couple of doors down. Of course, anybody who wanted to know where they'd gone could have put a gun in the manager's face. Or a fifty-dollar bill.

Hopping on one leg, Zafer pushed the other into his pants. *Why didn't I go with my first instinct and change hotels?* But they *couldn't* have come into the room and grabbed Drew without his knowing. *Couldn't* have. If they'd used something—spray or gas—he'd be groggy or nauseated. His arms and legs would feel like they were filled with cement.

Pulling on his jacket to hide the pistol he was wearing, he woke up Kadir.

"*Eh? Saat kach?*"

"Never mind what time it is. I'm going out to find Drew. Don't answer the door. If anybody so much as knocks, call my cell phone."

Zafer stepped out into a dimly lit hall paved with faded blue and yellow tiles.

In the lobby he asked the manager if he'd seen Drew, but the manager insisted his long-haired friend had not been in the lobby this morning. Unsure about his next move, Zafer decided to take the elevator up.

At the end of the hall, he found the exit to the roof. He pushed open the door and got slapped by a wave of hot air. Nothing much to see up here—no hint of the Nile, no glimpse of the pyramids' summits, just a bird's eye view of the empty street below and a cross-section of downtown Cairo.

Drew was sitting at a table, scribbling away in his notebook. He looked up and waved to Zafer.

Zafer shook his head. "You scared the shit out of me."

"Today's my wedding anniversary. Would've been six years. Only made it to four."

Zafer nodded. "All right. I'm going back down. Kadir is probably pissing his pants."

"He's probably pissing *on mine*."

"Might be," Zafer conceded. "Are you done here?"

"Almost."

"Well, hurry up."

The Turk disappeared down the stairs.

Pushing his sunglasses farther up on the bridge of his nose, Drew re-read his letter.

Dear Yasemin,

Some days I wake up, and all I want is to find you next to me again. I wait for the ache to subside, ignore it the way someone who has an incurable illness—nothing that'll kill him—ignores the pain. There's nothing else I can do.

I couldn't live with you the way things were. I know this is hard for you to understand. I know you don't think I had anything to complain about, although you have to admit, <u>something</u> made me leave. You were home to me, wherever you were was home— sometimes I myself don't know how I left.

I can distract myself for a while, but the ache is always there, the same ache I feel now as I write this.

I know you loved me, but I don't understand why you made me feel so unloved. I wish I knew why you snapped at me so much, criticized me so often, fought with me so much. I wish I knew why you made me feel that just about everything I did was wrong. The _why_ haunts me most of all. If you would just tell me why, I might be better at waiting out the pain.

Remember that morning when we got into a fight because I didn't make the bed? I kept looking at it logically, adding up all the things that proved I cared about you. But you kept insisting that if I really cared about you, I would make the bed once in a while. And that made me furious.

Only now do I realize I missed the point: you were defending an insecurity, a leftover from childhood. You were defending the way my neglect of the bed made you _feel_. What you needed was reassurance—a little affection to remind you that I was your husband. All your arguing was just covering up a vulnerability, and all of my arguing was just covering up my own insecurities and making things worse.

We used to wonder who loved whom more—now we know.

I'm in Egypt now and you wouldn't believe how much I miss you. It's even worse being abroad. I know it's impossible in this hotel, but if I were to come upon a pair of your shoes or a shirt of yours, I'd probably cry.

I tried dating a few times, but I can't look at her, whoever she is, and say anything in Turkish that doesn't remind me of you. I just can't. There are so many things I can't say to her because I said them to you first.

I don't think I'll ever be at peace with this period of my life. I will always remember how you pushed me away every time you were upset with me. We should have stayed together, Yasemin. We should have been buried in the same little plot. Don't you wake up some mornings and feel it? Don't you look around for your husband and feel that without him there, the horizon is too far away? If you don't, then you're not the fool, I am.

A line from Kundera's Unbearable Lightness of Being *has been boomeranging in my head for two years: How can we know what we want, because, living only one life, we can neither compare it to our previous lives nor perfect it in lives to come?*

Leaving you was the biggest mistake I ever made. Even before the divorce was final, I begged you to take me back, but your refusal made made me convince myself it was for the best. If I had known how much I loved you, I never would have left. Forgive me for that if you can.

Here it is our anniversary—you're in Istanbul, I'm in Egypt. You're with someone else, I'm alone.

Maybe Kundera was wrong. Maybe we get another chance. Maybe we keep coming back until we get it right. Maybe we'll meet as two different people in another restaurant in some other city, and what seems like instinct or intuition, but is actually dim memory will guide us, and this time we'll stay married.

I don't think I'll write anything like this again. I'm emotionally drained. I hope this is the last weight I need to lift off myself.

You're an everlasting fool Yasemin Karaja, and I'm an everlasting fool for you.

5: 5

FROM STEPHEN CUTHERTON

Sweat left wet trails on his forehead, was running down his face by the time he got back to the room. Making hot weather hotter was one of the drawbacks of long hair.

Colors inside the hotel didn't seem quite right, either, and he realized that his vision had been singed by the Egyptian sun. He tossed his notebook onto a bed.

Kadir, who was shirtless, his short legs covered by cuffed jeans, gave him a disapproving look. "Ya, my everywhere hurts."

"Your everywhere? You only got hit in one place last night." There was a nasty-looking bruise above the collarbone. Drew turned to Zafer. "Fire up your laptop, will you? I want see what I can find about the Ebionites. I still don't think they have anything to do with Raymond and his pal Jean."

Zafer unzipped the black case and slipped the slim computer out. "What better way to get Kadir to hand over the scroll?" He unplugged the phone. "Posing as Ebionites and giving us that cover story about how the scroll actually belongs to them?"

Drew frowned. "But they can't be Sicarii. They didn't even *mention* the other scroll."

Zafer seesawed a hand. "Maybe, maybe not. They might be feeling us out, seeing what we know. Which is what we were trying to do last night."

"I don't know. I just … I mean, on a gut level, I believe those guys."

Kadir, dragging a chair behind him, went into the bathroom and closed the door. He needed the chair for the mirror.

"Look." Zafer flipped open the laptop on the small desk. "Even if they're not Sicarii, a Girl Scout could infiltrate their little church." He pressed a button and stepped back. "All yours."

Drew sat down to the computer, but instead of going on line, he started typing the letter he'd written to Yasemin.

The bathroom door opened. Kadir came out freshly shaven, although there was still a noticeable shadow on his face. He and Zafer could grow a full beard in about seventy-two hours.

"What's all that clacking?" Zafer asked. "I thought you were doing a web search?"

"Just putting together an e-mail."

"An e-mail or a dissertation?"

Saving the letter to Yasemin on a flash disc, he got started on his search. There was more information than he expected, including a website with Father Hawass's smiling face on it. The Ebionite church and its monastery were modest but attractive in an austere way.

"Find out when that website went up." Zafer tapped the computer screen. "Can you do that?"

"I can e-mail a friend of mine who can do that."

On another website Drew found an edited-down passage from Gibbon's *The Decline and Fall of the Roman Empire.* According to Gibbon, the first fifteen bishops of Jerusalem were all circumcised Jews; and the congregation over which they presided united the Law of Moses with the doctrine of Christ.

Drew's eyebrows went up. The first fifteen bishops had been Jews?

After the destruction of Jerusalem and the Temple in 70 AD by the Romans, the Jewish converts, now called Nazoreans, retired from the ruins of Jerusalem to the little town of Pella beyond the Jordan, where that ancient church languished above sixty years in solitude and obscurity.

Just like the Ebionites today, Drew thought.

They spread themselves into the villages adjacent to Damascus, and formed an inconsiderable church in what is now Aleppo in Syria. The Name of Nazarenes was deemed too honourable for those Christian Jews, and they soon received the contemptuous epithet of Ebionites—poor ones.

Although some traces of that obsolete sect may be discovered as late as the fourth century, they insensibly melted away either into the church or the synagogue.

"Not quite," Drew murmured.

"So what do you have?" Zafer was standing behind him again, broad hands on his hips.

"Gibbon seems to confirm everything they said last night, and the location of the monastery on their website coincides with their last known whereabouts—Aleppo."

Drew logged into his e-mail account, vaguely hoping for something from Yasemin. Nothing, as usual. But there was a message from pembroker@tiscali.com, an email address he'd never seen before. The subject box read: *From Stephen Cutherton.*

It couldn't be.

Drew looked up at Zafer, who was busy rearranging something in his duffel bag, then back at the computer screen.

The Sicarii?

He was afraid to open it. He was afraid even to show it to Zafer.

Cutting and pasting the letter that he'd typed to Yasemin, he sent it off. This gave him a minor sense of relief, as though some small promise had been fulfilled. No matter what happened in the next few days, he wanted her to have that.

From Stephen Cutherton.

He clicked on the message.

> *Dear Mr. Korchula,*
>
> *I am a friend of Stephen's. He sent this to me with instructions that, if he did not contact me in a week's time, I should send it to you. You and I, as we are now joined in grief for a dear friend, are now ourselves friends of a sort though we have never met. Let me say, in closing, I hope we have the opportunity to rectify that some day. Stephen thought so very highly of you.*
>
> *With deepest sympathy,*
> *Dr. Richard Pembroke, PhD*

The professor's message followed.

> *My Dear Drew,*
>
> *If you are reading this e-mail, it means that I am not able to speak to you myself. Perhaps it is just an old man's sense of foreboding or the*

dramatic, but after you and your friends left this evening, I felt I might not have the opportunity to say some of the following. Can you hear my sigh of regret? Well, perhaps I am fretting over nothing. Perhaps this is all bosh, and we'll have time for a few more glasses of wine and a few more conversations. This, then, is just a safety valve of sorts ...

As you know, I never married. Instead of rearing children, I have watched my students mature, embark on careers of their own, publish, and make names for themselves. It fills me with immense gratification. Be that as it may, with a single exception, I never grew as emotionally attached to any of them as I have to you. I believe that I can sum up what I am trying to say rather succinctly in this way: If I had had a son, I would have wanted him to be like you—slothful tendencies and all. Oh, I could sit here and list your endearing qualities, your formidable intellectual gifts, and so on, but it goes beyond list-making. You are simply a wonderful presence. There should be more of you in our classrooms ... and our lives.

With love,

Stephen

Drew pushed the heel of a hand against the corner of one eye and smeared wetness over his cheekbone.

"Be hurry," Kadir said. "We must go for seeing Amal."

Drew signed out of his e-mail. "Yeah, I just—I need a minute." Shrugging a shoulder to his face, he wiped his nose on his T-shirt.

To distract himself from Stephen's e-mail, he glanced again at the website for the Ebionite church. At Father Hawass's smile and white teeth. Drew recalled something Nathan had said yesterday and slammed the desk with the flat of his hand. "He *couldn't* have been!"

"*Ne?*" Kadir and Zafer were both looking at him.

"Jesus *couldn't* have been the Messiah." Drew felt like Descartes emerging from a nightlong meditation with the cornerstone of his philosophy. "The Dead Sea Scrolls," he said without explaining. "That's why the Ecole Biblique refused to let scholars look at them for so long. That's why the Sicarii want the Habakkuk Commentary so desperately. And *that's* why Stephen said Jesus was not the Savior."

The two Turks just stared.

"It's obvious." Drew pressed his palm heels to his forehead. "It's so obvious."

5: 6

THE BOOK OF NUMBERS

A HORSE-DRAWN CART loaded with empty propane tanks clanked past in the cramped Islamic Quarter. Drew couldn't help being reminded of the Gypsies in Istanbul—distant cousins—who had fitted the same wooden carts with car tires, hitched them to horses, and rode through the streets as though they'd just emerged from another century.

Using the mosques as landmarks, most of which seemed to be famous for one reason or another, Zafer led them through the warren of narrow streets and alleys, stone houses, apartment buildings, and medieval workshops whose fronts opened like garages. Men with arms blackened from hand to elbow glanced up from machines and tools that looked like they belonged in a museum. Leaning against the wall of one shop was a broad sheet that was so black with grease and dirt only the splintered edges were identifiable as wood.

Zafer, as usual, had the satchel slung over a shoulder. Drew lugged a duffel bag that Zafer had packed.

"This is it. This is where she lives."

Three children looked up from their play, a dusty, yellow ball between them. It had been scuffed by their impetuous feet, the walls and cobbles it bounced off of, the harsh sunlight. There was no space between houses here. All made of the same stone, which, beneath the uneven coating of grime, was honey-colored. A street of old gold, tarnished like those icons he'd seen more than a decade ago in Professor Wittier's office—the gold of late afternoon sun through a dusty shop window, of ancient maps and gilded rose compasses. Gold wasn't supposed to dull, but somehow it had, and the treasures of the tombs, as well as the word itself, *Egypt*, no longer called up the splendor they once had.

The double-winged door they stopped in front of, its bottom ragged with rot, was plain. The stone archway above it, however, was an astonishing display of intricately chiseled leaves, vines, grapes, and Islamic designs. Directly above the door a shuttered *gamba* was obscured by laundry that had been hung across its width to dry.

The house directly across from Amal's was apparently abandoned, the handles of its doors were chained and several uncurtained windows broken.

They went through one wing of the outer door, which led to a tiny courtyard and a stairway. At the top of the first flight of stairs, Zafer knocked on the nearest door.

The door only opened a few inches, but it was enough for Drew to get a good look at Amal. Younger than Drew had expected, she was covered entirely in black except for her face. She was also more attractive than he'd expected. Black bangs protruding from under her headscarf, she had high cheekbones and full lips. Like a handful of other Egyptian women he'd seen, her eyes, thickly outlined in black, were a startling gray-green—all the more startling in contrast to her dark skin.

Zafer greeted her in Arabic, and she opened the door.

The apartment was not as depressing as the building's exterior. High ceilinged, the rooms were otherwise small but comfortable. Handsome carpets covered the floor, and, though the paint had faded, the walls were clean. Framed photographs and Arabic calligraphy had been tastefully arranged.

Zafer and Kadir sat on a low couch while Drew took a cushioned stool and set the duffel bag down at its feet. Amal brought in a tray with glasses, tea, and two tin bowls. One was heaped with almonds the other with dates.

Drew accepted a glass of tea and thanked Amal—"*Shukran.*" It was one of the few Arabic words he'd picked up. The tea was syrupy with sugar and mint.

Kadir, who always drank his tea plain, tried to hide his disgust.

Speaking in Turkish while Zafer translated, Kadir offered his condolences. He had Amal alternately smiling and wiping at tears as he extolled Tariq's virtues and told little anecdotes, including the one of how they met in Souq al-Gama'a, where Kadir was bargaining for scraps of ancient papyrus. Even Drew, recalling the pleasant man he'd met in Kadir's shop, began to feel a certain affection for Tariq.

Finally, Zafer took a sheet of paper out of the breast pocket of his shirt. Pressing a finger to his lips, he handed it to Amal.

After she had read the note, Kadir asked, "Did you know that Tariq had two scrolls?"

"*Aiwa.*" She nodded. Her gray-green eyes were watery and red.

"I have one. Do you know anything about the other one?"

Bracelets clinking as she reached for another tissue, Amal gave a lengthy reply.

Zafer translated. "The men have been here looking for it. First, an Egyptian came to talk to her. She told him she had nothing to do with her husband's business. He offered her one thousand Egyptian pounds to look through her husband's notes and book of numbers—" Zafer halted, realizing he had mistranslated. "His phonebook. She refused. When the offer went up to two thousand pounds, she gave him the phonebook."

"*Hay Allah!* We came too late."

Zafer held up a finger. "Wait ..."

Amal put down her tea and folded her small brown hands in her lap.

"She said there was nothing in the phonebook she gave the Egyptian. That was not Tariq's business phonebook. He always kept that with him. It was returned with Tariq's other belongings and his body."

Amal sipped tea from a water glass while Zafer translated.

"About a week after she was given two thousand pounds, the house was broken into while she and the children were in the marketplace. The place was turned upside down, but nothing was taken. She thinks they were looking for the other phonebook."

"Ya, did they find it?" Kadir asked.

Zafer shook his head. "Tariq was a good husband. He didn't stay out with his friends to late hours without calling. He never gambled. His family was his life.

"This man who gave me two thousand pounds ... I know this was one of the men who took my husband from me. The ones who took from our children their father. We gave Tariq a proper burial with insurance money.

Because of my husband's wisdom, we are not poor at the moment. But no amount of money can give a wife back her husband or give children back their father."

"But the phone book?" Kadir whispered harshly.

Zafer's glare let Kadir know that he was being unspeakably rude. Nonetheless, he translated some version of Kadir's question.

"I burned the phonebook so they would never get it."

Kadir threw up stubby arms. "*Hay Allah!*"

Turning over the note Zafer had handed her, Amal wrote something down.

Zafer slapped his thighs. "Looks like we came a long way for nothing." He took the note from Amal, glanced at it, and nodded. Tucking it in his pocket, he began writing his own note.

"Ya, isn't there anything you can tell us?" Kadir sounded truly desperate. "Did he do business with someone besides Nabil? Someone who might know?"

Zafer translated, but didn't look up from what he was writing. "She didn't get involved in her husband's business." He handed the note to Amal.

Amal stood up and excused herself.

Drew wondered why she was leaving the apartment, but since she left the door ajar, he assumed she would be back. He glanced at Zafer, but the Turk just held a rigid finger over his lips.

Lowering his hand, Zafer looked at Kadir. "Well," he asked in Turkish, "what now?"

Kadir shrugged. "We talked with Nabil, and he told us talk with Amal. Amal isn't know anything so we may as well go back to Istanbul."

Drew watched Zafer fold a one-hundred dollar bill in half and put it under his empty tea glass.

"Then what?" Zafer asked.

"How I am able to know? If we cannot find one scroll, it is better to sell the other."

Zafer smiled and held up a thumb.

Amal returned as quietly as she had left, pulling the door closed softly behind her. She nodded at Zafer. When she sat back down, she saw the money and began to protest. The back-and-forth with Zafer seemed to encompass more than a simple refusal of money. Kadir joined in, speaking in Turkish, and for the next few minutes, the little salon became as noisy as a coffeehouse.

Amal finally accepted the gift with profuse thanks and began to cry again.

"She says Tariq was lucky to have you as a friend, Kadir."

A little bored with the next few minutes of polite conversation, Drew almost jumped when he heard the mechanical wail of a police siren.

Amal went quickly to the window and peered through the slats of the shutters; they had been designed to allow women to look out on the street without being seen.

Zafer went to look for himself. Turning to Drew and Kadir, he smiled. "A police car at each end." He grabbed the duffel bag and quietly unzipped it. Tapping a rigid finger against his lips to remind Drew not to speak, he threw a wadded-up *jalabiya* at Drew. A red-and-white-checked *keffiyeh* to cover his head followed.

I'm going to look like a Kurdish peasant, Drew thought. While he put the gown on over his clothes, he heard an electronically amplified voice speaking in Arabic. A cop was talking into his car's loudspeaker.

Drew looked at the *keffiyeh*, wondering how he was going to put it on, but Zafer pulled it out of his hands and, as though knotting a tie for a child, deftly wrapped Drew's head. Then, motioning for Kadir and Drew not to move, he went back to the window.

A small crowd had gathered at both ends of the narrow street, which was about fifty yards long. A policeman in short sleeves was taking a huge pair of lock clippers out of the trunk of a car, but another officer with a walkie-talkie shouted at him.

The two policemen took off at a run, bystanders parting as they sprinted past.

Zafer was glad the Egyptians had had the sense to send a man around back. Tipping his head toward the door of the flat to indicate they were leaving, he stepped away from the window.

After the three men had exchanged farewells with Amal, they dropped down the chipped stone stairs. Zafer stopped in front of the door to the street.

"If the Sicarii are smart, they've put spotters in a few places. It's almost impossible to hide a dwarf, but we'll give it a try. Kadir, you go first. Take a right out the door and then another right at the end of street through that little tunnel. I'll go next. Drew, you're last. No more than three meters behind me. Scream like a bitch if anybody stops you."

"Scream like a bitch?"

Zafer grinned.

Drew wondered if that was what Zafer thought of him.

A couple of seconds later, Zafer and his grin were gone.

Drew hesitated. *What the hell am I afraid of? Neighbors are all over the street, the cops are here, and Zafer is five steps away.*

Waving away a pair of flies, Drew stepped out into the sunny day. Zafer had gotten too far away. Walking briskly to make up the distance, Drew saw the police round the corner with a man handcuffed between them. He looked European. Jean Saint-Savoy? Drew glanced peripherally, trying to be nonchalant, but the Sicarii stared him down to let Drew know he'd gotten a good look at him.

Drew turned the corner and entered the short tunnel that allowed the narrow street to bore through an apartment building. As dark as a cave, it was littered with broken stone, empty bottles, and crumpled papers. Zafer and Kadir were waiting for him.

"I think I saw Jean Saint-Savoy."

Zafer nodded. "So did I."

"So let me see if I have this figured out ... you knew the Sicarii would use that abandoned house across from Amal for surveillance. You knew her house was wired and her phone was tapped. So you wrote her a note telling her to call the Egyptian police from a neighbor's phone and say, what?"

"I told her to say a man is watching her and taking pictures. In Egypt if anyone but the police catch you, that's enough to get you killed."

Zafer smiled. "I'll give my friend at MIT a call and see if he can get the Egyptians to pin something on Jean to keep him locked up."

"Is that why we didn't meet Amal somewhere else? So you could play your little chess match with the Sicarii?"

Zafer shook his head. "If they were listening, they know she burned Tariq's business phonebook. They'll leave her alone now."

"What about that slip of paper she gave you? What did she write?"

"A number and a name. Before she burned Tariq's book, she memorized them. We're going to Antakya."

"Turkey?"

Zafer nodded. "I recognized the area code."

"Who are we going to see?"

"Iorgos Serafis," Kadir said. "A famous seller of antiquities."

"But before we do that, I want to see if we can draw the Sicarii out of hiding."

"How are we supposed to do that?"

Zafer put a hand on Drew's shoulder. "We put you out for bait."

5: 7

THE GAME

Before his first trip to Cairo, Drew had imagined a city of palm trees and untrammeled desert light. He had imagined Nile sunsets with the silhouettes of the pyramids looming on the horizon. Staying in downtown Cairo, however, was more like living in a basement with dirty windows. No view of the Nile or the pyramids unless you could afford one of the swank hotels along the riverfront. No view of anything, really, aside from other buildings—generally taller than the one housing the hotel—and the packed streets.

This morning, leaving their first hotel, Zafer had pointed at a street-sweeper. "That's the most important man in Cairo. Without him, the city would be buried by sand in about six months."

The sweepers were always out early with thatch brooms that looked like small, denuded bushes tied to handles. The sand they missed, if left to accumulate against the curb long enough, became so black and clumpy it looked like it had been used to filter oil.

Cairo's downtown was organized around "squares," which tended to be circular and, fed by an overpass or two, were particularly good at snarling traffic. The city was like a Gulliver tied down by its own system of roads. What made things worse was the Egyptian penchant for beeping. If they had to choose between a car with no wheels and one with no horn, Drew was sure they'd take the car without wheels. At 1:00 a.m., even with wads of waterlogged toilet paper plugging his ears, Drew was sometimes awakened by a spate of horn-blowing.

They were in Orabi Square now, not far from their second hotel, and back in their own clothes. They'd changed in the taxi, the driver casting bewildered glances at them.

"Why am I the bait?" Drew complained. "Why not you? You can handle the Sicarii a lot better than I can."

Zafer looked at him critically. "You want me to rely on *you* for backup? And forget about dangling shorty out there—he won't do it."

Kadir shook his head. "There is no chance of this."

"Besides, if he needs to run, he's not exactly an Olympic sprinter. No, it's you."

Drew sighed in resignation. "So...?"

"We find an Internet café. You sit there for twenty minutes, half an hour. I'll watch the door. You've got your new cell phone, and you handled Nabil's gorilla, right?"

"What if there are two or three Nathans?"

"Don't worry, you're no good to them dead. They want a bargaining chip. So keep your eye on the door and don't let anyone stand behind you."

Drew shook his head. "I really don't like this."

"Keep your cell phone out. If it rings, you know it's me. Except for Kadir, no one else has your new number. But if I call, you better answer."

Drew's hands, even in the Egyptian heat, had turned to ice. He took a deep breath and let it out. "Okay."

"Now, as you're walking, stay away from the street. If a car pulls up anywhere near you—run. Fast. We don't want them to force you into a car before I can get there. All right?"

"Yeah. All right." He tried to calm down by telling himself it was a game. *An oversized game using Cairo and Istanbul for the board.* But recalling that both Tariq and Stephen had been killed in this game, he didn't feel any better.

Zafer jerked his chin. "Get going."

5: 8

JESUS AND JOHN:
WHO BAPTIZED WHOM?

DREW NAVIGATED the crowded sidewalk, casting nervous glances over his shoulder and eyeing traffic. He remembered the sign he'd seen at the airport and wondered, *was* he going in a wrong way? Hadn't his father always worried he'd take after his Gypsy heritage and make his money through underhanded dealings of one kind or another?

A black car pulled over just ahead of Drew and double-parked. Drew hugged a shop front. He couldn't see in the tinted windows, but his heart drummed a warning.

Breaking into a trot as though he were a few minutes late to the café where his girlfriend was waiting, he passed the car and finally got a look at the driver through the windshield. An Egyptian woman who looked thoroughly bored.

Drew turned down a side street.

He turned again, following a zigzag pattern from where he'd started.

A few blocks down he found El Shams Internet Café, the sign written in both English and Arabic. Its logo was a yellow sun.

The café reminded him of the ones he'd been to in Istanbul—kids absorbed in video games, a few serious-looking men, a couple of whirring fans affixed high on the plastered walls, a lot of smoke and flies. There were only two vacant computers. He took the one farthest from the door. The computer's tower had no housing, and the dusty electronic guts were exposed.

Drew put his phone on the table, the wooden veneer peeling, exposing pressboard. A boy slipped the corner of a receipt under the monitor stand. Drew pulled a balled-up tissue out of his pocket and wiped grit off the screen. Glancing at the glass door, he reminded himself that Zafer was watching, that this was Cairo—not Baghdad—that kidnappings didn't happen to foreigners checking their e-mail.

When he saw an e-mail from Yasemin, he felt a vague tingling in his legs. He regretted every accusatory word he'd written this morning. She was going to ask him not to write anymore, not to call, not to have anymore contact with him.

The subject heading was *Your letter.*

Dear Drew,

He took a deep breath and held it.

This is the first thing you've written to me since we split up that has made me feel something. I mean, the other ones made me angry or bitter, but this one ... something in me broke.

Relieved, he exhaled heavily, and the little slip of paper held down by the monitor fluttered.

You can't imagine how I would love to go back to the night I met you in a restaurant in Taksim and start all over again. Really, Drew, I never loved anyone the way I loved you. That's why I married you. And your letter seemed to hit me in all of my weakest places. I'm crying now as I write this. Especially remembering all those photos of us.

Look, no promises, no big decisions over the Internet. But let's talk. I love you, too.

Yasemin

PS – When are you coming back from Egypt? And why doesn't your cell phone work?

"Yes!" he hissed and raised his fists as though he'd just won a world title. He started typing so rapidly every other letter was a typo.

Yazz,

We *can* start over. We can still have a family. No doctor has been able to find anything wrong with you or me. We'll go to the best clinic in Istanbul. I'll be back from Egypt in a day or two. I'll explain when I get back.

Love always, Drew

He wanted to take the next flight back to Istanbul. He wanted his wife back. He wanted their life together back. Well … half of him did. The other half was desperate to see this thing through to the end. Especially now that he understood why Jesus couldn't have been the Messiah. It was so obvious, he still couldn't believe no one else had noticed. Or, if someone had, he hadn't gotten the chance to tell many people.

How ironic: Yasemin used to accuse him of having no ambition, of letting life carry him along, and now he was city-hopping looking for an ancient manuscript that was responsible for the deaths two men, at least, and might force scholars to rewrite Christian history. Some of it anyway.

He zipped off an e-mail to Rob Mearns, a website designer who'd been a close friend in high school. Cyberspace had its own archaeological deposits, and Rob knew how to excavate it. He'd be able to tell Drew when the Ebionites' website went up and the last time it had been modified.

A kid screamed as though a snake had bitten him. Drew snapped his head around, but no one seemed to need a paramedic. Probably an on-screen spaceship had been blown up or someone had failed to save the computer-generated world.

Drew's eyes flicked to the door again.

The fan and the weak air-conditioning didn't help much; he was pouring sweat. Swiping at a fly on the monitor, he began an e-mail to himself called DEAD SEA SCROLL EVIDENCE.

It seems clear that at least some of the scrolls were written in the second half of the first century. The coins found on the site corroborate this and so does some of what the scrolls actually say. If that's true, how could the authors, some supposedly writing about James and Paul, fail entirely to mention Christ's ministry, his death, his resurrection? How could they mention James and not in the same breath refer to him as the brother of the Messiah? Even IF Jesus, not James, was the Teacher of Righteousness, there is nothing about a resurrection after the Teacher's death. There is nothing about the Crucifixion.

No way it could have gone unnoticed. And if James was the Teacher of Righteousness, then where was Jesus? It would be unthinkable to write about James as though he were the Messiah—it is through the Teacher that "the faithful will be saved"—if his brother had been the Messiah.

He sent it off to his own email. He might lose his notebook or his flash drive, but the file he'd just written was now stored in a server.

Stephen must have known years ago that Jesus was entirely absent from the Dead Sea Scrolls. Maybe that was what he had been hinting at every time he reminded Drew that the Scrolls were primary source material—no Christian scribe could have added or deleted anything.

But if Jesus wasn't the Messiah, who was? The obvious candidate was John the Baptist. John had been put to death for exactly the same—alleged—reason as Jesus: he was a threat to the ruling authorities. In John's case it had not been Pontius Pilate, but Herod Antipas.

And what about the Teacher of Righteousness? Could he have been John rather than James? John, after all, must have had ties to the Qumran community.

There was something else. John was descended from Zadok, which meant he was an heir to the title of high priest. It was even possible that James was not Jesus' brother but *John's*. According to Luke, John and Jesus (and therefore James) were cousins, which might have been an allusion to their actual kinship. Hadn't the Essenes been waiting for a messiah descended of the line of David and a savior from the line of Zadok?

"Why not?" Drew asked a little too loudly.

A few faces turned his way, but most likely assumed his world had flown apart in sparkling pixels or his virtual hero had been lasered out of existence, and went back to their screens.

Opening another e-mail, Drew jotted down parallels between John and Jesus:

1. *Just as the angel Gabriel told Elizabeth's husband that Elizabeth was going to bear a child who would be great in the sight of the Lord, Gabriel tells Mary she's going to conceive.*

He did a quick search and re-read Luke 1:15, which mentioned the birth of John.

2. *While the Holy Spirit was reputed to be the father of Jesus, it was prophesied that John "shall be filled with the Holy Spirit even from the womb." Pretty damn close.*

3. *Both were the products of miraculous births—Jesus to a young virgin; John to a barren, middle-aged woman. (A kind of reversal here.)*

4. *John was an itinerant preacher who gave sermons in the wilderness.*

Jesus also had a wandering ministry, preached in rural areas, and ventured into the wilderness, where he was tempted by Satan.

5. *John's following became large enough that he was perceived as a threat to the authority of Herod Antipas; Jesus was executed for being a threat to Roman rule.*

6. *John, like Jesus, was a passionate speaker who warned of the coming apocalypse. When the Sadducees and Pharisees come to hear him speak he scolds them: "Brood of vipers! Who warned you to flee from the wrath to come?"*

That was somewhere in Matthew. Another search and Drew found it. He read through chapter three, stabbing a finger at the monitor when he found what he was looking for. John's trademark chant was "Repent, for the kingdom of heaven is at hand!" A few verses later, Jesus shouts, "Repent, for the kingdom of heaven is at hand!"

7. *Jesus' ministry is based on John's. There's a passage from Matthew that even foreshadows Jesus' resurrection: "At that time, Herod the Tetrarch heard the report about Jesus and said to his servants, 'This is John the Baptist; he is risen from the dead, and therefore these powers are at work in him'." (Matt. 14:1)*

Drew recalled there was also some confusion in Luke about who the Christ was. He pulled up Luke 3:15: "Now as the people were in expectation, and all reasoned in their hearts about John, whether he was the Christ or not ..."

He started typing again.

8. *Jesus doesn't seem to exist before he is baptized by John. Mark, the earliest Gospel, gives no account of Jesus' birth—virgin or otherwise. And nothing of Jesus' childhood. Jesus simply goes to John, who quietly bows down to him, yet scholars have always been puzzled as to why the Messiah would have an inferior baptize him.*

"Because John *wasn't* inferior," Drew muttered. The more Drew thought about it, the more sense it made. In all the Gospels, Jesus is tried by Pontius Pilate, but Luke added an extra trial under Herod Antipas, who was *John's* executioner. Had Luke inserted that deliberately as an allusion to what really happened? Had John been the real-life Savior, the actual Teacher of Righteousness, on which the legend of Jesus had been based?

The glow of the screen seemed to intensify.

Drew punched in a few keywords and came up with a quote he could recall only in fragments: "Truly, I say to you, among those born of women, there has arisen no one greater than John the Baptist." John and Jesus were nearly the same age and both had had mortal mothers, so was Jesus just being humble? Or was Matthew in effect *saying* John was the Savior? And why had Drew never noticed this before?

If John had been the Savior, then Jesus' baptism in the Jordan hadn't been an actual event but a metaphor: John was passing the torch. Not to his superior but to a fiction created by the Gospel authors. Didn't John himself say something to that effect?

In a dusty, stifling Internet café in Cairo, among screaming kids, virtual invasions, and video combat, Drew thought maybe, just maybe, he was peering over the edge of revelation.

He punched in another set of search words, and a quote in bold letters popped up on his screen: *He must grow greater while I must become less.* John 3:30. There it was in John the Baptist's own words. He was passing the torch.

Drew had always treated the Bible as a literary work open to interpretation, but he now realized that there was more to it than that. Much more. The Gospel authors had left allusions and written in double-meanings, which, if deciphered, revealed entirely different Gospels. Seen from this perspective, Luke's addition of Jesus' interview before Herod Antipas was a way of signaling that, if Jesus and John the Baptist weren't one and the same, they were inextricably related.

And then there was Jesus' temptation in the wilderness—*John's* milieu—which had never made any sense to Drew. How could Satan, powerful as he was, tempt the Son of God? What could anyone offer the Son of God that He didn't already have? But what if *John* was the one who had been tempted? Not by Satan but by Herod Antipas? What if John had been brought before Herod and offered a handsome reward to give up his ministry? A scenario like this made far more sense.

The door opened, and Drew whipped his head around.

A kid in jeans and a ragged t-shirt with *Purdue University* written across it came in.

Relieved, Drew sent the e-mail to himself.

His cell phone rang.

5: 9

THE KNIGHTS OF MALTA

DREW PICKED UP THE PHONE. "Zafer?"

"I just spotted Nathan."

"*Shit.*"

"Stay where you are. *Don't* leave the café. I'll be right there."

"I'm at the last computer on the left. Hurry."

He'd hardly ended the call when the door swung open.

Nathan was in jeans, a T-shirt, and black sneakers. No jacket under which he could at least pretend to conceal a weapon. All he carried was a manila folder.

"Good to see you again, Drew."

"How the hell did you find me?"

The door opened again, and Zafer came in with Kadir.

Nathan acknowledged them with a nod. "Nice move you guys pulled back at Amal's."

"You were there?" Drew asked.

"We knew you would go so see Amal—you *had* to. The Sicarii knew that, too. There are only a three ways to get to Amal's street, and when you guys came out ... well, wearing *jalabiyas* wasn't a bad idea, but two guys and a dwarf are hard to miss. And you know if *I* could follow you here—"

"So could the Sicarii." Zafer finished the sentence.

"This is for you ..."

He opened the folder, and Drew saw a photograph of the man the Egyptian police had carted off.

"This is Jean Saint-Savoy." Nathan's dark hands sorted through more photos taken from various angles and distances. "Thirty-five years old, former agent for SGDN—French intelligence. Trained in hand-to-hand, various weapons, surveillance.

"And this is his pal Raymond Duvall, thirty-seven, French national. These two work together in Cairo. There is at least one more Cairo operative—maybe several—but we don't know who they are. And there are at least two more in Istanbul.

"Raymond made captain in the French Foreign Legion before he changed allegiances. Since he seems to travel the most and had the highest military rank, we think he's the team leader."

Raymond's blond hair was cut to stubble. His eyes were eerily pale in the black-and-white photo, and his face had no excess flesh, making the cheekbones and jaw line severe. Something about his eyes, beyond their strange pallor, worried Drew. Even in flat reproduction, they seemed to have the crackle of static electricity.

Nathan looked at Zafer. "He knows weapons, explosives, surveillance techniques, hand-to-hand."

He slipped another photo out of the folder.

"This is one of the Istanbul operatives."

Drew looked down at a pale man with a thin face, a mustache, and black hair cropped short on the sides but surprisingly long on top; it looked like he used the wind for a comb.

"Francis Collins, 36, American. A university professor when he's not employed by the Ecole Biblique. Comparative religion. Paid for college by serving in the Air Force."

Nathan closed the folder. "This is all the background information we could gather on these three. We're working on the others. We think there are a dozen or so hardcore Sicarii. But there are more who do small jobs—surveillance mostly." He handed the folder to Zafer.

Zafer nodded appreciatively. "Nice work."

"You should also know about the Knights of Malta. Members have to be Catholic, and they have to have a military background. The Knights are a legitimate organization with Permanent Observer status at the United Nations. We think the Sicarii are an elite within the Knights."

"They're recognized by the UN?" Drew asked.

Nathan nodded. "They have an interesting history. After World War II, quite a few high-ranking Nazis were smuggled out of Germany to Australia, Argentina, Canada, even the US. The Vatican called it Operation Ratline."

"In honor of their cargo?"

"Fitting, but no. A ratline is an old nautical term. It's a rope ladder that leads to the top of the main mast. It's the last place a sailor can go when the ship is sinking. Catholic Nazis were provided with Knights of Malta passports and new identities. Reinhard Gehlen, who ran Hitler's intelligence operations on the eastern front, was flown out of Germany in General Eisenhower's personal airplane and made an officer in the US Army."

"You're kidding."

Nathan's smile was close-lipped and ironic. "I wish I were. But you have to understand, this was not the Church. This was a handful of men maneuvering secretly within the Vatican, just as a handful of men within the United States' government operated without President Truman's knowledge."

"Why Nazis are important for us?" Kadir asked.

"Because you need to know who you're dealing with. Allen Dulles was a Maltese Knight. He was director of the Office of Strategic Services in Switzerland during World War II. He engineered Gehlen's escape to the US. William Donovan, another Knight, helped Dulles transform the OSS into the CIA. John McCone, director of the CIA after Dulles, and William Casey, director under President Reagan, were both Knights. For years, CIA Counter Intelligence and the CIA's Vatican desk were headed by a Knight named James Jesus Angleton."

"Jesus? Was his father a preacher?" Drew asked.

"Not exactly. He grew up in Italy and was assigned to the Rome desk of the OSS after Italy surrendered to the Allies in 1943. The Maltese Knights, it just so happens, are headquartered in Rome. Angleton and Dulles funneled millions into the Vatican to make sure Italian communists lost in the elections after World War II, so the Vatican repaid the CIA by opening doors for Nazis desperate to escape Germany and prosecution." Nathan paused. "Do you understand now?"

"Yeah," Zafer said. "The Sicarii don't recognize national boundaries."

"Exactly. A Knight's first allegiance is to other Knights. You also need to know that the Vatican has its own intelligence service. Worse, Casey not only opened up CIA files to the Vatican, he gave the Vatican access to CIA resources, like satellite reconnaissance. I think it's safe to assume that the Sicarii are able to log into the CIA's database. This puts us at a very serious disadvantage." Nathan tapped the folder Zafer was holding. "This is a show of good faith. All we want is the Habakkuk Scroll."

"How much you can pay?" Kadir asked.

"Why should we pay you? It's ours."

"Abu did not get this scroll in a legal way, but you say it was his." Kadir shrugged. "I did not get it in a legal way, too, but it is mine. My friend is dead because of this scroll. The *hoja* is dead because of this scroll."

"Look, Kadir, we won't keep anything but the photographs. The scroll is going to be returned to the Israeli government. They have a policy of generous compensation. There's your money."

"How much?"

"I don't know."

"After we find out how much, we'll talk," Zafer said. "We'll contact you in Istanbul. You have my word."

Nathan sighed heavily.

Kadir reached up with a hand. "It is a deal?"

Nathan took Kadir's child-sized hand in his own. "All right then, Istanbul. Now, if you guys don't mind, I'd like to talk to Drew for a couple minutes."

Zafer shrugged.

Kadir found an empty computer near the door and hopped up on a chair. Zafer stood next to him, arms folded over his chest.

Standing over Drew, Nathan said, "I have a confession to make ..."

Aware of a tingling in his groin as though he had to pee, Drew glanced over at Zafer.

"I'm not an Ebionite."

Why is he telling me this?

"I'm an atheist. Like the professor."

"Then why—?"

"I don't believe in God, but I can accept a religion that completely rejects violence."

"So you're using the Ebionites."

"My agenda is no different than Stephen's. Hasn't the world had enough of blind faith? Imagine a group of religious fanatics getting their hands on a nuclear weapon—9/11 would be nostalgic. And right now the best way I can think of to deal with that possibility is through the Ebionites. Don't get me wrong. I don't expect to change two thousand years of belief by disproving it. Most people aren't interested in the truth unless it reinforces what they already believe."

"What are you getting at?"

"I know this scroll means a lot more to you than it does to them." Nathan tipped his head to indicate Zafer and Kadir. "Just be careful who you trust. The Sicarii aren't the only ones who don't want you to know the truth."

What Nathan was saying, in effect, was that he was the only one Drew could be certain was above suspicion. But for the first time since they'd met, Drew didn't trust him.

5: 10

AHWA

"**Y**OU STILL THINK NATHAN is Sicarii?"

They were in an *ahwa,* a coffeehouse. Every square inch of wall space had been taken up with one kind of decoration or another: a bust of Nefertiti on a wall shelf, a mirror inscribed *Welcome to Egypt,* a painted belly dancer framed by a pattern inspired by the twists of vines and the soft undulations of leaves, a portrait of a Turkish Sultan—all dulled by the smoke they'd been saturated in for years.

Zafer took the stem of the *narghile*—a *shisha* to the Egyptians—out of his mouth. "What were you doing in that Internet café?"

"Checking my e-mail."

Drew had ordered *helba,* which the Egyptians also called *yellow tea* although, as far as he could tell, it was some kind of bean infusion. It had a subtle taste and seemed to mellow out the stomach riot that often followed a spicy Egyptian meal.

"No, you were in that Internet café because you were bait. And what did we catch? Nathan. It's classic good cop, bad cop. He feeds us some names, tells us who the bad guys are, winks and says, *Don't worry, I got your back.*"

Drew sucked hard on the *narghile.* Exhaling, he searched the cloud of white smoke for something meaningful. "Maybe you're right."

"He told you he's an atheist. An atheist who works for a church? Does that make any sense?"

"I don't know. Today was the first time I started to wonder who he really is."

"Never mind who is Nathan," Kadir said. "We're going to Antakya to see Serafis."

Drew was elated that there were no flights between Cairo and the airport near Antakya. It meant that after they arrived in Istanbul, he could meet Yasemin.

"Who is this guy, Serafis?"

"A Greek," Kadir said. "He is knowing the black market very well. I have heard of him, but I never met to him. Tariq was plan to see to him if we do not find buyer in Istanbul."

Drew wiped sweat off his forehead with the back of a hand. "You can't sell it to him, Kadir."

"Why I can't sell it?" Water bubbled as he inhaled through the coiled arm of the *narghile*.

"Because ... you *can't*. Scholars have to see it. This is ... this could change *history*."

Kadir shrugged. "Abu didn't change history."

"Yes but ... don't you understand? Everything Christians believe might be ... might change."

"Serafis is Christian. If the money is enough, I am saying goodbye to this scroll, and he can change everything he wants."

Drew leaned closer to Kadir. "Stephen didn't die so you could make money."

"Did he die so I could be poor?"

"He died—" Drew straightened up. "He died for something he *believed* in." His voice had sharpened to a blade.

Reaching across the little round table, Zafer grabbed Drew's wrist. "You knew sooner or later we were going to sell the scroll. You want us to sell it to Nathan? We won't get anything. The Ebionites are broke. Even if he's *not* Sicarii. If he is, we lose money *and* the scroll." He withdrew his hand.

"My friend is dead too." Kadir had switched to Turkish. "I can't do anything with a two-thousand-year-old roll of paper. I can do something with five million dollars."

Drew stood up. "Listen, you money-grubbing, little bastard—"

Zafer, who'd jumped up at the same time, seized Drew's wrist.

Drew broke the hold and retracted his arm. "Not that easy when the other guy has some training, is it?"

"Don't challenge me, Drew."

Drew's heart had kicked up a couple of gears, and now some of the Egyptians at other tables were looking at them.

"Sit the fuck down." Zafer patted the table with his hand.

Drew sank into his chair.

A waiter knocked gray embers off the tops of their *narghiles* with tongs and replaced them with coals glowing a healthy orange.

"Look, Kadir, what if this scroll were part of the Qur'an? Or the Hadith?"

"If it tells the same things as the Qur'an and the Hadith, who can need it? If it tells something different, it is *haram* and must be burned." Kadir shrugged. "Instead of burning, I would sell."

Drew let out an exasperated breath. "What if ... what if it had some—some *new* information about Muhammad? About his life?"

Kadir drew meditatively on his pipe. White smoke drifted past his face as he exhaled. "I would sell. Not to the black market, but still I would sell."

"Exactly!" Drew poked a long finger at him.

"Infidel. Still there is a problem ... it is *not* about Muhammad, it is a Christian writing."

"Jewish."

"Yes, Jewish. I am Muslim. So why I am caring about a Jewish writing?"

"You want money, right? Then what about the Israeli government? Nathan says they'll pay."

Zafer shook his head. "It's not that easy, Drew."

Reappraising Zafer's wide-set shoulders, his bull neck, and the thick bone of his brow, Drew was glad he had sat back down.

"What if they don't pay?" Zafer asked. "What if they just take the scroll? Then what?"

"And we don't know the how much." Kadir shook his head, which despite his diminutive body, was almost as big as Zafer's. "Ten thousand? Twenty?"

Drew raised both of his hands as though acknowledging a foul in a basketball game. "All right, all right. Just promise you won't sell it until you at least find out how much they'll give you." Drew looked at Zafer. "You have a friend in MIT. He can find out, can't he? Don't they have clerks or something who can do that? You know ... fact-checking? Bullshit work?"

Zafer nodded. "I'll talk to him." His cheeks hollowed as he drew on his *narghile*.

The American looked at Kadir. The dwarf was maybe three-and-half feet tall. No wife. No kids. It couldn't be easy. To watch a woman walk by, to know there was no point in talking to her no matter the clamor in your chest. To know that ... what? Ninety-eight percent of all women fell into the category of Unattainable. His whole life must be one knot of frustration. Getting on a bus was a task. Shaving meant dragging a chair into the bathroom. Walking attracted jeering kids. No wonder Kadir, sitting on a stool outside his shop, subsisted on a diet of cigarettes and pulp sci-fi in which he journeyed to far-flung worlds, bathed in the leaden light of blue stars, explored the ruins of ancient Martian cities.

Drew had had long talks with him after Sahaflar Charsisi had been mostly closed for the night, and the outdoor shelves cleared. Light from Kadir's shop spilling into the cobbled alley, moths and gnats would make a scattered cloud over their heads. On more than one of those late nights, Kadir had listened to him whine about his divorce. And whenever he'd had one *raki* too many, Kadir would talk about moving to southern Turkey and living on a boat. It was the only dream Drew had ever heard him mention. A boat on the Mediterranean.

Drew backhanded sweat off his forehead. "I'm sorry, Kadir."

"I'm also sorry." He sat sullenly smoking.

Zafer's cell phone rang. Glancing at the number, he smiled. "Perfect timing."

The Turk did very little talking, but from what Drew overheard, he assumed it was his friend at MIT.

Zafer put the phone back in his pocket and grinned. "Looks like Jean is going to be on ice for at least a month. That's one down, eleven to go."

Drew smiled, but he noticed that Zafer hadn't said anything to his friend about the Israeli government or its policy of compensation for returned antiquities.

5: 11

THE TERRORIST NETWORK

T HE ALLEY, LIKE MOST in downtown Cairo, was dimly lit
in spite of the hooded lamps hung from sagging cables strung between
buildings. A small crowd of men clogged the passage. They were
watching a television that had been set up above the doorway of a dingy
coffeehouse. Drew and the Turks slowed to a stop, and he looked up at
the screen. "What's this all about?"

The television camera swept across a ruined street: an apartment
building had been shorn in half and chunks of cement dangled from the
steel rods used for reinforcement. A rug hanging over a rough lip of floor
reminded Drew these were homes he was staring into.

"Where is this?" Drew asked in English.

"Baghdad," Zafer said.

The television cameras were rolling in a hospital now. Drew's jaw
involuntarily lowered—slowly, like a drawbridge slightly too heavy for
its counterweights. He'd never seen anything like the scorched face of
the man on screen whose arms were suspended by cables because, Drew
realized, in any other position they would have caused him intense pain.
Yes, he'd seen burn victims, equally hideous, but not in the same way. He
was bandaged from head to foot, only the lower part of his face visible.
Spots of crimson had soaked through. The lips were absurdly swollen
and deformed. Black, they had bubbled, and the bubbles had in turn
grown smaller bubbles, which seemed to have hardened into a crust.

Drew wouldn't have believed human tissue could do this—that this *could be done to* human tissue—if he hadn't seen it.

"How…?" was all he could say.

"Cluster bombs," Zafer said.

An Iraqi boy with a blackened chest lay in a hospital bed. Bandaged stubs had replaced his arms. He looked up as though he had been caught naked on camera. He had. He would never be able to cover up. He would never be able to hug anyone, not even himself.

"Is this Al Jazeera?"

"Bush calls it the terrorist network." Zafer snorted. "Embedded journalists. What a joke. Did you ever see anything like this on CNN?"

Drew shook his head. "If Americans had seen images like these every night, the war would have been over in a week." He prayed silently that was not a lie.

Zafer aimed a finger at the TV. "See that guy … the one who lost his face?"

Drew nodded.

"What do you think he'll do when he gets out of the hospital?"

"Join a group of terrorists?"

Zafer didn't bother to answer.

The report lasted another twenty minutes, at the end of which Kadir was bored. "*Hadi, gidelim,*" he said. "I want to go back to hotel."

Their new hotel was only a few blocks away. Eight stories high, it occupied the whole building. It also had a fairly posh lobby with a floor of green marble tile and graceful wooden archways beneath a high ceiling. The furniture was the sort you might expect in an English drawing room—amply cushioned and highly polished.

Drew's head snapped back for a second look at the woman sitting on the velvety green couch. "Is that…?"

Looking up, she seemed to mirror his own startled expression.

Her black hair was a little longer, her face now had mature lines and sharper angles but was as freckled as ever.

"Jesse?"

She stood up. "Drew?"

Jesse Fenton. After all these years—years that had taken her from a good-looking girl to … Christ, if she smiled at him he was probably going to lose bladder control. It wasn't that she had a model's looks, it was more the way it all added up: the slash of her dark eyebrows against her pale forehead, the curvy upper lip and slight overbite, the bright green eyes and, of course, the freckles.

Walking toward her, Drew held up the one-minute finger to Zafer and Kadir, who were standing in front of the elevator.

"What are you doing in Cairo?" He couldn't help leaning forward to hug her, although they'd never had any such physical intimacy in college. To his relief, she hugged him back. He straightened up and gave her some space.

"I really shouldn't be. I'm supposed to be in Syria finishing up some research on Suriani Christians and monastic Christianity. But Egypt is so close I thought I'd make a side trip to take in the pyramids. My grant won't cover it ..." She shrugged. "But what the hell? Tomorrow night I have to fly back to Aleppo."

"So you're still in the field?"

"Oh yeah. I'm a professor at Loyola. I'm on sabbatical."

"Why didn't I ever see your name on the web? I did a dozen searches."

She smiled up at him. "Probably because you were looking for Jesse *Fenton*. I publish under my married name: *Willard*."

"Oh." He nodded. "I see." In college, a boyfriend. Now, a husband. History repeats.

5: 12

A MODEST PROPOSAL

JESSE AND DREW SAT AT A TABLE on the hotel's roof. The view consisted of a cluster of neoclassical buildings that formed an artificial canyon stretching away to the east, the roof of an adjacent building a couple of stories lower, and a confluence of broad avenues that would become unbearably noisy in a few hours. Zafer and Kadir were a couple of tables away. A pair of tourists who looked to be German had the only other occupied table.

"I'm sorry about last night, but things are … complicated."

Last night Zafer had interrupted their unexpected reunion, pulling Drew away by an arm. He'd barely managed to get Jesse's card and room number. Drew had been fuming on the elevator. "What the *fuck* did you do that for?"

Zafer was impassive as usual. "Aren't you the one who can't wait to get back to Istanbul to see his ex-wife?"

"It's nothing *like* that." If Drew had been facing someone other than Zafer, he might have grabbed him by the shirt. "She's married. And she's a *scholar*. Someone who can *read* those goddamn photographs you carry around with you everywhere."

"Like the professor?"

"Yeah, like the professor. Only a lot younger and a lot better looking."

"You want her to end up like the professor?" Zafer asked.

"No," Drew took in a deep breath. "I guess not."

"Wait till morning. Then invite her to breakfast or something if you still feel like dragging her into this. Then give *her* a chance to think it over."

He raked back his long hair with his fingers. "You're right."

"How do you know her?"

Drew smiled and shook his head. "College. I haven't seen her in like twelve years."

The elevator had stopped. The double doors had to be swung inward manually and then a gate that folded like an accordion had to be drawn back. "You can't tell her much. *Nothing* about the scroll we're looking for, Drew. *Nothing.*" Zafer had closed the gate behind Kadir. "Nothing about Antakya or Serafis. And don't give her any way of contacting you. Except your e-mail address. That's it. You call *her* if you need to."

Drew had nodded.

"Drew, I need your word on this."

"All *right* … I promise."

Now here he was sitting across from Jesse, squinting in the bright sunlight and wondering how to explain the situation to her. "Have you ever heard of Stephen Cutherton?"

"Sure. He and de la Croix were archenemies."

"Yeah, well, it doesn't matter anymore. He was murdered last week in Istanbul."

"*Murdered?* I wasn't a big fan of his work, but … that's awful."

"To me Stephen was … in some ways, he was like a father." Drew looked away. "I didn't actually see it, but I was there a few minutes later."

"You were *there?* What exactly *happened?*"

"One of the Dead Sea Scrolls is involved."

"*What?*"

Drew let out an exasperated sigh and summarized what he'd been through since Kadir had given him an unmarked package to take home. He was careful to edit out everything about the second scroll.

Jesse's coffee cup clacked softly against the saucer. "Drew, is this some kind of joke?"

"Not remotely. So before the conversation goes any further, you have to decide whether or not you want to be involved."

"Do I get to see the scroll?"

"I can show you photographs but not here in Cairo." Drew jerked a thumb in Zafer's direction. "The big lug over there will keep an eye on you when you're with us, but you might be followed."

"Followed?"

"Stephen's dead. Tariq was an accident, but he's dead, too."

Jesse buttered a piece of toast. "You know, it's against my better judgment—I mean, guns, the black market, violating I don't know what laws, but how could any scholar say no?"

Drew nodded. "If I could take it all back and save Stephen, I would. But for the first time in my life, I'm *after* something. I need to find a way to get this scroll to scholars. I need to know if it changes our understanding of Christianity."

She looked at him skeptically. "What do you mean, *our understanding of Christianity?*"

"I think ... I don't think Christ was the Messiah. There was *some*one regarded as the Messiah, but it wasn't Jesus."

Jesse rolled her eyes. "That one's been tried before."

"Look, you know about the Teacher of Righteousness, the Liar, and—"

"The Wicked Priest? Mm-hm."

"Doesn't it strike you as odd that the scrolls never once mention the crucifixion or a resurrection? I mean how could the scrolls mention the Teacher—James the Just, the *brother* of the Messiah—without mentioning the Messiah?"

"Drew, I have news for you. The Teacher of Righteousness was *not* James. The Teacher was probably the *founder* of the Essenes. Which means he lived about two centuries before Christ. You have to remember, dating these manuscripts is an imprecise process. Scholars assume they can narrow it down to fifty years plus or minus—that's a range of one hundred years."

"Even if that's true, *some* of the scrolls are clearly from the first century AD, yet none of them makes any reference to Jesus."

Jesse shrugged. "So the Essenes didn't recognize Jesus as the Messiah. Jews generally didn't—and don't." She put a hand on Drew's. "You should have gotten your PhD."

There was a lot more to this argument, but this morning, before catching a plane back to Cairo, probably wasn't the time for it.

"Just to play devil's advocate," Jesse said, "here's a tidbit for you: ever heard of Philo of Alexandria?"

"Sure."

"Did you know he went to see Emperor Gaius Caligula around 40 AD, about ten years after Christ was probably crucified? He went to talk the emperor out of putting a statue of himself in the Temple in Jerusalem, but while he was there, he apparently offered testimony about the brutality of Pontius Pilate's rule in Palestine."

"Philo wrote about *Pilate*?"

Jesse tapped a hardboiled egg with the back of a spoon until it cracked. "Yes, but he never mentioned Jesus."

Drew swallowed a lump of disbelief. "How could you be a Jew, author works analyzing Judaism, be an exact contemporary of Jesus, write about Pontius Pilate's barbaric treatment of the Jews, and *never* mention Christ or the crucifixion?"

"Not so fast." The shell of the egg, still held by a rubbery membrane, peeled away with a soft sucking sound. "The second part of Philo's *Mission to Gaius* was lost, and that's probably where he wrote about Pilate in detail. It's the only thing Philo wrote that didn't survive. It's also where he would most likely have discussed Jesus." She smiled as she salted her egg. "Keep reading, Drew. You'll get there."

It was maddening that he couldn't tell her about the second scroll, which turned Jesus Christ into a mirage Paul had glimpsed wavering in the heat on a desert road. Drew pushed a clump of hair, still wet from the shower, off his forehead. "Okay, here's a question for you: is it pure coincidence that we have *all* of Philo's works except the one section where Christ, if he had been crucified under Pilate, *had* to have been mentioned?" Was that, Drew wondered, why Stephen had mentioned Philo? As more evidence of Church tampering?

"What are you saying? That early scribes just ... *threw away* every copy of Book Two of *Mission to Gaius*?"

"If you can add to Josephus, you can subtract from Philo."

"Not likely, Drew."

"Considering that Christian scribes were responsible for preserving nearly every text that's come down to us from antiquity, do you really think they'd copy something that contradicted their faith?"

Jesse salted her egg. "I think they'd toss out the whole book."

"And Seneca?"

"What do you mean?" She took a bite.

"Remember my paper for de La Croix? While I was reading up on Augustine, I came across a passage in *City of God* where Augustine tries to explain how Seneca could have written a book called *On Superstition* and criticized every foreign religious sect known to the Romans without ever mentioning Christianity. We have like ninety percent of everything Seneca ever wrote, but somehow *On Superstition* disappeared."

Jesse smirked. "Like I said, the Church probably tossed the whole thing. Why do you think all that's left of Celsus and Porphyry are fragments? They made vehement attacks on Christianity."

There was a loud exchange between car horns on the street below.

"True enough, but you're proving my point—the Church had a deliberate program of censorship. For centuries. And there's Tacitus. He writes a year-by-year account of the reign of Tiberius, but the end of 29, 30, and the beginning of 31 AD are somehow the only sections missing. Isn't 30 AD the accepted year of the crucifixion?"

Jesse nodded. "It's possible Tacitus skipped over the Crucifixion and the Church deep-sixed those chapters, but he does mention the crucifixion when he's talking about Nero." She shrugged. "History goes to the conquerors."

"I suppose." Drew looked down at her hand as she spread jam on a croissant. "Where's your ring?"

She wiggled her fingers as though she'd just freed them from a trap. "Divorced. Almost two years."

"Really?" He suppressed a smile. "Me too."

5: 13

RUBRICS

DIVORCED. It might have been better if she had still been married. Here he was, in a taxi on his way to the airport, and in a few hours he'd be back in Istanbul. He'd call Yasemin. He'd be elated to see her because for the first time in two years they were talking about reconciling. He finally had a chance to get his wife back, his old life. The pain he'd been living with since their separation was on the verge of disappearing. So why was his mind still on a hotel rooftop overlooking Cairo?

The taxi approached the enormous statue of Ramses II. The pharaoh stood in a green island dividing the highway, his granite shoulders like an etching on the sky. Drew turned as the taxi passed, bent down to see Ramses's face through the rear window. Impassive. No advice to give. Forever staring at the stream of cars flowing into the city. And drivers ... they hardly glanced at this giant out of their own past.

At the airport, Zafer led them through customs and passport control with nothing but smiles from the officials.

Taking a seat at the gate, Drew pulled out his King James Bible, which used red ink whenever Christ's exact words were printed. Kadir had opened an old science fiction novel he'd probably already read twice. Zafer looked restless.

Inspired by the conversation with the Ebionites, Drew had decided to re-read Paul's letters. About half way through Romans, it occurred to him that he hadn't seen any red ink. He skipped ahead to the end of the letter. No rubrics. He skimmed 1 Corinthians and found a single quote—instructions to eat bread and drink wine in ritual remembrance. In the whole body of letters, Jesus uttered only one more sentence.

An icy tingle shot up Drew's spine.

In his hands were translations of the oldest Christian documents, written within two decades after Christ had died, but all of Christ's parables, prophecies, sayings, and miracles were entirely absent. Nor did Paul ever mention Mary, Joseph, the Virgin Birth, Bethlehem, Galilee, Pontius Pilate, or Nazareth. Although Pilate was mentioned in Timothy, Timothy—as Drew had written in a footnote from his college days—was long known to be a forgery:

Word analysis shows more than 1/3 of words used in Timothy don't appear in genuine Pauline letters. Of those 306 words, 175 appear nowhere else in New Testament, but 211 are common in works of Christian writers of 2ND century.

Paul actually complains in 1 Corinthians that the Jews request a sign—a miracle. Instead of expounding on a few of Jesus' thirty-odd miracles, he criticizes their attitude as though he knew of no miracles. Nor did he consider the voice that spoke to him on the road to Damascus worth mentioning.

While Paul had never met Jesus, he was supposedly in direct communication with him. He also knew James and Peter and all or most or of the other apostles. Why hadn't he found even *one* of Christ's miracles worth mentioning? Even one of his proverbs or predictions worth quoting?

A hand on Drew's shoulder startled him.

Zafer stood up. "Time to board."

Drew hadn't even heard the boarding call.

"Don't look," Zafer whispered in Turkish. "Blondy. At the end of the line. I think he's Sicarii. If he knows we spotted him, he'll call for a replacement."

Drew sighed. Why the hell did Zafer *tell* him if he couldn't look?

After they'd taken their seats on the plane, Drew thought he caught a glimpse of the man Zafer had mentioned. American, British, Polish, German—he could have been any of two dozen nationalities. In his early forties maybe. He took a seat five or six rows ahead but didn't so much as glance at any of them.

A cheerful stewardess asked Drew to buckle his seatbelt. Smiling weakly, he complied and opened his Bible.

Drew re-examined Romans. He noticed that every chance Paul had to quote the historical Jesus, he quoted earlier scripture. In Romans 15:3 Paul wrote: *For even Christ did not please Himself, but as it is written, "The reproaches of those who reproached You fell on Me"*. Referenced by the Bible's editors, the quote was taken directly from Psalm 69.

Romans 5:8 said: *But God demonstrates His own love toward us, in that while we were still sinners, the Messiah died for us*—which sounded exactly like a New Testament gospel, but was taken almost word-for-word from Isaiah, one of Paul's favorite sources.

"That's it," Drew hissed. "That *has* to be it."

"Shhhhhhh." Zafer held a finger to his lips and smiled. "Blondy."

The captain advised the flight crew to prepare for takeoff.

Drew barely lifted his gaze from the Bible on his lap. He found it difficult to believe, but it seemed that Paul had constructed a general messiah and put various pre-existing sayings and prophecies into his mouth. It made sense, though, when Drew recalled how Matthew had famously used a mistranslation of a passage from Isaiah, asserting that *a young virgin shall conceive* when the actual words were *a young* woman *shall conceive*. The same passage also predicted this son would be named Immanuel. But Paul was writing before Matthew, and, since Paul had already established a following with *Christ Jesus*, Matthew apparently discarded Immanuel.

Drew couldn't help recalling Paul's accusation in Corinthians 11:3-4 that the apostles were preaching *another Jesus*. Another savior ... or a Jesus who offered different teachings? And if it was a different savior, could it have been John the Baptist? But John was dead by the time Paul was writing and deliverance from the Romans—expected of the Messiah—was nowhere in sight. And if John had been the Teacher of Righteousness, who had the Liar been? Herod Antipas had executed John for reasons that had nothing to do with the priesthood or the Qumran community. And the Liar, scroll scholars had observed, had arisen from *within* the Essene community at Qumran—ruling out King Herod.

The engines began to whine as the plane picked up speed, and as the whine flattened into a windy roar, the acceleration pressed Drew's head against the seat. The plane lifted off. Through the window he glimpsed Cairo, the city shrouded in a hot haze and surrounded by desert.

Somewhere down there was a monastery dedicated to Paul, whom the Ebionites believed was the Man of a Lie, the Scoffer, and an Essene. He had seduced people away from the Teacher by exempting them from the Law of Moses—circumcision, dietary restrictions, the rigors of ritual purity. His followers were referred to as Seekers-After-Smooth-Ways. The accusations fit Paul's ministry perfectly. In letter after letter Paul elevates faith above Jewish Law. In letter after letter he justifies casting the Law aside.

The Acts of the Apostles claimed Paul was on his way to the synagogues of Damascus when he had his vision of Christ on the road, which he never bothers to mention in his letters. But why would Paul go to Syria? It made no sense to send someone from Jerusalem to serve warrants from the high priest when the Sanhedrin—the Jewish high religious court—had no authority beyond the vicinity of Jerusalem.

The answer, perhaps, could be found in the Damascus Document, one of the Dead Sea Scrolls in which, for reasons scholars still didn't understand, Qumran was referred to as Damascus—another of Stephen's keywords. Was it possible that Paul had not been going to Syria but to the Essene community in Qumran? Qumran was only thirteen miles from Jerusalem. Why else would Stephen have mentioned Damascus?

The Qumran community believed it would be saved by faith in the Teacher of Righteousness—the Messiah. If the Essenes were tied to the early Christians and James had been the Teacher of Righteousness, then James might have been the other Savior Paul warned against in 2 Corinthians.

Drew flipped to 2 Corinthians.

For such are false apostles, deceitful workers, transforming themselves into apostles of Christ. And no wonder! For Satan himself transforms himself into an angel of light. Therefore it is no great thing if his ministers also transform themselves into ministers of righteousness, whose end will be according to their works.

The keyword was *righteousness*—another translation for *just* and a possible reference to James the Righteous—twice. Not only in the word *righteous*, but also it was James who steadfastly insisted that Jewish Law be upheld, James who insisted on good works.

If James had been regarded as the Savior, it explained why one of the last things Stephen had said was that Paul had to have been the Liar.

Why the Gospel writers had waited so long after the death of Christ to write down his story had always puzzled scholars. But if James had been a savior figure, then Mark would have had to have waited until after James's death to reinvent his life. James died in 62 AD, while Mark was written around 70 AD. Roman archives had been burned after the rebellion in 66 AD, clearing the way for the insertion of events that never happened, and with James dead, he could not argue with how his legacy was altered.

Backdating some forty to forty-five years, Mark could have claimed the Savior had died during the tenure of Pontius Pilate, and there would be no records to dispute his claim. Moreover, most of the generation that would have witnessed the crucifixion had already passed away.

James as the Savior also explained why there was no mention of anyone in the Dead Sea Scrolls who could be identified with Christ. But how had James gone from The Teacher of Righteousness to the *brother* of the Messiah? He had been virtually invisible during Christ's ministry—not even one of the twelve apostles—and then suddenly, after Christ's death, he emerged as one of the leaders of the Church in Jerusalem. It made no sense.

Nathan had said that a razor had never touched James's head. Was that where the image of the long-haired Christ had originated? From James, whose hair had never been cut? James was also said to be holy from the womb. Nazarite, as Drew now knew, was the word for someone who was holy from birth, who didn't anoint himself with oil or cut his hair, who abstained from wine and even vinegar. He scribbled a question at the top of a page of his Bible: *How far is it from James the Nazarite to Jesus the Nazarene?*

BOOK 6: 1 - 10

PLATO'S GOSPEL

The disciples said to Jesus, "We know that you must leave us. Who shall be our leader then?"

Jesus said to them, "Wherever you find yourselves, you shall go to James the Righteous, for whose sake Heaven and Earth came into being."

— Gospel of Thomas

6: 1

SAFE HOUSE

STANDING AT THE BAGGAGE CAROUSEL, its shifting sheets of steel like the oversized scales of a mechanized lizard, Drew glanced around as discreetly as he could for Blondy.

He didn't see him.

He leaned close to Zafer's ear. "Looks like you missed your guess."

"Maybe. Maybe he passed the ball." Zafer yanked Kadir's leather bag—as long-suffering as his vest—off the belt and led the way toward the exit.

The customs officials, who were arguing about a soccer match, didn't so much as ask where they were coming from.

Not exactly Midnight Express, Drew thought to himself.

Relatives, friends, and drivers holding up signs with names on them pressed up against the tubular fencing outside the exit. They reminded Drew of the times Yasemin had been waiting for him after a visit to the States.

Outside, Istanbul was not as hot as Cairo, but it was a lot more humid.

Ignoring the taxi drivers, Zafer walked toward the metro station under the airport.

"Where to?" Drew asked in Turkish.

"Safe house."

"You have a safe house?"

Zafer nodded.

"What do you need a safe house for?"

"Business. That's why I call it the Office."

As they were going down the escalator (Kadir hated stairs), Zafer whispered to Drew: "Don't turn around."

Drew felt the blood drain from his hands. "Blondy?"

"Should be at the top of the escalator right about now."

The train, which was modern and clean, was waiting. Zafer walked past the first two cars and got on the third.

"Stand in the back, don't sit. And don't look at the door. Relax. Talk to Kadir."

Kadir grinned up at Drew. *"İstanbul'da olmaktan memnum oldum."* *I'm glad to be in Istanbul.*

A chime announced that the doors were closing. Drew was dying to look at the door, but he kept his eyes on Kadir. "So am I." Even gazing down at the dwarf, however, he knew the blond man had beaten the hissing doors.

The train pulled forward with a jerk.

Drew's hands felt like he'd been making snowballs without gloves. As casually as he could, he glanced up. Zafer was near the doors looking bored. The blond man was just opposite him. He checked his watch as though he were late for a meeting.

Although the train was air-conditioned, sweat trickled down the small of Drew's back. Blades of sunlight sliced through the windows as they emerged from beneath the airport. The train made its second or third stop, and the car began to fill with passengers. Zafer and the blond man held their positions.

The doors swished open again at Zeytinburnu, and villagers from eastern Turkey pushed their way in before disembarking passengers could get off.

The chime rang.

Drew glanced up. Zafer worked his way closer to the blond man as the last passengers squeezed themselves in. The Turk moved so fast when the chime went off Drew almost missed him grabbing the blond man by the lapels of his jacket, ramming his forehead into his face, and shoving him off the train.

There were raised eyebrows from the men, a collective gasp from women layered in scarves and clothing in spite of the heat.

The doors closed.

"Bana burcu var!" Zafer shouted. *He owes me money.*

Some of the men smiled and nodded.

Zafer made his way to the back of the car.

"Christ, Zafer. He could have been a tourist."

"Oh yeah? Where's his luggage?" Zafer scanned the car as though there might be someone else he needed to toss.

"Okay, so he's on a regular commute ..."

Zafer shook his head. "He's meeting people here. By now the Sicarii have their own safe house in Istanbul."

The trio got off at the last stop in Aksaray and walked to a taxi stand.

"Don't put anything in the trunk," Zafer said. "Keep your bags on your laps."

He told the driver they were going to Zeytinburnu—the direction they'd just come from.

"What—?"

"When the car stops, get out."

They hadn't gone far when Zafer yelled at the driver to pull over.

"Let's go!" Zafer threw a five-lira note on the seat and jumped out. "Across the street!" He grabbed Kadir's bag.

A grassy island divided the four-lane road, but dodging the traffic—all of it speeding—was a tricky. Zafer, who made one car come to a screeching stop, waved them on.

On the other side, he stepped in front of a taxi and criss-crossed his arms.

The driver was shouting at Zafer as the three of them got in.

"Ajelemiz var!" Zafer shouted back. *We have an emergency!*

The driver forgot his anger and pulled away.

Zafer scanned the other side of the street. "Well," he said in English, "unless they've got a helicopter, I think we're ... how do put it?"

Zafer's English was so good, Drew sometimes forgot he wasn't a native speaker. "In the clear."

"That's it. In the clear."

The taxi took them over Galata Bridge and the Golden Horn, dropping them off at the base of the hill crowned by Taksim. A broad flight of concrete stairs had been built into a steep slope.

"Ya, I don't want to climb over steps," Kadir whined.

Zafer took his bag. "Come on."

With Kadir sweating and cursing, they went up the weathered steps. Near the top they switched to a narrower stairway that ended at a gate. Kadir bitched right up to the gate.

Three boys with dark faces and stained shirts hanging out of their pants were playing on a cement landing. They looked up inquisitively as the men passed.

Zafer led the way along winding streets until they emerged on Istiklal Caddesi—as usual, awash in foot traffic. Zafer let Kadir get out front, and the dwarf ducked into a passage beneath a building that opened onto a small courtyard. Couples sat at tables in the cobbled square drinking tea, Turkish coffee, sodas, but Drew didn't see Kadir anywhere; the little guy was easy to lose in a crowd.

Zafer took Drew into a small arcade of clothes shops. At the back of the last of these, Kadir was talking to a man behind the counter.

"How are you, Atanur?" Zafer asked.

Atanur smiled. "Passing through?"

Zafer nodded.

Atanur pulled aside a rack of clothes hiding a fire exit.

Following Zafer and Kadir, Drew found himself outside again.

They followed a series of narrow streets until Zafer stopped in an End-of-Empire neighborhood a lot like Drew's. White curtains billowed out of an open window, brushed against a stone sill, and retreated back inside. With some of these buildings, it was amazing that weather still broke against their worn edges, that the carved masonry, which was at its most impressive when given the excuse of a window or a door to frame, was still intact. The Turks who lived here were like squatters who inhabited a palatial past.

Zafer entered a tiny, gated alley between two buildings. This brought them out onto a short street with three hooded lamps hanging from cables strung between buildings. "Here we are."

"I've lived in Istanbul for *years*," Drew said, "and I have a pretty good idea of where we are, but I couldn't have tailed you. Even without that little stunt in the clothes shop."

"That's the point."

Wide by Istanbul's standards, the building looked like it was about to collapse. There were no *jumbas* although the windows were set off by blocks of elaborately worked stone. Once an optimistic yellow, the paint was now jaundiced and streaked with soot. Plaster had crumbled away in patches, and underneath the first floor windows—caged in wrought iron—teenagers had spray-painted their names. Another piece of European architecture eroding like an oversized tombstone, its cracks filling not with the green of moss or lichen but the black of pollution.

A huge double-door was crowned by half a rusty starburst. Zafer unlocked one wing and pushed against the steel.

The foyer was dank and full of debris—wood, unused tiles, the blade of a shovel, bottles filled with grime.

"No light in the hall, so be careful."

A zigzagging staircase took them to a steel door on the third floor. It was the one thing in the building that didn't look like it pre-dated the twentieth century.

"I'm the only one renting a flat here."

"You're the only one who would."

Stepping inside, Zafer punched a combination on a small keypad. "Welcome to the Office. This is home until this business is finished."

Drew bent down to untie his sneakers, but Zafer said, "No point in taking off your shoes. I don't."

Not a window open, the air was stifling and dusty. Drew dropped his bag by the door and wandered around the rooms. It was one of the biggest flats he'd ever seen in Istanbul. The ceiling was unfinished, exposing the joists and the boards of the floor above. In a living room almost as spacious as Drew's entire apartment were two worktables, each with its own goose-necked architect's lamp—each with enormous magnifying glasses built into them. The worktables were cluttered with pencils, pens, papers, tubes and bottles of glue. Most of the shelves were metal. There were also filing cabinets, a photocopy machine, a fax machine, and a computer.

Zafer opened a window and a breeze swept through the apartment.

Although the finish on the parquet was dull with wear, the floor didn't have a creak or a loose slat in it. There were no rugs to warm the place up or to get in the way of the push broom Drew imagined Zafer used to sweep up paper scraps. Three things kept the walls from being entirely bare: a cork board with various papers tacked to it, a map of Turkey, and a huge street map of Istanbul.

The only homey touches were a couch, a wooden stand for the TV, and an odd-looking coffee table that had a rough slate top and sides like a chest, rather than legs like a table.

"I got document training in Special Forces because sometimes that's what we were after, documents." Zafer swept a hand in an arc to take in his worktables. "I went a little above and beyond the call of duty and learned forgery techniques as well."

"This is how you make money?"

Zafer nodded. "I put official signatures and stamps on paperwork for people who don't want to waste hours in line. I do passports, driver's licenses, IDs. A good passport—Canadian say—to the right buyer … you're talking 30,000 or 35,000 US."

"Damn. I hope you're not selling to terrorists."

"I charge them extra." He smiled. "It's usually a miserable Turk who just wants out. Americans really don't know how lucky they are. Most of you woke up on third base and you think you hit a triple." He disappeared into another room.

Drew thought for a second. "That's about right."

Zafer came back into the living room and threw something at Drew.

He caught it with both hands because, judging from the way Zafer had tossed it, it was heavy. He was holding an automatic pistol.

6: 2

CHOOSE YOUR WEAPON

THE THREE OF THEM STARED down at a small cache of weapons—Zafer, with his hands on his hips and a paternal glint in his eye, Kadir, as though he were wondering how much money he could get for the collection, and Drew, in sheer amazement.

"Glock 9 millimeter, M9 Beretta." Zafer pointed at a pair of pistols. "AK-47s. Half a dozen grenades. A few smoke grenades."

Zafer kept the weapons hidden in the odd-looking coffee table. He and Kadir had lifted off the slate top and let it sink into the couch cushions.

"Are you planning to invade a country?"

"You think I joined the military because I'm an Ebionite?"

"How about a little paranoid?"

"I'm not paranoid." Zafer grinned. "I'm prepared." He lifted his chin at the pistol in Drew's hand. "You know what to do with that?"

With his thumb, Drew depressed a button near the trigger-guard and, as the clip slid out, caught it with his free hand. It was empty. He pulled back the slide to make sure the chamber was empty, too. The slide made a satisfying sound as it rammed home—the sound of metal parts machined to fit together perfectly. Holding the hammer back with his thumb, he pressed the trigger and eased the hammer into place. Then he handed the pistol and the magazine to Zafer, who nodded appreciatively.

"So you at least know weapons etiquette."

"My dad has a .45, a shotgun, and an old, bolt-action 30.06. My mother said if he was going to have guns in the house, he had to teach us how to use them. Once a week, every week, for a whole year, he made me, my sister, and my brother handle them."

"He have any military background?"

Drew shook his head. "Lyndhurst isn't particularly rough. He just wanted a little insurance. But if you don't mind ..." Drew waved a hand. "I'd rather not deal with one of those."

Zafer shrugged. "As long as you know how to use one. In case you change your mind."

"What about Jesse?" Drew asked.

"You trust her?"

"I, uh, kind of had a crush on her back in college."

"I'm pretty sure you still do. Before you answer, think with the *right* head: do you trust her?"

"Yeah I do. She's a scholar of comparative religion, so the political ramifications of an ancient manuscript don't matter to her."

"So, if we need to, we can use her the way we used the professor?"

"Exactly."

"All right. Just be careful. I don't care how much you trust her, if she starts asking you questions in bed, she's *using* you. Do you understand that? It means she wants information, not kids and a life happily ever after. The other thing is, you're making her a target by involving her. And we can't bring her here—"

"Why not?"

"Bad enough *you're* here. Besides me, you and Kadir are the only two people who have ever set foot in this place. *Ever.* If the Sicarii somehow get hold of her, she'd lead them right to us. How long's she going to be in Cairo?"

"She'll be in Aleppo tonight. Maybe she can give us a better idea of what the Habakkuk Scroll is worth." He was actually hoping Jesse could come up with *some*thing in the scroll that would keep it off the black market. "It's already a Dead Sea Scroll, but if it has important information scholars have never seen before, the Israelis will pay more for it. Maybe we can start negotiations with them before we talk to Serafis."

Zafer looked at Kadir.

"It doesn't important who we sell the scroll to. Price is the important."

Jesse, Drew realized, was the only ally he had. Nathan was a possibility, but he might be Sicarii. There was another problem: Zafer had Nathan's card. Drew had no way to contact him. But then, even Zafer had to sleep some time.

6: 3

ENCRYPTIONS

SITTING AT THE COMPUTER on Zafer's desk, Drew sorted through his e-mail. There were three messages worth opening: one from his friend in New York, one from Yasemin, one from Jesse. Business first.

"Okay, here's an update for you," he called to Zafer. "My computer geek in New York says the Ebionite website has been up since two thousand. The last time the home page was altered was about two years ago."

Zafer was standing beside the steel door. "All right, but we still keep Nathan at arm's length."

"Where're you going?"

"To check up on those business cards we got from Nabil, see if the Ecole's number is valid. It's not hard to print up a business card." He smiled. "Take it from a forger."

Kadir was on the couch, feet dangling above the floor, reading *The Stars, My Destination* for the fifth time. His vest was draped over an arm of the couch like the hide of an animal that had recently been skinned.

Zafer hovered in the doorway. "Don't leave the flat. Don't answer the phone. Ever. I'll be back in a little while."

Zafer closed the heavy door behind him, and Drew heard the deadbolt click into place. Now they *couldn't* leave the flat. Unless Kadir knew where to find a second set of keys or they jumped out a window.

Drew opened Jesse's message.

I still can't quite believe that, after all these years, we wound up at the same hotel in Cairo, not to mention this business about a Dead Sea Scroll! I'm unbelievably excited. A find like this is something scholars barely have the courage to dream about, let alone hope for. I'm a little scared, but this is my field, and, no offense, Drew, but you're not qualified. You're smart as hell, but you don't have the training. You NEED someone like me. This is the kind of thing on which lasting reputations are founded—why not mine?

No one could say she lacked ambition.

Glad to see, by the way, that you haven't cut your hair. You might not believe this, but I used to envy you back in college. If I try to grow mine out, it just frazzles at the ends. Are you part Native American or something?

Now she was flirting. Zafer had warned him.

I really enjoyed our breakfast at the hotel, and although we weren't all that close in college, from time to time (even when I was married), I used to wonder what you were up to. I went on to get my PhD, but it seems you've managed to get hold of a far more valuable document. The Lord really does work in mysterious ways. Please let me know what our next move is. I'm DYING just to see the photographs you've got.
Jesse.

Our next move. As sure of herself as ever. Drew began typing.

My colleagues here are giving me a hard time, but they've agreed to let you look at the photos of the scroll before putting it on the black market. We have to keep them from doing that. I'm not sure how, but I'm working on it. It was great to see you, too. In fact, since you came clean about your long-hair envy, I may as well admit I had a major crush on you back in university. The last time we talked—December rain, the mall—remember? I was seriously disappointed to find out you had a boyfriend. He isn't by any chance the guy you wound up marrying, is he?
All for now – Drew
PS – not Native American, Gypsy

Drew wasn't flirting. He hadn't enjoyed sitting across from someone so much since he'd met Yasemin. Just seeing her in the hotel sabotaged his equilibrium, as though he'd stepped off a carnival ride. But his infatuation for Jesse was incipient; it was nothing like what he'd felt for Yasemin—for years. Even as he clicked on his ex-wife's message, his hands were a little shaky.

Drewjuh'um,

All it took was adding the Turkish *juh'um*—roughly the equivalent of the English *my dear*—to make his stomach feel as papery as a wasp's nest.

When are you going to be back in Istanbul? I read your last letter three times! There is so much of *us* in there, so much history together, and though a lot of it is painful, so much of it is beautiful. I really need to talk to you. In person.

Call me as soon as you get back. The waiting is killing me.

Yasemin.

No "love" this time. She'd cooled off. Drew sighed and glanced at the clock on the computer. She was still at work.

"Hey, Kadir …"

"Yes, infidel, what is it?" He lowered his science fiction novel.

"You think Zafer will let me out of here tonight? Yasemin wants to see me."

"It is possible. Ask to him."

Sensible enough.

Sitting down to re-read his notes, Drew noticed something odd. The Essenes and the Pharisees were both virulently opposed to Maccabean rule. The Maccabees had taken power after they overthrew the Hellenized Syrians in 164 BC. Under Judas Maccabee, the Temple was cleansed of Greek elements and rededicated—an event now celebrated during Hannukah. While the Jewish people overwhelmingly supported a Maccabean king, the Essenes and the Pharisees were furious that the Maccabees had appropriated the office of high priest for themselves—an office that rightfully belonged to a Zadokite. Having a dynasty that was not of the line of David, it seemed, was acceptable to Jews. Having a high priest who was not a Zadokite was not.

The settlement at Qumran was an attempt to establish a priestly community of unblemished ritual purity. Their main concern was restoring a Zadokite high priest. The archaeological record showed that the Qumran community was active under the Maccabeans, but, with the coming of Herod the Great, who ended the Maccabean dynasty in 40 BC, the Essenes abandoned Qumran.

Why? The simplest explanation was also the most convincing. Herod, affecting respect for the religious purity of the Essenes but in reality more concerned with effacing all traces of the Maccabees, removed the last Maccabean high priest. Jonathan Maccabee, a boy of eighteen who would have been the next high priest, was drowned while frolicking in a swimming pool at the palace. Herod then replaced the Maccabean high priests with Zadokites. The restoration of the Zadokites to the Temple explained the Essene desertion of Qumran: their goal had been accomplished.

After the death of Herod, however, Romans once again imposed direct rule on Palestine. In 6 AD they allowed the Zadokites to be ousted and installed a new high priest. Qumran, as much a military outpost as a religious community, was rebuilt.

The year 6 AD stopped Drew from reading any further.

According to the Gospel of Luke, Jesus was born during the census of Quirinius taken in 6 AD. Was it coincidence that Jesus' reputed birth in Luke overlapped with the downfall of the Zadokites? With the re-establishment of Qumran and the renewed ferocity of Judas of Galilee's rebellion?

Drew scissored fingers into his back pocket for the folded-up sheet of paper listing the professor's keywords. He scanned the names, halting his descent—as if down a ladder for eyes only—when he came to *Judas of Galilee*. He pulled his knapsack onto his lap and groped around inside until he felt the kind of hardcover heft that could only belong to his copy of Josephus. The index was written in type so small he would've picked up a magnifying glass if one had been handy. Judas of Galilee had touched off his revolt against the Romans in 4 BC, rushing—armed—into the opening left by Herod's death. Give or take a year, that was about the time Matthew placed Jesus' birth.

A pattern, like a single recognizable word in an otherwise undeciphered text, resolved itself: Matthew had used Judas's first revolt to mark Jesus' birth, drawing the obvious parallel between Judas of Galilee and Jesus of Galilee. Luke, on the other hand, had used the Essenes' return to Qumran and the ousting of the Zadokites from the office of high priest. Matthew emphasized the *political* messiah embodied by Judas of Galilee, who'd crossed swords with the Romans. It is Matthew's Jesus who says, "I came not to bring peace but a sword." Luke, however, emphasized the *priestly* savior. Traditionally, the first would be descended of David, while the other was an heir of Aaron and Zadok. Conveniently enough, Jesus was descended of David on his father's side—assuming his father wasn't the Holy Spirit—and of Aaron and therefore of Zadok on his mother's. That made Jesus both messiahs in a single person.

James the Just, possibly the Teacher of Righteousness, and John the Baptist, also a savior figure, were brother and—at least in Luke—cousin to Christ. John in many ways was actually more like a brother than James. Both Matthew and Luke make much of the fact that Elizabeth's and Mary's pregnancies overlapped, with John being born six months earlier than Jesus. Which raised another question: if John and Jesus were the same age, how was it that John had built up a huge following by the time of Christ's baptism in the Jordan, but there wasn't a single word about Christ's ministry until then? What was Jesus doing all that time? The gospel account made sense only if John was passing the torch—not as *the* Messiah but as *a* messiah.

Judas of Galilee was far more central to the Gospels than Drew had realized. His story seemed to end with his sons, Simon and James, who were crucified by the Roman procurator Tiberius Julius Alexander although they led no popular uprisings—a pre-emptive strike apparently—but Josephus was strangely silent on the fate of Judas himself.

"Crucifixion most likely," Drew said to himself. But why omit the account of it?

There was a Simon on the list, as Drew recalled, who had squared off with Rome in 66 AD. He glanced at the list. *Simon bar Giora.* Drew found Simon's quixotic drama in Book 4 of Josephus's *Jewish War.* Although he was of peasant stock, Simon's skill with a sword and natural gift for leadership eventually brought an army of 40,000 under his command. According to Josephus, Simon entered Jerusalem in the third year of the revolt *as a savior and a preserver.* He reigned as king, had coins struck with the motto *Redemption of Zion,* and was thought by many to be the Messiah.

The Romans, however, overran the city in 70 AD and destroyed the Temple. Simon and a handful of stonecutters took refuge in a cavern under Jerusalem, hoping to escape by burrowing under the city walls. But the digging was so impeded by rock, their provisions ran out.

Simon hit on a new strategy. He put on a white robe and a purple cloak and appeared out of rocky ground where the Temple had been as though he'd risen from a tomb. The Romans were astonished—they *stood still where they were* as Josephus put it. It didn't take them long, however, to figure out Simon wasn't an apparition. Refusing to identify himself, he insisted they call their captain. The men *ran* to their captain, Rufus Terentius, who arrested Simon.

"Hm." Drew rested his chin on his fist. When Jesus was crucified, a purple mantle was thrown over him to mock his supposed claims to royalty ... but the resurrected Jesus wore a white robe. And the astonishment of the Romans seemed to mirror the astonishment of the women who find Jesus' tomb empty—a tomb, as Drew recalled, *newly* carved out of rock. The women in Mark run to tell the disciples the same way the soldiers run to tell their captain. Had Mark pilfered these details? Or was he alluding to something?

Simon was put in chains and loaded onto a ship bound for Rome, where he became part of a triumphal parade. He was haltered like a horse, flogged, and beheaded.

Drew wrote three names on the back of Stephen's list: *Judas, James, Simon.*

Oddly enough, these were three of Jesus' four brothers: *And are not his brothers James and Joses, and Simon and Judas?* Were the names veiled references to James the Just, Judas of Galilee, and Simon bar Giora? Then what about Joses?

Drew flipped back to the passage about Judas of Galilee. He had broken into the armory in Sepphoris—not five miles from the site on which Nazareth would later be founded. Drew shook his head. "This can't be coincidence."

"*Ne?*" *What?* Kadir had closed *The Stars, My Destination.*

"The Gospels. In one sense they're fiction, but in another ... there are things that go beyond metaphor and symbol. There are references to historical events and people that we don't usually connect with Christ. Clever allusions that maybe a certain elite within the early Christian Church would understand but that would mean nothing to the uneducated."

Kadir shrugged and went back to his book.

Drew typed out *hidden, Mark, allegories* on the computer keyboard. Seconds later he had the quote he was looking for:

And Jesus said to them, "*Things are hidden only to be revealed, and made secret only to be brought to light. If any have ears to hear, let them hear.*" *And he kept speaking to them in allegories, according as they could hear, and he said nothing to them without allegories, but privately to his own students he always gave the key.*

Had the Gospel authors written in allegories so that the illiterate took away only the surface meaning while learned Christians understood the deeper meanings encoded in the Gospels?

The overwhelming need he had felt to pray during the conversation with Nathan and Father Hawass had been replaced by anger. Was Stephen right? Had the Gospel writers *invented* a messiah—a messiah for whom wars had been fought? In whose name thousands of men and women had died after tortures that equaled anything their role model had supposedly endured on the cross?

The lock to the front door clicked over and Zafer came in.

Drew stood up. "I'm going to need some books from my apartment. *The Collected Works of Philo, Ancient Christian Gospels*, Eusebius's *History of the Church*—"

"Yeah, sure." Zafer smiled indulgently. "Write them down and give me the key. I'll get them for you tomorrow."

So far Drew had been letting Stephen's keywords come to him. Not anymore. He was going to track down each one, starting with *James the Just. Time to find out what the fuck went on two thousand years ago.*

6: 4

RECOGNITIONS

"DREW. OVER HERE ..." Zafer beckoned with a hand. He was sitting on the couch next to Kadir.

The photographs of the three Sicarii were laid out on the coffee table. Drew sank into a cushion next to the ex-commando.

"I spoke with my *kankardesh* at MIT. He didn't have as much for me as I'd like, but then MIT has no reason to have files on these guys.

"Looks like Nathan isn't connected with the Ecole Biblique—not on the surface anyway. These other three are, probably only as a front." Zafer tapped one of the pictures with a finger. "Memorize these faces."

Drew looked at their names again: Raymond Duvall, Jean Saint-Savoy, Francis Collins. "It won't be hard to remember *him*." Drew pointed at the picture of Duvall. Stubbly blond hair, eyes a ghostly blue, face raw-boned.

"Which is why he probably never does sidewalk surveillance himself. For that you have to have a face people forget as soon as they see it. He's probably the most dangerous, too—a Maltese Knight, a Sicarii, a couple of medals with the French Foreign Legion in Operation Daguet during first Gulf War. Should have gone higher than captain, but he doesn't like taking orders. He was thrown out of the Legion for challenging a superior officer. Pulled out a knife and said, 'God will decide between us.'"

"Damn." Not someone Drew wanted to meet.

Zafer handed him color copies of three of the photos. "Keep them with you."

Drew stared again at Raymond's pale eyes.

"Kadir says you have a date with your ex-wife tonight."

Drew glanced at the dwarf. "Maybe. I haven't spoken to her."

"Well, figure it out."

"Give me a minute." Drew pulled out his cell phone and texted her the time and place he wanted to meet. A message came back in seconds: *Seni bekliyorum. I'm waiting for you.* Zafer's dusty warehouse of an apartment became palatial, the steel furniture seemed plunder from a sultan's chamber, and even the grit on the floor might as well have been tracked in from an imperial garden.

"I'm meeting her on the Asian side."

"Good. It's better if you stay out of Taksim."

Something in Drew's chest unknotted.

Kadir smiled. "Good luck."

"One thing," Zafer added. "I spoke with Serafis. We have a flight to Adana tomorrow."

"Antakya doesn't have an airport?"

"No. We leave at three."

"Not a problem," Drew said.

"When you want to come back, call me. I'll meet you in Karaköy. Just to make sure you didn't grow a tail while you were straightening things out with your ex."

"Will do." Drew stood up.

"You know what? I'll walk you down. Safer that way."

Kadir was still grinning. "Tonight I will see you."

"I hope not."

6: 5

THE OLDEST MYTH

ZAFER SCRUPULOUSLY AVOIDED ISTIKLAL. It was always crowded, but if the Sicarii were watching, they'd definitely have eyes there.

A leather jacket Zafer had loaned Drew was draped over an arm. The air was warm, but with the Sun down, it wouldn't take long to cool off.

They took narrow streets that skirted the westerly slope of the hill, angling east. Through a break in the static procession of buildings, Drew glimpsed the Golden Horn, a smooth absence of architecture surrounded by sprawling city. The water was slate-colored in the bluish dusk, tinted orange where it caught the last of the sky's light.

"Wanna take the funicular down?" Drew asked

"Nah. I could use the walk."

The walk, down a cobblestoned street, became steeper.

"So what does she do, Yasemin?"

"She's an editor at a publishing house. Blue Amber Books."

Zafer nodded. "Mavi Ambar? Good one."

The street was hardly more than an alley canyoned by a mix of narrow, Ottoman-style tenements and their European counterparts.

"She was a literature major. Bohazichi University." Mentioning Bohazichi in Turkey had about the same effect as name-dropping Harvard in the States.

"Impressive."

Yes, she was. "You know how she got her first promotion?"

"Can't wait to find out."

"She was an editorial assistant—answering phones, opening mail, doing bullshit work basically, and reading manuscripts at home."

"A step up from the guy who sweeps out the office at night?"

"Exactly. The two editors who run the house, both men, pride themselves on their taste in books, but they don't like to roll up their sleeves and *edit*. One day they're arguing over a novel they just bought. Neither wants to work on it. One's shouting, it's *your* turn! The other is yelling back, *you* do it! And the rest of the office can hear them they're so loud. So imagine … here's Yasemin, smart, confident, assertive, but still a grunt. She walks up and knocks on the office door. One of them answers, all pissed off, and asks her what the hell she wants. 'Give the manuscript to me,' she says. The guy is shocked. First of all she's just an editorial assistant. Second—you know how it is in Turkey—she's a woman. Third, she's barely out of college. Fourth, she just admitted she was eavesdropping. Her boss thinks he's misheard her and asks again what she wants. 'Give me the manuscript,' she says, 'I'll edit it.' This guy looks at the other editor like *what the fuck*? Yasemin says, 'If you don't like what I do with it, give it to someone else. And you can give my job to someone else too if you want.' The second editor nods, waves a hand, and she gets the book. She turns it in a week later. A few days after that, boom, they move her up to assistant editor. Now she's a senior editor, and the company can't live without her."

"Looks like neither can you."

"Yeah, maybe." Some of the same things that made Yasemin so good at the office in a male-dominated society—and some of the very things he admired her for—also made her a bitter adversary when they fought. She took shit from no one. She was headstrong, sure of herself, and could make him think he was wrong even when he wasn't. He'd never learned how to back off, let things cool down, try a different tack. And it had cost them their marriage.

The two men came to the bottom of the hill not far from Galata Bridge. Somewhere within a tangle of roads on the far side of the bridge, Tariq had been hit by a truck.

"All right, you can take it from here. I'm going to find a place to plant myself and watch, make sure nobody's tagging along." Zafer whacked Drew on a shoulder. "*Iyi shanslar.*" Good luck.

"Thanks."

Drew hopped a low, iron-bar fence and crossed a four-lane street divided by an island of paving stones. It was a lot shorter and easier—and more dangerous—than crossing legally. Galata Bridge was a couple hundred yards to his right. The ferry station in Karaköy lay at an oblique angle to his left. Across the Golden Horn, just beyond the bridge brooded the New Mosque. Behind it, half a dozen other mosques, like steps ascending the urbanized hill in which they were embedded, gazed out at the water.

Drew glanced over a shoulder. No one else had jumped the fence.

He cut through a small maze of alleys that brought him out to the waterfront.

The quay edging Karaköy was always crowded with fishmongers, sailors, commuters, tourists. Brothels had attached themselves like barnacles to a slope above the quay. The skin trade in Istanbul was tolerated but strictly segregated. A house of ill-repute could hire either foreign or Turkish women, not both. Foreign men were forbidden to so much as approach the Turkish lovelies leaning out of windows and smiling impishly, but Turkish men had their pick. Police stood sentry, checking IDs and passports to make sure there was no crosspollination.

Drew dropped a token in a slot and pushed through a turnstile. He was gently bumped along by a crowd moving like an oversized caterpillar up the gangway. The ferry, probably a holdover from the 60s or 70s, held a few hundred people. He took the stairs to the upper deck.

How many times had he made this crossing? How many times to see Yasemin? The Asian side of Istanbul, where they had always lived, recalled North Jersey. It was mostly residential, and the sights that drew tourists were almost all on the European side, which had its counterpart in New York.

The breeze off the Bosporous lifted Drew's hair and whipped it behind him. He slipped into the leather jacket. Zafer was shorter by a few inches, but also broader. It balanced out to a reasonable fit.

Drew gazed out over the railing, the shifting screen of the water slingshotting him back to first time he'd gone to the cinema with Yasemin. Looking over at her almost as much as up at the screen, he'd watched the silvery blue light fade and intensify on her face, watched her react to what was going in the film. She caught him staring and a smile appeared in the dark. Leaning in, she whispered, "What are you doing?" He shook his head. He didn't know how to explain he was more interested in watching her than the movie. In that light her face had the marblesque allure of Classical statuary, and he knew if he wasn't in love, it wouldn't be long.

How many moments had been so full that one more drop of anything and he'd have to deal with the overflow? Moments when every sentence spoken was a line of poetry, every movement graceful. When they were suspended by something almost tangible that had formed between them.

It got so bad that when he was away from her for more than a few days just seeing her again felt like an event, the kind that attracted people with cameras and binoculars, faces gazing up or off, expecting something to define itself, to show through a universe they'd grown bored with, to be struck by the wonder men and women in ancient times thought might have something to do with magic.

This was exactly the problem. They were living the oldest myth—not the oldest in the book because it predated books. What was more human than wanting back what they'd once had?

6: 6

NOTES

Too many things in the apartment still reminded her of Drew. He'd been lucky. He didn't have to go on living in the home they'd shared even before they'd gotten married. Well, maybe not that lucky. One day when he was packing up, he sat down, cried into his hands, and mumbled an apology on the way out. He'd left the box he'd been filling in the middle of the floor, flaps open.

She had taken down all their photos except one in the living room, a wedding picture she liked because her parents and two brothers were also in it. She had draped a bolt of silk over Drew and his smile so that she wouldn't have to answer his stare, celluloid or not.

When they lived together, Drew used to leave little notes all over the place—under a vase, between the pages of a book, mixed in with the post-its on her desk. At first she found the habit terribly sweet, but after he moved out, she came across a few more, and they never failed to upset her. Two days ago she'd taken one from the pocket of a coat she never wore anymore. *Miss you so much*. He must have left it when he was boxing up his things.

The morning after he had finally finished moving out, the empty spaces on her bookshelves and in the bedroom, even in the bathroom, made her feel as though she had been trying out a coffin and someone had closed the lid—suffocating and terrifying at the same time.

She padded into the living room in her stockings, pushing an earring into its back by feel. The walls were lined with bookshelves, but there were no longer gaps. Her heart had scarred over. She hadn't replaced Drew yet, but she could imagine a future without him. Did she really want to put everything in reverse now?

She sat down in front of the coffee table and picked up a letter from atop an uneven stack. He had sent emails too, but he took more time with the letters and decorated the envelopes with Xeroxed photos (usually of them) and images cut or torn from magazines. He'd written the one in her hand when he was on vacation in America.

Yazz, everything makes me miss you more … drinking, going out, seeing other couples, even visiting familiar places—because I want to share them with you. I'm starting to think now that W.I.F.E. is an acronym for W.oman of my I I.F.E. Okay, not really an acronym, but you get the idea.

In a bar right now doing a little beer sampling, but it doesn't help much. Writing this out (on a couple of napkins) helps a little.

Did I ever tell you I love being yours? I wish I had your hand in the dull red light of this bar (as if the star the planet circles were in its last, dying years). I'm going to fall, I'm going to make mistakes, I'm going to do fool things, but don't let go. We're married now. Quoth the raven: forevermore. I want to fall asleep next you, wake up next to you, eat with you, read next to you, raise children with you, dream with you.

What I wouldn't give to have you here for one night before I come home. One night of soul-diving for pearls shining on the murky bottom. We won't come up for air until morning!

Love always, Drew.

Ironically, he was the one who had let go. And yet she was going out tonight to meet him, this man who was a strange collection of conflicting impulses. He loved her desperately but had left her. He was smart but lazy. He was talented, but he had no ambition. He could be unbearably charming but still lose his temper like a stubborn child.

Maybe it was better to call it off, just send him a text and tell him she wasn't coming.

Returning the letter to the stack, she picked up her phone and stared at the little screen.

She missed the way he made her feel when nothing had mattered to them but each other. She missed being married. She missed having her husband home. Sometimes, when she rolled over and saw Mehmet, she was shocked he wasn't Drew. A pair of Mehmet's shoes faced the wall in the foyer. Some of his clothes were in a drawer in her bedroom, and he'd insisted on framing a photo one of his friends had taken of them. It was on her nightstand, but she hardly noticed it anymore. It had become a fixture, like the lamp.

Yasemin lowered her phone and stood up. She went to the kitchen and took her purse off a chair. She'd placed a pink pill, a tiny oblong, next to a glass of water. To remind her. She drank the water and shouldered her purse but left the pill where it was.

6: 7

SAMARKAND

DREW HAD NEVER SEEN A BAR like Samarkand. In Turkey or anywhere else. Four floors of Ottoman Gothic: brick alcoves with Moorish arches; unglazed interior windows that turned the smoke-blurred faces they framed into animated portraits; intricate latticework, polished wood paneling, and trim carved to satisfy the Oriental fetish for the elaborate. The loft-like sections of the upper floors were joined by plank walkways with wrought-iron railings. Hanging lamps of tarnished brass extruded light through star- or crescent-shaped perforations, casting geometric patterns on the ceiling. Riveted sconces smoldered against the walls.

Drew descended the steps, dropping below street level. He could never tell whether the plastered-over stone had been stained by shadows or the dampness sweating through them. Overhead, the stairs and gangplanks traced out an M.C. Escher sketch.

He took a table near an other-century fireplace of aquamarine porcelain, its fire-blackened interior cold. Samarkand had been Yasemin and his favorite place for a wine, a beer, a smoke.

She was late, but that was normal.

He sat with a half-liter mug, his hands colder than the beer. He was wearing jeans, docksiders, and a blousy, white shirt. With his long hair and earring, the shirt made him look vaguely 18th century.

The music in Samarkand was anything from seventies rock to

unclassifiable bands like Dead Can Dance. Right now it was an '80s song by Sisters of Mercy.

Yasemin came down the steps in a black skirt, black stockings, and a shirt that, like the one she'd worn the last time he saw her, fit her a little too snugly. His heart felt like it was beating inside a fist.

He raised a hand to let her know where he was. Her boots made soft echoes on the ceramic tiles.

He was afraid to risk anything more than a routine kiss on both cheeks, but she pulled him close and hugged him.

"Why do you always smell so good?"

"Frequent showers."

"It doesn't matter what you do. You always smell good. I miss that about you."

A good omen?

She slipped out of her jacket and draped it over the back of her chair. "You're not going to break anything today, right"

This was typical Yasemin: follow up a compliment with a criticism.

"If anything's going to break, it'll be in here." He thumbed at his chest.

"Oh stop." She smiled that soul-expanding smile of hers; she was in a good mood.

The waiter had followed her—what guy wouldn't have?—and she ordered a Merlot.

"So ... what's the plan? Make laughing stocks of ourselves and get married again?"

The rush of blood to Drew's head made it hard to answer. "If we get back together, I'll be the one laughing. And the rest of Istanbul ... I don't care what they do."

"That's the man I married." She said leaned across the table and kissed him.

His heart locked up for a second. At least a whole second.

"Of course it's not going to be that easy. You have some changes to make before I let you back into my life."

He nodded. "I know. I ... listen. We both have our insecurities and weak spots. But we can't ... we have to make some allowances. I mean, remember the infamous bed incident?"

She grabbed his hands with both of hers and squeezed so hard he got a little worried. "You were right in your e-mail! *That's* why I was so upset! I just needed reassurance." She pulled him across the table and kissed him again.

He felt like he was underwater. The music was submerged and distant, his head full of rising bubbles.

As she sat back down, she wiped away a tear with one hand. The other held tightly onto his. "Why did it take you so long to figure this out? Why did you put me through a divorce?"

He was above water again, everything sharp and in focus.

"Hey, hold on. It wasn't all me. I'm not the only one who needs to break a couple of destructive habits."

She dragged on her cigarette.

He knew she didn't have the flawless looks of a model, but in that brief flare of orange, he couldn't imagine a more beautiful woman.

"Look," he said, "I've apologized for the things I did wrong—for all the times I lost my temper, for the times I was lazy or inconsiderate, and I'm apologizing now for not being more understanding, for not trying to see things from your point of view. For my failures as a husband. But don't you think you owe me a couple?"

The edge of her jaw hardened. "For what?"

Drew shook his head. "If I have to ask, this isn't going to work."

"For sleeping on the couch when I was mad at you?"

"For starters. I mean, distance can't be your solution to our problems. Putting your back to me in bed—when you actually slept in our bed—was like putting a sheet-metal fence between us. I never got any sleep those nights. It was like lying on a plank I was afraid to fall off. And let's not forget walking out of the room in the middle of a conversation, then not talking to me for days."

She tapped ash from the end of her cigarette into a black tray.

"*Ordering* me to do things, instead of *asking* me, as though I were your kid, not your husband. Making decisions on your own—do you remember the time you came home and announced we were going to apply for adoption papers? Didn't it occur to you that adopting a child is something you should talk over with your husband?"

"All *right*, Drew, all right. I don't really want to deal with this tonight, okay? I'm childless, divorced, and I'm very vulnerable right now."

Tears glazed her eyes; the candle gave them orange tints.

He took one of her hands in both of his. "All I need right now is for you to say you'll *try*. Just tell me I'm not completely crazy and there are things we *both* need to work on. Can you do that?"

She nodded and put her other hand in his. "I'm not making any promises—"

"Just tell me you'll *try*. We'll talk. You'll listen to me, I'll listen to you."

The corners of her eyes crimped, and then her whole face crinkled as she began to cry in earnest. "I never wanted to be divorced."

"Neither did I." He squeezed her hands. "I wanted to be married once in this life, just *once*. To you. We can start over, Yazz. You still love me, right?"

Her face smoothed out and she nodded. "That's why I hate you so much."

He laughed. "That's love all right."

The door to the bar opened and Drew glanced up. Maybe it was all the looking over his shoulder he'd done in the past week—why else would he let anything—*any*thing—distract him now? But he was glad he did.

"Uh ... Yazz. I think your boyfriend just walked in."

6: 8

HOME AGAIN

ABOUT YASEMIN'S HEIGHT, curly hair, and a face that probably appealed to girls, he reminded Drew of any number of kids he'd taught over the years, but his eyes had the unmistakable glare of someone who had gone through his options and discarded all of them except one: violence.

Drew let go of Yasemin's hands as though he were a student caught cheating on a test. Straightening up, he pulled back across the table. His temper was Yasemin's biggest complaint, and now was the time to prove he was serious about controlling it.

"Mehmet!" Yasemin stood up. "What are you doing here?"

"Why are you holding his hand?"

Drew didn't like how close he brought his face to hers. His hands latched onto the edge of the table.

Yasemin poked Mehmet in the chest with a finger hard enough to make him take a step back.

Drew almost laughed; he knew that poke well.

"What I do is none of your business. Do I follow you when you go out with your friends?"

Instead of answering, Mehmet stepped around her, grabbed her glass, and threw the wine on Drew.

Drew caught most of it on his chest.

"*Erkeksen gel!*" Mehmet shouted. *If you're a man, come on!*

No Turk would have tolerated the taunt—let alone the wine; better to die with honor than live with shame. Clamping his mouth shut and breathing through flared nostrils, Drew stood up slowly. The veins in his forearms swelled with trapped blood. Mehmet was all of 150 pounds and almost half a foot shorter. Drew could bounce him off the water-stained walls if he wanted to—and he wanted to. Desperately.

"I'm going to the bathroom." Drew looked at Yasemin. "I don't want to see him when I get back."

To go to the men's room he had to go right past Mehmet. Drew watched him out of the corner of an eye as though the boy were too insignificant to worry about. Mehmet felt the insult and reached for Drew's shoulder. It was all Drew could do not to take the unprotected wrist, step in and drop Mehmet on the stone tiles. Instead, Drew knocked his arm away without turning his head.

"Mehmet! If Drew doesn't kill you, I will. Now please go."

The ladies' room and the men's room, right next to the entrance, were directly opposite each other in an alcove. In between them were a sink and a mirror. Just before a wall cut off his view, Drew glanced over his shoulder. Mehmet was pleading with Yasemin and, from the looks of it, had broken down into tears. He was probably in love, and this was the most pain he'd ever had to confront. Poor kid.

Drew glanced in the mirror. He looked like he'd been in a duel—and lost. A fucking white shirt. Why couldn't she have ordered a white wine? After rinsing his face, he used paper towels to soak up what he could. Just as he finished up, he heard hurried footsteps first on the tiles and then on the wooden stairs. That, he assumed, had been Mehmet.

And there was Yasemin, sitting at the table, alone.

"I'm really sorry." Standing up, she brushed at the burgundy stain. "I love this shirt."

The touch of her hand made Drew tingle under his skin. "Did you tell him you were meeting me tonight?"

"I'm honest with him."

"Did you also happen to mention where we would be meeting?"

"No. But he knows I come here a lot ..."

"Do you come here with *him*?"

She shrugged. "Once or twice." Her thick eyebrows bunched together. "Don't start, okay? We're divorced. Where I go, who I go with—"

"Just asking." Drew sat back down. His mouth was bone-dry, his hands trembling slightly. Lifting his mug, he downed most of what was in it.

"That was impressive by the way."

He held up his mug. "Finishing off my beer?"

"He threw a glass of wine on you, and you didn't beat the shit out of him."

"Yeah, well, it's not like I didn't want to."

"But you didn't. Is this the new Drew?"

"I'm trying." He lifted his chin. "You want another wine?"

"Let's go home."

"Home?"

"Yeah, you know, where you used to live? With me?"

Standing up, Drew dug in a pocket and pulled out two crumpled bills and dropped them on the table. From the back of the chair he took the leather jacket he'd borrowed from Zafer.

He reached for her hand and was relieved when she laced her fingers with his. As he took the stairs, he wondered if Mehmet was waiting outside.

He pulled on the door and springs whined.

No Mehmet.

Stupendous. For once, his luck was holding out.

"Their" apartment was barely a ten-minute walk from the bar. It was on a quiet street with a mix of palm and deciduous trees sprouting from small but lush gardens in front of apartment blocks. From the fourth floor there was a view of the building across the street. Just above it, the sky dissolved into the darker blue of the Sea of Marmara. During the day anyway.

Yasemin unlocked the outside door. "The place is really a wreck. Just give me a few minutes to tidy up."

"Sure."

The lock clicked in place as the door closed behind her.

He knew she wasn't going to straighten up. Yasemin was never a meticulous housekeeper, and he had seen her at her worst. Right now, she was hiding photographs of Mehmet. Maybe throwing some of his clothes in the hamper. Mentally he shrugged: no point in denying her this little fiction.

A moment later, the door buzzed and he pushed it open.

He took the steps two at a time.

"Sorry about that." She was standing in the doorway.

He bent down and kissed her. He'd meant it as a way of saying he didn't care whom she'd been with as long as she was willing to take him back. She surprised him by slipping her arms around his neck and pushing her tongue into his mouth.

Cold light shivered through him. He splayed his long fingers on her back and pulled her closer. His legs felt hollow and weightless, while the rest of him seemed to be filling with liquid warmth.

Her cell phone rang.

She broke off the kiss and looked at her purse on the coffee table. "Let me get that." Digging in a front pocket she held the phone up as though reading the temperature on a thermometer.

Drew was slipping out of his shoes. "Mehmet?" The kid really had to be suffering, but Drew had been suffering for two years.

Yasemin nodded and turned off her phone. "While I'm at it …" She disconnected the house phone as well.

On the buffet, Drew noticed a wedding photograph he'd taken with Yasemin and her parents; a scrap of silk was draped over one end so that his face was covered. Must've missed that.

"He doesn't have a key, does he?"

"I'm not *that* stupid." She took one of his hands in both of hers. "Cold as ice, same as always."

"So I'm excited. Or nervous. Or both."

She smiled and lifted one eyebrow. "There are other ways to tell." Turning away, she let her arm dangle behind her as she led him toward the bedroom.

They kissed again at the edge of the bed. Yasemin's hands followed his flanks to his waist. Breaking off the kiss, she looked down to undo his belt. His pants dropped to the floor, buckle clinking.

Stitches strained as he yanked at her blouse before getting a button fully undone.

"Ea-zee."

Slipping his fingers under her bra, he stretched it up and over her upraised arms without unhooking it.

He pulled his shirt over his head instead of unbuttoning it and tugged his hands through the cuffs. So much of her skin against his own raised goose bumps. This was all he needed: the curves of her body conforming by some weird trick of geometry almost perfectly to his. The hard nubs of her nipples pressed against his chest. Her mouth joined to his.

He felt the anger, the bitterness—whatever would have resisted him—drain from her limbs.

As she lay back and he eased into her, something inside him collapsed. From fingertips to toes he dissolved in the swarming sensation sluicing through his veins. He closed his eyes, and a thought at the back of his mind flared like a firefly almost too distant to see. It vanished against pure black before he could recognize it.

He whispered her name hoarsely in her ear. She said something in Turkish he couldn't quite make out—and didn't care. Her arched neck revealed the underside of her jaw, the Mongolian swells of her cheekbones. Her mouth half-open, she began to moan. He kissed her and trapped the sound in his chest.

He wanted to promise a thousand things—they would get married again, they would never leave each other again, they would make a home together, they would start a family, they would stop doubting each other—but they had achieved something as miraculous as levitation, and he was afraid that one wrong word and they would fall.

Slipping in a broth of sweat—his hair clumped with it—they pressed against each other, the last of the space between them gone, and Drew's muscles quivered in the final moment as though contending with some great weight. Dizzy, he tucked his head between her neck and shoulder.

"Don't move." She tugged on his flank to keep him where he was and let her heels come to rest on the backs of his thighs. "Just for a minute."

The fears that began to rise even as his blood cooled and the rush of lovemaking receded she calmed by whispering, "I still want a baby."

6: 9

UNMARKED GRAVE

DREW HAD ALWAYS LOVED watching Yasemin sleep. Before drifting off, he'd imagined waking up next to her: ephemeral tan lines from last summer across the deeper caramel of her chest and shoulders, mascara an endearing smear under her eyes, her short hair a sexy tangle. He turned over.

"It's not going to work."

He hadn't even been aware she was awake. He rolled to his back, pressed the heels of his hands against his eyes. He was well-acquainted with her habit of incubating problems overnight. The negatives seemed somehow allied with darkness and dreams, seemed always to outweigh anything good that had happened the previous day. "I thought ... didn't you say you still want a baby?"

"What if you leave me again?"

Despite her beauty, her intelligence, the confidence that glossed her gestures, there was this black hole of insecurity at her core that Drew had never learned to deal with. "I won't leave, Yasemin." He turned to face her again. "I promise you."

She was staring at the ceiling, refusing to look at him.

"You broke your wedding vows, Drew." She turned to him, her eyes distant, cold. "How can I still trust you?"

He should have pulled her close. He should have reassured her, as a remote voice in him urged, but he was hollowed out, and anger shouted down the voice. He rolled out of bed, separated his underwear from his jeans, and slipped into them.

"Of course you're leaving. That's always your solution."

He stood and pulled his pants on, aware that he was doing exactly the wrong thing—reinforcing her fears—but he couldn't stop himself. He turned to face her. "What else is there to say? You've made up your mind." He could at least try, but he was tired. He was frustrated. He was angry. Maybe if she had waited a whole twenty-four hours before pulling this shit.

"Go ahead then, leave!"

Her words turned into a screech, and she hurled a pillow at him as he bent over to grab his socks and shirt. It bounced off his back.

He went to the hall, collapsed on a chair, and pulled on his socks. The living room was aglow with sunlight spilling through windows he couldn't see from where he sat.

She was out of bed now, too. Her shape under a thin robe was disarming, but her face had that ugly set to it—as though it were composed of shards of glass that didn't quite fit together.

He stood up to put his wine-stained shirt on.

"I was wrong last night. I was wrong to think you had changed." She stabbed him in the chest with an index finger as she spoke.

He looked down at her finger. "Why are you doing that?"

"Does it hurt?" She poked him some more. "Am I hurting you with my little finger?"

"It's insulting, Yasemin, and you wouldn't like me to do it to you."

"And what are you going to do about it? Punch me? Throw me on the coffee table like you did in our first apartment?"

He wanted to go in with a clean move and lift her over his head—just to scare her a little. But that was how he'd dropped her on the coffee table. "That was an *accident* and you know it."

"My back hurt for a week."

"You *know* I didn't do it on purpose."

"You're ..." (poke) "a man. And you ..." (poke) "should know ..." (poke) "your limits." *Poke.*

He couldn't stand her poking him. "You've made mistakes in this relationship too, but you can't admit it, so you've never apologized for them, and it still hurts." He tapped his chest. "Yeah, more than your finger."

"Don't forget this." She pulled Zafer's leather jacket off a peg and held it out it to him.

He snatched it, swooshed his arms through the sleeves angrily. "Well now you can go back to your twenty-year-old."

"*Siktir git!*" *Fuck off!* She started slapping at his chest and arms, which made loud smacking sounds against the leather. "*Siktir git!*"

He closed the door behind him.

"You just couldn't help it, could you?" he said to himself as he dropped down the stairs. "Pride. Spiteful, fucking pride."

He hit the buzzer to unlock the door and stepped into stunning September weather. The kind for a sweatshirt and shorts. He squinted in the sun as a mild breeze stirred fallen leaves. They were like sepia-stained photographs whispering against the paving stones.

Drew walked toward the Sea of Marmara. Hardly thirty yards ahead was a sparkling view. The land fell away steeply just beyond the sidewalk. He had to use his hand for a visor. Maybe there was enough sun-beaten water to wash away the pain of a failed marriage, the guilt he felt for the disrespect both he and Yasemin had shown their love. It was still there after all the bickering, the pride wars, the smashed glasses and broken furniture—like a child looking up at them with uncomprehending eyes. This child would forever wonder how two people who loved each other so much could hurt each other so often. The child would eventually die of neglect—the most beautiful thing either of them had ever held or felt or seen. There would be no funeral, but one day they would know that somewhere inside each of them was an unmarked grave.

His phone rang. He prayed that it was Yasemin, that she had calmed down enough for him to apologize and talk her into going out to breakfast in a tea garden overlooking the water. Why else had they been given this absolutely perfect weather?

The number on the screen was Zafer's.

"How'd it go?"

"I was winning up until the twelfth round. I got TKOed with about a minute left."

"Sorry to hear that, *dostum*. You on your way?"

"Yeah."

"I'll meet you in Karaköy, the ferry station."

"I'll call when I'm on the boat."

He pressed the red icon to terminate the call and stared at the phone as though he could make it ring. He could call her now, put on his most charming persona—the manic one that courted extravagance and always had something witty or funny to say. He could promise her a champagne brunch on the Bosporus. They could erase this morning and go back to last night.

He shook his head and put the phone in pocket. There had been too many *this mornings*, not enough *last nights*. It was time to let go.

6: 10

BETRAYAL

Drew FILED OFF THE FERRY with a throng of impatient Turks and walked along the quay.

Zafer spotted him and his smile turned to laughter. He pushed back a flap of black leather. "What happened? She *stab* you in the twelfth round?"

"Nah. Her little boyfriend showed up. Threw wine on me."

"Did you wreck him?"

"Yasemin wrecked him." Drew tapped his left breast with a finger. "In here. Besides, he's twenty and half my size."

"Turning into an Ebionite?"

Drew shrugged. "I don't know."

They walked past half a dozen waterfront restaurants with professional hawkers waving and trying to talk them inside even though it was way too early for lunch.

"I got a box for you back at the Office."

"My books?"

Zafer nodded. "Couple of my boys picked them up. They know what they're doing."

"What a way to live." Drew shook his head. The upside was he'd sneaked his much-thumbed-through Thoreau, collected Emerson, and a Whitman compilation onto the list of books to be rescued from the apartment.

"Don't worry," Zafer said. "We'll have the scroll sold in a few days."

Drew had almost forgotten about the scroll: how the hell was he going to keep it out of Serafis's hands? Nabil was a minor player on the black market; Serafis was somewhere near the top of the hierarchy. If the scroll was worth five million dollars, Serafis could offer four million and still sell it at a profit of a million. How would Drew's opportunistic pal be able to resist? Serafis would be offering Kadir his boat and his dream life on the Mediterranean. No matter how many times Drew turned the problem over in his mind, there was only one solution: at some point, he was going to have to betray them.

6: 11

SIX WORDS THAT REWROTE HISTORY

DREW WANTED TO PULL out his hair, scoop up dirt, and pour it in fistfuls on his head the way King David might have after hearing about the death of his rebellious son, Absalom. He was grappling with a two-thousand-year-old riddle. Worse, some of the evidence had been deleted, false information had been inserted, cryptic allusions made—allusions that might be impossible to track down in the historical accounts that had survived Christian book burnings and the glacial grind of the centuries. He didn't have Stephen's training or the knowledge he'd accumulated after a lifetime in this field. What he had before him was a palimpsest of texts, histories, and scholarly commentaries—often conflicting—from which he was supposed to separate the ghosts of previous passages from later overwrites, truth from spin, likelihood from falsehood. A single word could mean a turn in an entirely wrong direction.

The most famous example of one-word derailment was the Immaculate Conception as it occurred in Matthew. Matthew didn't know Hebrew and read the Book of Isaiah in the Greek Bible. What Isaiah wrote in Hebrew, however, was *a young* woman *shall conceive and bear a son.* Young woman (*almah* in Hebrew) was translated into Greek as *parthenos,* which generally meant *virgin.* The Old Testament mentioned a virgin some fifty times but always using the word *betulah.* So the concept of a virgin birth in Matthew hinged on a mistranslation—and the milieu of the first century Levant, which was rife with the miraculous births of various demigods and heroes.

Drew pulled out the list of keywords Stephen had mentioned the night he'd been killed. "Two thousand pigs?" What did *they* have to do with anything?

"Eh?" Kadir looked up from the TV.

"Nothing." Drew skipped the pigs and typed in *James the Just.*

James was barely mentioned in the Gospels, and when he was, he wasn't particularly distinguishable from the other brothers. Which was very odd since he was important enough for Josephus to write about, and—as one article pointed out—there was as much or more extra-biblical literature devoted to James as there was to Jesus.

Drew pulled Eusebius's *History of the Church* out of the box of books Zafer brought back. He found the passage on James, which Father Hawass had quoted, by the second century historian Hegesippus, an Ebionite whose works, except for a few fragments, had mysteriously disappeared.

He did not anoint himself with oil, nor did he go to the baths. He alone was allowed to enter the Holy of Holies, for he did not wear wool, but linen and he used to enter the Temple alone, and was often found upon his bent knees, interceding for the forgiveness of the people, so that his knees became as callused as a camel's because of the constant beseeching he did and kneeling before God and asking forgiveness for the people.

For James to have had the rights of a high priest to enter the Holy of Holies, to have been one of the leaders of the Church after Jesus' death, and yet, in the Gospels not to have been so much as one of Jesus' apostles, to be nowhere present at his brother's trial before the Sanhedrin and Pilate—*someone* had to be lying.

The simplest explanation was transference: if James had been the Teacher of Righteousness and had been viewed, at least until his death in 62 AD, as the Savior, then it made sense to strip him of his stature in the Gospels and transfer his saintly qualities to Jesus. That is, assuming Jesus was a fiction the Gospel authors needed to elevate well above any other messiah figure of the first century.

James was mentioned in the Pauline letters as a pillar of the Jerusalem church—and yet Paul was his lifelong enemy. That Paul and James were enemies was clear in the Letter of James: *Don't you realize you Empty*

Man that Faith without works is useless? Paul, whose emphasis was always on faith alone, was a ringer for the Empty Man.

Drew supposed scholars could argue that James was not a believer or follower of Jesus during the latter's ministry but only became a devout Christian when his resurrected brother appeared to him. The problem was that by all accounts James was, as Saint Hegesippus had put it, *Holy from his mother's womb.* Moreover, while Paul claimed that the resurrected Christ appeared to James, it wasn't mentioned in any of the Gospels—the process of diminishing his importance had already begun. Drew recalled John the Baptist's words in the Gospel written by another John: *He must grow greater while I must become less.*

James played a much larger role in Acts of the Apostles than he did in the Gospels although he doesn't even appear until chapter 12. Oddly, he shows up without introduction as if the reader were already familiar with who he was. Some scholars theorized that James had been written out of earlier chapters of Acts to downplay his importance.

Like Jesus, James was condemned by the Jewish high religious court, the Sanhedrin, and suffered a wrongful death. Rather than being crucified, he was stoned. The real reasons for James's execution had been recorded by Josephus. The Roman governor of Judea had died in office. While awaiting the arrival of the new governor, Ananus the Younger, then high priest, saw an opportunity to eliminate a rival for power. Convening the Sanhedrin, he had James and a number of his followers condemned on charges of blasphemy.

Ananus, high priest for only three months, was himself murdered and his body desecrated.

Of particular interest to Drew was a passage in Josephus's account that had been recorded by Saint Origen, Eusebius of Caesarea—the Father of Church History—and Saint Jerome. According to all three men, Josephus states that the reason for the fall of Jerusalem was the murder of James the Just. This passage, however, couldn't be found in any existing copy of Josephus.

"I wonder why," Drew said sarcastically and typed in the keywords for a web search. Saint Origen, writing in the third century AD, had paraphrased Josephus.

So great a reputation among the people for Righteousness did James enjoy, that Josephus, when wishing to show the cause for why the

people suffered such great misfortunes that even the Temple was razed
to the ground, said these things happened to them in accordance with
the Wrath of God in consequence of things which they had dared to do
against James ...

Later Church fathers fulminated against this passage as an outrageous lie, insisting that the crucifixion of Jesus was the reason for the fall of Jerusalem and the destruction of the Temple. Which, of course, made no sense since the Church held that Christ was crucified in 30 AD, and the Temple wasn't destroyed until 70 AD. This was eight years after the death of James, but there were hints that the stoning of James was one of the reasons for the revolt of 66 AD, only four years after James's death.

Much more interesting, however, were some of the details surrounding James's death. Saint Hegesippus and a third century Church father named Clement of Alexandria had written that, while addressing the Temple crowd on the Passover of 62 AD, James proclaimed *the Son of Man sitting in Heaven on the right hand of the Great Power and coming on the clouds of Heaven.* This was what Jesus supposedly said at his trial—in Mark, which was written *after* James's death. More intriguing still, in the accounts given by Hegesippus and Clement, James was not stoned to death but thrown from a pinnacle of the Temple.

His legs broken, but still half alive, raising his hands to Heaven, he
said, "Lord, forgive them for they know not what they do." Then, struck
on the head by the club a laundryman used to wring out wet garments
with, he died.

Words that, once again, would later be put into Jesus' mouth. It could be argued of course that Jesus had uttered them on the cross and they were then attributed to James—but why? Wouldn't it be blasphemy to take the words of the Son of God and put them in the mouth of his brother? Of course, if Jesus were fictional, a statement like this from James's actual death would be a wonderful bit of realism to add to his portrait. It might also help explain why there were three different versions of what Jesus said while he was on the cross. If the Gospel writers were *not* witnesses to the crucifixion, nor even privy to first-hand accounts, they would have had to search scripture and contemporary events for suitable quotes. Not surprisingly, in three of the four Gospels, Jesus' last words were taken from various psalms.

Oddly, there was no *biblical* account of the death of James, in spite of the fact that he was one of Christianity's great leaders and the first bishop of the Jerusalem Church. Odd also that no complete copy of Clementine's *Institutions,* which *does* describe James's death, had survived.

So James, holy from birth—like Jesus and John—was a Nazarite. Although a Nazarite took his vow for a specified period of time, Saint Epiphanius, an early Church historian, insisted James had been a lifelong Nazarite. No haircuts, no shaving, no wine. Even vinegar and grapes were forbidden. James was also a strict vegetarian.

"Wait a minute," Drew muttered, "how could James have been a Christian?"

If he rigidly abstained from drinking wine, he could not have participated in the only sacrament that Jesus himself had commanded. What's more, he also strictly avoided the consumption of blood—symbolic or otherwise.

"James was an observant Jew," Drew said, his voice rising, "and wine was a *Greek* addition to Judaic worship that came straight out of the Mystery cults—courtesy of Paul, who was the first to mention wine as a sacrament."

Drew rummaged through the box of books at his feet until he found *Mystery Religions of the Ancient World.* Flipping to a dog-eared page, he found a quote highlighted in fluorescent yellow. *He who will not eat of my body and drink of my blood, so that he will be made one with me and I with him, the same shall not know salvation.*

Any Christian would immediately identify that quote as belonging to Christ. It was actually an inscription referring to Mithra, a Persian god first mentioned in the second millennium BC. Nor was it only Mithra to whom wine and bread were sacred. Dioynsus, who had his own Mysteries, was god of wine, and a wheat cake went with his rites.

"Now it makes sense." Drew closed the Mysteries book with a *whump.* "There are *two* layers here ... one is Jewish, but the other is Hellenic."

Kadir glared at him.

Just as the Church made Jesus' birthday coincide with the birthday of the Sun as celebrated in Mithraism and other pagan cults, various aspects of James had been transferred to a non-existent older brother; if you were building a messiah, it made sense to use real parts. Didn't novelists model their fictional characters on actual people?

Drew grabbed his volume of Josephus and re-read the passage about James.

Ananus convened the judges of the Sanhedrin and brought before them a man called James, who was the brother of Jesus, who was called the Christ ...

Drew had found six words that, if they were later insertions as he now suspected, had altered history's trajectory. He took them out and was perhaps the first person in a millennium and a half to read the passage Josephus had originally written: *Ananus convened the judges of the Sanhedrin and brought before them a man called James, who was called the Christ ...*

6: 12

LETTER TO THE TWELVE TRIBES

His NAME HAD BEEN Ya'akov ben Yosef. In the Greek of the New Testament, Ya'akov became Iakubos, and from there, the more correct English translation would be Jacob. But when the New Testament was translated into Latin, Iakubos became Iacomus, which was later Anglicized to James.

Jacob the Christ. James the Christ.

Even if James had been regarded as the Messiah, it was impossible to prove.

On the surface Jesus and James were nearly opposites. Whereas Jesus often displayed a relaxed attitude toward observing Mosaic Law, James wouldn't abide a single point of it being violated. While Jesus was accepting of gentiles, James would not allow the disciples to so much as share a table with the uncircumcised—that is, the Greeks. Hence, the confrontation between Peter and Paul outlined in 1 Galatians. Whereas Jesus embraced the impure, James would have nothing to do with them. While Jesus was portrayed as cosmopolitan—perhaps *Hellenized* was a better word—James was thoroughly Jewish.

So why were there so many disturbing parallels between the two men, right down to quotes pulled from one mouth and put into the other's? Not to mention a detail found only in the writing of Saint Jerome: *This same James, who was the first Bishop of Jerusalem and known as Justus, was considered to be so Holy by the People that they earnestly sought to touch the hem of his clothing.* There were instances in the Gospels where fingers reach for Jesus' hem, and this struck Drew as exactly the sort of realistic detail a Gospel author would graft onto his fictional Christ to lend him credibility.

James was said to have been a life-long virgin. Jesus' virginity was never mentioned in the Bible, and yet that was the time-honored image of him. A razor never came near James's head, which meant he didn't shave his face either, but Jesus was always depicted with long hair and a beard. James was a vegetarian who abstained from consuming blood in any form—the peaceful, hippie-like Christ Drew had come to love was James.

Was that why Saint Hegesippus's writings disappeared? Because he made James appear as holy as Jesus?

Drew picked up his King James copy of the Bible and opened to the Letter of James.

In voice, tone, and especially in content, it sounded exactly like James as he came across in Acts. James 2:13 seemed expressly directed at Paul's insistence that faith alone would lead to salvation: *What does it profit, my brethren, if someone says he has faith but does not have works? Can faith save him?*

Christ was mentioned by name at the very beginning of the letter (*James, a servant of God and of the Lord Jesus Christ ...*) and then, just once more. Twice in the entire letter. The letter that followed it, attributed to Peter, mentioned Jesus nine times in the first 13 verses alone. And why didn't James identify himself as the *brother* of Christ in his opening? Only as a servant?

Drew checked the letter for quotes from Jesus, which, in his Bible, would show up in red ink. There were none. Not once did James quote his "brother," not even when he wrote things Jesus had supposedly said. Drew examined the letter more closely. The Bible editors had referenced the wisdom sayings in the Letter of James that paralleled those found elsewhere in the Bible. One of Jesus' speeches in Luke, in which Jesus says *"Blessed are you when men hate you, and when they exclude you and when thy revile you, and cast out your name as evil for the Son of Man's sake,"* had its counterpart James 1:2: *Count it a joy when you fall into various trials, knowing that the testing of your faith produces patience.* But in James, there was no mention of Jesus, only to faith in God, which meant he was not quoting Jesus but a wisdom source such as the Gospel of Thomas. The earlier version of this saying belonged to James's letter since the biblical epistles were all older than the canonical Gospels. Luke had embellished it, as Luke loved to do, and attributed the saying to Christ rather than God. The saying was there in Matthew, too, almost identical to the way it had been recorded in Luke.

"All three come from *Q*!" Drew shouted.

Zafer looked up from a worktable. "You all right over there?"

"No. I'm *not* all right. *Nothing* is all right. The history of Christianity is falling apart in front of me."

"Sorry to hear that, but it's almost show time."

"Show time?"

"We have a plane to catch, remember?"

"Just ... give me a minute."

Drew skimmed the letter. There were more of these common quotes, many more.

"Why would James write them without mentioning his own brother?" Drew asked the open Bible. Why would he say nothing of his brother's death? No token remembrance of their childhood? Not a single phrase to connect him to Jesus by blood. It made absolutely no sense ... unless James had had no knowledge of a Savior whom Paul had called Christ Jesus.

Drew hurled his pen at the desk. It bounced up, hit the wall, and landed on the desk again.

Zafer and Kadir were both looking at him.

"James didn't write this," he said as if they had been following his research. "Or the letter would be in Aramaic. But it's in Greek. It must be a summation of his thought written by a Christian scribe who inserted *a servant of the Lord Jesus Christ* in the greeting. The scribe wasn't aware James was Jesus' brother—because James *wasn't*. That was an innovation of the Gospels, which the scribe clearly had not read. The letter isn't even addressed to the Christian community. It's addressed to the Twelve Tribes."

The sayings weren't borrowed from Christ or the Gospels; they were taken from Q, just as Stephen had theorized.

"Does this make increase the price of my scroll?"

"If James was regarded as the Savior and the Teacher of Righteousness, yes."

"Iyi o zaman." Good, then.

"Now that I think about it, there's nothing in this letter that's particularly Christian—nothing about Jesus' life, his crucifixion, the resurrection. James takes just about every chance he gets to praise Jesus and praises God instead."

Zafer stood up. "Time to rock."

Drew looked around at the books and papers he had amassed. He started gathering things up absentmindedly, still trying to synthesize all the information he'd taken in. But there were still too many unanswered questions.

James was not one of the twelve apostles and yet, after the death of Christ, he was universally acknowledged as leader of the Church in Jerusalem—even by Peter. Early sources claimed that Jesus *chose* him as his successor. Why would Jesus choose a successor who was in so many ways his opposite? Why not one of the Twelve? Unless there *was* no Jesus.

Jesus' brother Judas, Drew recalled, had written a letter in the New Testament as well. He dropped the stack of books in hands and picked up his Bible. He flipped through it until he found The Epistle of Jude.

Jude, a servant of Jesus Christ, and brother of James ...

How could *no one* have noticed? Jude mentioned James as his brother but not Jesus! The original salutation must have been *Jude, a servant of God, and brother of James*. A scribe had substituted *Jesus* where he saw the word *God*.

The Ebionites must have known all along. But there was something about James they were hiding. Maybe whatever the Ebionites knew had been the reason that they had disappeared from the pages of history. Maybe the Habakkuk Scroll, which they so desperately wanted, was the key.

BOOK 7: 1 - 19

ANTIOCH ON THE ORONTES

Jewish historians have written that Joshua ben Perachiah was Jeschu ha-Notzri's teacher. They say also that this Jeschu lived during the time of King Jannai; the historians of other nations, however, have written that Jeschu was born in the time of Herod and was hanged in the days of Archelaus, Herod's son. This difference is a great one, a difference of more than 110 years.

— Abraham ben Daud, circa 1100 A.D.

And the Teacher has said: "Yeshua practiced sorcery and corrupted and misled Israel."

— Talmud

7:1

ADANA

THE FLIGHT TO ADANA was a little over an hour. The plane taxied to a stop in front of a dinky terminal that turned out to have a single baggage carousel. While Zafer stood at a counter signing the paperwork for a car rental, Drew's phone rang. He glanced at the number. *Yasemin?* Sighing in anticipation of a string of accusations, he pressed the green icon.

"Hello...?"

"Drewjuh'um, why didn't you cook me breakfast this morning?"

"What?"

"Ya, my job is making the bed and bitching at you for being lazy. You're supposed to cook me breakfast at least." She was speaking with the voice of a little girl. "What's the matter? You're afraid of a little temper tantrum?"

This was the one-eighty he'd been hoping for while he was walking to the ferry station. "I don't know, Yazz." He was answering the question they both knew was behind the one she'd actually asked.

"I'm sorry about this morning, Drew." Her voice had reverted to a woman's. "My emotions have been a little volatile since the divorce."

"Since the *divorce?*"

She giggled. "Okay, maybe before that. But it's worse now."

"I've noticed."

The baggage carousel jerked into motion. Kadir stood next to it, looking up at Drew as though the taller man were telling the Sicarii the address of Zafer's safe house.

"Drew, there's something else."

"I'm listening …"

"I've been in therapy for the last three months."

He was surprised she'd admitted it, but more surprised she'd finally given in and started seeing a shrink.

"I'm supposed to be on medication."

"Supposed to be?"

"I haven't been taking it."

"It doesn't work if you don't take it."

"I know. But I hate the idea of being on drugs."

"It's medication."

"Whatever you want to call it. I took one after you left. And I do want us to try again. I'm sorry."

Drew sighed. "We can't keep playing this game, Yasemin." Maybe they loved each other, but their love wasn't the healthy kind.

"After all the work I put into you, why should someone else get you? Mehmet gave you a chance to lose your temper in Samarkand, and then, just for good measure, I gave you another in the morning."

He almost laughed. "Is that what you were doing?"

"Of course. You're a little lazy, okay, but without your temper, you're the man I always wanted."

"Maybe we can split your prescription."

He heard a stifled giggle.

"Sure. Why not?"

"Look, Yazz, I can't let you take all the blame here. The truth is, I did lose my temper. I didn't throw anything or smash any family heirlooms, but I shouldn't have taken off like that. I should have stayed. Not even gotten out of bed. We should have talked things over. I know that's what you needed, I just … I'm still adjusting, okay? I'm still getting a handle on my anger. I'm working on it."

"*That's* what I wanted to hear, Drew."

She sounded like she was close to crying, even with the mood-flattener. "Drew, you're still my husband."

"That's what *I* wanted to hear. But listen … I'm not in Istanbul right now. We'll—"

"Where are you?"

"I'm …" Reflexively, he lied. "I'm in Ankara."

"*Ankara?* What are you doing there?"

"It's too complicated to explain right now."

"Drew, don't you have to start school?"

"I'll be back in three or four days."

Probably making a genuine effort to preserve the spirit of reconcili-ation, she didn't dig any deeper. "Okay. I'll see you then. *Seni seviyorum.*"

"*Ben de seni seviyorum.*" *I love you, too.* He closed the phone and put it back in his pocket.

Kadir was grinning up at him.

"What the hell are you looking at?"

"Ne kadar tatli." How sweet.

"Let's get out of here." Zafer jerked a thumb toward the exit. Their bags were piled at his feet.

As the glass door leading to the parking lot slid back, it was a rerun of Cairo: a wall of dry heat that seemed to melt the cars, the asphalt, and the fencing.

"I hope you got something with air conditioning."

Zafer pointed at an Audi. "I'm more interested in what's under the hood than what's under the dashboard."

"Not bad." It had to be the ugliest green anyone had ever picked out for a car.

"They were all out of Porsches. They were all of out of gray and black, too. This was the best I could do on short notice."

Downtown Adana was crumbling buildings, exposed brick, unpainted cement. Unlike Istanbul and Cairo, however, these buildings had *never* been particularly inspiring. Drew was glad when they pulled onto the highway and Zafer hit the accelerator. Another two and half hours or so and they would be in Antakya, where he had to find a way to meet Jesse.

Drew had called her from the airport in Istanbul. "Don't worry," she'd said, "I'll be there." Only how the hell was he going to get away from these two? How was he going to get the photographs out of the satchel Zafer carried around with him? And even if he managed to pull off both of those tricks, how were he and Jesse going to stop an ex-commando from selling the scroll to Serafis?

7: 2

CONFESSION

FOUNDED IN THE FOURTH CENTURY BC on the Orontes River by one of Alexander the Great's generals, Antioch had swollen, not two hundred years later, to a cosmopolitan city of a quarter million. The apostle Peter had been drawn to its bustling precincts, and the church he founded in a shallow cave—on land that belonged to the apostle Luke as legend would have it—was reputed to be among the oldest in the world.

With mountains to the north and south and hills to the east and west, modern Antakya sat in a broad river basin. The Orontes was now known as the Asi River. Although the outskirts of the city reminded Drew of a Mexican border town—buildings unevenly painted, walls carelessly patched up, roofs of corrugated tin or dirty yellow fiberglass held up by rusting brackets—Stephen had fallen in love with the quiet valley and its ring of hills and mountains.

Zafer drove them south down what turned out to be Istiklal Avenue although it was nothing like the one in Taksim. It was lined by concrete boxes six or seven stories high that might have been part of some Soviet-inspired—or rather, distinctly *un*inspired—construction plan. As was usually the case with Turkey's southern cities, motorcycles and scooters were popular. Drew had tooled around Istanbul on a motorcycle for a while, but too many near collisions with cars had convinced him to get rid of it.

He glanced up at a hotel towering over the street. For all he knew, Jesse had booked a room there. Sweat had broken out on Drew's forehead despite the car's air-conditioning. *I'm going to have to tell them about Jesse.*

They went over the Old Bridge that spanned the Asi, which was hardly a river anymore. Both of its banks either sheathed in concrete or lined with stone, it looked like a drainage canal. Drew had difficulty believing Roman ships had once followed it from the Mediterranean.

Navigating winding back streets, Zafer brought them to a stately hotel. Apparently erected before architects had learned to cheat everything into concrete, it had shuttered windows, balconies with stone balustrades, and a vertical row of faux Moorish arches framing the windows.

The lobby of the Hotel Antiocha was small but elegant, with red marble tiles and the sort of Victorian furniture that could have come out of a Dickens novel. Zafer handled the paperwork and surrendered a passport that Drew was sure did not have his real name on it.

Cramming themselves and their baggage into a tiny elevator with a glass door, they took it to the fourth floor.

The room was clean and spacious, with three beds, a wardrobe, and a small writing table. The back window opened on the eastern hills—wooded where they weren't craggy with rock—against which the city had backed itself. Most of the flat-roofed houses dotting the slopes were white. Picturesque from a distance, Drew knew that up close they lost most of their charm. It was a poor quarter where Arabic was spoken more often than Turkish, the roads were often dirt, and the homes were generally in desperate need of repair. But with the dramatic backdrop of hills and a flock of birds wheeling gracefully overhead, Drew had an inkling of what Stephen had seen in this Arabic-Turkish backwater.

He pressed a hand to his sweating forehead; his fingers were as cold as a can of refrigerated beer. "So what's the itinerary?" He tried to sound casual.

"Bad news first." Zafer held up his phone. "I got some texts from my pal at MIT. The Israelis might have given us around $500,000 US for the Habakkuk Scroll, depending on its condition—"

"That's the *bad* news?" A surge of anger swept away Drew's nervousness.

"The problem is, when they investigate its provenance, Abu's wife is probably going to get the money, not us."

"Okay, fine. Just promise me one thing: don't agree to anything—no matter how much Serafis offers—until we've had a chance to come back here and talk over our options."

Kadir nodded. "I am never give my word at the time of bargaining. If you give your word, you cannot change it. This is the law of bargaining everywhere."

"That's all I'm asking."

Kadir nodded. "*Oldu.*" *Done.*

So he'd postponed the inevitable. "When do we meet with Serafis?"

Zafer looked at his watch. "In about two hours. In Harbiye."

Harbiye was a sleepy hill-top town just south of Antakya. The town's claim to fame was a gorge that myth had marked as the place where Apollo had pursued Daphne, and she, after imploring the gods for salvation, had been changed into a laurel tree. (This part of Turkey was so saturated with Greek myth the Turkish word for *laurel* was *defne.*) Shaded by cypress and laurel groves, cooled by clear pools and waterfalls cascading down the gorge as though a niagara had been hammered into dozens of shards, it was no wonder wealthy Romans had built summer villas in Harbiye.

Two hours before they met Serafis … two hours for Zafer to cool down.

"Guys … I, uh, I have something I need to tell you …"

7: 3

SERAFIS

"WHAT THE FUCK is wrong with you?" Zafer was at the wheel of the Audi and Drew was afraid a seventeen-year-old in a souped-up Fiat was going to cut them off, get out of the car with an attitude, and get beaten into a coma. Then again, there was always the possibility Zafer was going to lose patience and pummel *him* into a coma.

From the backseat, Kadir said, "What you can expect? He is infidel."

It was more joke than accusation.

"I didn't say a word about Serafis or what we're doing here. She doesn't know our hotel, she just knows we're here. She doesn't even have my cell phone number."

Zafer had been so angry at first he'd gone completely silent. Finally, as the meeting with Serafis approached, he started talking. "I can't believe you did that. Why exactly do you want her here?"

"After we talk to Serafis, we can show Jesse the photographs. She'll have a much better idea of what the scroll is worth than Stephen did."

Zafer's hands, crowned by knuckles like rocky outcroppings, relaxed a little on the wheel. "*Could* be useful. To keep Serafis from bullshitting us."

"After Serafis makes an offer, we can give Jesse a chance to study the photos. A few phone calls and we'll know exactly what we have."

"That *might* work, but ..." Zafer took his eyes off the road to look at Drew. "Don't go behind my back again. *I* know what I'm doing. You *don't*. All right? If I can't trust you, you're no good to us."

No good to us made him sound like a wrench that was the wrong size for a repair. A euphemism for *worthless*. He nodded, a little hurt, and prayed he could keep his word.

Harbiye crowned a hill and spilled down its side. The Sun, at the bottom of its arc, appeared in bright bursts where streets spaced out buildings.

Zafer suddenly slowed. "There they are."

A gray Mercedes Benz, tail lights aglow, was parked with its nose pointed down a side road. Black-tinted windows made it impossible to see inside. Slowing the Audi, Zafer flashed his high-beams—virtually invisible during the day, except to someone watching. The Mercedes pulled out.

After fifty yards or so, the asphalt devolved to paving stones. The houses on either side of them were typically two flat-roofed stories with a vine, its trunk as thick as a man's arm, crawling up the side. Rooftops were crowned by latticework carpeted by leaves and hung with clusters of grapes. Property dotted by olive and lemon trees was marked off by crumbling cinderblock walls. Here and there, a goat or a cow was tied to a pole, and chickens inspected the ground before pecking.

As the westerly road bent away to the south to avoid tumbling over what was probably a sheer drop, they got a breathtaking glimpse of a broad valley hemmed in by hills, of a sky flushed with early sunset. The road, now marked as private and no longer lined with houses, ended at a wrought-iron gate. Surveillance cameras mounted over the entrance reared like mechanical cobras.

Beyond the gate Serafis's house bore no resemblance to the balconied, concrete homes they'd passed. Nor did it have anything to do architecturally with the more expensive houses they'd seen. Clearly Greek, it was a two-story cube of honey-colored stone. Some of the stone blocks were perfectly smooth while others had been left rough. The mason had used these differences in texture to create subtle designs around the mirrored windows and the front door. Two huge palm trees flanked the entrance, which was sheltered by a portico covered in Spanish tile. Strips of garden lined the stone walls around the house. The Mercedes stopped under loose latticework covered with wisteria. Drew was surprised to see, not a burly chauffeur in sunglasses and a dark suit, but an attractive blonde in sandals and a denim shirt hanging loosely over her shorts.

Even Zafer raised an eyebrow.

"Remember," he told Drew as he opened his door, "not a word of Greek."

Drew nodded. Serafis was fluent in Arabic, Greek, Turkish, and English. If the dealer spoke Greek to keep something private, Zafer wanted Drew to listen in.

The woman approached Zafer. "Hello, I'm Dr. Courant-Ancuri. A pleasure to meet you."

In spite of the French-Italian surname, her English had what Drew thought was a German accent.

"I'm sorry." She smiled apologetically. "My Turkish is awful. What little there is."

"English is fine." Zafer put out his hand.

A little mannish but pretty. Blue eyes, sprinter's legs, nervous smile.

"*Iyi akshamlar!*" Serafis was standing in the doorway in a short-sleeve shirt with the top buttons undone. After his Turkish *good evening*, he switched to English. "I see you've met Francesca. A first-rate archaeologist without whom I would simply be lost." He went straight to Kadir and thrust out a pudgy hand. "I'm Iorgos Serafis, the man who is going to make you rich."

Serafis, while he towered over Kadir, could not have been more than five foot two. Balding, he kept what was left of his black hair short. Gold rings choked his thick fingers and a huge cross of lumpy gold bedded in black chest hair exposed by his shirt.

When Serafis grabbed Drew's hand and pumped it energetically, Drew saw that he was wall-eyed. *Shit, you can never tell what the hell this guy is looking at.*

On either side of the carved wings of the doors were enormous terra cotta urns that probably pre-dated Peter's church. Now they were being used as pots for a couple of broad-leafed plants.

The front salon was an echoing space with a distant ceiling and tall windows that admitted girders of sunlight. A stunning mosaic of Apollo pursuing Daphne covered half of the tiled floor. The walls were lined with climate-controlled cabinets in which Serafis kept an assortment of vases, pitchers, urns, plates, and ceramic oil lamps in an impressive array of styles. A Corinthian capital had been covered with a cushion and made into a seat. But nowhere did Drew see a bookshelf.

He stepped closer to a cabinet to get a better look at a large Greek vase. It showed a bearded man on a stake being attended by four women. On his toga was a wheat motif, and stalks of wheat sprouted at the base of the stake.

"You didn't know that Christ was Greek, eh?" Serafis stood next to him.

"What?"

"Dionysus, of course. See how he is set on a stake? The word *stauros* in the New Testament has been translated as *cross*, but it means *stake*."

Drew almost said *I know*.

"Look ... on his head is a crown of ivy instead of thorns. And what have the women brought? Loaves of bread and jars of wine. Dionysus worshippers ate a little cake called the *makaria*, which means *blessedness*, but it's the Eucharist, of course—another Greek word!"

Drew nodded as if this were all new to him.

"And, if you look closely, you can see a little bit of purple coloring left on his tunic. Just like the purple robe Jesus wore on the way to Calvary."

"How ... how old is this?"

"Sixth century BC."

Sixth century BC! The ritual of the Mass predated Jesus by half a millennium.

"There are many such vases already in museums showing almost the same things. Christ was a Greek before he was a Jew! But come." He waved a hand that flashed with gold. "Forget about the trifles on my shelves. The true beauty is on the terrace."

After the guests had removed their shoes and slipped into flip-flops that Serafis provided, their host led them up a granite staircase and onto a terrace. Here, in addition to tropical plants in ancient pots, four columns no longer supported anything but Serafis's affinity for the trappings of his livelihood. There were also several pieces of classical sculpture including a *kouros*, arms at his sides, shoulder-length hair falling in waves of white marble, placid face staring out over a view of the river basin that almost made Drew forget to breathe.

The vista, not the antiquities, must have been the beauty to which Serafis had been referring. To the north, where stunted mountains roughened the horizon, Haribiye and Antakya was spread out below them. To the west, where the Sun had already disappeared behind the mountains, was a gently undulating quilt of square fields and groves. The distant valley seemed as peaceful as a vineyard that had been abandoned to honeybees and swallows. Even the view from Stephen's house hadn't compared with this.

"Are those as old as they look?"

"This?" Serafis kicked an urn overflowing with green fronds. "A cheap replica made in Cairo. But ..." He held up a finger. "Importing these replicas is one way of getting a genuine antiquity out of Egypt. You paint it over in watercolors—a crude job of course so as not to attract attention—mix it in with a crate of similar replicas for the tourists, and no one is the wiser! Out from the port in Alexandria, into the port at Iskenderun not an hour's drive from here." He smiled gaily at his own ingenuity. "Please sit, sit. Francesca will bring us tea."

There was a single long table with a glass top. The four legs were fluted columns that even Drew could tell were plaster fakes.

"Take a good look around you. Would you believe I was born in Istanbul the son of a cobbler? My father had to stare at the bottoms of shoes all day—God rest his soul." He made the sign of the cross. "You know what an insult that is to the Arabs? The bottom of a shoe? Even in Istanbul, say thirty years ago, if you sat with one leg crossed over the other on the tram, the man next to you had every right to knock your teeth out."

Francesca arrived with a tray of glasses and a double-boiler of tea.

"I couldn't bear my father's life. The same dingy shop for ten or twelve hours a day." He squeezed his eyes shut and shook his head with brisk distaste. "Of course, my occupation has its own drawbacks. Everything about the antiquities market flows like mercury. If you like your things in boxes or neatly on their shelves, as my father did, this is not the business for you. The market is shadowy, not black. Difficult to tell what is solid from what is not, what is counterfeit from what is real, what is valuable from what is worthless. *But* ... if you have the talent for this, you can make a great deal of money. Tariq understood this." Serafis turned to Kadir although his eyes going off in different directions made it hard to be sure he was looking at the dwarf. "You and he were good friends, weren't you?"

Kadir nodded.

"Tariq worked for Nabil, but for me he also did a few things. Of

course you know something about our dealings or you wouldn't be here."
His rings glinted in the dying sunlight as he waved a hand dismissively.
"His job was to let me know about antiquities surfacing in Cairo." He
sighed wearily. "A shame he is gone. A very likeable man."

Zafer and Kadir had listened quietly, but Drew felt compelled to break
up Serafis's monologue. "If you don't mind my asking, why Antakya?
Why not ... Cairo or Paris? It's not just the port at Iskenderun, is it?"

"My boy, I have a villa in Rhodes. I have an apartment in Zurich—
Switzerland, you know, is an absolute haven for looted antiquities. Any
time you have artifacts from a violated tomb in Italy or an illegal dig in
Greece, you send the merchandise to a freeport in Zurich and store it
there for a while. The Swiss don't bother about what you've got as long
as you pay your rent, and, best of all, there are no Swiss duties to pay.
That is why they are called freeports. Then you have someone swear out
an affidavit saying the objects came from somebody or other's attic. The
goods are then shipped from Switzerland as though that had been their
point of origin. Wonderful isn't it?"

Drew looked at Francesca. Probably in her early thirties, she had a
PhD in archaeology, and here she was serving tea to this Greek *maganda*
with a gold cross around his neck big enough to sink him in the river.

"You see," Serafis continued, although it was impossible to tell who
he was looking at, "no one wants to know how you get hold of these
things, not even the museums. The thinnest of cover stories will do. And
the next thing you know, your acquisition is being displayed in the Met
or the Getty.

"As for Antakya ... one of the best routes for antiquities being smuggled
out of Egypt has always been through Syria—hardly eight miles from
here. When Egypt passed new laws and enforced them more strictly, I
actually considered giving up my little summer home here. Ah ... but the
war in Iraq changed the antiquities trade." He clapped his hands together
and smiled impishly. "A single car seized by the Iraqis was loaded with
nearly four hundred artifacts from the Baghdad museum. A stroke of bad
luck they were caught at all! At this very moment, illegal digs are going
on all over Iraq and Syria—day and night since there is no longer any
central authority to stop them. Peasants with shovels are turning up great
numbers of objects. And once again, much of it is coming through the
porous Syrian border. Business has never been better!"

Francesca seemed to be avoiding eye contact with everyone at the table.

"Be at ease, enjoy the view, drink your tea ..." Serafis pushed up off his thighs as he rose. "I have something to show you that puts your scroll to shame."

Serafis came back with a shoebox and pulled out something rectangular wrapped in newspaper. He grinned as he peeled away paper and spread three tablets on the glass table. They were engraved with tiny rows of odd, fingernail indentations.

If that was Sumerian cuneiform, Drew was looking at the oldest writing in the world.

7: 4

GOD'S ONE GIFT

THE BROAD TERRACE was a tiny marble echo—smooth and barren and white—of the green expanse it overlooked. Its pots, its columns, its pieces of classical sculpture cast shadows that felt almost as old as Sumer's time-razed ziggurats. The Sun had dropped well below this edge of the world, crowning the hills with hot embers. Above their red glow the sky was a burnt orange that gave way to shades of darkening blue—like perfectly blended waterlines staining the western sky. The underbellies of long clouds were purple smudges. Insects, invisible among the greenery, chewed the fringes of the otherwise still evening.

"More than four thousand years old." Serafis smiled; his cross glimmered.

Francesca nodded gravely.

Drew had never seen cuneiform that wasn't behind the glass case of a museum. "What ... what's written on them?"

Francesca shrugged. "I can't read cuneiform, but I would say these tablets most likely contain verses from a Babylonian epic. The *Enuma Elish*."

It was a few seconds before Drew could speak. "You ... you don't even know what you're selling?"

Serafis lowered his eyebrows and pulled his head back as if he were a turtle and had a shell into which he could withdraw. His gesture—*Don't be ridiculous*—fattened his already round face. "My boy, what's the difference? They're already sold. The buyer was sent photographs, and perhaps before he agreed to a price, he found someone who could translate them." Serafis shrugged. "Tomorrow they will be gone."

And what was the buyer going to do with clay fragments from a Babylonian epic, Drew wondered. Use them for paperweights?

Serafis seemed to have his diverging eyes on Drew. "I took one look at you, my boy, and I saw that you don't care about money. From the same look I can tell you something else: you don't have any. No great riddle. But I also know that you are rather proud of your poverty."

Drew smirked with appreciation.

"Well, I *do* care about money. What I don't care about is what these things mean—history, archaeology, scholarly *theories*." He scrunched his chubby face and waved a hand as if dispelling noxious vapors. "God save us from any more *theories*." He put both hands out as if he were pushing away an overfriendly dog. "Most of my merchandise is pottery—baked clay for which fools pay hundreds of thousands of dollars. I don't want dirty pots—I want dollars. Freshly printed euros.

"Nothing bores me more than reading. Why do you think I've hired Francesca? I don't mind looking at pictures or paintings. Vases are fine for decoration. I like to drink. I like food. I love my wife. I like to laugh. If some old clay pots buy me these things and the time to enjoy them, why should I care?"

"What about the rest of us?" Drew was aware he sounded hopelessly naïve, but he couldn't help it. "You don't feel any sense of responsibility?"

"*Responsibility?*" Serafis seemed to dislike the word even more than *theory*. "My responsibility is to *me*. Let me tell you something: God made me the way I am. If He doesn't like it, he has no one to blame but Himself! Why fight against my own nature?" He spread his arms wide. "Does it look like God is punishing me?"

"You could sell frostbite to a polar expedition."

Serafis chuckled and glanced at Kadir. "Your friend here, he is like I am. He's not interested in crumbling parchment, old pots, long-winded poems. He cares about the one gift God has given us all: *life*. And about making his life—the only one he or any of us is going to get—*worthwhile*.

"Money is freedom my young friend—freedom not to spend your life in a tiny shop hammering at the bottoms of shoes. Freedom to travel where your heart leads you. Freedom to love whomever you choose. You and he, you're nothing alike. And this one …" He looked at Zafer and laughed. "A mercenary! With good business sense." He wagged a finger collared by a thick ring at Zafer. "I hope you don't have a conscience. A mercenary with a conscience sooner or later winds up dead."

"Sooner or later," Zafer said, "we all wind up dead."

"Hah! True enough, true enough. Sooner is what I meant." He turned his spreading eyes back to Drew. "And everyone else with a conscience winds up poor."

Drew imagined borrowing Zafer's pistol and emptying the clip into Serafis. *Ventilating* him as they would have said in the old gangster movies. The way they'd done to Stephen. Stephen, with his singularly wonderful mind, was dead, but here was this ignorant homunculus selling off the world's heritage, interested in nothing more exalted than financing a villa here, a mistress there, maybe a wine cellar to compete with Louis XIV. This gnome, with his house and its palatial pretensions, trafficked in fossils of the human psyche—these clay tablets and the painted ceramics filling Serafis's glass-sheathed shelves.

Guessing what Drew was thinking, the dealer said. "Do you think Greece's glorious past ever propped up the drachma?" He shook his head. "That's why after 1300 years, we Greeks gave it up without a groan. Now it's euros, not drachmas."

Placing the tablets in front of Francesca, who began re-wrapping them in newspaper, he rubbed his hands together briskly as if to remove dirt from a grave. "Now that philosophy is out of the way, are we ready to do business?"

"We are ready." Kadir pointed at the tablets Francesca was putting back into their shoebox. "These are very much older than our scroll, yes, but our scroll is worth very much more. So the shame is put on them."

"Hah! You're a shrewd man, Kadir." Serafis toggled his finger rapidly. "I saw that right away. Let us not make any foolishness about our deal. Please, would you show the photographs to Francesca?"

Zafer lifted the flap of the leather satchel still slung over a shoulder, took out a manila envelope, and put it on the table in front of her. She pulled out the stack and examined them. Drew guessed, however, that she was once again out of her element. Someone who dealt primarily in classical antiquities would not be able to read Aramaic. Nonetheless, her nod seemed to be the confirmation for which Serafis had been looking.

"Well the scroll certainly *appears* to be authentic, and although I know of course where it came from, there's no need to speak of that." He lowered his head and focused intently on Kadir. "What do you say to two million dollars IF ..." He sliced the air with an index finger. "*If* my experts can authenticate it. *If* it is indeed one of the Dead Sea Scrolls. Two million dollars in cash."

Kadir shook his head. "Nabil even offered more than this."

"*Nabil?* He...?" For the first time, Serafis seemed to lose some of his carefully composed façade. The episode with Nabil was a blank in his data banks.

"Then I will make the unprecedented offer of three million dollars!" He held up three fingers for emphasis. "One million for each of you!"

Drew prayed that Kadir wouldn't crack. *Please, Kadir, please.*

Kadir was as impassive as the *kouros* sunk in evening shadow. He shook his head.

"My friend, what is it you think you have there, the Rosetta Stone? A gospel signed by Jesus himself? Perhaps some undiscovered verses of the Holy Qur'an? Do you want a roll of old parchment or three point six million dollars—yes, one point two million for each of you?"

Drew couldn't believe Kadir's reserve. The sum Nabil had mentioned was as imaginary as a unicorn; here was a man who could actually produce $3.6 million. Cash.

Kadir shrugged. "I am thinking maybe I will not sell."

"*Not sell?*" Serafis's voice betrayed his agitation. "Look my friend, we are here to do business, yes? I am offering you a fortune—an absolute fortune for a long sheet of ragged paper. You must realize you cannot sell the scroll on the open market because it is stolen property—twice stolen in fact. It has no provenance, no history of legal ownership. Universities won't touch it. The Israeli government will give you a tenth of my offer if they don't throw you in jail first. Without me, this scroll is worthless."

Kadir shrugged again. "Maybe the only one offering millions of dollars is not you."

Even Drew wasn't sure whether or not Kadir was bluffing.

"Is this your last price?" Kadir looked like he was about got get up.

"*Dort buchuk! Son fiyat!*" He shouted in Turkish. *Four and a half! Last price!*

Although Kadir looked slightly more interested, he slid out of his chair. "We will call you tomorrow morning and say you yes or no."

Drew was relieved—and astonished.

Zafer collected the photographs and put them back in his satchel.

"Think well my friend, think well." Serafis jumped out of his chair as if to drag Kadir back to the glass table. "One and a half million dollars for each of you. Think of what that kind of money can buy. No scroll has ever brought such a price!" He opened the glass door covered with iron leaves and vines.

As they descended the stairs, as they crossed the salon with its huge mosaic of Apollo in pursuit of Daphne, and even as they walked the tiled courtyard toward the green Audi, Serafis kept talking, insisting that no one could make good on an offer of more than $4.5 million. "I alone, Iorgos Serafis, can put this sum of cash in front of you the moment we are sure the merchandise is authentic!"

Driving them through the iron gates, which opened automatically, Zafer said. "They're here."

"Who?" Instinctively, Drew looked over his shoulder.

"The Sicarii."

"They followed us?"

Zafer smirked. "They've been in Antakya since we left Egypt."

7: 5

IN THE BAG

ZAFER DROVE AS FAST as the serpentine backroads—half of them unpaved—would allow. "The games are over now," Zafer said.

"What do you mean?"

"I mean the Sicarii could predict our moves up until now. They knew we'd have to go see Tariq's wife. They knew we'd come here to see Serafis—or Serafis would come to Istanbul to see us. But once we finish our business with him …" Zafer shook his head. "If this guy Duvall is any good, we can't hide for long."

"Even at the safe house?"

"If they pick us up in Istanbul, and they put enough people on us, they'll find us there, too."

When they pulled onto the two-lane highway connecting Antakya and Harbiye, Drew glanced in the side-view mirror, but he didn't see anyone behind them.

With good pavement under the wheels, Zafer kept the needle at around 135—about eighty miles per hour. He passed illegally at will and constantly checked his rearview mirror for another vehicle doing the same.

A hairpin turn made the tires squeal as Zafer took them down a side street. Hitting the brakes, he cut the wheel so hard the car fishtailed. By accelerating at the right second, he got the car to do a complete 180. Pulling to the side of the road, he brought the Audi to a rough stop that snapped Drew's head forward. Zafer kept the motor running, turned off the lights, and looked at Drew. "If I get out of the car, slide over and take the wheel. And I mean *fast*." He twisted his head around to talk to Kadir. "I'd tell you to keep your head down," he said in Turkish, "but no one can see it anyway."

"Defol git." Piss off.

Zafer scrutinized every car that turned down their street. He'd wait until the car was about fifty feet away and then turn on his high-beams. All they saw were a surprised family, an old man who looked like he was about to collapse behind the wheel, and a woman in a headscarf.

"She'd be great for surveillance work," Zafer said as the covered woman passed. "Not very likely though. The car she's driving is older than I am and has local plates."

When a fourth car turned down their road, Drew knew right away something about it was wrong. It was going too slowly, as though the driver wasn't familiar with the roads. The car glided under a streetlamp, a black BMW.

Zafer flicked on his lights.

The man squinting in the beams didn't look Turkish. He had dark hair, pale skin, and looked English if anything. It was the American that Nathan had given them a photo of: Francis Collins.

Collins had the sense to turn on his own brights and speeded up as he passed.

"Get ready, Drew."

The car's back bumper had hardly cleared the driver's door when Zafer leapt out, pulled out his Glock and squeezed off six or seven shots inside of a couple seconds.

Drew climbed over the stick shift, landed in the driver's seat and released the parking brake.

The BMW sped away with a peel of screeching rubber.

Zafer sprinted to the other side of the car—

Drew hit the accelerator before he'd even closed the door.

"Make a right up here." Zafer dropped the clip from the Glock, which Drew noticed wasn't empty. "I don't think Collins will follow us. I'm pretty sure I took out his rear tire." Zafer slammed a fresh clip into place with the palm of his hand.

Drew cut off a small truck to make his right turn, incurring angrily flicked headlights and a blaring horn, but he hit the accelerator and rapidly outdistanced the truck.

"There's a *dolmush* stop about two or three miles up. You're going to make a left down the street right after it."

Drew took them back up the hill, passing the road where they'd met Francesca in the Mercedes.

"There!" Zafer pointed. "Make a left."

Drew saw the line of *dolumushes*—white minivans here in Antakya—and zipped past an oncoming car to make the left.

"Now ... the next right, find a place to park."

Drew's hands were practically numb, but they were surprisingly steady on the wheel. Was he getting used to this business? Pulling over, he stopped the car and yanked the emergency brake into place.

"Pop the trunk."

As he got out of the car, Drew looked sympathetically at Kadir. This wasn't going to be fun.

Zafer took a huge canvas bag out of the trunk. Unzipping it, he looked at Kadir. "In you go."

Kadir muttered a curse in Turkish and climbed into the bag.

"Now ..." Zafer pulled a *keffiyeh* out of the trunk. "We cover that goddamn long hair of yours."

After wrapping Drew up like a Kurd, Zafer tied one around his own head. This was why Zafer insisted Drew dress in long pants despite the heat. Now he could pass for a local. Taking off his jacket and shoulder holster, Zafer put them in the bag with Kadir. His pistol went into the satchel. "Try not to move around in there, all right?"

"*Defol!*"

With the bag zipped, Drew and Zafer each took a handle strap.

"Shit. He's heavy for a little guy."

Pulled toward each other by the weight between them, Zafer and Drew lugged Kadir toward the *dolmush* stop, about 150 yards away.

"One thing I can't figure out ... Collins *couldn't* have followed us all the way from Serafis's—there was no one behind us. How the hell did he find us?"

"They already knew what kind of car we were driving—I'm sure they saw us leave—and they knew sooner or later we'd come out to the highway. Collins was just lucky enough to see the street we turned down."

"I don't know if I'd call that *lucky*."

They heaved the bag with Kadir in it onto the first *dolmush* in line. The minivan was almost empty.

Zafer paid for four places so that they could put Kadir next to them on the row of seats at the back. He sat down next to Drew. "So ... how the hell are you going to talk him—" he tipped his head toward the luggage—"out of four and a half million dollars?"

Hermes or some other god of thieves had inspired Drew as Serafis and his guests had been walking over the mosaic of Daphne and Apollo in the antiquities dealer's palatial house. The answer was so obvious, he didn't know why he hadn't thought of it sooner. He leaned closer to the ex-commando. "I'm *not*. We should take Serafis's offer."

7: 6

ONE-ON-ONE

WITH THE BAG HOLDING KADIR sagging between them, Zafer and Drew walked, a little stiffly, into a hotel a couple of miles from the one into which they had checked in earlier. Zafer, who had already booked reservations, handed in another passport and got their room key. He and Drew, still in their keffiyeh's, carried Kadir onto the elevator.

Zafer unzipped the bag. "Free ride's over."

Kadir climbed out, pouring sweat. "*Ya*, it's like a *hamam* in there." He wiped his face with his hands.

They got off on the third floor, the canvas bag now under Drew's arm.

Zafer unlocked the door to 324. "A new hotel, a new room. No bugs. No surveillance. Even if they happened to post someone here, they'll be looking for *him*." He jerked a thumb at Kadir. "Not a couple of Kurds."

Their luggage was already in the middle of the room, waiting for them. About half an hour before meeting Serafis, Zafer had telephoned the second hotel to arrange to have their bags picked up.

"All right ..." Zafer pulled off his *keffiyeh* and raked out his curly hair. "So why do you want to sell to Serafis all of a sudden?"

"We set him up with the antiquities police." He looked from Zafer to Kadir and back again. "We take Serafis's money, he lands in jail, the scroll goes back to Israel, the Turkish government takes the credit, and we give the photos to the Ebionites. Everybody wins except that little bastard Serafis."

"You see the gaping hole in your plan, don't you?"

Drew shrugged. "It's a first draft."

"Even if we don't get arrested *with* him, how do we keep the money?"

Kadir shook his head. "It doesn't work."

"It might, it might." Zafer rubbed his jaw with two fingers. "Let me think about for a while."

When he'd come up with the idea, it had seemed perfect, but if Zafer couldn't find a way to set up Serafis without losing Serafis's payment, the scroll was as good as gone. He needed to see Jesse *tonight*.

"So, now that that's settled, you mind if I show Jess the photos? She might be able to tell us something important."

Zafer shook his head. "I don't like it, Drew. I got us locked up, safe and sound."

"Look, I'll call a taxi. I'll go straight to her hotel—as soon as I find out where she is. I'll keep my *keffiyeh* on. I mean, what if Serafis tries to put something over on us at the last minute?"

"The professor already looked the photos over."

"*Barely*. He didn't have time to read more than a few lines. He was interested in the other scroll, remember?" Drew tried to keep his voice from sounding desperate. "Jesse can tell us exactly what we have and how much it'll bring in." It was only half a lie.

"We know how much the scroll is cost."

Drew looked at Kadir. "According to *Nabil*. Maybe it's really worth seven, eight million dollars. How do you know it's not worth ten? Serafis went up to four-and-a-half million pretty quick, don't you think?"

Zafer sank into the edge of a bed. "He wouldn't offer that kind of money unless he already had a buyer lined up."

"The Ecole Biblique?"

Zafer shrugged. "Or the Vatican. Who else is going to front that kind of money?"

"Okay, then. If he's already got that kind of money lined up, you ought to be able to squeeze another half million dollars out of him—if not more. Especially if Jess can find something in the scroll that's damaging to the Church."

Kadir had taken off his shirt, balled it up, and was using it to wipe down his face. The muscles in his short arms tightened into knots as he plied himself with the makeshift towel.

"But you need to know what you're going to do *before* you make your phone call tomorrow morning. Once you agree to his price, that's it, bargaining's over."

Kadir tossed the shirt on the floor and exchanged looks with Zafer.

Zafer turned the corners of his mouth down and raised his eyebrows. "Half a million dollars for a couple of taxi rides might be worth it." He exhaled heavily. "All right, go ahead, take the photos over, but don't stay the night. And call me before you come back. I'll meet you in front of the archaeological museum."

Drew offered a silent prayer of thanks. "No problem." He grabbed the satchel; its unexpected weight reminded him that Zafer's pistol was still in it. He hesitated.

"Take it," Zafer said. "You might need it."

"No, I don't think—"

"Better to have and not need, than to need and not have."

"What about—?"

"I have another one."

Drew didn't like the idea, but he let the weapon stay where it was.

He slipped the strap of the satchel over a shoulder. The steel lump bouncing against his hip, he opened the door. "See you in a couple of hours."

He felt a little silly stepping off the elevator in sandals, jeans, a button-up shirt and a *keffiyeh*, but the hotel manager offered only a perfunctory smile.

The night air was sultry. The hotel was on a quiet street a couple of miles from the center of town. He found a public phone about a block away and punched in Jess's number.

"*Where* have you been? I have been waiting all *day* for you to call."

"I'm lucky Zafer didn't break my ribs. I had to tell him about you."

"He didn't—?"

"No, I'm fine. Where are you?"

"The Hotel Orontes. On Istiklal Jaddesi."

"What's your room number?"

"Three-twelve."

"See you in five."

Trotting back to their new hotel, he hopped into a cab that had just dropped off a well-to-do Turkish couple.

Although Antakya didn't have much nightlife, tourists in shorts and sandals mixed with locals on the streets, and restaurants were still open.

They passed the Old Bridge—one of the few river crossings that accommodated cars—and a small plaza dominated by *kunife* shops whose chairs and tables overflowed onto the stone tiles. *Kunife*, a pastry made with syrup-soaked shredded wheat and a buttery cheese, was an Antakyan specialty. More than once Drew had shared a table here with Stephen. It was hard to believe, on this end-of-summer night in a quiet Turkish city, that he would never sit across from him again, never hear him carry on about some obscure fact he'd unearthed in his research, never hear his clear laugh.

The Hotel Orontes was a block or two from the river. Drew had barely stepped out of the taxi when he sensed the urgency of the footsteps approaching him from behind. By the time he lowered himself into a wrestler's stance and whirled around, it was too late. The night blurred as he grappled with an opponent whose moves were precise, fluid, and unfamiliar. Drew hadn't been on a mat in more than a decade. His reflexes were off, and this guy was good—*really* good. After a trip combined with a throw, finished off with an arm-lock, Drew found himself on his back, the pistol in the satchel smacking loudly against the sidewalk.

When he looked up, he recognized the swarthy face and the broad grin.

"What the fuck, Nathan...?"

7:7

CHURUK ELMA

ZAFER CALLED GÖKHAN from the same payphone Drew had used a few minutes earlier.

"*Kankardeshim*, I need a favor."

Gökhan sighed. "What else is new? Look, Zafer, I know this black market business of yours is worth a nice piece of change, but I have to watch my ass. If anything backfires, I can't take the heat for you. You're my *kankardeshim*, but I'd be telling you this even if you and I had the same mother."

"Understood. I'll make sure nothing can be traced to you. All I need right now is a little information. There's a guy named Iorgos Serafis who deals in antiquities. I met with him today. He's as dirty as they come. He's got himself a villa here in Antakya and another in Istanbul. No way he can be set up like this without paying somebody off."

"And you want me to find the *churuk elma*, right?" *Rotten apple.*

"*Some*one is on the take in the Department of Smuggling and Organized Crime, and I need to know who."

"I'll tell you this much, the antiquities police here are as tough as any except the Italian Carabinieri. In a good year they'll recover something like 10,000 artifacts."

Zafer nodded to himself. "See if you can find someone in the Istanbul or Antakya branch who's under investigation. Maybe you can say you've got a tip from one of your informants. But don't tell anybody what you're looking for. I don't want the bad apple implicated in any way. See what you can dig up on Serafis while you're at it."

"I'll take care of it, but give me a clue here—what's going on?"

"I'm going to sell something for a lot of money—and some of that will be coming your way. The trick is going to be not to get arrested."

"Make sure you don't because if you do, you're on your own."

"Yeah, I know."

7: 8

THE PAST EXHUMED

Nathan's eyes were on the satchel. "What's in the bag, Drew?"

Zafer had been right: Nathan was Sicarii. But what raised the hairs on the back of Drew's neck in spite of the warm night breeze was the realization that Jesse must have set him up.

"Photographs."

Nathan snickered. "Something else? A little heavier?"

"A Glock 9 mm."

He shook his head in parental disapproval. "Keeping the wrong company." Stepping back, he tugged Drew to his feet by the arm he'd trapped.

"So what was the point of racking me up like that?"

Nathan held up an index finger as he walked toward the street. "Wait here." Opening the door of a gray Opel parked in front of the hotel, he leaned inside. Drew took a good look at the Opel, just in case it showed up somewhere else.

"Here." Nathan held out the envelope. "A few more Sicarii."

Still trying to get me to trust him? Drew stuck the envelope in his satchel without opening it. "Thanks."

"Did you sell the scroll to Serafis?"

If Nathan was Sicarii, he'd know. Either that or the Ecole hadn't approached Serafis about the offer. But they *must* have.

"No. It's not even in Antakya. How the hell … how did you find me?"

That bright smile in his dark face again. "You found *me*."

"What?"

"Jesse. We started following her in Egypt."

"You mean, after the Internet café, you tailed me to our hotel?"

Nathan shook his head. "My partner, Josh, tailed you."

"But … Zafer. He's always jumping out and switching taxis, taking pedestrian overpasses—"

"All well and good. Unless you have a dwarf and a guy with long hair with you. Then, a few inquiries to doormen at various hotels or nearby shopkeepers, and even in a city the size of Cairo, you can get lucky. Especially when you've got a couple dozen well-meaning Ebionites at your disposal. They're useless for tailing someone like Zafer, but since they have the patience of monks—some of them *are* monks—they're pretty effective when you put them in front of a hotel and tell them to watch the door for a few hours." Nathan lifted his chin to indicate the *keffiyeh*. "That was pretty clever. Although you still have to take a dwarf around with you."

We have you there, smart-ass.

"We knew sooner or later you'd be coming here, and when Jesse showed up in Antakya …" Nathan shrugged. Then the expression on his face changed. "Drew, you have to find a way to keep them from selling. It'll go to the Sicarii and disappear in a vault under the Vatican. If they don't burn it."

"Why? What the hell is so important about the Habakkuk Scroll?"

Nathan sighed. "You really want to know?"

"That's a rhetorical question, right?"

Nathan nodded as though he were being forced to do something against his will. "There are a few controversial lines in the copies of Habakkuk that scholars have seen, but they still date it to about the end of the first century *BC*—well before Jesus was born. In the full scroll though, the one Kadir has, there's proof it was written after the destruction of the Second Temple, in 70 AD. The author of Habakkuk recognizes the Teacher of Righteousness as the Messiah, but never mentions anyone resembling Jesus. That's the most important reason the Sicarii need this scroll to disappear."

"How can you possibly know that without the scroll?"

"We've had the photos for years. But without the original, they're worthless."

"There's something you're not telling me."

"There are a lot of things I don't tell you, but that's neither here nor there. Drew, you have to find a way to keep them from selling to Serafis."

"What do you think I'm doing here?" He opened his arms to the hotel. "I'm hoping Jesse and I can put our heads together and come up with an alternative."

"Steal it."

"What?"

"Steal it, and get it to me. I'll turn it over to the Israeli government. The publicity and the photos we already have will do wonders for the Ebionite church. Of course, after you steal the scroll, Zafer or Kadir might come at you with a kitchen knife—"

"Zafer doesn't need a knife to kill me."

"You're right about that." Pulling out his wallet, Nathan handed a card to Drew. "Let me know when and where the sale is going to be, and *I'll* steal it. Then you're in the clear. I've tracked you this far, haven't I? Who's to say I didn't figure out how the sale was going down?"

That could work, Drew thought. Nathan and his partner nail Serafis; Zafer and Kadir make off with the Ecole's money; the Ebionites get the scroll. It was *perfect.* "What's the other reason the Sicarii want the scroll?"

"It shows that Paul of Tarsus murdered Jesus' brother."

7: 9

THE DEATH OF JAMES

"**W**HAT IS THAT doing on your head? You look like you lost your herd of goats. And what took you so long?"

Drew didn't know if it was Jesse's freckles or the front teeth that were slightly rabbit-like because of the curl of her wavy upper lip or maybe the white shirt that she filled out in what was probably considered an unscholarly way, but he was having trouble focusing on the business at hand. A blade of guilt under his ribs reminded him of the conversation he'd had with Yasemin earlier in the day.

"You're being followed. And this ..." He pulled off the *keffiyeh*. The air-conditioning made it feel like he'd dunked his sweaty head in a cool stream. "... makes me less visible."

"I'm being *followed?*"

"Since we met in Cairo."

"Okay ... by whom?"

"The Ebionites."

"The *Ebionites?* They fell off the face of the Earth by the fifth century. And even if they were still around, why would they follow *me?*"

Drew took a deep breath. "I'll explain ..."

"Here ..." Jesse pulled a chair away from a small desk for him and took the edge of the bed for herself. She listened, barefoot and in shorts, while Drew filled her in on Nathan and the Ebionites.

"This guy's outside my *hotel?*"

Drew nodded. "I just lost a wrestling match with him." He took the scroll photos out of the satchel. "Here. What you've been dying to see."

She took the 8 x 10s but still had an eye on the satchel. "What's in there that's so heavy?"

"You don't need to know."

"You know why I'm a scholar, Drew? Because when I ask a question, I want to know the answer. Even if it takes years. This one better not."

Drew sighed. "A pistol."

"You brought a *gun* into my room? A *gun*? Drew this isn't—"

"I told you in Cairo what you were getting into. I didn't want to bring it. Zafer insisted."

"Can't you ... *put* it somewhere?"

"You want me to leave it in the lobby with the receptionist?"

"I just don't ... *like* it."

His forearms resting against his inner thighs, he watched her leaf through the photos.

"*Wow.* The quality is fantastic."

Drew straightened up in the wooden chair. "You mind if I use your laptop?" Sitting on the desk, it was open and plugged in.

She didn't look up from the photograph she was holding. "Go ahead."

She'd already forgotten he was in the room. He turned to the computer. He knew there were two accounts of James's death, and they didn't match up. In Josephus's version the Jewish Sanhedrin had been convened, sentence had been pronounced, and James was stoned to death in 62 AD. Clement and Saint Hegesippus, however, had James—at the insistence of the scribes and the Pharisees—addressing a crowd from the pinnacle of the Temple on Passover. When James was asked about Jesus, he replied *Why do you ask me about the Son of Man? I tell you he is sitting in heaven at the right hand of the Great Power, and he will come on clouds of heaven.*

This was not what the scribes and Pharisees wanted to hear.

So they went up and threw down the righteous one. Then they said to each other "Let us stone James the Righteous," and began to stone him, as in spite of his fall, he was still alive. But he turned and knelt, uttering the words: "I beseech Thee, Lord God and Father, forgive them; they do not know what they are doing."

Saint Hegesippus, Clement, and Josephus agreed James had been stoned to death; they disagreed on the circumstances. But either way Drew couldn't see how Paul could have been James's murderer. Unless Paul—

"Drew!"

Jesse's voice startled him.

She was on her feet and flapping a photograph as though trying to shake the letters from it. Floorboards creaked under the Turkish carpet. "This scroll *could* be late first century AD. It mentions that the Kittim— the Romans—"

"Sacrifice to their standards?"

Jesse deflated a little. "Yes."

"Which means it wasn't the republic. Rome had an emperor."

"You knew?"

Drew nodded. "So, all the stuff about the Liar, the Wicked Priest, and the Teacher of Righteousness in the scroll fits in pretty well with Paul, Ananus, and James the Righteous?"

"I still think it's a long-shot. The Dead Sea Scrolls aren't my specialty—at all—but scholars have been over every millimeter of the Habakkuk Scroll, and the general consensus is that it is late first century *BC*, not AD."

"So I heard. Nathan says there's something in there that shows up in the full scroll but not in the version scholars currently have."

Jesse held out a photograph. "This must be what terrified the Church and the Ecole Biblique—a scroll written in the first century AD that mentions the Teacher of Righteousness but *not* Jesus. The Gospels, the histories, even Josephus have been tampered with but not *these*."

"Well," Drew said, "I think I figured out how Paul killed James."

She sank into the edge of the bed. "Somebody e-mail that to you? Last I heard, Ananus had James killed, and Paul wasn't even in Palestine anymore."

He shook his head. "I'm not so sure. James was stoned to death, whether by order of the Sanhedrin or a Temple mob. That much we know. But let's suppose Josephus is right—"

"He is," Jesse assured him. "His account fits much better with what we know."

"Then all it takes is for Paul to be in collusion with Ananus in convening the Sanhedrin, and he's just as guilty. *That* must have been why Professor Cutherton had counted Ananus as a key player.

The air conditioner hummed.

Jesse shook her head skeptically. "There's one little problem ... in 62 AD Paul was awaiting trial in *Rome*. We know because Acts tell us that Festus, the Roman governor of Judea, sent him there. And James was killed shortly *after* Festus died."

Drew smiled. "That's where you're wrong."

"Oh *really*?"

Drew closed the laptop. "Let's try recreating the scene. Around 60 AD, after years of preaching among the Greeks, Paul returns to Jerusalem, where he meets up with James. As always seems to happen when Paul is around, there's trouble ... Paul is accused of casting aside the Law of Moses and bringing uncircumcised Greeks into the Temple. There's a riot, Paul's arrested by a Roman centurion and brought before the governor of Judea, Felix. And what happens?"

Jesse hesitated. "Nothing."

"That's right—nothing. Although Paul is a Roman citizen, nothing happens for a full two years. At which time Festus takes over for Felix, and *he* doesn't do anything either. Instead, he ships Paul off to Rome."

"So what are you saying?"

"Acts of the Apostles ends abruptly—without ever mentioning a trial or an outcome for Paul."

"I'm aware of that." Her tone added *So what* ?

"Look closely. Paul is hauled in front of Felix in 60 AD, exactly two years *before* James is killed. When Acts ends, Paul has been renting a little house for himself for two years—exactly two years *after* the death of James. The axis of the symmetry is James's death. I mean *please* ... for some Temple indiscretion in Jerusalem that only marginally involves the Romans, Paul is still waiting for his trial *four years later*? It's obvious horseshit."

Jesse's face darkened like a thumbnail whacked by a hammer. "Drew, I'm modern and all that, but please, let's try to keep the Bible separate from farmyard metaphors."

"Sorry."

"I take your point though. *Some*thing is off."

"Yeah, and this is what it is: Ananus and Paul both had strong motives for killing James—Ananus because James's popularity was a threat to his own power, Paul because James's brand of Christianity was diametrically opposed to his own. It was too Jewish. All those purity laws didn't appeal to Paul or the Greeks. Paul was the silent partner in the conspiracy. *But ...*" Drew stabbed a finger at her. "Paul *wasn't*, as the Bible says, arrested two years before James died, nor was he brought before Felix. He was arrested when Festus was already governor—and James was already dead. He went to Rome either because Festus died in office and Paul invoked the rights of his Roman citizenship to be tried in Rome or, more likely, he exiled *himself* to Rome, where it was less likely his hand in James's death would be discovered. In fact, the whole trip to Rome might be a fiction to make it look as though Paul is in Rome at the time of James's death, and for nearly two years after that. Luke could hardly make him appear more innocent. And don't forget why Luke wrote Acts—"

Jesse nodded impatiently. "To reconcile Jamesian Christianity with Pauline Christianity, which was very Hellenized. That's why, although Paul is clearly the hero of Acts, James settles the central dispute about admitting gentiles to the Church."

Drew waved a hand. "There it is."

"It's an interesting theory, but ..."

"Don't take my word for it." Drew pointed at the photographs. "Nathan says there's material in the Habakkuk Scroll that clearly implicates Paul. I also got the distinct impression that the Ebionites were persecuted nearly out of existence because they knew Paul murdered James. They still call him the Enemy."

Jesse nodded. "That's what bothers me—too much of what you're saying makes sense. I really have to ... I have to read the whole scroll." She lifted a handful of the 8 x 10s.

"Then you're going to have to come to Istanbul. You can take all the time you want while I try to work out more of these Gospel encryptions."

"What Gospel encryptions?"

7: 10

SUBSTRATA

"WELL ... LOOK, YOU KNOW there are a lot of contradictions between the Gospels and things that don't add up within a particular Gospel. But what if that's intentional? What if the authors of the Gospels used allegory to encrypt historical events?"

"An alternative history?"

"Unless I'm completely off, there are disguised references to historical events and to ... a substrata of history I guess you could call it. Bethlehem is a good example. All the Gospels record this as Jesus' birthplace. Luke even goes out of his way to get Joseph and the pregnant Mary, who already lived in Nazareth in his version, to Bethlehem. What was so important about Bethlehem?"

Jesse had been leaning to one side, a straightened arm propping her up on the bed, but now she sat up. "Micah 5:2 ... *a ruler of Israel shall come out of Bethlehem.*"

Drew pushed back sweat-soaked hair with his fingers. "That's exactly how a Jew would read it. But we know from Saint Jerome that Bethlehem was a center of worship for Adonis long before it was Christ's birthplace. *Adonis* is a Greek name taken from the Phoenician *adonai* for *lord*—identical to *adonai* in Hebrew." Drew put both of his hands out. "There it is. Our Lord was born in Bethlehem—the same message for Jew or gentile. So the other side of the coin, the hidden side, is how a Greek would read it. Jesus was another in a long line of dying-and-rising gods who were venerated in the Mystery cults, a divine lord born in Bethlehem."

Jesse sighed. "Yes, that's been the trend in modern scholarship ... to call Jesus another Dionysus or Mithras or Adonis..."

"It makes sense. In Judaism, there was no precedent, no prophecy about a Messiah resurrected from the dead."

"That's true," Jesse admitted. "But the Adonis cult in Bethlehem ... that's pure coincidence."

"Maybe, but *all* the Mysteries venerated a dying-and-rising god. Mithra might be the best fit of all. He was born to a virgin on December 25. He's depicted with a halo, had twelve disciples, his holy day was Sunday—the day he was resurrected—he was worshiped on Vatican Hill in Rome, before the Catholic Church existed of course, and the leader of his cult was a pope. I mean, that tall hat bishops still wear is called a mitre, from the Latin for Mithra—Mitra. It's adding up."

Jesse nodded, a little wearily maybe. "So you think the Gospel authors plagiarized the myths of the Mystery cults?"

"At first that's exactly what I thought," Drew conceded, "but I realized the stories were too well-known to steal. I think on one level the Mystery elements were landmarks for pagans, particularly the Greeks— it was the Greeks after all who took to Christianity, not the Jews. Greeks would feel at home with a Mystery cult. So the Gospels were meant both for the Jews and for an audience versed in the Mysteries—pagans all over the Levant. Why else would Matthew be so ready to write that a *virgin* would *conceive and bear a son*? A virgin birth wasn't strange to him because he was a *Hellenized* Jew surrounded by the Mystery cults in which any number of god-men had been born to virgins."

Jesse shook her head. "Scholars have made these connections before— and dismissed them. Except for a couple of wingnuts with PhDs."

Drew sighed. "Okay. Let's rewind a little ... James was a Jew first and foremost. To him following the Messiah meant observing the Torah and showing your faith through good works. Paul, who was thoroughly Hellenized, wasn't interested in Judaic Law. For him faith justified everything. He's the one who popularized a savior resurrected from the dead like every other god-man in the Mediterranean world."

Jesse's smile was condescending. "You should have gotten your PhD, Drew. You can't support all this."

"Well, I'm not done digging yet. I'm not even sure Jesus was the Savior."

She rolled her eyes. "Now you're *way* out in left field."

"Look, even in Saint Hegesippus, James is described as holding debates on the Temple steps as to whether or not Jesus was the Christ. If it was common coin that Jesus had actually risen from the grave, would there really be any doubt? No. Which means the resurrection *wasn't* accepted among the Jews, it was a Pauline invention."

"So who *was* the Savior?"

"James." Drew was far from convinced, but he wanted to see how she countered.

"Hold it, hold it right there. You mean to tell me—"

"Jess, didn't you just say the Teacher of Righteousness and James look like a good fit? What does the scroll—" he lifted his chin toward the photos spread out on the bed— "say about the Teacher? *All those who observe the Law whom God will deliver because of their suffering and because of their faith in the Teacher of Righteousness...?* Not only does the Teacher *sound* like the Messiah, but stressing Judaic Law sounds exactly like James. And the Teacher *can't* be Jesus because there is nothing about the crucifixion or the resurrection or anything else to indicate Jesus."

Jesse frowned. "I'd rather read the whole scroll before rearranging centuries of scholarly interpretation."

"Okay, but look at their deaths. In the stylized version of James's death—"

"Stylized?"

"Josephus gives us the historical account. Clement and Hegesippus give us the stylized accounts, where James is thrown from the pinnacle of the Temple and stoned. Isn't it curious that Acts of the Apostles leaves out James's death entirely? The first bishop of the Church of Jerusalem, brother of the Lord? Acts and the Gospels deliberately suppress James as often as possible. They *had* to. His holiness takes away from Jesus'."

Jesse waved a hand in vigorous denial. "They were suppressing Jamesian Christianity in favor of Pauline Christianity."

"No argument there. But there are too many similarities between James and Jesus. In the stylized version of James's death, James is addressing a crowd on Passover just before he's killed; Jesus is crucified on the eve of Passover. Jesus and James both see *the Son of man coming on the clouds of Heaven* before they are killed. Both are unjustly accused of blasphemy. Both ask God to forgive their killers. It's not one or two things, Jess, it's about a dozen."

"Why wouldn't it be the other way around? Why wouldn't pieces of Jesus' life have been grafted onto James's?"

"Because that would diminish Jesus' stature and elevate James's. And as you just admitted, the New Testament writers sympathized with *Paul* and went to great lengths to suppress James's importance. Paul was bringing in Greek converts on his missions but James was a stay-at-home kind of guy who barely converted any Jews." Drew snapped his fingers. "Justin Martyr! He *proves* what happened. When Saint Hegesippus describes the death of James, he cites something in Isaiah as a prophecy, something like *Let us take away the Just One ...*'"

"Let us take away the Just One, for he is abhorrent to us, wherefore they shall eat the fruit of their doings," Jesse finished. *"The Septuagint's mistranslation I might add."*

"Right. Anyway, the point is that for Hegesippus the Righteous One is *James*. Hegesippus was born around 100 AD in Palestine. But by the time we get to Justin Martyr, who's writing a couple of decades later, the Righteous One is no longer James, it's *Jesus*. It makes sense. Even if there *was* a historical Jesus, his worshippers would have wanted him looking down on every other prophet. Why do you think Mark sticks that line in John the Baptist's mouth about not being worthy to loose Jesus' sandal strap? If John were really so unworthy, Jesus would be the one baptizing *him*. And Jesus wouldn't be repeating some of the same things—word for word—John had already said."

Jesse smirked ironically. "There's a gaping hole in your theory. If James was the Savior figure in first century Palestine, where did the crucifixion narratives come from? There's nothing in the history of James to explain that."

"Paul doesn't mention the Romans or Pilate."

"Nonetheless, the crucifixion narrative came from *some*where."

Drew thought of the vase—centuries older than Christianity—that he'd seen at Serafis' house, the image of Dionysus impaled on a stake— *stauros* in Greek but translated into English as *cross*. *There's your dying-and-rising god*, he thought, but that image was still a long way from the detailed crucifixion narratives in the Gospels. "Like I said, I'm not done digging."

"Well," Jesse held up the photographs. "If this scroll ever sees the light of day, the Church is going to have some explaining to do."

"I think I've got that covered."

"You found a way to keep them from selling it to Serafis?"

Drew nodded.

"*How?*"

"It's not important."

"So why don't you tell me?"

"Because the less you know, the safer you are."

"Oh, come *on*, Drew. I'm up to my neck already."

"Look, Jess, I took a *huge* chance having you meet me here. I already lost Zafer and Kadir's trust. It's not a good idea for me to lose any more."

She sighed. "So what now?"

"I have to get back to my hotel."

"And leave me here? Under surveillance? Drew, I'm not staying here tonight."

"I can't take you with me, Zafer would freak out. We have to get you to another hotel."

"How are we going to do that? Maybe you haven't noticed—I'm a *Caucasian* dressed like a tourist. I'm a dead giveaway."

Drew smiled. "I'll take care of that."

7:11

THE MARKET, AFTER HOURS

SITTING IN A CAR PARKED across the street, Nathan saw a couple step out of the hotel. He glanced at his watch. Nearly midnight. The woman wore a scarf over her head and an ankle-length skirt. Head down, she held her husband's arm as the two of them walked south on Istiklal Avenue.

Where the hell was a conservative Muslim couple going at this hour?

Nathan got out of the car and followed them at a pace that would be fast enough to overtake them but not to draw attention. He slipped off his watch and pushed it into a pocket. He would simply ask the time—almost everyone here spoke Arabic—as an excuse to get a good look at them.

Still on the opposite sidewalk, they turned down a narrow street. He trotted across Istiklal. As he turned the corner, he nearly bumped head-on into the man, who was now walking in the opposite direction.

"*Affedersiniz.*" *Excuse me.* The man looked at him curiously and stepped around him.

Nathan realized at that moment that the covered woman had *not* been his wife. He took out his cell phone.

Just as Jesse reached Drew, Drew spotted Nathan. "Shit."

Drew had found the Turkish couple in the lobby of the hotel. He'd explained that although his wife wasn't Muslim, she wanted to dress more modestly, tonight, and offered an exorbitant price for a set of clothes. He promised the man an extra 25 lira if he would walk Jesse around the block. He himself had climbed out a window at the back of the hotel.

Jesse looked over her shoulder.

"That's him on the corner. We'll have to lose him in the car. Come on."

Drew had the satchel against one hip and Jesse's laptop bouncing off the other. The straps intersected over his sternum and his spine.

"My rental is this way." Jesse pulled him by the hand.

On either side of the street was Antakya's central market, a warren of alleys and winding streets. Slouching and leaning, their awnings of corrugated tin or fiberglass, the shops and stalls looked as though they had once been on the move, their advance had been suddenly halted, and they'd settled into these haphazard arrangements.

Jesse pointed at a Fiat. "Here."

A car facing them started up, and its high-beams flared to life.

"Wait." He caught Jesse by the arm.

The car pulled out with a shriek of rubber.

Instinctively, Drew pulled Jesse down onto the sidewalk with him. Automatic gunfire erupted as the car passed. Glass exploded into tiny shards that rained down on them and danced on the concrete.

"They shot at us!" She sounded astonished more than anything else.

The thought of the Glock he was carrying flashed and disappeared, leaving the same blankness that followed a nighttime display of lightning. A pistol against submachine guns—that was suicide. Scrambling to his feet, he tugged Jesse up by her hand.

The side windows of the Fiat had been shot out.

Tires squealed as the car did a 180 near the corner.

"This way!" Drew yanked Jesse into one of the narrow streets of the market place where a few Turks, their faces curious and tentative, gathered to peer at the Fiat in its glittering setting of broken glass.

Drew knocked into an empty vendor's cart as he took Jesse around the corner.

"Do you know where we're going?"

"No!"

The car screeched to a stop, and a flashlight beam found them.

Realizing the curve of the road would make a clear shot nearly impossible, Drew pushed Jesse ahead and broke into a sprint.

Another burst of automatic gunfire unstitched the quiet. Drew heard pings off metal, ricochets off stone, the shattering of glass. Most of it over their heads. As they rounded the curve, Drew heard the whine of a car in reverse. A few seconds later, headlights cast Drew's and Jesse's elongated shadows in front of them as the car sped up the narrow street.

Drew glanced over his shoulder. Above the glare of the high-beams, he saw the silhouette of a man leaning out of the car's window.

"Shit."

"This way!" Jesse pulled him down an alley far too narrow for a car. Just as they emerged onto another street, there was another spurt of automatic fire. Stone shattered but the alley was already behind them. Drew stopped suddenly, slipped off her laptop, and handed it to her. "*Go.*"

A Turk, who'd been sawing wood in his shop, stared up at them in disbelief.

Drew pulled out the Glock, a weird pistol to him because it had no hammer. He looked at the carpenter. "*Chabuk eh'il, abi.*" *Get down fast, brother.*

The Turk ducked into the recesses of his workshop.

"Where am I supposed to go?" Jesse shouted.

"Get behind something." Drew dropped to one knee behind a wall. Aiming with both hands, he trained the Glock on the mouth of the alley maybe thirty feet away.

A man carrying what looked like an Uzi trotted into the street.

Drew squeezed the trigger. A burst of sparks showed where the bullet scarred the dark cobbles at the Sicarii's feet. The man leaped back into the alley, and Drew fired off two more shots in rapid succession.

"Let's go!" Grabbing Jesse's hand, he sprinted up another curving street.

"Did you hit him?"

"Didn't try to. I just wanted to give them something to think about."

They ducked into another alley as the Uzi opened up.

A motorcycle approaching from the far end brought them to a sudden stop. Drew prayed a Sicarii wasn't riding it. He and Jesse flattened themselves against the corrugated steel rolled down over the front of a shop to let the bike pass, but at the last second Drew jumped out. Using a long arm bent slightly at the elbow, he caught the rider under the chin.

It *hurt!*

The Turk, who had no helmet on, flipped over backwards while his riderless machine toppled on its side and scraped a line of sparks on the cobbles until it came to a stop, back wheel spinning.

"Drew!"

"He'll be all right." Drew grabbed the bike, and kicked the starter. Once, twice, three times, but the engine didn't turn over.

"Damn it!" He glanced up at the mouth of the alley and kicked twice more. The engine caught and idled roughly for a few seconds. Drew gave it a little gas and revved the engine. It was a Honda Scrambler, which had probably been discontinued in the seventies. A top speed of eighty-five or ninety—when it was *new*. This one needed a tune-up. "Great."

While the Turk, an eighteen- or nineteen-year-old kid, struggled to a sitting position, Drew pulled the bike up in front of Jesse. "Get on!"

She climbed on the back, hampered by the long skirt.

"Keep your leg away from the tail pipe. It's a little high on this thing." Drew let out the clutch too fast, and the front wheel jerked up as they sped out of the alley. While the acceleration was enough to make Jesse constrict his waist, it was disappointing to Drew.

Instinctively, he made a hard left. Letting out a cry, Jesse fought against him as they leaned to one side, and the ground rose up toward them.

Drew brought the motorcycle to a stop. "You can't do that. If *I* lean, *you* have to lean. You have to be my shadow, okay? Or you'll throw us off balance."

"I'm sorry, I ... I've never been on a motorcycle before."

Police sirens rose over the sound of the idling engine.

Drew checked the only side-view mirror he had left; the other had snapped off in the fall.

As soon as he saw the high-beams of an approaching car, he knew without a backward glance who it was.

"Hold on."

Jesse's arms tightened again as he gunned the engine, and the motorcycle jerked forward.

No helmet, he thought, *no mistakes*. Which wouldn't be all that easy with a car full of professional killers on their asses. He concentrated on the stretch of asphalt in front of him. Swerving to avoid a startled Turk, he angled for a turn down a street narrow enough to slow it down some. He heard two pistol shots just as the bike leaned into the turn, and this time Jesse moved with him, the blurred asphalt rising up, then receding as the bike righted itself. Drew opened up the throttle a little more.

Tires screeched behind them as the car struggled to make the same turn. Drew glanced in the remaining mirror and saw the car take out a pole holding up a tin awning. It collapsed with a crash.

Drew wove from one side to the other side to make them a more difficult target. Jesse would be the one hit—unless the shot went above her head, in which case it would shatter his.

The back of the bike fishtailed as Drew fought its momentum to make a turn. Every turn was to their advantage: they didn't have to slow much, and they could accelerate faster.

They emerged onto a wide street, and Drew shifted into fifth. There was a rising whine as the gear wound out. The *keffiyeh*, which he hadn't properly wrapped around his head, flew off behind them. By the time the car was in his side-view mirror again, they had opened up a good deal of distance.

That was when a second car showed up—coming from the opposite direction. Switching lanes and gunning the engine, it headed straight for them.

"Shit!"

Drew steered the bike to the right—the car's left—as though he were going to shoot through the narrow space between the car and the buildings. As soon as the driver moved to close off the space, Drew cut hard to his left and went through the opening—the wide side of street— he had created. Jesse's arms choked his waist, but she didn't fight the bike as it tilted.

With both of the cars behind him now—how many were there?— Drew raced down every narrow street, up every alley, hugged every curve until it straightened out. Poles, barrels, crates came at them at high velocity; he veered and they missed.

The road broadened unexpectedly into a two-lane avenue divided by a grassy island, and the market fell behind them. He cut the motorcycle's lights. The avenue was well lit and traffic was sporadic in either direction. Drew eyed the cars suspiciously and checked his side-view mirror every few seconds. He could see Saint Peter's Grotto Church on the slope of a distant hill, its façade bleached by floodlights.

Jumping the curb, he took the Honda over a footbridge spanning a concrete storm drain that was dry but deep. The other side of the bridge was a field with nothing in it but a couple of trees and the remains of stone walls.

He turned and lifted his voice above the idle of the engine. "I think we're okay now." Sliding forward in the seat, he slouched toward the handlebars. "Hop off."

He missed her hands around his waist as soon as she let go.

Dismounting, he dropped the kickstand with the toe of a sneaker and left the key in the ignition. Antakya was a small city; the cops or a good Samaritan would get the bike back to the kid.

"All right, hot shot, so how do we get back?"

He could see she was trembling. So was he.

"Back *where?* We show up on the street, we're likely to get shot at again. I think we should let things cool off for an hour or two." He looked up at the Grotto Church. Awash in chalky light, the façade the Crusaders had added in the 12th century had taken on an otherworldly look, as if it weren't the crude effort of knights doubling as masons but the handiwork of angelic artisans. "I know just the place."

7: 12

THINGS DONE IN THE DARK

"DREW, THIS IS *CRAZY*."

They were hiking up a road as steep as it was dark and so badly paved he wondered if it had been shelled at some point in Turkey's history.

"No better way to be out of sight for a while. Besides ... *I'm* the one toting the laptop."

Rounding the last switchback, they were rewarded not with a close-up of the church but of an official-looking building. Tickets were sold here during the day.

Jesse folded her arms over her chest. "I'm just guessing but I'd say the gate is locked."

"Y'think? C'mon." He tipped his head toward the hill. "There's a trail."

Wide enough for two, the path was rough with exposed rock and loose stones.

After about five minutes, Jesse stopped. "I can't take this thing anymore." She pulled the silk scarf off in a single smooth movement as though unveiling herself. "Oh that's *sooo* much better."

Drew put his hands on his hips and faced west. They were well above the church now. The city sprawled over the river valley below. It looked as though a small star had been crushed and the pieces scattered—thickly in places, sparsely in others. On the horizon he could see the hard lines of mountains, darker than the sky, and a few clouds like floating shadows.

Jesse drew a sharp breath. "It's beautiful."

"This is why Stephen loved it here."

"Stephen?"

"Professor Cutherton. He had a house here. For when he couldn't take English weather and London's pace anymore." Drew lifted his chin to indicate a direction. "Ready?" Without waiting for an answer, he started back up the trail. Cutting south across the slope, it brought them to a stone shelf surrounded by rock outcroppings.

"*Where* are you taking us?" Jesse asked.

He pointed. "There."

"That ... *hole?*"

Drew nodded.

"What is it?"

"The church had an escape tunnel in case the Romans decided to crash the party. This is where it comes out."

"It looks like a shortcut to the underworld."

"Don't worry." He dug in a pocket and pulled out a lighter.

"You smoke?"

He gave a half shrug. "Cigars, *narghile*. But I'm not having a nicotine fit. This has a pen light. The thing is, I'm kinda ..." He held up a hand and waffled it. "Claustrophobic. Not on elevators or anything, just when I can't see the way out. Dark makes it worse. A lot. Do you, uh, mind going first?"

She sighed. "It's easier than being shot at."

He tossed the lighter. "Good catch. I might have to hold onto you, okay?"

She snickered. "It'll be payback for clinging to you on the motorcycle. Ready Professor Hardwigg?" Jesse clicked a switch, and the lighter generated a tidy beam.

Drew smiled appreciatively. Professor Hardwigg had headed up the expedition in Jules Verne's *Journey to the Center of the Earth*. "After you, Hans."

The tunnel was a natural formation, its rough walls—in the circle cut by the light—the color of sand. Widened in places by industrious Christians, the passage was large enough for Jesse to stand, but Drew had to stay hunched over. They put out their hands to the chisel-scarred stone for support. The ceiling or the western wall would fall suddenly away as they walked, exposing the city below.

The passage narrowed during its sloping descent, and the air cooled. Drew felt like they'd been swallowed by a stone gullet. Panic began to rise, and he put a hand on Jesse's shoulder. Her warmth and firmness reassured him. He carried her computer bag in his other hand.

When the passage became so tight they had to crawl, Drew's limbs grew cold and numb, and his heart constricted like it was caught in a fist. Sweat beaded across his forehead as he pushed the laptop in front of him.

"Drew, I think we should go back ..."

"Just a little ... further." One more word and his voice would have cracked.

The tunnel widened again, but they were still hunched over like early humans—

"Long arms and tough knuckles would come in handy right about now, huh?"

Drew was too tense to laugh.

"I can see light, Drew."

The fist around his heart relaxed slightly.

Jesse straightened up in a small chamber, its mossy walls glistening with dampness. It led to a much larger chamber into which she wandered, her head tipped back as she gazed overhead. "So this is it, the first church in Christendom. Or close to it."

Once upon a time, he thought, Christianity was one of those things done in the dark.

They were in a natural cavern, the air noticeably warmer than it had been in the tunnel. Light, harsh and white, sliced through windows and a pair of starburst designs cut into the façade. The back wall looked almost as though it had been formed by the drippings of countless candles. It *had* been created by a flow—the eternal seepage of water. The front of the cave had been tamed by chisels and rudimentary masonry. The plastered ceiling was water-stained and cracked. Square columns built from stone blocks of varying sizes supported brick arches and shallow vaulting. Crevices between the stones were clogged with moss.

The altar was a stone box with a few simple carvings. Behind it was a squat throne that had been crudely cut from limestone now stained by the centuries and darkened by the damp. Like the façade, these accoutrements had been added long after Peter's time.

Besides their own breathing, there was only the faint sound of trickling water.

Jesse ran an open palm over the altar as though it were a coffin holding the body of a saint. A tiny pool had collected just beyond the altar. "They must have used this for baptisms."

Drew put the laptop down. Slipping off the satchel, he put it on the altar's smooth, white surface. The Glock made a muffled click through the leather.

Jesse put her handbag next to it.

Instead of aspiring to lofty heights, the grotto church had burrowed into the dark. An intimate space where faith wouldn't echo. A reminder of an age when a cavern was entry into the body of a goddess, when darkness was gestation and germination.

"I better give Zafer a call." Drew squeezed a hand into a pocket and took out his cell phone. He glanced down. "*Shit*. Battery's dead." He looked up. "Can I borrow yours?"

"Sure."

"Sorry. I don't have his number memorized ... I have to switch SIM cards." Her phone, however, wouldn't recognize the card. "Where did you buy this?"

"In the States."

"It must be wired differently. It just keeps saying *code error*. I guess Zafer will have to wait." Replacing her card, he handed the phone back to her.

"I wonder what it was like ..." She dropped the phone in her purse and leaned against the altar. "When Saint Peter was preaching here. Don't you sense it, Drew? An aura?"

"There's something here ... yes." Drew was trying to get used to Jesse in her borrowed clothes: a loose aquamarine vest, a silky blouse the yellowed white of ivory, and an ankle-length skirt covered by a field of printed flowers.

Jesse turned around. "So what happened in college?" Her face roughened by shadows, she looked like a piece of classical sculpture. "Why didn't you major in religion?"

Christ, he thought, *she's beautiful*. Mentally he regrouped. "The feeling you get from this place? I get it from a poem ... or a good novel. Even when I studied Christianity, it was the stories that interested me most.

They're not so different really, fiction and religion. I mean, God may be real, but religion is the fiction we dress Him up in. Or Her. I guess what I'm saying is you can't take the Bible *literally*. Philo of Alexandria right? It's allegory, fiction."

"That's taking it a little too far, don't you think? Calling religion a bundle of lies?"

"Fiction isn't a bundle of lies. Okay the events never actually occurred, but the stories still reflect some kind of truth, psychological or social or whatever." Drew didn't like standing across from her, like a face-off, but, arms folded over his chest, he didn't move. "Religion is basically a fiction people agree to believe in."

Jesse frowned. "That's *all*? That's all religion is to you?"

"What do you mean, *all*? The world is run by fictions."

7:13

TRUE STORIES THAT NEVER HAPPENED

DREW REACHED INTO A POCKET and pulled out a ten lira note. "This is the greatest fiction going—fiat money. Without faith, it's just a piece of paper. Back in 2000 I watched the lira lose more than half its value in *one day*. Because a couple of politicians had a fight that created a crisis of confidence. Suddenly, my paycheck was more than cut in half." He pushed the bill back into his pocket. "Even a nation is basically a fiction with an idealized identity and a sanitized history—a collection of stories that are half true at best. The Greeks have *The Iliad*. The Brits have their Arthurian legends. The Romans had Romulus and Remus. The Jews have the Old Testament."

Jesse cocked an eyebrow. "I have a feeling the Jews would disagree with you."

Drew shrugged. "Faith *has* been known to override logic. What worries me is that substituting fiction for reality used to take centuries—not anymore. Look at how Nazi Germany revived German mythology to galvanize a sense of German superiority."

"And the Gospels?" She looked like a teacher patiently interrogating a student.

"Fiction of course. That's why those guys were shooting at us tonight."

"Maybe the Gospel of John," Jesse conceded. "Although M—Professor de la Croix argued otherwise."

It sounded like Jesse had started to say something that began with *M*.

The professor's first name? No, it was Amanda. Jesse had probably been on a first-name basis with de la Croix, just as he had been with Stephen. For all he knew, her nickname was Mandy.

"It doesn't mean the Gospels should be dismissed. It means they should be read another way."

Crossing the floor, Drew turned around to lean against the altar. Now they were both facing the church's façade. Light streaming in lent the place … yes, an aura. It was easy to understand how, of all the attributes God might possess, nearly every culture agreed God was luminous.

"I mean," Drew continued, "why is Matthew the only gospel to have the flight to Egypt? He's alluding to something." His heartbeat had picked up.

"There is, of course, no historical evidence for the slaughter of inno-cents under Herod," Jesse admitted. "Matthew lifted the incident from the life of Moses. Along with a couple of other things."

"I'm sure that's how Jewish converts would have seen it …" But Drew had a feeling there was more to it.

"I don't think Matthew was writing for anyone else, Drew. Anyway, it must be after one, and I'm exhausted."

He watched her chin tip up as she gazed at the ceiling.

"I still can't believe what happened." She fixed her eyes on him. "We were *shot* at. *You* shot at somebody. And then took us on a roller coaster ride—only without tracks. We could have wiped out at any time."

"Since Stephen was murdered … nothing seems so strange anymore." He turned toward her so that his left hip brushed the edge of the altar. "I'm sorry I got you into this."

She smiled. "I'm not."

He put his hand out as though asking for a dance. She took it. Tugging her gently toward him, he bent down and kissed her. She opened her mouth to his and slid a hand up to his shoulder. He felt her fingers spread on the back of his neck. Something electric rose from his toes, made his ribs tingle, and short-circuited his balance. Letting go of her hand, he slipped both arms around her to steady himself. Pressed up against her, he felt her stiffened nipples through their shirts.

The way his heart was hammering against his chest, he was surprised it didn't echo. Slipping a hand between their bodies, he cupped one of her breasts and traced a circle over the nipple with his thumb. She moaned and he broke off the kiss. He was in too much of a hurry for buttons and pulled the vest over her head. He tried to do the same with her shirt, but she laughed—"Wait, wait."

While she unfastened the sleeves, he yanked his shirt off and let it drop to the floor.

Her shirt fell on top of it.

They kissed again, her tongue exploring his mouth.

He had held this woman in a secluded place inside him for years, and now, with her bare skin against his own, he was afraid he was going to pass out. His fingers found the clasp to her bra and unhooked it.

She put her arms out and let it tumble to her feet.

"Why do you smell so good?" she whispered. "And why did this take so long?"

A thumb followed the back of her jaw and tucked itself behind an ear. "Um ... because the Lord works in mysterious ways?"

She laughed and slapped his chest. "And I thought the night couldn't get any weirder." He reached under her skirt with both hands, tucked his fingers inside the elastic band of her panties, and tugged until she could step out of both.

He ran a hand up the inside of a thigh and sank a finger with a soft kissing sound. She sucked in a breath so sharply he thought he had hurt her. At first she worked her hips against his hand, but then her fingers began digging at his belt.

Stripping off his pants and underwear, she grabbed him by the waist and leaned back against the altar, pulling him with her.

He bent at his knees and lowered himself as she reached down with a hand to guide him.

The sound that came from her was like a timber cracking. Her nails sank into his arms, and he froze, paralyzed by how good it felt. In that moment, he would have given her anything she asked for—a wedding ring, Serafis's five million dollars, both scrolls.

"Oh, *God* ..."

He didn't even know which one of them had said it. Lifting her legs, he pushed all the way inside her; she gasped and clawed his shoulders. As demanding as the position was, they worked frantically against each other until Jesse finally shoved him away and spread their clothes on the stone floor. Maneuvering herself under him, she locked her legs around his waist.

It might have lasted an hour, it might have gone on longer, but when it ended, their skin shone with sweat, and she was on top, a shirt cushioning one knee, socks padding the other. Only then, with Jesse still breathing hard and trembling against him, did he give any real consideration to the promises he'd made to Yasemin.

7:14

THE CHRISTOS MOSAIC

DREW WOKE UP IN HIS UNDERWEAR, his pants folded into an unleavened pillow. The smell of damp stone was familiar, comforting—the Earth's body odor. A leisurely dripping sound came from somewhere behind him. Outside, a few birds made lively chatter while insects chirped and whirred.

The feeble light seeping through the windows and openings in the grotto's façade had traveled more than ninety million miles to be with him—and Jesse—in this sanctified cavern. But sky, stars, God's projected affection (did it dispense with distance as effortlessly?) were often distractions. Next *to us*, Thoreau had insisted, *the grandest of laws are continually being executed*. Next *to us is not the workman we have hired, but the workman whose work we are.*

Next to him, Jesse was still asleep, a hand resting on his flank. She was in her panties and the ivory blouse but no bra. All they needed now was for the guy who collected money from eager tourists to find them.

He raised himself up on a single palm. "Shit." The right side of his body was numb from pressing against the stone floor, and his biceps were sore as hell where he'd caught that kid under the chin. Holding up his arm, he saw a dark blotch.

He glanced at his watch. Six-thirty. And Zafer had no idea where he was.

His gaze dropped back down to Jesse's face. The perky upper lip. The cinnamon freckles. The nose ... not small or dainty but as sculpted as a cat's. The dark eyebrows like slashes from a painter's brush. The angular jaw and the nearly invisible cleft in her chin.

What the hell was he going to do when they got to Istanbul?

Gently, he took her hand off his side and sat up. Pulling on his pants, he tried stretching some of the ache out of his muscles. The grotto felt like a tomb.

They had fallen asleep in front of the altar, on an apron paved with rectangular stones. The rest of the floor was pretty chewed up. Here and there were fragments of a mosaic that had once been mostly white but was now a dusty gray. Buttoning his shirt, he walked barefoot to one of the larger fragments. He looked down. In that underground dusk, he made out the remnants of a simple geometric design, nothing like the stunningly rendered scenes of Classical life—gods, goddesses, shepherds, athletes—preserved in Antakya's museum, but he finally understood. He was standing on the answer. He started to laugh. "That's it! That *has* to be it! I'm so *stupid*."

"Drew?" Jesse's eyes were only half open.

He smiled at her, probably a little maniacally. "There wasn't *one* Messiah. The Christos is a *mosaic!*"

She sat up. "What are you talking about?"

"Stephen was *wrong*! I thought I was looking for a single savior, one man on whom the Christ of the Gospels was based, but Christ wasn't based on James or John the Baptist—he's *both* of them. He's a Mystery cult figure. He's Judas of Galilee. He's *all* of them."

"Judas of Galilee?" She used four straightened fingers like a pick on her tangled hair. "What are you talking about?"

"Yesterday you asked me about the crucifixion, where it came from. The sign over Jesus' head—*The King of the Jews*—shows up in all four Gospels. But that sign wasn't over Jesus' head, it was over Judas of Galilee's."

"You're not making any sense." She was tugging the floral-patterned skirt over her hips and her breasts jiggled under the shimmer of her blouse.

"Look, Judas of Galilee began a revolt in 4 BC, right after the death of Herod.

Jesse turned her back to him to take off her blouse and slip into her bra.

He forgot his excitement just long enough to be disappointed that she wasn't comfortable getting dressed in front of him. "He's from Galilee, but not *anywhere* in Galilee, he's from Sepphoris—a stone's throw from where Nazareth was later founded. In fact, when the revolt began, Judas and his followers broke into the palace in Sepphoris to steal weapons from the armory, right? In Luke, Jesus tells his followers to arm themselves. '*He who has no sword, let him sell his garments and buy one.*' This totally contradicts Jesus' ministry, his command to bless your enemy. It's more likely Luke alluding to a piece of the mosaic."

Jesse buttoned up her blouse. "You're not the first to point that out."

"Before he died, Stephen gave me some words to track down. One of them was *Iscariot*. That's all he gave me, Judas's last name. Why? What does *Iscariot* mean?"

"No one knows for certain. It might just ... designate his village."

"Cut it out, Jess. It's derived from *Sicarii*. And we know from Josephus that Judas of Galilee founded the original Sicarii."

"Okay, Drew. If Judas Iscariot is an allusion to Judas of Galilee, and Christ is in some ways *modeled* on Judas of Galilee, why does Judas betray Jesus?"

"The Jews expected someone to save them from the Romans, right? But Judas of Galilee came up short. Then the revolt of 66 AD tanked, and the Temple was destroyed. Mark was writing *after* the sack of Jerusalem, so he knew if Christ was going to be the Savior, he had to be a *spiritual* savior, not a kingly messiah. Judas Iscariot's betrayal and death were a way of rejecting armed revolt as the way to defeat Rome."

Jesse shook her head. "Sounds like literary analysis, not historical scholarship."

"Think about it," Drew urged. "The Gospels quietly acknowledge Judas of Galilee's challenge to Roman rule by naming one of the apostles after him—he's a piece of the mosaic. I mean, there's no question that Jesus sometimes has the tendencies of a Zealot. But in the end, the swords stay in their scabbards, and Judas is cast as a betrayer."

Jesse frowned dismissively. "You'll need something a lot more solid."

"How's this—Acts 5:37?" He'd reread the whole book a few days ago. "*This man, Judas of Galilee rose up in the days of the census ...*" Drew closed his eyes, trying to envision the passage. "*He ... attracted numerous followers,* or something, *but he and all those who fought with him perished.*"

"Yeah, okay…?"

"Then it says something like *And now I say to you, keep away from Zealots for …* I don't remember the exact words—"

"*If this work is of men, it will come to nothing, but if it is of God it cannot be overthrown,*" Jess finished for him. "Gamaliel's counsel."

"You see? Clear rejection of a military solution—with Judas the Galilean as the poster boy. And there's one other thing the Gospel authors took from Judas of Galilee."

"What's that?"

"His death."

"Judas wasn't—" Jesse stopped herself. "Acts says he was killed but not how. And Josephus never says what happened to him. At all."

"Not in the copies we have of Josephus."

Jesse adjusted a shoe strap. "Are you saying he was crucified, and a sign, *King of the Jews*, was put over his cross? That Josephus wrote about it, and the passage was deleted?"

"The passage Josephus wrote attributing the fall of Jerusalem to James the Just rather than Jesus—which Saint Origin, Eusebius of Caesarea, and Saint Jerome *all saw*—was deleted. We know that. And don't forget what Josephus said about the revolt of Judas of Galilee … the chaos and strife it caused in Palestine was all in *order to raise himself out of an ambitious desire of the royal dignity*. I underlined that yesterday. More importantly, both of his sons, James and Simon *were* crucified, around 48 AD. And Menachem, a grandson, led Zealots in the rebellion of 66. Menachem put on a crown, the royal purple and, as Josephus says, entered Jerusalem *in the state of a king*. The entire family aspired to dynasty."

"That still doesn't mean he was crucified as king of the Jews."

"Maybe it's not definitive proof, but the Romans didn't crucify criminals. Sedition was a *political* charge. We both know the Greek word *lestai* in this context doesn't mean *criminal*. Jesus wasn't crucified between two *criminals*, they were *Zealots*. How much you wanna bet the three of them on their crosses in the Gospels represent Judas and his two sons?"

Jesse folded her arms over her chest. "I can't even tell you how unscholarly this is."

"Is there any scholarly proof for a charge of sedition?"

Jesse exhaled with obvious exasperation. "Jesus admits to considering himself king of the Jews—"

"It's tacked on at the very end, Jess. You never hear about that during Jesus' ministry. And the Sanhedrin accused him of blasphemy—the same trumped-up accusation they leveled against James. And like James, if there was a real Jesus, he was probably stoned."

"So there *was* no Crucifixion?"

Drew raked his fingers through his hair. "A dozen scholars have pointed out that it makes no sense for the Jews to be screaming blasphemy at Jesus' trial while the Romans accuse him of sedition. He was either tried before the Jewish Sanhedrin or Pilate—not both. And if Pilate actually said, 'I find no fault in this man,' he would have let him go. The sedition charge, Jesus' last-minute admission that he's a king—even though he acknowledges Rome's authority when he shouts '*Render unto Caesar what is Caesar's*—was a Gospel invention to create the drama of the Crucifixion."

Jesse's face was full of morning light—the light of Antakya, of ancient Antioch, strained through a stone façade built by the crusading knights moonlighting as masons. Her back to the dark stone of the grotto, she seemed to be waiting for him to say something else.

"Mark was trying to give the Jews their own dying-and-rising god, just as Philo of Alexandria tried to interpret the Old Testament according to the Mystery cults—and the cross fits in perfectly. All the Mysteries god-men are associated with trees, and some of them actually *were* crucified. The cross, or the *stake* if we translate literally from the Gospels, is Jesus' tree. Doesn't Peter's epistle say Jesus was hung from a tree? So does Paul. And Peter says it in Acts. Christianity was a Jewish version of the Mysteries. The Romans had to be pulled into Jesus' death because crucifixion was forbidden among the Jews."

Jesse shook her head. "A few coincidental dates, a few unexplained facts—"

"I have a few more unscholarly tidbits for you: Jesus had four brothers, right? Three of them were named Judas, James, and Simon, which just happen to be the names of Judas of Galilee and his two sons."

"They were common enough names, Drew."

"I'm not done yet. The Jesus of the Gospels is a fictitious figure with two basic layers—one Jewish, one Greek. In the Jewish stratum, there are at least three models: John the Baptist, James the Just, and Judas of Galilee."

"So, a couple hundred years of biblical scholarship and you're the only one to notice these connections? Or the only one who doesn't realize how absurdly tenuous they are?"

Drew hesitated. He heard water dripping at the back of the grotto. He recalled the thousand-fathom strangeness of those deep-sea fish with ugly, oversized mouths and skewed saucer eyes—and saw them as analogous to the alien aspects of beliefs centuries distant.

"Most scholars have assumed they were reading *history*, not a carefully constructed fiction. Even scholars tend to believe what they want to believe, and that usually corresponds to how they've been conditioned by their upbringing and training. We see what we've been conditioned to see."

Jesse smirked. "Well, you've been re-conditioned, and now you're finding what you expect to find."

"Look, I still believe in God. I just don't … know how to relate to God anymore."

"From what I've heard, you don't know how to relate to Christianity anymore, either."

"All right, so maybe you can help me. Let's take the Apostles … there's a John and a James—both sons of Zebedee—a Judas, and Simon the Zealot. These are precisely the names of the men whose lives became the basis for the Jesus of the Gospels. Three of the four also happen to be the names of Jesus' brothers. What do you make of that?"

Jesse backed herself against the altar, and, bracing herself with the heels of her hands, lifted herself onto it, letting her legs dangle over the side. "Drew, I can barely stand to listen to this nonsense, but tell me: why isn't there a brother named John? And besides James the son of Zebedee, there is a second disciple named James—the son of Alphaeus. Why are there two?"

"John's pretty close—he's Jesus' cousin."

"Only in Luke."

"Maybe. But the Bible gives us more information about John the Baptist than it does about James the Just—and forget about the other brothers. They're just ciphers. Don't you see the reversal? John's mother is old and used up, while Jesus' mother is an immaculate young virgin—she symbolizes a new start. Jesus' ministry began *precisely* where John's left off. The torch was being passed. Not only that, John's birthday is celebrated June 24th—the summer solstice. After which the days become progressively shorter. When is Jesus said to have been born? December 25—the *winter* solstice on the Julian Calendar. After which the days become progressively *longer*. *'He must grow greater, while I must become less'*. It's all *symbolic*. The Gospel writers knew exactly what they were doing."

Jesse shook her head. "The relationship between John and Jesus is allegorized somewhat, true, but that's because the Gospel writers wanted to lure Mandaeans and other sects loyal to John over to Christianity. Otherwise this is really just a lot of colorful theorizing."

Drew glanced down at the floor with its patch of dirty, white mosaic. "You don't think there's *some*thing in this, Jess? The Jews on whom Christ was modeled are *all* included in Jesus' family—John as a cousin, the rest as brothers. And they're all included again as apostles."

"Highly unlikely. And what about the second James?"

"Zebedee is derived from the Hebrew. But the other James was the son of Alphaeus—clearly Greek. There you have the dual heritage of the Jesus of the Gospels: half Jewish, half Greek."

Jesse rolled her eyes.

"Remember the first two Apostles who were called ... actually *called*?

"Simon and Andrew." Jesse frowned. "Simon is a Jewish name, but Andreas—"

"Greek," Drew finished. "Look at Acts of the Apostles ... James the son of Alphaeus is never mentioned anywhere. He simply disappears. In chapter 12 of Acts, James Zebedee is executed by Herod Agrippa. Oddly, Herod merely arrests Peter. Why doesn't he kill him, too? Because it's a killing of convenience—there was no actual James Zebedee, no historical son of Alphaeus. To make that clear, James Zebedee is killed right at the beginning of Chapter 12—the same chapter in which the *real* James makes his first appearance. The stand-in is no longer required."

"You really believe James the Just was the model for Jesus?"

Drew shook his head. "*A* model. A mosaic is the only way to explain all the contradictions of the portrait of Jesus in the Gospels. I mean, one minute he talks like a Zealot— *'Do not think that I came to bring peace on Earth. I did not come to bring peace but a sword.'* —the next he says, '*Put*

your sword in its place, for all who take the sword will perish by the sword.'
One minute he's full of the apocalyptic rhetoric of John the Baptist,
saying, '*I came to send fire on the Earth, and how I wish it were already
kindled*'. The next he giving us long-winded advice on how to be kind
to sinners. In other words, he's *not* saying forsake this world because it's
already doomed, he's telling us how to make it better, as if it *won't* be
destroyed and we should make the best of it. In Mark he cites Moses:
'*Honor your father and your mother. He who curses father or mother, let him
be put to death*'. But then in Matthew he says *He who loves father or mother
more than me is not worthy of me*'." Drew shrugged. "I don't have to tell
you this is just a handful of contradictory messages."

"These inconsistencies are already well known, Drew. And have been
explained by actual scholars."

"Yes, but every scholar—actual scholar—who wrote about Jesus
picked *one* aspect and tried to make that cover the whole of the Jesus
presented in the Gospels. Someone argues for Jesus as a kind of Jewish
sage influenced by the Greek Cynics. Someone else insists Jesus was an
itinerant Essene. Another scholar sees Jesus as a magician and healer,
based on Greek miracle-workers like Pythagoras and Asklepius. Still
another says Jesus was a Zealot who was remade by the Gospel authors
into a pacifist. But they all see a historical Jesus at the core. *That's* the
mistake. No single theory explains all of the contradictory elements.
Jesus is all of them."

"Great. Just one thing." Jesse raised a sarcastic eyebrow. "Jesus had a
fourth brother, Joses. To whom exactly does he correspond?"

"I'm still working on that. But I have a feeling that Joses is somehow
related to Matthew's flight to Egypt. He might be the last piece of the
mosaic."

"I don't think so, Drew. You've come up with one or two interesting ...
details, but the rest is wild speculation. Some revisions of our portrait of
Christ are probably in order, but there's no call for the radical assumption
he never walked the Earth."

"I don't think we're going to settle that right now. So how about we
get out of here?"

"The way we came in?" She slid off the altar.

Drew grabbed the satchel and gestured toward the back of the cave.
"Would you, uh, do the honors?"

She led the way to the rough chamber they had entered last night and disappeared head-first into the stony throat.

Going back wasn't nearly as difficult for Drew. There was more light, and, having done it once, he was more confident. They emerged into daylight as though they'd just been born. A warm breeze fluttered Jesse's skirt and lifted Drew's hair off his shoulders.

Jesse shielded her eyes with a hand. "Wow. The view is even better during the day."

"Hey … over this way. I want to show you something."

A huge face, its features nearly obliterated by the elements, had been carved into an outcropping of rock. Sphinx-like, it loomed twenty-five or so feet over them although it was only a kind of relief, not a statue, and only from about the chest up. The head was wrapped in a hood or maybe a wimple. Streaks of dark gray running through the ashen-colored stone gave the face a melancholy cast, as though it had been stained by centuries of tears. On one shoulder stood the comparatively tiny figure of a robed man, his outlines all but effaced.

"It's beautiful, Drew. I had no idea Mother Mary was carved into a hillside in Antakya. Why didn't I ever read about this?"

"You just proved my point, Jess."

"What point?"

"The early Christians thought this was Mary too. But this was sculpted around 200 BC. It's not even a woman. It's Charon. Ferrying a soul across the Styx to Hades—the small man on his shoulder." He could tell Jesse didn't appreciate his smirk, but he couldn't help it. "You saw what you were conditioned to see."

7: 15

THREE MORE

H E KNOCKED ON THE DOOR of the hotel room and, to make sure he didn't get a palm-heel to the face or a Glock under his chin, shouted, "It's Drew."

Kadir opened the door. "What happened about you? Why you didn't call?"

"Battery's dead. I'm lucky I'm not dead, too. They tried to kill us last night."

"*Oyle mi?*" Zafer's eyebrow's went up. He was wearing a button-up shirt with short sleeves and an empty shoulder holster. "Fill me in."

After Drew recounted the meeting with Nathan, his failed ruse to get Jesse out of the hotel unseen, the motorcycle chase, and their overnight stay in the grotto church, Zafer shook his head. "If they had wanted you dead, they wouldn't have tried a drive-by."

"What was the point then?"

"Scare us into selling the scroll to Serafis."

"Which reminds me. You didn't call him yet, did you?"

"Not yet."

"Good. Go up to five million. Jesse found something *very* damaging to the Church."

Zafer snickered. His arm shot out unexpectedly, and he hit Drew's shoulder with a meaty palm. "Not a bad night's work. You saw some action and probably got us another half million dollars. One thing bothers me—Nathan. He shows up everywhere the Sicarii do."

Drew shrugged. "They're after the same scroll. Which reminds me …" He took out the yellow envelope. "He gave me this."

"Nathan gave you that? *Lanet olsun!*" *Damn!* Zafer snatched it out of Drew's hand and ripped it open. Photographs clipped to sheets of paper fell out. Zafer scrutinized the envelope as if he expected to find something written in invisible ink. He went through the photographs and papers one by one. "He's *kurnaz*, that one." *Cunning.* "I thought he might have bugged the envelope, but he's too smart for that. He'd have planted it on you while you were wrestling. Strip down."

The three of them went over every thread of Drew's clothes, but turned up nothing. "I still don't trust him," Zafer said.

Drew was relieved. "I thought you were going to kill me after I didn't make it back last night."

"We are not wanting to be at your funeral," Kadir grinned, "but if it is necessary, we will buy for you a very wonderful tomb with the money from Serafis."

"Yeah, thanks."

Zafer's eyebrows lowered and his forehead furrowed. "How the hell did you fall asleep on the stone floor of a church?"

Drew didn't answer.

"In the church?" Zafer laughed. "You better leave that little episode out next time you talk to Yasemin." He glanced down at one of the photographs in his hand. "Three more Sicarii."

Drew skimmed the briefs. *Jan Miskovicz, Polish national, age 59. Height: 5' 11" Weight: 175 lbs. Oxford educated, professor of Christianity and Judaism, retired from teaching. Now works for Ecole Biblique as a researcher and contributing editor of* Revue Biblique. *Three years of military service in Poland, ages 18 to 21.*

Round glasses, eyebrows pointed like gothic windows, curly hair that had once been blond but was now turning wispy and white, Jan had taken on something of the Einstein look.

Gary Strahan, American national, age 34. Height 6' 2". Weight: 225. Ten years with the FBI. Now heading security details for the Vatican.

Crew-cut black hair, a bull neck like Zafer's, dark green eyes, a broad face. He looked like a rugby player.

Kurt Hohenzollern, German national, age 36. Height: 5' 10". Weight: 185 lbs. Employed by the Vatican, specializes in Hebrew, Aramaic, and Syriac paleography. Eight years in the German army before attending university. Sniper training.

His dark hair was practically shaved on the sides but long enough on top to comb—a style more common during World War I. Hohenzollern had the drawn cheeks of someone who never got enough to eat, sharp cheekbones, a mouth like a slot.

"Quite a crew they got. One former intelligence agent, one former FBI agent, one from the Foreign Legion, three with significant military training." Zafer looked up. "And all I got for back-up is you two."

"I think I could take out the Pole." Drew tapped his photo. "But Strahan looks like he could chew through barbed wire. And the German, wouldn't surprise me if he keeps a razor in his shoe."

"Razors and knives I don't mind," Zafer said. "I've got my own. But I don't want to be a headshot for a sniper. Of all the ways there are to die, I'd hate to be killed from a distance. No honor."

Drew glanced at the photographs. "So what's the plan?"

"We call Serafis and arrange to sell him the scroll in Istanbul. Then we pick up the car and start driving. Airport's too risky. It'll take us a day to get home."

Drew nodded. "What about Jesse?"

"I'm sure the police have traced that shot-up Fiat to her. They've probably figured out where she checked in yesterday, too. If I were her, I'd leave town without my toiletries and clean panties."

"So she can come with us?"

"Why not?"

After breakfast in the hotel dining room, Kadir called Serafis from a public phone. It took about ten minutes of haggling before Serafis finally agreed to a round sum of five million dollars. Serafis would meet them in Istanbul in two days.

Zafer leaned over to pat Kadir on the back. "*Aferin.*" *Well done.*

He turned to Drew. "You charge your phone, Double-oh-seven?"

"Yeah."

"Well don't use it to call Jesse. Use the hotel phone and tell her we'll pick her up in about fifteen minutes."

After Zafer had squared up their bill, and the three of them had left behind the lobby with its Dickensian furniture and red marble tiles,

Zafer disappeared. He came back behind the wheel of a black Audi.

"Where's the green one?"

"Right where we left it. I have someone taking care of it."

"Where did you get this?"

Zafer glanced at Kadir. "This isn't our first trip to Antakya. And Serafis isn't the only black market dealer we know. Let's go."

Jesse's hotel was on Ataturk Avenue, which was the show-off street in Antakya. Lined with shops and expensive hotels, it was divided by an island that supported a long row of small palm trees. The contrast with Istiklal Avenue—running more or less parallel on the other side of the Asi River—was startling.

Jesse was in the hotel lounge still wearing the skirt that looked like a field of ironed-flat flowers and the ivory blouse. She had left off the headscarf and the vest. She stood up and bandoliered herself with the laptop. The strap sank a furrow diagonally across her breasts. She looked like an educated peasant—like she could plant two bare feet in the grass, wrestle him to a draw, then kick his ass at Jeopardy. That was about as sexy as it got as far as Drew was concerned.

He bent to kiss her and was relieved she didn't pull away. Her breath was cool with the fading mint of toothpaste. He tipped his head toward the door. "Let's go."

A uniformed hotel employee held the glass door open for them.

Jesse slid into the back seat of the Audi.

Kadir and Zafer, both in the front, greeted her with grins and polite hellos. Kadir's seat was pulled all the way up to give Drew some legroom.

Pulling out onto Ataturk Avenue, Zafer glanced at Jesse in the rear-view mirror.

"Thanks for letting me come with you. I feel a lot safer."

Safer with us? Drew wanted to ask. *Might as well climb an aluminum pole during a thunderstorm.*

At a circle crowned with a statue rising out of a fountain, Drew looked in the direction of the grotto church, a gouge in the stone face of a hillside, a hard nest for faith where prayer had once seeped through the rock and wept down the rough walls. He couldn't get his mind off the missing stones in the Christ mosaic.

7: 16

ISKENDERUN

ZAFER WOVE THROUGH TRAFFIC, constantly checking the rear-view mirror.

How the fuck is anyone going to keep pace with you? Drew thought. Zafer rarely let the speedometer's needle fall below 110 kilometers an hour.

The coast road took them west, past Iskenderun and its enormous port. Once known as Alexandretta, the city had had a cameo in an Indiana Jones movie. Dug into the slope of a small mountain facing the Mediterranean, it must have been a lovely seaside town when Roman ships were docking in its harbor, but there wasn't much to see now. The port itself was a tangle of towering derricks and loading cranes like mythical beasts with impossibly long, steel necks; the Old World charm of sails, ropes, and sea-weathered wood was long gone.

"This is where Serafis makes pick-ups," Drew muttered.

"It turns my stomach to think of the scroll going to him," Jesse said.

Drew had to stop himself from clamping a hand over Jesse's mouth.

Zafer looked in the rearview mirror and grinned. "I'm workin' on it."

Dark clouds had drifted over the low mountains on their right. A flash of lightning backlit blunt peaks. A few seconds later, there was the distant rumble of thunder.

"But you're going ahead with the sale?"

Back off Jess. Drew glanced over a shoulder, but the port was already lost to view. What had Serafis said? *Out of the port in Alexandria, into the port in Iskenderun.*

Zafer kept grinning. "Oh we're selling it all right—before one of us gets killed."

Big drops of rain spattered against the windshield so hard Drew flinched. Scattered at first, the rhythm became increasingly frantic, as though the rain were desperate to get in the car. Water washed down the windshield in sheets turning other cars into blobs of color. They turned into cars again when the wipers swept past. Zafer eased up on the gas, and the speedometer's needle dropped to eight-five.

"Alexandria!" Drew shouted loudly enough to make Jesse jump. He looked at her with a hysterical grin on his face. "*I have called my son out of Egypt!*"

"What—?"

"Zafer, stop the car!"

"What the hell for?"

Zafer, his eyes locked on Drew in the rear view mirror, frowned. But he slowed the car.

Lightning x-rayed the road and a boom of thunder vibrated the car's glass.

Drew leaned forward between the seats. "Just pull over."

"Drew, are you all right?"

Zafer crossed lanes and guided the car onto the shoulder.

"Open the trunk. Be back in a minute." Rain drummed on the roof, drowning out the radio as Drew hopped out of the car. The warm downpour doused him before he had a chance to use the trunk as an awning. Digging through a pocket of the bag in which he kept his clothes, his upper body was sheltered, but his lower legs and feet were taking a shower. He pulled out a sheaf of papers, slammed the trunk closed, and jumped back in the car.

Drops of water tickled his scalp, and one slid down his face. He shook the pages at Jesse. "*This* is the missing piece."

7: 17

JESUS PANTHERA

ZAFER TURNED OFF the air conditioner and hit the defroster; the moisture coming off Drew had started to fog the windshield. "What is that?"

"The Talmud. Quotes anyway." Drew picked through the pages he'd downloaded from the web. The paper was spotted where rain had scored hits, making rough circles of print on the other side visible.

"The Talmud?" Zafer cocked an eyebrow.

"*Please.*" Jesse's voice was pure irritation. "You don't mean that anti-Christian propaganda about Jesus Panthera?"

"Hold on a minute, Jesse. Remember what I said this morning? That the original charge against Jesus must have been blasphemy? That he was stoned to death like James? The flight to Egypt in Matthew makes no sense if taken literally—people in Matthew's day would have known that there had been no slaughter of innocents. Matthew had to be alluding to something else."

"Yes, I told you—Moses. Jesus was a second Moses for Matthew."

"Right, I got that." Drew shuffled through the damp pages. "What if there *was* a flight to Egypt ... just no Holy Family?"

Jesse tilted her head back and raised her hands, exasperated. "What are you talking about?"

Drew pushed wet hair off his forehead. "King Jannai, the Maccabean who ruled Palestine from ... let's see ... 104 to 78 BC. The Pharisees accepted his claim to the throne, but they were outraged that the Maccabeans had usurped the office of High Priest, which should have gone to a Zadokite."

"Right …" Jesse said cautiously.

Kadir and Zafer had given up following what was going on in the back seat and were speaking quietly in Turkish.

"The Pharisees rebelled around 94 BC, but six years later, Jannai won, decisively. He crucified eight hundred Pharisees and forced them to watch as soldiers slashed the throats of their wives and children. Another eight thousand fled Judea—including Jesus ben Perachiah, the most respected Pharisee at that time." Drew flipped over a water-stained page. "He wound up in Alexandria."

Jesse nodded. "So far, so good."

"When Perachiah escaped to Alexandria, his favorite pupil, Jesus ben Panthera, went with him. There's your flight to Egypt—to escape the wrath of Jannai, not Herod."

"That's just not true," Jesse protested.

"According to the Talmud, Panthera learned magic in Egypt, became a religious teacher, and attracted five disciples."

"Exactly," Jesse said, "this is where legend kicks in."

"Jesus had his twelve apostles, but how many does Jesus actually *call?*"

"Drew …" Jesse shook her head. "I'm getting tired of this."

"Five. It's right there in Mark. He called *five*. The rest show up later."

"*Fine,*" she snorted. "A numerical coincidence."

"So … Panthera had his five. Eventually he was accused of sorcery and executed on the Eve of Passover. Christian scholars like to say the Talmud is simply disparaging Christ, but if this is a parody of Jesus, why not give him the recognizable twelve apostles? Why not line up the other details—crucified in the days of Caesar Tiberius, by order of Pontius Pilate, and all the rest? Why locate this all nearly a century earlier? Parody doesn't work if you don't recognize what's being mocked."

Jesse sighed. "Here it comes …"

"Because the Talmud authors were genuinely trying to identify a crucified Jesus in history—the best they could do was Panthera. We both *know* there weren't twelve apostles. The Gospel writers chose twelve to line up with the twelve tribes of Israel, the twelve signs of the zodiac, and I don't know what else. Most of them are barely even mentioned in the Gospels. The Gospels don't even agree on their names."

"Yes, but—"

"What if the so-called magic was simply the practices of the Egyptian Essenes, the Therapeutae, living on the shore of Lake Mariout? Which is right next to Alexandria, where Panthera and Perachiah exiled themselves? The Therapeutae were Essenes who had elements of the Pythagorean Mysteries mixed in with their beliefs. What if it wasn't sorcery that got Panthera into trouble but following the practices of the Therapeutae?"

Jesse was about to say something acidic—he could see it—but he raised a hand. "Hold on. After Jesus was born and the Wise Men showed up, Matthew says Herod commanded the slaughter of innocents, hoping to kill the Messiah-to-be. The episode serves two purposes. First, it alludes to the executions under King Jannai, which included children. And let's not forget, Pharisee initiates were called *innocents* or *infants*. This would be recognizable to Greek converts as a stock episode in the life of the divine child—Hera sent snakes to kill Herakles in his crib, the child Dionysus was attacked by the Titans, Attis's grandfather commanded the baby to be left in the wilderness to die of exposure."

"And *Moses*," Jesse added. "Pharoah tried to kill Moses when he was an infant."

"Sure," Drew conceded, "that would make Jewish converts happy."

A sudden gust of wind drove rain into the passenger side of the car; it sounded like someone had tossed a handful of raw rice at the window.

Jesse glared at him, probably wrestling with the desire to head-butt him.

"Like Christ, Panthera was killed on the Eve of Passover. The accounts of his death differ, from being hung on a tree or a stake to being stoned, or being stoned and then hung out as a warning, which is exactly what is prescribed for blasphemy. Paul, who was writing *before* the Gospels were composed, clearly implies in Galatians that Jesus was *hanged on a tree*."

"And how exactly do you fit Jesus' fourth brother into all this?" Jesse asked.

"The missing part of the mosaic is Jesus Panthera, but you can't have a brother with the same name. Joses is about as close to Jesus as you can get."

"It's a variation on *Joseph*," Jesse snapped.

"Right, but it's *not* Joseph. It's shortened. Jesus Panthera is the earliest Jewish model for Jesus of Nazareth. Symbolically at least, he's Jesus' father—Joseph. And isn't it curious that in Jesus' genealogy Luke includes Jannai a little earlier than the time when there *was* a King Jannai? Saint Epiphanius actually inserts Panthera into Jesus' genealogy as Christ's grandfather, which would have been about the time there *was* a King Jannai."

Jesse looked as though she might slap him. "So why did the Gospel writers fix the death of Jesus under the rule of Pontius Pilate?"

"For the drama of the Crucifixion. And the Romans didn't arrive until 63 BC. Panthera was already dead by then," he answered. "Since the Gospels were written after the Jewish revolt, after the sack of Jerusalem, and after Roman records had been burned, there was no way of knowing who had been crucified under Pilate."

"It's all just a little too neat, don't you think?"

"But it makes sense. The death of the original Jesus was shameful. Being hanged was a curse. That's right out of *Deuteronomy*."

"For once we agree."

"The earliest model for Jesus of Nazareth died an embarrassing death, and the whole drama of the Crucifixion covers it up. Isn't it clear? For *centuries*, scholars have tried to explain the Gospels' absurd portrayal of Pontius Pilate, one of the most ruthless rulers in history, as a compassionate man."

"The Gospel authors did that for incredibly obvious reasons, Drew. Palestine was still under Roman rule. They had to avoid antagonizing the Romans."

"Except that there was no need to exonerate Pilate," Drew said. "The Jews had complained openly about Pilate for years—Philo of Alexandria was still complaining about him to Caligula even *after* Pilate had already been recalled to Rome in disgrace." Since their conversation in Cairo, Drew had discovered a few other things about Philo: his family had put up the money to sheath the Temple gates in gold and silver, and his nephew had actually been married to Herod Agrippa's daughter, Berenice, who puts in several appearances in Acts of the Apostles. And yet Philo never mentioned Jesus of Nazareth.

Jesse shook her head. "So Jesus wasn't crucified by the Romans, he was hanged by order of the Jewish Sanhedrin before the Romans had even taken Palestine?"

Drew shrugged. "It's not impossible. In Matthew, Pilate pardons a man named Barabbas. *Bar Abbas* is about the extent of my Aramaic, but I know it means *Son of the Father*. Matthew is telling us that Jesus the Son of God the Father was *not* crucified under Pilate. Not only that, but Jewish Christians would have *known* what *bar Abbas* means. Gentiles— the Greeks—wouldn't have noticed. And that's who the whole passion play of the Resurrection was for, the Greek converts who were used to the dying-and-rising gods of the Mystery religions."

"Oh *please* ..." Jesse seemed unable to find words to match her disgust.

Drew was undeterred. "In Mark, we're told that Simon of Cyrene carried the cross for Jesus. *Simon* carried the burden. *Simon* was the one tortured, not Jesus."

"Simon of Cyrene was tortured?" Jesse asked.

"No, Simon of Cyrene is a stand-in for Simon bar Giora. Giora, Josephus says, entered Jerusalem in 69 AD as its *savior and preserver.*"

Jesse nodded. "And then he was dragged to Rome, paraded in a halter, flogged, and *beheaded—not* crucified. But even if he *had* been crucified, you can't possibly know Giora is the Simon being referred to. There are so many—"

"Simon of Cyrene's son was named Rufus, which also happens to be the name of the Roman captain who took Simon bar Giora captive."

Jesse sighed theatrically. "I was wrong when I said you should have gotten your PhD in comparative religion. You're exactly where you belong—fantasy."

Even though Zafer had switched the air-conditioning back on, Jesse looked like she was beginning to sweat.

"Except that my interpretation explains why there's no reference to a crucified Savior in the Dead Sea Scrolls, how Jesus the Nazarite became Jesus the Nazarene, why Philo never mentions Jesus although he has plenty to say about Pilate, why Paul never quotes Jesus, mentions his miracles, or any of the biographical stuff in the Gospels, why the only Jesus the Jews knew of died around 90 BC, and why the historical record doesn't show a trace of Jesus of Nazareth."

There was a sound like a gunshot, and the car fishtailed. Swearing in Turkish, Zafer fought to control the wheel.

7: 18

THREE-SIXTY

INSTINCTIVELY, DREW GRABBED the headrest of the front seat with his right hand. As Jesse's hand clamped onto his wrist, Zafer cut the wheel hard in the opposite direction. If it hadn't been raining, he might have righted the car, but they were already sliding into the middle lane. A horn blared, and the car beside them suddenly filled Drew's window. The Audi whipped around again, this time in the opposite direction.

Although they had managed to miss the car beside them, they were now staring into the headlights of oncoming traffic. Drew prayed the car had enough momentum to keep going.

It turned nearly a complete 360, but not quite, skidding forward at a lopsided angle, half in the right lane and half in the center. Another horn was distressingly loud. Zafer cut the wheel again, shifted gears, and accelerated. With a jerk that snapped Drew's head back, the car straightened out, and the pressure on Drew's wrist eased.

They'd avoided an accident, but there was still something wrong with the car's back end; it felt like the right rear wheel was thumping over neatly spaced potholes.

"Blowout," Drew said.

He and Jesse looked at each other at exactly the same time. He had to fight the overwhelming urge to kiss her. She smiled—grateful, relieved—and let go of his wrist.

"Allah'a shukur," Kadir murmured, exhaling a held breath.

Zafer hit the hazard lights and pulled over to the shoulder. Yanking the parking brake into place, he cut the ignition. He looked over his shoulder at Drew. "C'mon. Let's have a look."

The rain had abated to a softly descending mist. Most of the traffic zipped past them at a blur, but cars in the right lane went past slowly enough for Drew to see the inquisitive looks from passengers and drivers.

Zafer squatted down beside the rear right tire. "Blowout all right."

So much rubber had shredded in one section that *hole* wasn't the right word. The steel belt looked like a ribbon of silvery bone exposed beneath thick black skin.

"You don't think someone shot it...?"

"Can't tell. But a bullet wouldn't make sense … we're *selling* the scroll. Unless there's something I'm missing." He jerked his chin toward the trunk. "You know how to change a flat, right? Get started. I'm going to keep an eye on the traffic." He swept his eyes over the rugged terrain on their right. "And on the hills."

"Kadir …" Drew mimed pressing a button with his finger. Kadir nodded and the trunk popped open. Drew was relieved to see there was a real spare, not a doughnut. While Drew unscrewed the tire lugs, Zafer paced back and forth, and Jesse and Kadir stood on the shoulder glancing around nervously.

No rusted bolts to deal with, Drew had them back on the road in fifteen minutes.

Zafer drove noticeably slower. The weather shifted again, and by the time they began to head west toward Adana, they had bright sunlight and dry asphalt.

Zafer picked up speed.

Less than an hour from Adana, they angled north or they might have passed through Tarsus, where the apostle Paul had been born. Educated in a school founded by the Cynics—Greek philosophers—he was as much a Greek Roman as he was a Jew. Tarsus was also the heart of Mithra's cult. Was it coincidence that, to Paul, the central fact of Jesus was not what he taught, but his resurrection? Jesus was a dying-and-rising god. The cities Paul preached in were all cult centers of similar gods: Antioch was famous for the Mysteries of Adonis, Ephesus for those of Attis, Corinth for Dionysus. Making Christ into the god of another Mystery cult fit in perfectly with Paul's tasks of converting Greeks. No one was more familiar with the Mysteries.

By afternoon they weren't far from the so-called fairy chimneys of Cappadocia. Paul had been there too. Oddly, despite all his years in Turkey, Drew hadn't.

In the evening, as they approached Ankara, Drew took the wheel.

Zafer didn't waste any time flirting with Jesse. He entertained her with jokes and by recounting quirks of Turkish history. At one point, Drew's and Zafer's eyes met in the mirror and Drew tried to convey how pissed off he was, while Zafer's expression said, *Hey, you've got an ex-wife waiting for you in Istanbul.*

Drew happily gave up the wheel after night had set in, and at around two in the morning, they were back in Istanbul.

"So …" Jesse asked, "what're we doing with me?"

"We're getting off in Sultanahmet," Drew said, "where I'm going to find you a hotel."

Zafer gave him an accusing look in the mirror before he shifted his gaze to Jesse. "I'm sure you'll be safe with Drew." A last skeptical glance in the rearview.

"Would you mind, though, letting me keep those photographs of the Habakkuk Scroll for a few days?"

"I'll bring you clean copies."

"Great."

"How about the Sarnich Hotel?" Drew asked Zafer.

"Shouldn't be a problem."

It was on a narrow cobblestone street not far from the Byzantine cistern after which it had been named.

"You know the drill," Zafer said to Drew. "Call first." He smiled at Jesse. "It's been a pleasure having you aboard our Antakya-to-Istanbul non-stop. We'll hope you'll choose us again."

"But in future time, don't bring with you the American." Kadir smirked like a goat.

Jesse laughed and leaned through windows to kiss their cheeks. Bag in hand, Drew watched the Audi disappear around a curve.

Jesse shook her head. "What a pair." The laptop, in its black case, was at her feet.

Drew nodded absently. "Look, I don't know how you feel about me staying …"

"I would've killed you if you had left me here and gone with them. You're spending the night with *me*."

"Oh." He couldn't believe it was so uncomplicated.

His cell phone rang.

Drew dropped his bag on the sidewalk and pulled out his phone. Yasemin. *Shit*. It *wasn't* going to be so uncomplicated.

7:19

SLOWNESS

"*YA, DREWJUH'UM* ... I couldn't sleep. Are you in Istanbul?"

Drew offered a silent prayer of thanks that Jesse didn't speak Turkish. "I just got here." As soon as he said it, he damned himself.

"Hadi, gel."

"Now?"

"Ya, I miss you. *Hadi, gel."*

"Yasemin ... I can't come over right now."

"Why? What are you doing that's so important?"

"Look, I can tell you everything tomorrow, okay? And I can probably stay tomorrow night."

"What's all this secrecy? What were you doing in Ankara? Why can't you tell me anything?"

"Look, I can't. But if it works out ..." He suddenly realized that he didn't want to make any promises. He was no longer sure he wanted a future with her. As much as they loved each other, they had never been able to live together. "If it works out, it'll be worth a lot more than my salary."

"For the month?"

"For the year."

"Drew." Alarm sharpened her tone. "You're not doing anything illegal, are you?"

Illegal but not, he reasoned, immoral. "No."

"You're lying, Drew. First, you quit your job. Then a trip to Ankara. Now you're doing business at two in the morning—"

"Yasemin, ya, *lütfen … please* can't this wait until tomorrow?"

"Wait? That's what you told me when you were in Anakara: wait. I'm tired of waiting. I waited our whole marriage for a child. I waited for you to be responsible—"

"Please, *please*, let's not do this now. I promise, we'll talk tomorrow."

"Fine. Good night."

He looked at the phone and shook his head.

"Who was that at two in the morning?"

Drew sighed. "My ex-wife."

"Some kind of emergency?"

"Something like that." He could see that she was waiting for more. "Look, Jesse, she and I have been talking about reconciling … but I don't think it'll work. I don't think the two of us are capable of going a whole week without a fight. And I can't live like that anymore. I just can't."

"But you still love her." It wasn't a question.

"Yeah … till the day they stick me in my grave. But love's not enough for a marriage. Not by itself."

Jesse folded her arms over her ivory blouse and switched her weight to one leg, making one hip suddenly higher than the other. "Okay, and, uh, where exactly do I fit in?" Her voice had begun to shake.

"I didn't have to tell you that was Yasemin on the phone. I didn't have to tell you I still love her. So you have to believe me when I tell you that there's a reason twelve years after university just seeing you again in Cairo rearranged my insides. I'm not playing games—"

She stepped close enough to him to put a hand on the back of his neck. "I understand … you have a history with her. You have nothing with me but a lot of ifs, maybes, and an infatuation leftover from college that might or might not turn out to be solid."

He smiled. "Lots of maybes." She scraped the back of his neck lightly with her fingernails, and tiny hairs stiffened.

"Fine. I'm used to fighting for what I want, and tonight I'm not letting anything come between us." Her fingers sent splinters of ice to melt somewhere under his scalp. "If you still want her after we've spent some time together …" She shrugged. "At least I'll know she didn't get you because I didn't show up to the match."

She pulled lightly on his neck. Night-cooled air replaced his blood when they kissed.

As much as he didn't want to, he pulled back. "This is Turkey." He smiled apologetically. "We can't do this in public."

Her upper lip curled back to expose her prominent front teeth—a smile girlishly innocent and mischievously womanish at the same time. "So let's get a room."

Drew took her hand.

The hotel had been modeled on the distinctive wooden Ottoman houses that had mostly either burned down or fallen into ruin around the city. The first floor housed a bar where even at this hour tourists holding drinks and conversations were silhouetted against yellow light.

The man behind the desk, in a suit and tie, spoke excellent English. The room he showed them was a tasteful blend of east and west—European furniture, Turkish rugs, and antiques.

Drew dropped his bag at the foot of the bed. "Looks a little more comfortable than the floor of a cave."

Jesse put a hand on the back of his neck, a thumb behind an ear, and pulled him into a long kiss. In Antakya everything had been rushed, as though they had expected to be interrupted at any moment. Tonight, they moved with deliberate slowness. Drew wasn't sure who had decided on these soft, underwater movements, but there wasn't any dissent.

Jesse, slippery with sweat, was still arching against him with teasing sluggishness when the room seemed to grow lighter. It might have been the nighttime glow of a city he was approaching from a distance or something luminous rising from ocean depths. It *couldn't* be dawn. It wasn't blinding, the room wasn't flooded with it, but the walls—the room itself—seemed to have dissolved in a soft smolder. If someone could make you see stars by hitting you hard enough, maybe someone else could sink you into a star by making you feel the right way.

They were both trembling after he shuddered against her a final time. Jesse grabbed one of the pillows and threw it off the bed.

"Why'd you do that?

"I don't want to be that far from you."

Drew could have cried. He and Yasemin had gotten into a fight about six months into their relationship because there was still only one pillow on his bed. *You're selfish*, she had accused, *you don't think about me*. He tried to explain that he'd thought it was more romantic to share a pillow, but she never forgave him.

The cell phone beeped to let him know he'd received a message. "Sorry …" He rolled over and picked up the phone. *Pawns so far. Tomorrow we take a rook. Brush up on your Hebrew. Zafer.*

He put the phone back on the night table, and Jesse nestled her head in the crook between his neck and shoulder. A flowery smell rose with her body heat. They fit together so seamlessly they might have been formed in the same womb. Something told him this was the way it would always be with her.

Just as he was dozing off he murmured, "Hebrew?"

BOOK 8: 1-14

HIDDEN SENSE

The Therapeutae have been recognized throughout the centuries as identical with the earliest Christian Church of Egypt. They were known to Philo at the very latest as early as 25 A.D., and they must have existed long before. If the canonical dates are correct, they could not have been Christians, in the sense of being followers of Jesus; and yet they were so like the Christians that the Church Fathers regarded them as the model of a Christian Church. We are, therefore, confronted with this dilemma; either Christianity existed before Christ, or the canonical dates are wrong.

— GRS MEAD

8: 1

PROFESSOR DE LA CROIX

W HEN DREW AWOKE, Jesse was standing over him, brushing hair off his forehead with a finger. Groaning, he sat up and rubbed his face.

"Time to get dressed." She bent and kissed him lightly. "I'm starving."

She modeled her Turkish clothes in front of the dresser mirror. "I look like a damn Gypsy." Both hands flew to her mouth. Cautiously, as if something else might escape, she lowered her hands. "Drew, I didn't mean—"

"I know what you meant." He tried not to stare at the freckles below her throat, exposed by the top three buttons of her blouse she'd left undone. What *was* it about those warm flecks of color…?

She pulled aside the curtains with a *whoosh* and flooded the room with sunlight. "I'm dying for some eggs."

Drew squinted and turned his head away. "Eggs," he muttered as he pushed off the bed. He tugged on a pair of shorts, washed his face, and tied his hair into a ponytail. Letting a t-shirt hang over his cargo shorts, he slipped into his sandals. "All set."

She shook her head. "You really are the textbook definition of a slacker, aren't you?"

"Professor de la Croix thought so. Couldn't stand me."

"Because you got good grades in spite of your sloppy habits. And because you're a *man*. I hate to say it, but my mother bore a grudge against all of you."

"Your *mother*? Professor de la Croix is *your* mother?"

Jesse nodded.

He shook his head. "I can't ... I just can't put the two of you together."

"My father's last name was Fenton, but my parents never married. In fact, I hardly ever saw him."

"He ran out on her, huh?" Drew couldn't really blame him for that.

"Pretty much."

"I'm sorry. It must have been tough for her, being a single mom. And tough for you."

"We managed."

"And I thought you were teacher's pet because you were the best student."

"*We* were the best students."

"I guess that explains why you didn't take my side that day she lost her temper in class."

She nodded. "Conflict of interest."

"What about now? Is your mom—?"

"She died seven years ago. Sort of an accidental suicide."

"Jess ... I'm so sorry." If he took one step forward and reached for her, he could wrap her in a hug, but something in her face kept him from taking that step.

"I've come to terms with it."

"Can I ask ... what happened?"

"Well ..." Jesse was looking at the floor now, as though deciphering something in the pattern of a rug. "You know she sometimes lost her temper in class. The head of the department covered for her more than once. Add to that the fact that she was seen as a kind of dinosaur by most of her colleagues ... with her literal belief in the Bible. She was basically forced into early retirement. About a year later, the book she considered her life's work came out, *The Gospels as Eyewitness Accounts*. I guess you know that most of the reviewers panned it—including your hero, Stephen."

Drew's breath scraped past his teeth. "I know they didn't see eye to eye."

"No, they didn't. Anyway, she had no classes to teach. Her views were obsolete, except in the Deep South. Her life's work was a commercial and critical failure. One night, too much wine, too many pills ..." Jesse shrugged. "She just didn't wake up."

It was hard to believe that, however indirectly, Stephen had helped kill Jesse's mother. "Do you have any brothers? Sisters?"

"Mm-mm. Only child. Mom never married. She always said I would be all she needed in her retirement—me and her library."

"Jess, I'm so sorry." Before she could protest, he had both arms around her.

"Same shirt as yesterday ..." She pressed her cheek against his chest. "But you still smell good." She pulled away by half an arm's length. "I guess I was a little scared when I got married. My college boyfriend. I felt very alone after I lost Mom and ... I guess I didn't want to go through life that way."

"I still can't get over it. You and Professor de la Croix ... you're so different."

"In a lot of ways, yes. I'm sure if she could see me with you now—"

"She'd blow a gasket."

"That's one way to put it.

His cell phone rang. Zafer.

"Saint-Savoy is out of jail. Which means he'll probably be showing up in Istanbul."

Drew remembered the man he'd seen being hauled away in handcuffs by the Egyptian police. Neatly trimmed black hair, Roman nose, early thirties, dark eyes. "Yeah, I could pick him out of a crowd."

"I'll swing by the hotel in a couple of hours. We have a little blackmail on the agenda today."

"Who?"

"A police captain."

Blackmail and *police* sounded like an exceptionally bad combination.

8: 2

AYA SOFYA

THE CATHEDRAL OF DIVINE WISDOM—the Hagia Sophia—had been converted into a mosque after the Turkish conquest of the city. Centuries later, at the insistence of Mustafa Kemal Attaturk, the founder of the Turkish Republic, it was turned into a museum. It was only a five-minute walk from the hotel, and Drew thought it would be a great diversion after breakfast.

The avenue, inlaid with tram tracks, took them along the massive, crenellated wall Mehmet the Conqueror had built. Or rebuilt. Drew didn't remember which.

Rising above trees and the city wall, the Aya Sofya, as the Turks called it, was a tiny city unto itself—a minor skyline crowned by a lead-covered dome. Four minarets surrounded the monument like sentinels. Once painted red, the cathedral was now a drab gray with only hints of ruddiness.

Tourists thronged the entrance.

As soon as the cathedral took them in, Drew felt as though light and heat had been swallowed as well. They stood in a kind of vestibule facing a set of doors a giraffe could have gone through without ducking. Sheathed in brass with a patina of green, the doors were as smooth as porcelain. A mosaic of the Virgin Mary with the infant Jesus glittered on the wall above the threshold. The figures were set against a background of gold slightly tarnished by the dimness. The entire interior, Drew had read somewhere, had once been covered by something like four acres of gold leaf.

"There are better mosaics inside. C'mon."

Their footsteps echoed on a floor paved with marble tiles.

"Wow." Jesse tilted her head back to take in what, nearly a millennium and a half ago, was regarded as the antechamber of heaven.

"The largest enclosed space for something like a thousand years," Drew said.

"The architecture is ... stunning. Really. I can't believe how high the center of the dome is. And how intricate the ... I mean, the capitals of those columns look like lace, but they're *stone*."

Double-tiered colonnades of green marble, parallel to the nave, receded into the gloom. Rows of windows honeycombed the walls with sun and fragments of sky. Here was the artfully worked glass staining Shelley's white radiance of eternity. Just below the dome itself, a ring of arched windows created the impression the dome rested on a foundation of light.

A pigeon circled near the overarching ceiling. Thanks to the acoustics, the feathery rustling reached them more than 150 feet below.

"Just for a second I imagined we'd startled an angel." Jesse was still looking up.

"Definitely a pigeon. Ask the guy who has to clean up the shit."

"Oh don't be such a killjoy. This is an amazing monument to faith. Imagine if people really dedicated themselves to common goals, to shared values. Imagine if we weren't always fighting each other, if we didn't pour billions into weapons and wars."

"Sounds like a John Lennon song."

"Well he was right, wasn't he?"

"You know who did the most damage to this church?"

"The knights of the Fourth Crusade?" She smiled. "Surprised? Good old Catholics under Enrico Dandolo, a Venetian."

Drew nodded. "You're a hard date to impress. Dandolo used to have a tomb around here somewhere, but the Turks destroyed it. There's a marker now with his name carved in it. Up in the gallery. The Crusaders were supposed to be fighting the Muslims—"

"But they were broke," Jesse continued, "and when they saw the wealth of the city, they decided to pillage it themselves."

"Exactly." Drew led her by the hand back into the vestibule where there were illustrations of the earlier incarnations of the Saint Sophia and summaries of its history. He pointed.

The Latin soldiery subjected the greatest city in Europe to an indescribable sack. For three days they murdered, raped, looted and destroyed on a scale that even the ancient Vandals and Goths would have found unbelievable. They smashed the silver iconostasis, the icons and the holy books of Hagia Sophia, and seated upon the patriarchal throne a whore who sang coarse songs as they drank wine from the Church's holy vessels.

                                     - *Speros Vyronis*, Byzantium and Europe

"How can people can be so cruel to each other?" Jesse asked as they re-entered the cathedral.

"Let me show you the gallery upstairs. That's where my favorite mosaic is. I can spit on Enrico's marker while we're there."

"*Drew* ..." She frowned.

"You can spit on him, too, if you want."

She shook her head and followed him up a winding ramp of uncut stones polished by thousands of feet.

Standing between columns, they looked down on the tourists milling around on the floor.

"This way ..." Drew tugged on her hand. "Here it is ... The Last Judgment."

Hardly half of it left, the mosaic showed Christ flanked by his mother—only her face and a piece of her shoulder remained—and John the Baptist. Like Christ, John's legs were missing. Their faces beautifully rendered, the three robed figures were set against shimmering gold.

"Oh this is lovely ..."

Only now Drew didn't see Jesus; he saw James the Just. James, whose death had been left out of the Gospels. Who had prayed for those killing him. Who'd had no heavenly father to fall back on.

Jesse put both hands on his arm and pulled him closer. "You were right. This is something I needed to see."

"Every time you sink a shovel in the city, you turn up some piece of history. You know a carpet dealer found an entrance to the basement of Constantine's palace behind his shop? It's underground now because the city has sunk about six meters since it was founded. They estimate there are something like thirty blocks of city, pretty much intact, right under Sultanahmet."

Drew's cell phone rang.

Jesse let go of his arm.

"Duty calls," Zafer said.

8: 3

TARGET PRACTICE

DREW HAD NEVER FIRED a gun with a silencer.

"Smith & Wesson automatic," Zafer said. "The original hush puppy, as Americans call it. Paid a nice piece of change for it in Iraq."

After giving Jesse color copies of the Habakkuk Scroll, Zafer had taken Drew back to the Office with the usual tortuous precautions.

The basement was gray cement with a couple of bare bulbs for light, its windows boarded up. The space looked like a mini commando training camp. Two punching bags hung from the floor joists. There were weights, a leather jump rope, and a sheet of plywood with silhouette targets stapled to them. Behind the plywood was a stack of lumber the size of railroad ties. Cans dangled on strings from the ceiling. They varied in color and had been hung at different lengths and distances.

Zafer opened a leather bag full of weapons.

"You got an Uzi in there for me?"

"So you can shoot everyone in the room, including me? No."

He handed Drew the Smith & Wesson. "I want to see how you handle it." He gave Drew a pair of shooting glasses with amber lenses. "Put those on."

Walking over to the plywood sheets with the only gun Drew had seen in the Office that wasn't lethal, Zafer stapled up some fresh targets. Ch-*chnk*. Ch-*chnk*.

Drew stood about twenty-five feet away behind a yellow line painted on the floor.

Zafer walked back. "Take your time aiming and give me four shots."

Remembering what his father had taught him, Drew held the gun with both hands and aimed slightly below the bull's-eye: bullets traveled in an arc and, at close range, the pistol would shoot a little high. He squeezed off the first round. The gun jumped in his hand but made hardly any noise. All four shots probably took about six seconds. The acrid smell of gunpowder stung his sinuses. He'd always found the odor oddly appealing.

Zafer examined the target. "Nice group. One bull's-eye, the other three to the right. Unless this guy was wearing Kevlar, he's dead." Using a yellow marker, he circled the four holes and wrote *1st Grp*. "Of course, this is just a target. You had plenty of time to aim, and no one was shooting back. This time, bring the gun up from your waist and give me four more as fast as you can."

Drew let his hands hang at his side for a second before raising the pistol as though someone were aiming back at him. Four shots in about two seconds.

"Not bad. Two wide, two in the black." Zafer made an amoeba-like shape with the marker. *2nd Grp*.

Drew felt a little giddy. Despite the weak popping sound the pistol made, he was holding the power to kill another human being. *Jesus, no wonder criminals get addicted.*

"This time, I want to you to hit as many cans as you can as fast as you can. Nearest first. If you miss, shoot at the same can again. Go until you run out of ammo."

Drew took a second to gauge distances: the white can was closest. Then yellow, blue, green.

The pistol popped. There was a satisfying ping as the white can leapt up and back. He nailed the yellow can on the second try and took two more for the blue one.

The slide stayed open after the last shell was ejected, and a wisp of smoke curled out of the chamber.

"Not bad at all. You have the basics down."

"You gonna take a turn?" Drew held up the Smith & Wesson.

"Put another magazine in."

Zafer took the pistol after Drew had reloaded it. "Whenever you're ready, get the cans swinging. Then get your ass behind me."

Running with his arms out as though imitating an airplane for a game of charades, Drew knocked into all the cans. Zafer starting shooting. Pings followed rapid flashes from the muzzle, and cans jerked on strings. The clip was empty in a few seconds.

Drew had counted ten pings. "You missed."

"I missed twice. Fourteen rounds in the clip, I hit the cans ten times, and twice I aimed at the targets. Go look."

Drew shook his head. The bulls-eye was over the heart of the silhouette, but Drew only saw his own shots, which were circled and labeled.

"You missed."

"Look at the head."

One silhouette had a hole in the forehead, the other in the face.

"If he was wearing Kevlar, he's still dead."

Drew nodded. "Pretty fuckin' good."

"Get over here so I can fit you with a shoulder holster. You're going spend a couple of hours practicing your quick draw and pulling the slide. Just *don't* fire on the draw—you won't hit anything like that."

"Ok."

"Next week I'll show you how to work with C4."

"Plastic explosives?" The idea didn't appeal to Drew.

Zafer snickered. "You never know when you'll need to blow something up." He handed Drew a pistol. "Here, this is your new friend."

A Beretta automatic pistol with a tiny bore. Probably a .22.

"How come you're giving me a peashooter?"

Zafer took something out of his back pocket and flipped it to Drew.

Drew caught it as it fell. It was an official-looking ID card that said his name was David Katz. "Mossad? The Israeli intelligence agency? Are you kidding me?"

"No. And they like pea-shooters."

8: 4

SWORD IN THE CLOSET

HIS WRISTS STILL SMARTING from the shooting he'd done, Drew rang up Yasemin. She was as playful and seductive on the phone as she'd been when they first met. He hung up and grinned at Zafer. "Got a date!"

He walked into the room where he slept and stripped off his shirt. For his Mossad role, Zafer wanted him in the pearl gray suit he'd worn in Cairo.

He and Yasemin had to come to a decision tonight—try again or break it off and cauterize the leaks. Then he and Jesse could figure out what to do with their long-incubated infatuation.

Zafer stood in the doorway while he changed. "We're going to have a little talk with an antiquities officer who's probably taking bribes from Serafis."

"Probably?" Drew pulled up the silk trousers.

"My *kankardeshim* made a few phone calls. Captain Ozatalay has more money than he should. His house is just a little too nice, his car is a little more expensive than it should be, and his daughters go to a private high school."

Drew buttoned up a white shirt. "But ... what if he's not taking bribes from Serafis? What if someone else is paying him off?"

Zafer shook his head. "The two times Serafis's Istanbul residence was raided, Ozatalay was in charge of the operations, and Serafis came out without a scratch."

"Still looks pretty risky." Drew tucked in his shirt and cinched his belt.

"Listen, all you have to do is say *shalom*, sit there and look like you know exactly what's going on. In other words, he's dirty, you *know* it, and we're putting his balls in a vice. Your ID, by the way, is authentic."

"You mean a forgery of an authentic Mossad ID?"

"Right. Mine says I work for MIT. This is a joint Turkish-Israeli op to recover Israeli cultural property. My assumed name is Tayfun. Don't fuck up and call me Zafer."

Drew turned up the collar of his shirt and got started on his tie. "So we're going to double-cross Serafis—keep the scroll and his money."

"Right."

The length of Drew's tie was wrong. He took the knot out and started again. "Why? I mean I'm glad, but ... why not take the money and run?"

"I'm not in this for the money, Drew. It's a nice windfall, sure, but I'm a soldier, and right now I don't have an army. I mean, imagine you made a sword—you spent years on it, starting with choosing the right kind of steel. Hammered it, honed it, polished it. Until the blade whistled, and it was perfectly balanced in your hand. Then somebody puts it in a closet somewhere and lets it rust. I wasn't made for storage. I wasn't made to look good hanging from a belt. The best way to keep rust off something is to use it."

Drew nodded. "Gotcha."

"Turkey's been dealing with terrorists for decades. I want to go back into the field where I belong. Seek and destroy. And the ones I don't kill, I hope they stay awake at night knowing someone's looking for them."

Drew admired Nathan and his non-violence, but he admired Zafer's attitude as well.

"Right now, I don't exist—no army, no uniform, not even my real name. I'm in this game to beat the Sicarii. Then I'm going to take my name back. I'm going to get back into the military, one branch or another. I'm going to get back onto the battlefield, wherever it is."

Drew was convinced.

"Oh, and one other thing ..."

"What's that?"

"I want Raymond."

8: 5

CAPTAIN OZATALAY

MASSIVE AND UGLY, the Emniyet Station in Mejidiyekoy was a labyrinth of departments and floors manned by hundreds of personnel. It belonged in Mejidiyekoy, a business district choked with concrete overpasses and traffic. Something like the less glamorous sections of Cairo.

Drew and Zafer were in a parking deck next to the police station.

A steel door opened, and a man who looked like a lawyer emerged. He walked briskly toward his car.

"Our boy will be in uniform," Zafer said. "He drives a shiny Opel. Not too ostentatious, not a BMW or a Mercedes, something just in his range if he spends his money carefully."

The steel door opened again and two men entered the garage. Exchanging farewells, they headed in opposite directions.

"That's him."

Stocky, balding, visored, blue cap in hand.

Captain Ozatlay looked at the two men approaching him at first with what Drew took to be curiosity but mild alarm seemed to set in as he and Zafer got closer.

Zafer stepped in front of the officer. "Captain Ozatalay?"

"Yes."

Zafer flipped open his wallet and gave him a good long look at his ID. "Tayfun Akkaya, MIT. This is field agent Katz with Mossad."

Drew greeted him in Turkish; saying *shalom* had been a joke.

"The Israeli Mossad?"

"Do you know another one?"

Drew held out his wallet to display his ID.

The captain smiled almost as if he were embarrassed. "What can I do for two intelligence officers?"

"You can take us to Araf in Nishantashi and buy us a couple of beers. You know where it is?"

"I've been there."

Zafer gestured toward the Opel. "You don't mind if we ride with you, do you?"

"I ... of course."

The doors of the car unlocked with an electronic chirp.

Ozatalay slid into the driver's seat. "May I ask what this is about?"

Drew took his place in the back, while Zafer sat up front.

"It's nothing to worry about. But the Turkish government, which is cooperating with the Israeli government, is going to need your services."

The police officer pulled out of the parking deck onto busy street. "Shouldn't I have been notified by my superior?"

"Well, the truth is, captain, the chief of your department may be part of the problem."

"I see."

Drew thought the man relaxed visibly, although he could see no more than the back of the captain's head and a partial profile.

They pulled up in front of the bar, and Ozatalay surrendered his keys to a valet.

Zafer held the door of the bar open for him. "After you."

Araf was swanky, with a lot of polished wood and brass. Cylindrical lights dangled from a high ceiling by long cords.

They seated themselves at a corner table. Zafer flagged a waiter and held up three fingers. "*Üh tane kirmizi.*" *Three reds.* He turned to the police officer. "That's a nice Opel you're driving," Zafer observed. "You're doing well for yourself."

Ozatalay suddenly had the look of a rabbit whose long ears had caught the sound of a twig snapping somewhere behind him.

"Do you know a man named Iorgos Serafis?"

"Of course. An antiquities collector who deals on the black market. I raided his house in Istanbul twice."

"We've had his phones tapped for about six months now. We've also been intercepting his cell phone calls—he has several cell phones."

Now Ozatalay looked as though he felt something crawling inside his pants, but he was trapped in a foxhole and one wrong move might draw enemy fire. He simply had to endure it.

"And you think ... Serafis and the police chief—"

"No. We don't think, we *know*. We know that you and Serafis have had business dealings."

"I'm afraid I—"

"Shut the fuck up and listen. You're talking to a MIT field agent. I know about the scars on your legs you got from shrapnel while fighting the PKK on the Iraqi border. I know your wife's middle name is Emine. I know where you live. I know how many cavities you have, and I damn well know who you do business with."

You didn't have to be an expert interrogator to see that Ozatalay was putting all the will he was capable of mustering into trying not to look terrified.

"I see I have your attention. Good. You're wondering why MIT and Mossad are here, not internal affairs. Well, before we get to that, I have good news for you. We're going to give you a chance to redeem yourself."

Ozatalay's forehead had begun to glisten with sweat. He looked from Zafer to Drew and back again.

The waiter set down three beers and left.

Zafer took a glass mug by the handle and pulled it closer. "First, we want to know how much you've taken in over the years. We already have the figure Serafis mentioned, but we want to verify it. If they don't add up, you'll both sit in an iron room with no windows until your memory improves. Now, just to make you feel a little more comfortable, we're not wearing wires." Zafer turned out the collar of his jacket as if that would be enough to prove what he'd said. "Serafis involved himself in something a little over his head—that's why my friend David is with us today. Now, I'm only going to ask you once: how much has Serafis donated to your favorite charity over the years?"

Ozatalay spilled his guts like a slashed fish. "Ninety thousand US."

Zafer looked meaningfully at Drew.

Drew pretended he understood the look.

"Congratulations, Captain, you decided to cooperate. Now ... Serafis doesn't know he's being monitored—and it's going to stay that way, right?"

"Of course."

"Good. Because in addition to tapping his phones, he's under twenty-four-hour surveillance. If you try to contact him, we'll know."

"You have my word."

"Do I?" Zafer smiled. "I guess this is my lucky day. It just happens to be yours too. Not only do you get a chance to redeem yourself, but we're going to let you keep the bribes you've already taken. Can you believe that shit? We're going let your daughters stay in their private school. We're not going to repossess your Opel. There's just one catch: you're going to be the one who arrests Serafis." Zafer spread his hands out and held his shoulders in a shrug as if to say *what can you do?* "It's you or him, right? He played the game, he lost." Zafer put his hands down and leaned across the table. "Understood?"

"Absolutely."

Zafer looked at Drew. "You hear that, David? He knows we're not fucking around." He turned back to Ozatalay. "All right, Captain, let me explain what's going to happen. Tomorrow we're going to meet with Serafis. He has a scroll worth a great deal of money. This item is the property of the Israeli government. We are going to walk in with a substantial amount of currency belonging to the Israeli government, and we intend to leave with it. We are *not* going to buy the scroll."

Drew took a few gulps of beer. This was the part of the plan that worried him most.

"Immediately after we leave, you are going to raid the premises, confiscate the scroll, and arrest Serafis. We—" Zafer gestured to himself and Drew— "don't show up in any reports. Understand?"

Ozatalay nodded.

Zafer leaned back in his chair. "Now, we have reason to believe your superior is not entirely honest, either. That's none of your concern—it's ours. All you have to do is organize the raid. You'll have to inform him of the raid, of course. You're not going to say a word about MIT or Mossad. Tell him you're acting on a tip from one of your informants. If he opposes the bust in any way, we'll know he's on Serafis's payroll, too."

Ozatalay nodded again.

"The exchange will take place at Serafis's house in Tarabya Üstü. Tomorrow, you'll have to have men in place, but I can't stress enough that your men *can't be seen*. If Serafis suspects a raid, he'll call the deal off, and you'll be prosecuted for corruption."

Ozatalay had regained his composure. "I will arrange it. My best men—only my very best. Serafis will suspect nothing."

Zafer tipped his mug back and took a long drink. He put the glass down on the wooden table with a loud *thunk*. "I love this stuff."

Ozatalay smiled nervously and sipped from his own mug.

Zafer leaned over the table a little. "Now, I want you to see the beauty of this arrangement. You and your department grab the glory for thwarting an internationally known smuggler and recovering an extremely valuable artifact. When the Turkish government presents the scroll to the Israelis, Turkey comes out looking good in the eyes of the international community. David and I save the Israeli government piles of money, so we get a pat on the back from our superiors. You see? Everybody wins—except Serafis." Zafer opened his hands and spread his arms as if to receive a large gift. "Do you foresee any problems?"

Ozatalay shook his head.

"Good. There's one other thing: this is *not* a joint operation between MIT and your department. MIT is going to pull all of its on-site surveillance *before* the exchange takes place so that we don't have antiquities officers shooting at MIT agents. David and I are the only two agents you have to worry about. Everybody else is fair game. Understood?"

"Understood."

Zafer finished his beer and stood up. "If you have any problems, call me *immediately*." Zafer handed Ozatalay a card.

Ozatalay took the card, pulled out his wallet, and offered a card to Zafer.

"You're kidding, right?" Zafer tapped his head with a finger. "Five-three-two, two-five-five, seven-four-nine-nine."

"I apologize."

"Have a good evening, Captain."

Drew finished his beer and said "Shalom." An Israeli agent stationed in Istanbul would speak Turkish fluently, but he thought it went with Zafer's condescension and sarcasm. Following Zafer out of the bar, he glanced at his watch. In a couple of hours, he would be sitting down to a drink with Yasemin.

8: 6

BROKEN THINGS

Deniz Atı, THE *SEA HORSE*, crowned one of the ferry stations in Kadiköy. Drew had managed not only to get a table on the terrace, but also to reserve one that was pressed right up against the wrought-iron railing overlooking the Sea of Marmara. A rough trail of hammered platinum led across the water to a half moon just above Topkapi Palace and the Aya Sofya.

Yasmin was late, as usual.

Nostalgia soaked in brine scented the end-of-September breeze. A candle flickered at the bottom of a glass shaped like a truncated teardrop. The beer in his glass glowed amber.

When he glanced up from the table, there she was, scanning the terrace. She was in earth tones—a terracotta hobble skirt that accentuated the curve of her hips, a short blazer to match, and that caramel skin of hers.

She saw him and her face took on the aura of a fanned ember. She walked to the table looking him over incredulously, as though somehow he'd just emerged, dry as dust, from the Bosporus. "Is this the new Drew? Mr. Businessman?"

He was still in the silk suit. "I guess." They kissed on both cheeks and hugged warmly.

The spikes and barbs their past fights had left inside of him melted. How did this happen every time he saw her?

Yasemin caught the attention of a waiter in black tie and ordered a red wine. "So …" She looked at Drew. "What's this top-secret deal you're working on?"

"It involves, uh, an antiquity."

"An antiquity?"

"It's better if I don't say anything until after it's sold."

"Oh come on, Drew."

"What it is, isn't important. It's worth a lot of money, it didn't come from Turkey, and it belongs to friend of mine. He just … needed my help."

Putting her back to the breeze coming off the water and cupping the flame of the lighter, she lit a cigarette. "What do you know about antiquities?"

"Does it matter? It'll be sold soon and hopefully I'll make … I don't know, maybe $50,000."

She leaned closer to him, eyes wide. "You're *kidding*. Drew, this *has* to be illegal."

"Actually we're getting it back to the rightful owner, and there's a … reward for that."

"It still sounds to me like some kind of black market deal."

"Yeah, well, whatever it is, you should be happy about it. You and my old man never get tired of telling me how I haven't amounted to much, how everything I do is half-assed, or just a waste of my potential. Even *your* father was disappointed you married an English teacher."

The cigarette halted its approach to her mouth. "Are we going to start this again?"

"Yazz, *this* is what we have to deal with if we're going to try to get back together. You told me to deal with my anger, and I did—I am. I admit I'm still working on it. But I can't be the only one who makes changes. You have to make some changes, too."

Her eyes narrowed as she inhaled. "Such as?"

"You have to stop trying to squeeze me into the husband you want me to be. That's what so much of our marriage was about—you pushing, me resisting, then you punishing me … by shutting down and turning cold. You can't treat me like a child. I don't want to be married to someone who sounds just like my father."

She exhaled a plume of smoke that was swept away by a breeze. Her hair, short and thick, barely moved. "You can't keep acting like a child."

He shook his head. "You have to take responsibility for some of the things you've done, Yazz."

She shrugged. "Most of the mistakes were yours."

Drew leaned forward. "Was it *all* me? Am I a hundred percent to blame?"

"Eighty percent."

"I don't agree, but fine. Just tell me what you think your twenty percent is."

"I don't want to do this."

"Just give me one thing, one flaw. Not a mistake you've made ... something you do consistently. Like my bad temper."

"If I have so many flaws, why have you been begging me to take you back for two years?"

"Isn't it obvious why we behave the way we do? You ... sometimes it's like being too close to a fire—I get burned. But when I get too far away from you, I'm cold. I want to go back. Until I get burned again. Then freeze again. I guess it's the same for you. That's why we have all this back and forth. All I've been asking is for you to turn it down a little so I can be warm without being burned."

"I did turn it down. It didn't help."

"What did you turn down? What did you change?"

She stared at him.

"Name one thing in your personality we could both do without. Like my temper."

"That's enough of this."

"Just *one*."

She turned her head away and looked out over the water.

"You're not hypercritical or overly sensitive? You don't hold grudges? You don't punish me with my own love?"

"*Bunu duymak istemiyorum!*"

"You don't want to hear it because it's upsetting. Your father was like mine. He disapproved of you so much when you were a child, he made you think there was something wrong with you—"

"Don't talk about my father!" She stood up and flicked her cigarette at him.

It bounced off gray silk in a burst of tiny orange embers. "I was a fool to think I could live with you again."

She almost bumped into the waiter who was bringing her wine. He looked at Drew quizzically. Drew motioned for him to go ahead and bring the wine. He watched Yasemin—her angry steps shortened by the skirt she was wearing—disappear inside the restaurant.

The waiter set the glass down on the table.

There she went, the woman he'd been pining for for two years. Reconciliation had been just a few nods of the head and a couple of promises away, but he knew that if he was the only one who apologized and acknowledged his mistakes, the cycle that had ended in divorce would start all over again.

He glared out at the water, feeling like something had been amputated.

Her shortcomings weren't tragic, but if she admitted them, she would have some rebuilding to do. Maybe it was easier for her to let the marriage go.

"You always got so upset about a broken tea glass or a cracked chair," he said under his breath. Why didn't you ever notice the things that were breaking inside. Both of us.

"Drew."

He turned around.

"I'm sorry."

"You go off your meds again?"

"No. Or I wouldn't have come back."

He waited.

"Drew, if I take you back and you leave again, I might not get over it this time. I love you too much."

"I won't leave again."

"Even if I go off my medication? Even if I do the same things that made you leave in the first place?"

"I'll sleep at a friend's a house if I have to, but I'll come back. No more divorce court."

"Listen Drew … for two years I convinced myself it was over. I never fell out of love with you, but I believed—really believed—you were out of my life. I learned how to live without you. How to be a divorced woman in Turkey. How to think about having a future with someone else. And now … I want you back, I do, but I'm afraid. That's why my emotions are so volatile. I only wanted to be married once in this life, Drew, you know that."

"Do you want to sit back down?" He stepped around to pull out her chair.

"No. Not tonight. Let's take a little time. Both of us. Let's really think this through. No distractions, no one else. I'm done with Mehmet—that was a mistake. Can we do that? Give it some time and see how we feel?"

He put his hands on the back of his chair. "Sure."

"I have to go now. I have to be alone tonight."

He nodded.

"Love me?"

"Always."

"Then wait for me. And I'll wait for you."

He glanced at the sea, indifferently reflecting the moon. "I'll wait."

8: 7

GAME PLAN

B<small>Y THE TIME DREW</small> got out of bed, Kadir was at the stove atop a pair of vegetable crates making *menemen*—undercooked scrambled eggs, peppers, tomatoes, cheese and a Turkish pepperoni called *sujuk*. In the last few days, Kadir had taken it upon himself to do most of the cooking and all of the dishwashing. Spatula in hand, he grinned at Drew. "Today we are going to be riches. Five million dollars!"

Drew nodded sleepily. "Where's Zafer?"

"He is making recon."

Drew blinked. "Reconnaissance?"

"*Evet.*"

Drew looked over the dwarf's shoulder. "Smells good. You make enough for me?"

"*Ne eshek seni! Burasi Turkiye.*" *What a donkey you are! This is Turkey.*

He was right. It was unthinkable for a Turk to ignore his friends when it came to food. All these years and Drew still wasn't used to Turkish hospitality.

Kadir tipped his head toward the table. "*Otursana.*" Drew took a seat. "After the breakfast we are getting to the scroll."

"Where you been keeping it all this time?"

"In the bank. In a safety box."

"In a safe deposit box?" Drew's voice rose in alarm.

"Don't worry. It is very dry. You will see."

The tips of his fingers tingled as though with the caffeine buzz that came with gulping a liter of coffee. In a few hours he would be up close and personal with a Dead Sea Scroll, one that only a handful of people had ever seen.

After a steaming heap of Kadir's *menemen*, half a loaf of bread, and pint of orange juice, Drew got on the computer and checked his e-mail. Jesse had sent him a message.

> *Dear Drew,*
>
> *I just about laughed in your face when you told me in Antakya that Paul had murdered James. If he had, it might suggest Paul was the Liar in the Habakkuk Scroll and that the High Priest Ananus, who actually DID convene the Sanhedrin and have James stoned to death, was the Wicked Priest.*
>
> *As you probably know, the Wicked Priest wasn't killed by Jews but by Gentiles who defiled his corpse. Look at this passage from the scroll:*
>
> *"And the gentiles inflicted horrors of evil sickness and took vengeance upon his body of flesh ... "*
>
> *This is interesting because Ananus was killed during the revolt of 66 AD by the Idumeans—the Edomites—and his body was thrown over the walls of Jerusalem and left for the dogs and crows. This is an unthinkable desecration for a Jew. Gentiles killed the High Priest and defiled his corpse!*
>
> *But what got my scalp tingly is this: "After the death of the Teacher, the Man of a Lie was banished to the land of the Kittim." We know that Kittim is code for the Romans, and we know that Paul was sent to Rome around the time of James's death. This is NEW, from one of the missing sections. So current scholarship has never seen it—and it's a LOCK. Paul is a dead ringer for the Liar! I hate to say it, but I'm beginning to think James the Just really might have been the Teacher of Righteousness.*
>
> *I guess that's what that Ebionite meant when he told you we'd find proof in the Habakkuk Commentary that Paul had murdered James.*
>
> *There is also a passage about the "the last priests of Jerusalem" "whose riches and plunder" fall into the hands of the Romans. This sounds tantalizingly like the destruction of the Second Temple under the command of Titus in 70 AD. (the Temple wasn't plundered under Pompey in 63 BC). There's a problem though. Most scholars consider*

*this a prediction, not a record of what actually happened, but that's a
lot less likely if Paul is the Liar.*

That, Drew realized, must have been one of the controversial passages
Nathan had mentioned in Antakya.

*Looks like your dwarf pal is holding a late first-century scroll that
mentions the Teacher of Righteousness, but NOT Jesus. It's invaluable
to scholars, Drew. Please tell me you've figured out a way to keep it out
of Serafis's hands.*

Call me when you get this.

Jesse.

While he was debating whether or not to ring Jesse, Zafer walked in.
A motorcycle helmet under his arm, he was dressed in the red and yellow
of a DHL courier.

Drew smiled. "That was your cover, huh?"

He held up the helmet. "I can see out, nobody can see in." He walked
over to Drew and looked over the computer monitor. "What're you
working on?"

A pop-up in a corner of the computer screen announced: *JesFen has
just signed in.*

"Oh." Zafer nodded. "Focused on business I see."

Drew? You there?

"Jess is part of business."

"Yeah." Zafer snickered. "The fun part."

Drew messaged back: *Here.*

Any news?

Drew thought for a moment. "Everything's over with Yasemin.
Ended it last night."

Zafer looked confused. "You did?"

Drew waved a hand to shut Zafer up. "I just want to get her reaction."

"That's some devious shit."

Zafer's slang still surprised him.

Won't pretend I'm sorry, Jesse replied.

A straightforward enough answer although it was just as likely *she*
was playing *him.*

*Missed you the minute you left yesterday. Okay, yeah, I had a Dead
Sea Scroll to keep me company … speaking of which, did you read my
e-mail?*

Yes, Drew typed back. *Told you so.*

But what about the scroll?

Sorry, Jess. They're unloading it today.

Zafer nodded. "Good boy."

Drew! That scroll could rewrite the New Testament. Not to mention our current understanding of Christianity. If the Church gets it, it'll never see the light of day.

Jess, I don't even know where Kadir keeps it. Miracles are a little out of my league.

Zafer held up a thumb in approval.

What about the photos? Can you salvage those?

They're part of the deal.

This bastard gets EVERYthing?

I'm sorry, Jess.

UGGGH!! This is so UNFAIR. I guess there isn't much you can do, though, is there? You're not a CIA agent, are you?

Mossad, actually. *No.*

It's so hard to believe we came SO close …

I know.

Today, huh?

Yeah.

This isn't done. I don't know how … but this isn't done.

Drew didn't know how to reply.

Call me so I know you're safe.

I will. What did she mean, 'this isn't done'?

Please be careful, Drew.

I will. Talk to you soon.

Good luck. XO

Drew logged off.

Zafer slapped Drew on the back. His hand felt like a slab of wood.

"You're finally getting in character. Stonewall *everybody*."

"Thanks." Drew was about to sign out of his e-mail, but a new message had come in: *From Raymond*. Chills shot up his spine and broke out in goosebumps on his upper arms. He turned around to look at Zafer.

"Open it."

"How did he get my e-mail?"

Zafer shrugged. "Hacked into the professor's e-mail account or found it in his address book. What does it say?"

How are you, mon ami? This is a message for the Saracen.

"What the hell's a Saracen?" Zafer asked.

"That's what Christians called Muslim soldiers during the Crusades."

Tell him God has chosen me to be His champion. It is inevitable that we meet. Tell him I look forward to that time.

Raymond.

Drew shivered through another wave of chills.

"Don't worry." Zafer whacked him again—this time on the shoulder. "He's just trying to rattle your cage."

"It's not my cage I'm worried about."

"All right, forget about Raymond. Here's the game plan ... we meet Serafis at his house, which is a lot like the one in Antakya. The exchange takes place at 2:30. I already contacted Ozatalay and told him to keep an eye trained on the front door—from at least 300 meters. When we come out ..." He pointed at Drew and himself. "He and his boys go in."

Drew nodded.

"We're out of here at 1:30. Any questions?"

"Yeah ... isn't this kind of stupid? All the Sicarii have to do is shoot us when we walk in the door, and they save five million dollars."

"Except they still want the other scroll. And they're hoping we'll lead them to it."

Drew shook his head. "You're making an assumption that might get us all killed."

"What's that?"

"That the Sicarii haven't already found the other scroll. Maybe we've evaded them so far because they've been putting most of their effort into the *other* scroll. Maybe that's why Serafis didn't bargain all that hard with Kadir. These guys are fanatics—zealots, just like the original Sicarii. As long as they get these scrolls, they'll all go to their graves smiling."

"You done?" Zafer dipped his head and lifted his eyebrows. "While you were out burning your wick at both ends, Kadir over there was gathering a little intel for us."

Drew glanced at Kadir, who was grinning at him.

"Remember the bar we went to in Cairo right after Nabil turned on us? Remember the Egyptian Kadir met in the bar? His name is Jamal.

A small-time runner, like Tariq. We had Jamal call Nabil and tell him that he had a lead on the other scroll. Now, if you remember, when we sat down with Nabil in the coffeehouse, we promised him a five-percent finder's fee if he came up with the scroll. I knew that Raymond and Saint-Savoy had already promised him more, so he'd go to them first. Sure enough, Nabil insisted on checking out the lead immediately. Jamal was evasive. Jamal waited a day and then called Raymond—we gave him the number—and insisted someone meet him in person.

"Jamal never showed up for the rendezvous. Well, technically he was there, but he was watching from a safe distance. An Eygptian—probably an interpreter—and one of the Sicarii took the bait. If the Sicarii are willing to fly to Cairo at a moment's notice, it means they're still hot for the missing scroll. Any more questions?"

"Yeah ... you got an extra bulletproof vest?"

8: 8

THE EXCHANGE

DREW HAD NEVER IMAGINED that Kadir had been keeping the scroll in a bank in Levent—a suburb of Western architecture, brick fences, and green yards. Nor did he imagine that the exchange would take place, not after hours on some secluded backstreet in a dilapidated hotel—light from the chandelier in the lobby blurred by cigarette smoke—but on a sunny afternoon in a villa with a hillcrest view of the Bosporus.

The scroll, still sheathed in disintegrating leather, was in a plain wooden box. The bottom of the box was strewn with those packets of desiccants that sometimes turned up in the pockets of new clothing like tiny teabags with DO NOT EAT written on them. Not high tech, but effective. Drew had been dying to see the scroll in the bank, but Zafer had shaken his head. "You'll get to see it at Serafis's."

Long and narrow, the box wasn't more than five inches deep and was stowed in an aluminum brief case. There were two briefcases, identical. The idea was to go into Serafis's house as if they were carrying the money with which to *buy* the scroll. Inside, they would transfer the money to the briefcases and walk out as though, for some reason, the exchange hadn't taken place. After they came out, Ozatalay would send men around the sides and back to make a noose. Once Drew and Zafer had pulled away, the police would move in, Serafis and whoever was with him would be arrested, and the scroll recovered.

The three of them were headed to Tarabya Ustu in a gray Audi. Drew was armed with a .22 caliber Beretta pistol. Zafer drove. Serafis's house was located just below the top of a hill along a steep road that wound its way down to the European shore of the Bosporus. As in Antakya, a gated driveway of about one hundred yards led to Serafis's house.

"Hard to be inconspicuous in this neighborhood," Zafer said. "One road and a few rich neighbors with watch dogs and private security guards and nosy wives sunning themselves beside the pool or having friends over for tea.

"By now Ozatalay has replaced security guards with policemen, some gardener probably has an automatic weapon under his coveralls, and there are a couple of men peering from bedroom windows with binoculars."

Pulling up near the gate, but beyond the line of sight of the two surveillance cameras mounted on the brick walls, Zafer took out the hush puppy. He took aim through the open window. There was a pop from the gun followed by a soft crash—as if two toy locomotives had collided—and the tinkle of falling glass. He took out the second camera the same way.

He dialed Serafis on his cell phone. "We're here."

"What happened to my cameras?"

"Sorry, no pictures. We'll compensate you for the damage."

"What kind of way is this to do business?" Serafis yelled.

"Do you want the scroll or not?"

The wrought-iron gate jerked open and rolled aside on a track. The house was similar to the one in Antakya—a two-story, stone block—but this one had narrow *jumbas* decorated with carved pilasters.

Zafer pulled the Audi down the long drive but instead of parking beside the two cars already there, he turned around and positioned the car so that it was blocking traffic in or out. Then, well out of the sight of the security camera over the beautifully carved double doors, he took out the hush puppy and popped that one, too.

"He's probably going to scream like he's passing a kidney stone," Drew said. Although he was sweating, his hands were icy. In each he held the handle of an aluminum briefcase.

Zafer collected the ejected shell casing and replaced the pistol's clip. He looked at Drew. "Just in case we need a full one." He unscrewed the silencer.

Drew realized his knees were shaking. Ashamed, he commanded

them to be steady and walked stiff-legged a step behind Zafer. His stomach was a nest of fluttery activity. Rather than reassuring him, the weight of the gun against his body made him that much more anxious. His breathing rapid and shallow, he remembered a baby bird he'd once held in his fist, the needle-thin ribs pressing against his hand as the bird hyperventilated with panic. *You can do this*, he said to himself.

The door opened so abruptly Drew almost reached for his pistol.

"Just who exactly gave you permission to destroy my property!" Serafis screeched. His anger was slightly comical to Drew, partly because, with his wall-eyed gaze, it seemed to have no focus.

Zafer grinned. "Smith and Wesson."

"Smith and—?"

"Never mind. I told you you'd be compensated."

"This *isn't* the way business is done."

Drew and Zafer stepped inside. "Let's get on with it, Iorgos."

Serafis looked down at their feet.

Zafer shook his head. "Sorry, we won't be taking off our shoes."

"No, it seems protocol's been thrown over the side today."

Serafis led them into a sitting room with a floor of cream-colored, hard-baked tiles. Glass cabinets stuffed with urns, vases, and elegantly shaped ceramics lined the walls. There were also five monitors stacked against one wall; three of them were blank. As they entered, two men who had been seated at what might have been a dining room table for eight stood up: Jan Miskovicz and Kurt Hohenzollern. Sicarii.

Miskovicz had an unruly mop of white hair with a few glints of gold still left. Bespectacled and gaunt, he looked frail.

The German, with his sharp cheekbones accentuated by a military haircut and the slot-like mouth, was more intimidating in person than he had been in his photo. An expert on ancient Hebrew, Aramaic, and Syriac paleography, he'd undoubtedly been chosen to verify the scroll's authenticity. The Pole was probably there to second his assessment.

These were Serafis's "experts."

A small black suitcase lay on the table like a single piece of merchandise on display. Light came in through the tall windows making Drew feel almost as if the place, even without altar or pews, was a sort of chapel.

The two men eyed Zafer suspiciously. Zafer approached looking friendly enough, put both hands on the edge of the table and shoved it against the two men. They reacted predictably, putting their arms out and folding over at the waist to avoid the wooden edge. Zafer hopped up on the table and, as Miskovicz straightened up, caught him across the cheek with a vicious kick. The Pole collapsed. Hohenzollern took a step back and reached inside his jacket, but Zafer had already drawn his pistol and had it aimed at the German. "Don't!"

By this time, Drew had dropped the briefcases, but, unsure of whether or not he should pull his weapon, just stood there.

"Gentlemen, please! Please!" Serafis, both hands thrust out, looked like a referee far too small to separate a couple of heavyweights intent on mauling each other.

Zafer reached in Hohenzollern's jacket and took out a Glock.

Then he reached in the unconscious Pole's jacket and removed his pistol as well.

Hohenzollern knelt down beside Miskovicz. "Jan is an old man." The German's English was accented but clear.

"So was Professor Cutherton."

Anger warmed the back of Drew's neck.

Zafer glanced up at the light fixture, which looked normal enough to Drew, and then at Serafis. "Eye in the sky, huh?" He aimed the pistol he had just confiscated and fired it once. The light went out and glass shards danced briefly on the smooth white floor.

"For the love of God...!" Serafis raised his hands as if he thought a piece of the ceiling would come down as well.

"Now we can do business." He turned to Drew. "Show them what we brought."

Miskovicz was on his feet again although he had to be supported by Hohenzollern. Drew placed one of the aluminum briefcases on the table and opened it. He took out the wooden box containing the scroll and slid it over to the German.

The Sicarii snapped open the pressure latches and lifted the lid. Drew couldn't see what was behind it, but even Miskovicz, whose cheek had already swelled, seemed to revive.

Gingerly, Hohenzollern removed the scroll from the box. The leather sheath was ragged, and it was only with great care and agonizing slowness that the German was able to extract the scroll. For all his meticulous handling, a flake fell from the scroll to the table. Miskovicz tweezered it up and put it in a tiny box with a lid that snapped close. Drew realized that in spite of their Christian fundamentalism, they were still scholars, and this was an astonishing find.

Zafer took out the envelope with the photographs and slid that over to them as well.

After Hohenzollern had rolled about three feet of the scroll out on the table, the two men began comparing it with the photographs. Serafis, that balding, tubby, glorified used car salesmen who vandalized tombs, culture, and history with equal abandon, was standing in front of Drew, defenseless. Drew had his chance to *ventilate* him, and take out two of the men who'd been responsible for Stephen's murder. Instead, he stepped closer to the scroll.

The neat rows of Hebrew script were beautiful in a way Drew couldn't describe. Singed by time, the parchment had turned a golden brown, and the rune-like letters looked, not as though they had been inked onto the parchment, but burned into it. This was as close as human beings could get to speaking from the grave, to preserving an angel's words. The men and women who'd believed in heavenly visitations the way Drew believed oxygen and hydrogen combined to make water had gone to dust, but in this scroll some of the magic remained.

After conversing in whispers—and in German—Hohenzollern and Miskovicz looked at Serafis and nodded.

"Gentlemen ..." The chubby Greek addressed Zafer and Drew. "As promised, I, Iorgos Serafis, have arranged for payment in full. Five million dollars." Spinning the suitcase around on the table so that it faced Zafer and Drew, he opened it.

Drew's first thought when he saw the neat stacks of 100-dollar bills was: *We're not gonna fit all that in two briefcases.* He got to work on it while Hohenzollern gingerly rolled up the scroll. The German put it back in the box with the leather cover beside it. The latches snapped the lid down another millimeter as they locked in place.

Drew had stuffed both briefcases to capacity and there were still a few wads left over. He put a couple in his pants, and one in his jacket. Zafer took one and peeled off five thousand dollars. "I think that's a fair price for your cameras."

Serafis nodded.

Everyone turned when Nathan entered the room.

8: 9

PAWN TAKES QUEEN

Zafer had never trusted Nathan, and here he was about to fuck up a five-million-dollar deal. He must have picked the lock to the back door. *Damn* him. Zafer made a split-second decision.

"Hey, Kurt!" Zafer threw a Glock to Hohenzollern and pulled his own weapon. *Now*, Zafer thought, *we'll see who Nathan's working for.*

"He'll kill him!" Drew shouted.

Zafer aimed a finger at Drew. "Shut up and do what I tell you!"

As Hohenzollern looked up from the weapon he'd just caught, he took a generous dose of pepper spray in the face. The German fell to his knees with a cry. The pistol clattered to the tile floor. Miskovicz dropped to his knees and grabbed it, but Nathan was already on him. Seizing the weapon, he twisted it—and the Pole's arm. Hard. The snap of bone was accompanied by a shriek. Miskovicz rolled onto his back holding his mangled finger; it had been caught in the trigger guard.

Nathan put the weapon in a trouser pocket.

Zafer didn't see the red-headed Ebionite approaching from the foyer until he'd already gotten off a burst of pepper spray. Zafer raised a forearmed and spun around, but he wasn't quite quick enough; his left eye caught fire.

"Kahretsin!"

Drew pulled his Beretta and pulled back the slide in the same motion—just the way he'd practiced all day yesterday and this morning.

He aimed at Josh—this guy with crew-cut red hair had to be Josh—and fired.

Josh leapt to one side, and the bullet pierced the glass door of a cabinet, shattering the ancient urn behind it.

Not all that loud was one of a jumble of instantaneous thoughts that went through Drew's head. *What if that was an urn showing Dionysus as Christ?* was another.

Drew fired a second round. *Amazing how fast people react when you point a gun at them.* It ricocheted off a terra cotta tile conjuring an intricate web of cracks.

"Drop the fucking spray can and roll it over to me, or I won't miss the next time."

Josh did as he was told, but Nathan had his can of pepper spray out again.

"Don't!" Zafer's pistol was trained on Nathan. "Even blind I can hit you at this range."

A shot rang out from somewhere behind Drew, and he flinched. A tiny hole erupted in Nathan's buttoned jacket, and Nathan stumbled back. Drew turned and saw Serafis holding a small revolver. A second shot hit Nathan, and he fell like a boxer who'd just taken a sharp punch to the jaw. He sat there looking slightly dazed, the can of pepper spray still in one hand.

Without thinking, Drew reached the Greek in two long steps. With a vicious twist of his trunk and all of his weight behind his elbow, he caught Serafis under an eye.

The balding dealer collapsed as if he'd taken a bullet. His revolver fell a few feet away, and Drew snatched it up.

Zafer charged Josh. Josh threw the first punch, but Zafer—one eye closed—parried and landed a palm heel to the nose. Josh's head snapped back so hard Drew saw the entire underside of his jaw. Just to make sure he was out of the game, Zafer caught him with a knee to the temple.

To his amazement, Drew saw Nathan back on his feet.

"Put bracelets on Nathan's pal," Zafer growled at Drew.

Drew groped around in a pocket stuffed with money until he came up with a Kevlar tie; it looked like the kind used to cinch a garbage bag. Kneeling beside Josh, Drew was about to put the Ebionite's limp hands behind his back when he saw Hohenzollern flying at Nathan with a wicked-looking knife.

"Nathan!"

Nathan dropped the can of pepper spray and raised both hands in a block. Hohenzollern artfully retracted the knife and stepped away leaving no room for a counter.

The German could barely open his eyes—just enough, it seemed, to locate Nathan. He nonetheless swung the blade in an expert arc. Nathan evaded it, but Zafer, who wanted desperately to get out of Serafis's house before something else went wrong, skipped forward and hammered the small of Hohenzollern's back with the instep of his foot. The German flew forward and collapsed to his knees, the knife landing some distance away on the floor.

Zafer pointed his Glock at Nathan. "I know you're wearing a vest under there, but I've got a 17-round magazine. If I don't feel like breaking your ribs, believe me when I tell you I can take out your kneecaps. Even with one eye. So we're done now, right?"

"Believe him," Drew said.

Nathan held up his hands to signal surrender. "Done."

"Slide over the gun you snatched from the Pole."

Nathan took it out of his pocket and sent it skittering over the tiles.

"Now grab your pal, Nathan." Zafer tucked the pistol in the waistband of his pants. "Drew, get the money." He tried to open his left eye, blinked rapidly, then squeezed it shut again. "We're all leaving together."

Miskovicz was still on his knees moaning.

Serafis was holding onto the corner of the long table to steady himself.

"Sorry about the cheap shot, Kurt," Zafer said, "but we're all settled up now. Scroll's yours, money's ours."

The German's eyes were red and swollen, his cheeks glistening with tears like a repentant saint.

"Pleasure doing business with you."

Drew grabbed the aluminum briefcases, but before they reached the door, they heard pounding from the other side and shouting in Turkish. The word "Polis" was clear enough that even the Sicarii probably understood it.

"Fuck!" Zafer sounded angry, but—his back to the Sicarii—he was grinning.

Serafis looked at the only TV monitor still receiving a picture. Three police officers filed through the back door. "Impossible! They can't be here now!"

Drew dropped to his knees, took out his Mossad ID, and put his hands on his head.

Zafer did the same. "You, too, Nathan."

Hohenzollern lurched toward the table in what was probably a frantic effort to grab the scroll, but several officers pressed him to the floor with their hands and knees. Two stood over him with guns drawn.

Miskovicz, who looked sick with pain, put up no resistance.

One of the officers opened the front door while another threw Serafis against the table. He squealed in Turkish.

Captain Ozatalay, leading half a dozen more officers into the house, examined Zafer's ID as though he had never seen it before. He motioned for Zafer to get up.

"Ikisede bizimle geliyor." Zafer pointed at Josh and Nathan. *These two are coming with us.*

After Ozatalay checked Drew's ID, one of his men brought him the long wooden box containing the scroll.

Zafer flashed Hohenzollern his ID. "Bet you wish you had one of these." He tucked his wallet back in his jacket.

The German glared through eyes swollen to slits. "We'll kill you for this."

"No you won't." Zafer grinned. "We have something else you want."

"From that idiot, Nabil?"

"Nabil? We don't need him. We'll be in touch."

"Next time will be very different."

"Yeah ... see you in Egypt."

Josh, his nose streaming blood, was on his feet, his hands cinched together by the Kevlar bracelet.

"Keep quiet." He turned to Ozatalay. "Captain, would you escort us to our car?"

"Of course."

The patio surrounding the house was littered with haphazardly parked cars, only one of which was a marked police vehicle.

Drew opened the back door of the Audi for Josh. He closed it after Nathan had slid in next to them.

Leaning close to Drew's ear, Zafer said, "Not a word to those guys."

"You still don't trust—"

"Remember what I told you? Stonewall *everyfuckin*body."

Motioning Drew to join him, Zafer took up a place at an oblique angle to the trunk of the car. His left eye was still crimped shut and tears ran down the side of his face

Something beeped; Zafer checked his phone and then slipped it back into a jacket pocket.

"You came in a little sooner than expected, Captain."

"I ... got nervous. I thought you might need help."

"Well, we'd like to show our appreciation." He looked to Drew. "David ..."

It took Drew a second to realize he was David and to figure out what was expected of him. Instinctively, he reached in his pocket and pulled out a banded stack of bills.

Ozatalay looked around, but his officers were all either inside or preoccupied with searching the grounds. "Thank you, sir."

Zafer handed over a stack of bills. "I'm sure the Israeli government won't miss 100,000 dollars. We'll call it operating expenses. Be sure your men get something."

"Very generous of you, sir."

"Remember, we were never here. Make sure your men remember as well." Zafer looked a little comical assuming a position of authority with that shut eye shining his cheek with tears.

"I understand."

Drew took the wheel while Zafer got in on the passenger's side and wiped at his eye with the ham of his thumb.

He pulled out, not quite able to believe that they were getting away with nearly five million dollars.

"How the hell did you do that?" Nathan asked.

"I'm not as dumb as I look." Zafer craned his neck to get a look behind him. "So you're Josh, huh?"

"Yeah."

Zafer hawked and spat out the open window. "My eye is killing me."

"I think you broke my nose."

"That cheers me up a little."

They came to the end of the tree-lined driveway, and Drew made a left onto the road that led down the hill toward the Bosporus.

"The good news for you guys is that the scroll will probably go back to Israel. The good news for us is that we have enough money to retire."

"This was a set-up?" Nathan asked.

Zafer shook his head. "Not on our end. My guess is Serafis has been bribing Ozatalay all along, but this time, somebody high up got wind of the deal. Ozatalay had no choice but to make an arrest."

"But Serafis is sure to turn over on him."

Zafer shook his head. "It's not in Serafis's interest. Not only is he still guilty of trafficking in illegal antiquities, but bribing an officer is an additional charge. Even if Serafis *did* manage to take Ozatalay with him, the little Greek could be sure somebody would stick a knife in his back during his stint in prison. No, he'll get an expensive lawyer, do a few years, bribe the guards to get cushy treatment, and get back into smuggling antiquities when he gets out."

"And you ... why won't Serafis turn you two in?"

"Same reason. It won't save his skin. He' still guilty of receiving an illegal antiquity and, when he gets outs of prison in a couple of years, he'll be blackballed from the trade. Even if he does roll over, a security camera shows us going in there with two briefcases, not with a scroll. And we left with the same two briefcases—not with the scroll. We didn't buy anything."

"What about the Sicarii? They can still rat you out."

"If we go to jail, they don't get another little item we happen to have."

"What's that?"

"I could tell you, but then I'd have to kill you."

"I guess we almost fucked up a perfect deal."

"Almost."

The winding road had taken them to Tarabya, not far from where the Black Sea funneled into the Bosporus. Zafer pointed and Drew pulled over.

"Out you go, gents."

Black Sea fishing boats, with their distinctively upcurved sterns and bows, bobbed in the quiet harbor.

Josh held up his hands. "What about this?"

"That's Kevlar. I've got a knife, but I don't want to ruin the blade."

"C'mon, Zafer," Nathan said. "Don't you think we'll look a little suspicious?"

Zafer sighed. "All right." He got out of the car, opened the trunk, and pulled out a pair of lock clippers. Even then, Zafer had to strain to get through the bracelet.

Josh rubbed his wrists. "Thanks."

Zafer looked over the Ebionite's swollen nose and grinned. "Does look broken." He gestured with a hand. "There's a bus stop about a hundred meters from here."

When the Ebionites had covered about half that distance, Zafer opened the trunk again.

Kadir got out with a video camera in his hand. He had filmed through the clear plastic of the taillight; the inside of which had been removed leaving only the plastic cover. When Zafer's phone beeped, it had been Kadir letting him know he'd gotten a clear shot of the deal.

Zafer got back in the car. "Now we got a little something extra on Ozatalay to go with our conversation in Nishantashi."

"I heard that video doesn't hold up in court. Too easy to doctor."

"Maybe. But I've got two separate audio tapes to back it up." Zafer pulled the collar of his shirt down to reveal the microphone.

"What was that show you put on for the Ebionites? They're not Sicarii."

"No. I don't think anybody would take two bullets as part of an act. Especially from Serafis. The way he held the pistol, I'm surprised he hit anything he aimed at. In any event if the Sciarii have them under surveillance, it will look like we kept our end of the bargain."

"Does that really matter?"

"A little good faith might come in handy. We took a queen with a pawn, but the game isn't over yet."

8:10

AND THEN THERE WERE TWO

"WHADDA YOU MEAN YOU'RE *OUT*?"

Neat stacks of bills covered the slate-topped coffee table in the Office. A total of $105,000 had gone to Serafis and Ozatlay, leaving $4,895,000 to be divided up. Kadir set aside $500,000 for Tariq's widow. Drew's share—more money than he'd ever dreamed of having—was $895,000. Zafer got $1.5 million. Kadir, two million.

It was unreal, all this money, all this paper—the world's greatest fiction. He wished his father would call now and ask him what good studying *lidderacher* was. Or what he was going to retire on. Or what he was going to leave the kids he didn't have.

But the money hadn't diminished his desire to find the Q document.

Kadir, on the other hand, had lost all interest. "I will give my shop to my cousin. I will go into the south and buy to a boat. I don't want to getting killed for another piece of antique paper which is written with Jewish holy words."

Drew had gotten used to their team of three. "Zafer? What about you?"

"I told you, I'm in the game till the end."

"I guess, then, we need to figure out where Q is."

"Sounds about right."

"Well," Drew said, "Q wasn't stolen from Abu, so there was no reason for Tariq to take it out of the country. We need to track down whoever found it and contacted Tariq. He's probably near Cairo since that was Tariq's territory."

Kadir, who was filling a briefcase with 10,000-dollar stacks, paid no attention to the conversation.

"Zafer, can you get the photos of Q?"

The Turk went to one of his filing cabinets, took out a yellow envelope, and slid the photos out.

Drew spread them on the table.

The photographer had used a flash—something no professional would have done with such delicate material—so wherever the photos had been taken had been badly lit.

Drew looked up at Zafer. "What do you think?"

"The scroll looks like it was unrolled on ... that might be stone."

"A cave?"

"Maybe. Or an old basement with a rough floor. Could be an old church."

"The Dead Sea Scrolls were found in caves." Drew turned to Kadir. "Where did you say Tariq was from originally?"

"A village near to Sadat City."

"Do we have a map of Egypt?"

Zafer nodded. "I've got an atlas."

Kadir cleared the rest of the money off the table and Zafer spread the atlas over about half of it.

"Okay, Sadat City is here ... between Alexandria and Cairo."

"So?"

"Well, I'm thinking that Tariq had most of his contacts in the area he was from."

"Also many contacts he had south from Cairo. He had car."

"Yes, but this is a Jewish scroll, written in Aramaic. The largest concentration of Jews outside of Palestine when Q was written was in Alexandria. And remember, when Jesus Panthera fled Jerusalem, he settled in Alexandria. The Therapeutae that Philo wrote about lived near Lake Mariout, just south of Alexandria."

"Jesus who?"

"Never mind. The point is we need to find a system of caves, a monastery, a cemetery—the scroll could have been photographed in a tomb—somewhere between Lake Mariout and Sadat City. Cairo at the farthest. If we go to Egypt, maybe we can find whoever came up with Q."

Zafer shook his head. "Might as well be looking for a contact lens on the bottom of a pond."

Drew nodded. "I suppose you're right." He walked over to the desk Zafer let him use and pulled *The Collected Works of Philo* out of a stack of books. All he could think to do was reread what Philo had written on the Therapeutae. Which might improve the odds slightly—like looking for a *penny* on the bottom of a pond.

8: 11

THE PYTHAGOREAN THEORY

WHEN DREW HAD LEARNED about Pythagoras in high school, the ancient Greek had simply been an obscure mathematician—a name and a theorem to memorize in geometry class. It wasn't until he got to college that Drew learned that $A^2 + B^2 = C^2$ had been discovered not by a math teacher, but by a religious sage who, in many ways, paralleled the Christ of the Gospels. Pythagoras was commonly held to be the son of Apollo and Parthenis, a mortal whose name had its root in *parthenos*—the Greek word for virgin. So a god had been his father and a virgin his mother. According to Iamblichus, Pythagoras also performed any number of miracles, including *calming the waves of rivers and seas in order that his disciples might the more easily pass over them.*

Said to have spent twenty-two years in Egypt as a student of the Mysteries of Osiris, Pythagoras had lived some five centuries before the traditional date of Christ's birth. The Pythagoreans gathered for prayer at dawn, devoted themselves to the study of philosophy and mathematics during the day, and in the evening gathered for a meal sanctified by readings from their scriptures. Robed in white, they refrained from eating meat of any kind and tended to be celibate. This was almost identical to Philo's description of the Therapeutae.

Jesus Panthera had learned "magic" while exiled in Egypt. *Magic*, Drew figured, was the Pythagorean theology passed on to him by the Therapeutae. Panthera, like Pythagoras himself, had brought back knowledge that his countrymen simply didn't understand. Or accept.

If Panthera had been one of the models for Christ, then it wasn't surprising that Pythagorean concepts of numbers had been encoded in the Gospels. Twelve, for example, made a number of appearances in the New Testament: Jesus is twelve years old when he holds forth in the temple; Jesus has twelve apostles; Jairus's daughter, whom Jesus raises, is twelve; and the hemorrhaging woman whom Jesus cures has been bleeding for twelve years. All the more intriguing that the dodecahedron—a solid shape with twelve pentagonal sides—was the Pythagorean symbol for the cosmos.

"You can call them coincidences, Jess," he said as if she were in the room. "But they're adding up."

John seemed to have borrowed more heavily from Pythagoras than any other Gospel. In fact, the opening was stolen right from Philo of Alexandria, who had also been known as Philo the Pythagorean for his veneration of the Greek sage.

In his allegorical interpretation of Genesis, Philo had put forth his own concept of the *Logos* or Word, a theme that already been expounded on by several Greek philosophers, including Heraclitus. Philo had believed in two Adams: the first was a *heavenly* human who reflected the image of God; the second was the mortal Adam patted out of clay. The first was a perfect man inhabiting a realm consisting purely of God's thought— borrowed obviously enough from Plato, specifically his *Timaeus* and its realm of ideal forms. Philo calls this heavenly human God's Logos or Word. *Adam's father*, Philo wrote, *is God, who is likewise Father of all, and his mother is Wisdom, through whom the universe came into existence.*

Flipping to the opening of John, Drew read, *In the beginning was the Word, and the Word was with God, and the Word was God. He was in the beginning with God. All things were made through Him, and without him nothing was made that was made.* The *Word* and *He* in John had always been interpreted as Christ, but this was clearly Philo's concept of the Word tacked onto Christianity: instead of Philo's Man from heaven being Adam, it was now Jesus. Whereas Philo wrote that the universe came into existence through Wisdom—the personification of God's thought—John moved it to *Jesus* as the Word. This conceptual sleight of hand cleverly eliminated the feminine *Wisdom* from the equation.

By stealing Philo's concept and pronouncing Jesus—not Adam—a denizen of heaven, John had helped change the course of religion, and, subsequently, of history. The irony was that, as scholars had demonstrated, whoever had written John wasn't even one of the twelve apostles. His Greek came from outside the Pauline mission area.

Drew went back to the Therapeutae, this time as seen through the eyes of Eusebius, the so-called Father of Church History. Writing in the fourth century, Eusebius of Caesarea made a posthumous fool of himself by "proving" the Therapeutae were the first Christians. Anyone, he says, can see that Philo was writing about *the earliest preachers of the Gospel teachings and the traditions handed down by the Apostles from the beginning*. Eusebius didn't know of course that the Gospels were written well after Philo had composed his essay and that the Therapeutae and their practices predated Christ by as much as centuries. Eusebius insisted that the skeptical would find *proof that cannot be found anywhere but in the rituals of Christians who follow the Gospel*. And yet, not only did the Therapeutae follow these practices, so did the Pythagoreans, whose cult was established nearly half a millennium before the accepted date of Christ's birth.

Drew picked up his volume of Philo and underlined *They read scripture and make a philosophical study of this ancestral wisdom, comprehending it according to allegory, since they consider the literal sense to be symbolic of a hidden reality revealed in figures*. Drew underlined allegory twice.

Even two thousand years ago, neither the Therapeutae nor Philo took scripture as literal history but as symbolic—in other words, fiction. Not lies but truth in poetic form. Fascinating as that was, Drew was no closer to the location of Q. He closed the book with an angry *whump*.

"Kadir, don't you know *any* of Tariq's contacts?"

Kadir frowned. "There wasn't importance to know."

"Yeah, well there is now. And Amal burned his phonebook. What about ... is there anything near Sadat City—ruins, caves, an abandoned church maybe?"

Kadir nodded. "There is monastery."

"*What?*"

"When Tariq was child, he was living in monastery."

"I thought he was *Muslim*."

"Yes, he became Muslim. But he was Christian before."

Drew jumped out of his chair. "Why didn't you say something sooner?"

"Does it important?"

"Yes, it *does*! Which one? *Which* monastery?"

"I have no any idea."

"Zafer, do you have a ... a guidebook on Egypt?"

"Somewhere."

"Find it. That has to be the connection. It *has* to be."

Zafer scanned a few shelves, pulled out a book, and tossed it to Drew.

It thumped against his chest. Sifting the index, he found listings for all of Egypt's monasteries.

"There are four monasteries between Alexandria and Cairo." He looked up at Zafer. "That has to be Tariq's connection to Q."

"Easy, Drew. Even we find the right monastery, it doesn't mean we'll find the scroll."

"But at least now we know where to look."

8: 12

TRUST

"WHAT DO YOU *MEAN* there's a second scroll? Why didn't you *tell* me?"

Calling from a public phone as per Zafer's instructions, Drew hadn't thought the euphoria of the good news—the Habakkuk Commentary was in the hands of the Turkish government and two Sicarii had been arrested—would wear off so fast.

"Jess, you know how things work with Zafer and Kadir. They keep me on a short leash."

"Yeah, I understand, but they don't listen in on your phone calls, do they?"

"It's not a matter of trusting you, Jess. Zafer doesn't even trust *me*."

"So you're telling me there's a second scroll, probably in Egypt, an Aramaic version of Q1, and you're going to leave *me*—probably the only qualified scholar in Istanbul who's not in jail—and go off to find this thing on your own with a, a ...what is he? An ex-commando? Did he even go to college?"

"Considering the people we're up against, I don't think it's such a bad thing have to an ex-commando around. But listen, we don't even know if this thing is genuine."

"And what exactly are you going to do with it if you find it?"

"Get it to you."

There was a pause. "Really?"

"Like you said, you're the only expert we've got. How else are we going to know if it's genuine?"

"So you ... you know where to look?"

"Yes."

"Wow, no hesitation. You know exactly?"

"Pretty much."

"Drew this is ... this is incredibly exciting. Are you *sure* I can't come with you?"

"Not as long as Zafer is running the show. And without him, there *is* no show."

"Why don't you just ... just message me when you get there? I'll show up on my own and ... and make up a story."

"He's way too smart for that."

"*Shit*. Well, can I see you? Before you go? I miss you."

"I miss you too."

"I don't understand why I can't go with you. Is it because I'm a—"

"It has nothing to do with the fact that you're the only one of us who could model a swimsuit for *Sports Illustrated*. When we sold the Habakkuk Scroll, Zafer wouldn't even let Kadir go."

"Can you imagine how I feel? The greatest find in New Testament archaeology—"

"If it's genuine."

"Right. And who's going to find it? An English instructor and a guy who got kicked out of the Turkish army."

Drew kept the insult he felt out of his voice. "Hey ... who found the Dead Sea Scrolls? A Bedouin shepherd. If we do come up with Q, you'll be the first to translate it. Your name will be in the history books right next to Q."

"Well, now that you got my hopes up, you better not come back without it."

8: 13

THE MYSTERIES

DREW GAZED OUT A WINDOW. A tin-capped lamp, weighing down a cable strung between buildings, turned the street into a black-and-white photograph: cobblestones dark as cinders, crumbling doorways sunk in shadow, eroding faces carved into cornerstones—sepulchral, like tomb effigies.

He glanced at his watch. Two a.m.

The empty street should have been silent. He stopped breathing and listened. He thought he heard faint footsteps on the cobbles. No, what he'd heard were echoes of whoever had already walked these back streets. Maybe this morning. Maybe before he'd been born.

In spite of the fact that he was looking out of a third-floor window, he had found his way into an underworld. He had a pile of money but no job, and half the things he did were illegal. He had become a part of the city's shadow population—just as his father had always feared.

"Well," he said to himself, "I guess it was always in me."

He sat down at the desk he'd come to think of as his and lit a cigarillo.

The mosaic wasn't finished. The Jewish pieces were in place, but the Greek picture was still a tombstone in the fog.

From the cardboard box beside the desk, he pulled out his battered copy of *The Golden Bough*. Sir James Frazer had dug up the oldest of Christianity's roots—the worship of a god who dies only to be resurrected—and followed it to its elemental source: the cyclical death and rebirth of plant life. It was that simple. The turning of the seasons. Drawing upon examples from hundreds of cultures and peoples as divergent as African huntsmen and German peasants, Native Americans and Welsh farmers, Frazer had demonstrated that Christianity and a host of other religions reflected the death of the Earth in fall and winter and its rebirth in spring and summer.

If Christianity was essentially a Jewish Mystery cult, then the Gospel authors must have unwound a thread for initiates to follow. Jesse would have dismissed the idea as wild speculation, but the Mysteries had from the first worked through symbol and allegory: they were meant to be double-sided, deciphered, to be narrative double-entendres.

Drew picked up *Ancient Greek Religions* and skimmed the highlighted passages until something Plato had written stopped him:

It seems that those men who founded the Mysteries were not unenlightened but in fact had a hidden meaning when they said that he who goes uninitiated and unsanctified into the world hereafter will lie in the mud ... "

Drew tapped ashes from the tip of his cigarillo. Plato's statement was interesting but vague. Taking another drag on the cigar and surfing the index, he found a more explicit quote from Heliodorus, a hierophant of the Mysteries:

Philosophers and theologians do not reveal the meanings encoded in these stories to the uninitiated but instead use myths to instruct them. Those who have attained the higher levels of the Mysteries, however, they initiate into deeper knowledge in the sanctity of the holy shrine, in the light cast by the flaming brand of truth.

Drew snatched up his leather-bound Bible and scanned Paul's letters. His finger stopped on a passage in Corinthians.

However, we speak wisdom among those who are mature, yet not wisdom of this age, nor of the rulers of this age, who are coming to nothing; but we speak the wisdom of God in a mystery, the hidden wisdom which God ordained before the ages for our glory...

He closed the Bible and let it thump onto the steel desk. If it was already common practice among the Mystery religions to encode certain information, then it was almost certain the New Testament authors had done the same. Nearly two thousand years after the Gospels had been written, *we* were the ignoramuses, the inexperienced initiates who believed every word of a narrative that was never meant to be historical. Jesus hadn't been born to a virgin any more than Athena had sprung, fully armored, out of Zeus's head. What history the New Testament contained had been thoroughly disguised and placed in a mythic framework—a fiction. Hadn't Jesus said *"To you it is given to know the Mysteries of the kingdom of God, but to the rest of them it is only given in parables?"* Weren't the Gospels exactly what had been given *to the rest of them*—to us?

Drew recalled fragments of something similar a saint had said about Genesis. He tapped a palm heel against his forehead trying to remember which Church Father it had been. "Saint Origen?"

Drew grabbed *A History of the Gospels*, a hefty hardcover, and flipped back and forth between the index and the body of the text. "There it is," he muttered.

What man is found to be such an idiot as to believe that God planted trees in Paradise, in Eden, like a gardener? Every man must understand these things as images under which a hidden meaning lies concealed.

A few lines later Drew found something even better: *No one will doubt that these are merely figurative expressions that designate certain mysteries through the appearance of history rather than through actual events.*

"Straight from the mouth of a Church Father," he said and filled his own with cigar smoke.

Encoded information was plausible enough; deciphering it was something else.

Drew tilted his head back and exhaled a cornucopia-shaped cloud, which drifted toward the exposed rafters.

The high priest of the Mysteries, the hierophant, represented the dying god. Had this been Jesus Panthera's crime? Had he returned from Egypt as a hierophant?

The hierophant led initiates into a cave, the recesses of a temple, or some other dark enclosure where they were expected to bump heads with God. Hadn't Paul said *For now we see in a glass, darkly, but then face to face?* Hadn't Luke's Christ been born in a *katalemna*, a *cave?* Hadn't Dionysus been born in a cave? Hadn't Mithra been born out of rock and didn't his initiates meet in caves? Was it coincidence that the oldest church in the world, Saint Peter's in Antakya, was a cave?

Yesterday, when he'd taken Jesse to the Aya Sofya, the first adjective that had come to mind was *cavernous*—the whole interior of the Byzantine cathedral, its geometry of domes and semi-domes was a stylized *cavern*. They all were. Every church in early Christendom had been nothing more than an aboveground cave. Only centuries later did the heaven-tending steeple become popular.

Drew stood and went back to the window although all he could see was the building across the street. He gazed in the direction of the Cathedral of Saint Sophia. Here, in once-upon-a-time Constantinople, architecture had preserved Christianity's ties to the Mystery cults.

What if the tunnel in the grotto church in Antakya hadn't been a precaution taken against the Romans, who were barely aware Christians existed at the time Saint Peter was preaching, but part of an initiation rite? After the ceremony was held in the cave, where initiates were baptized, they may well have been sent through the tunnel to emerge on the hillside—a symbolic rebirth. Cave and tunnel would therefore symbolize womb and birth canal.

Everything had become part of a clear pattern that, until only a few minutes ago, hadn't existed. When Drew glanced down at the book in his hands and saw the Greek word for *initiates,* he understood the Mystery.

8: 14

A 2,000-YEAR-OLD COLD CASE

Dark sky backgrounded the mosques and their minarets. The Moon was setting somewhere behind the city. The Sea of Marmara, the Golden Horn, the Bosporus—he couldn't see any of them from the Office, but undoubtedly their surfaces had been silvered.

The word that sent his thoughts down a series of forking roads was *mystae*—initiates, derived from the verb *myein*, *to close* or *shut*. Novices, the *mystae* did not yet understand the Mysteries: their eyes were closed. After the hierophant had submerged them in the ceremonies, they were called *epoptae*—*those who had seen*.

The healing of Bartimaeus—a blind man in Mark—now took on an entirely new dimension. For centuries this was read as a simple miracle story, and so it would have appeared to Jews of the first century. But why does the blind man, whose name translates to *Son of Timaeus*, share the name of one of Plato's most famous dialogues? A dialogue in which a man named Timaeus distinguishes—at length—between the physical world and the eternal world? A dialogue in which Plato argues that sight is the foundation of philosophy because it is through sight that we recognize the intelligence and divinity blueprinted in the physical universe?

It now seemed obvious to Drew that Mark's Jesus in this passage was a hierophant opening the eyes of an initiate to the eternal. Bartimaeus had become an *epopt*, a witness; *he had seen*. No Greek or Hellenized

Jew could have missed it. To make the master-initiate relationship clear, Bartimaeus throws off his cloak and joins Jesus.

The Jews of antiquity could easily have confused a hierophant with a sorcerer—heirophants even carried wands. Was this the sorcery Jesus Panthera had learned from the Therapeutae?

Recalling another story revolving around a man who is closed off— he is deaf and dumb—Drew did a quick Internet search to pinpoint the incident. Mark 7:34. He reached for his Bible and fingered through the crepe-thin pages. The word Jesus utters in Aramaic, *Ephphatha*, was translated in red letters: *"Be opened."* And *Immediately his ears were opened, and his tongue was loosed.* To the Jews, who, as Paul complained, demanded a sign, the man had been miraculously healed; to the Greeks, who sought knowledge, a man who was closed, a *mystae*, had been opened to the wisdom embodied in the Mysteries.

As Drew read, smoking one cigarillo after another, he found more dual-sided incidents.

Jesus riding into Jerusalem on a donkey while an adoring crowd waves palm fronds at him served to "fulfill" a prophecy in Zechariah about a king *lowly and riding on a donkey.* Centuries before Christ, however, Dionysus was portrayed as being carried by a donkey. During the procession to the Eleusian Mysteries, a donkey bore materials that would be assembled into an effigy of Dionysus while a crowd along the road saluted the celebrants with sheaves of branches. To Drew, the critical detail was that palm fronds and branches were missing entirely from the verse in *Zechariah.* Palm Sunday was not a Jewish or even Christian tradition but a pagan one. While Jews reading Mark would pick up the reference to Zechariah, Greeks would see another version of their own Mysteries.

Drew could almost have convinced himself he was interpreting creatively, but his insomniac descent into history led him to a strange purification ceremony in which initiates took a piglet into the sea with them—as many as two thousand initiates at a time. The idea, apparently, was that the impurities of the bathers would be taken on by the unsuspecting animals. The pigs were later sacrificed by being thrown into a chasm, symbolizing the disappearance of Persephone, daughter of the goddess Demeter into the Underworld.

"Two thousand pigs," Drew muttered to himself and pulled Stephen's creased list out of a back pocket. He unfolded the square of paper and there they were: two thousand pigs. He opened the Bible again, Mark 5:9. The passage detailed the exorcism of a man who *dwelled among tombs*. He is possessed by a multitude of demons, which Jesus sends into a herd of two thousand swine. The pigs stampede off a cliff, fall into the sea, and drown.

To modern Christians and to ancient Jews, this was simply a bizarre miracle. But two thousand pigs? In a country where pork was outlawed? The swineherds could have been Greeks living in Palestine, but why didn't they demand reparation for the lost herd? Why didn't Jesus offer any? Even today two thousand pigs would bring a hefty price.

Because it never happened; the story was an allegory.

A few keyboard taps brought up Sir James Frazer's observation that the pig was sacred to Demeter, the fertility goddess at the center of the Eleusian Mysteries. Persephone was worshiped at the same Mysteries. Even as a kid Drew had known the myth of how Persephone had been kidnapped by Hades and taken to the Underworld. Icy needles formed in his spine when he read Frazer's version:

> *At the moment that Hades carried off Persephone, a swineherd called Euboleus was herding his swine on the spot, and his herd was engulfed in the chasm down which Hades vanished with Persephone.*

The demon-infested man in the Gospel *lived* in the tombs; what better way of recalling the Underworld, where Persephone presided over the dead for seven months of the year? Sending "unclean" spirits into the pigs was Mark's translation of impurities going from initiates into the pigs, while having the pigs run off a cliff and drown in the sea implied both the chasm Hades had opened and the briny Mysteries rite.

Drew no longer had any doubt that the Gospels were essentially attempts to reconcile Judaism with the Greek Mysteries. If he could dig up so many double meanings in a single night, surely scholars poring over the Bible could find plenty more—even the name *Jesus Christ* was an amalgam of the Aramaic-derived *Yeshua* and the Greek *Christos*.

The societies for which the Bible had been written were long gone, and what we knew about them hardly amounted to an epitaph on a grave marker. But rather than admit our ignorance, we clung to surface details without grasping the deeper meanings; we had the box but had lost the contents.

Drew recalled the vases at Serafis's villa in Antakya that had shown

Dionysus with loaves of bread and huge jars of wine set before him. The god of wine and fertility, Dionysus was intimately tied to the harvest, to wheat. At Dionysus's rites wine was drunk as a way of taking the god inside and communing with him. During the same rites, worshipers were given a wheat cake called *makaria—blessedness*. It was the Eucharist.

The great Roman orator Cicero criticized Mystery celebrants for taking their rites too literally: *Is anybody so mad*, he wrote, *as to believe that the food he eats is actually a god?* Again, the Eucharist. Since Cicero was dead at least four decades before Jesus had been born—if he'd been born—there was no question about who had borrowed from whom.

It was nearly four in the morning, but Drew went on smoking and reading. There were detectives who worked with bodies and forensic evidence; he was working with the translations of ancient texts, with a two-thousand-year-old cold case.

He studied Stephen's list to isolate what was still marked NFI – no fucking idea or CU – connection unknown.

- *John the Baptist – Model for Christ*
- *James the Just – Model for Christ, Teacher of Righteousness in Dead Sea Scrolls*
- *The Ebionites – Knew Paul was the Liar in D.S.S., insisted Christ was not divine*
- *Ananus – the Wicked Priest in D.S.S., colluded with Paul in murdering James the Just*
- *Damascus – Essene name (D.S.S.) for Qumran*
- *Judas of Galilee – Zealot model for Christ*
- *Simon bar Giora – Model for Christ*
- *Iscariot – Evidence of Jesus' Zealot ties*
- *The Sicarii – Founded by Judas of Galilee*
- *2000 Pigs – Mysteries connection*
- *Clementine Recognitions – Account of James's death*
- *Serapis – Egyptian god (CU)*
- *Ezekiel's Exodus – NFI*
- *Philo of Alexandria – Mentions Pilate but not Christ. Wrote about Therapeutae.*
- *The Therapeutae – Practiced Jewish version of the Mysteries, (link to J. Panthera?)*

- *The Bacchae – a play by Euripides (CU)*
- *Nag Hammadi Library – Collection of Gnostic Christian works deemed heretical (CU)*

Not only was his sleuthing incomplete, but also Stephen had only given him a partial list, the words that had come immediately to mind that night. For the hundredth time Drew wished the old hierophant could sit down with him, pour some wine, and help a novice make sense of so much murky history.

Drew turned to the computer, typed in *Serapis,* and waited for the list of websites to pop up.

"Well whaddaya know?" Serapis had been born in Alexandria.

BOOK 9: 1 - 16

ALEXANDRIA

For among the many worthy and indeed divine institutions which your Athens has contributed to humanity, none, in my opinion, exceeds the Mysteries. The rites are properly called 'initiations' and in truth we have discovered in them the first principles of life. We have gained the understanding not only to live in happiness but also to die with superior hope.

— Cicero, De Legibus II, xiv, 36, circa 49 BC

9: 1

ASHRAF

ARCHITECTURE ASIDE, Alexandria was nothing like Cairo. Founded near a fishing village by Alexander the Great in 331 BC, it eventually came to rival Rome itself as the empire's greatest city. Ptolemy, one of Alexander's generals, became the second Greek pharaoh—after Alexander. Scavenging statues and obelisks from older cities, Ptolemy used them to give Alexandria, conceived and built by Greeks, an Egyptian veneer. His vision was of a city that was a harmonious blend of Greek and Egyptian cultures.

Next to nothing remained of ancient Alexandria, but Drew preferred it to Cairo. It was right on the Mediterranean, with a beautiful crescent-shaped harbor. Two curving promontories, like protective, if spindly arms, left a small opening to the sea. At the tip of one of them had been the Pharos—a lighthouse that rose some four hundred feet in three magnificent stages, like a slender ziggurat.

Buses weren't as popular as trams, which, battered and gnawed by rust, rumbled along tracks that criss-crossed the city. Alexandria was neither as dusty nor as crowded as Cairo, the tang in the air was refreshing, the light seemed to be of a different quality—and there was more of it. Unlike Cairo, Alexandria was not a city of alleys and passages kept in perpetual shadow by highrises.

The day had started in the car. Zafer was sure the Sicarii would be waiting for them at Ataturk Airport in Istanbul so they drove to Sabiha

Gökchen Airport, which handled far fewer flights, none of which landed in Egypt. Instead, they flew to Anakara and took a connecting flight from there.

On arrival in Alexandria there were more games—switching taxis, doubling back the way they had come, alternating between traveling on foot and by car, weaving through crowds and ducking into a hotel and getting out through a back door.

They had only leather messenger bags slung over their shoulders. Anything they needed, Zafer had said they could pick up in-country. "Don't worry, Ashraf will take care of us."

Ashraf was a tall, swarthy Egyptian with singular markings: three quarters of his left eyebrow was white, and there were small patches of pigmentless skin just above it.

Drew thought of a friendly bear when Ashraf smiled.

"Don't let him fool you," Zafer said. "He's a dangerous bastard." Without turning to look at the Egyptian, who was a couple of feet behind him, Zafer let go with a back kick. Ashraf stepped to the side and parried it. Zafer turned into a Tasmanian devil, whirling and throwing elbows and palm heels and kicks. Ashraf—taller by four or five inches and a good deal heavier—had all he could do to keep the smaller man off him. The play brawl ended with an elegant trip, which put Ashraf on his back, and a wristlock that made him tap the floor.

Zafer let go of Ashraf's arm, hooked thumbs with him in a biker's handshake, and pulled him to his feet.

"Egyptian commandos are a lot better than they used to be," Zafer said, "but they still need some work."

Maybe they do, Drew thought, *but I won't try taking one down any time soon.*

Ashraf was no longer in the Egyptian military. He had become a small-arms dealer and used the flat they were in as a safe house. Although it was about half a mile from the Eastern Harbor, there was still a composite odor of salt and damp wood. The building was worn, its amber paint faded, although the shutters covering the long windows—framed by Ionic and Corinthian pilasters and faux lintels—were still bright green. Ashraf had a small network of lookouts—a shoeshine boy, a man who sold wallets on the street, a shop owner.

The first thing Zafer did was buy a pair of Glocks.

"You're not Mossad anymore." Zafer grinned at Drew. "You don't have to carry a peashooter."

They didn't wear suit jackets to conceal their weapons. Instead, they were both in shorts and T-shirts.

Zafer dropped the Glock into his messenger bag. "Car?"

Ashraf nodded. "Renault 406."

"Good." Zafer turned to Drew and tipped his head toward the door. "Let's go."

9: 2

THE MONASTERIES

ZAFER DROVE SOUTH on a highway that cut through desert. It was early afternoon as they approached Wadi Natrun, an area named after the substance found there in abundance and without which mummification would have been impossible. Natron, an earth-made salt, that, if used properly, more or less petrified dead flesh. Of the sixty monasteries that Coptic Christians had built throughout this arid terrain, only four remained.

Now that they were here, Drew was less optimistic about finding Q. How many caves and tombs could they search? Even if they found the place where the scroll had first been discovered, who was to say the site hadn't become a haunt for the wind while the scroll was tucked under a bed in some hut in a village that wasn't even on their map?

He didn't like being without Kadir either; it was like they'd left behind their good luck charm.

Zafer drove past a mosque on the side of the road, sand piled against its walls. The scenery reminded Drew of Arizona although it was considerably more barren, and instead of saguaro cactuses, palm trees grew in scattered clumps. There were even highway signs advertising food, gas, lodging—all in Arabic, of course.

The three southernmost monasteries were in a tight cluster. Zafer had decided to work more or less backwards, going to the monastery most distant from Alexandria first.

The first compound of walled-in buildings they approached looked like the adobe of Spanish churches in the American southwest. The small domes with crosses planted in them were more reminiscent of oversized kilns than the architectural marvels of the Aya Sofya.

Getting out of the car, Drew swept his eyes over the smooth, sandstone-colored walls. They looked to be thirty or thirty-five feet high. Drew was surprised to see a paved lot with a tour bus parked in it, and kids kicking around a soccer ball. It wasn't the desolate seclusion he'd expected.

Flies made a tiny cloud around his head, tickling his face when they landed. Waving them away, he followed Zafer through a small door rather than a capacious gate. They were greeted on the other side by a monk who wore a long, navy-blue gown and a cap that covered his ears. The cap reminded Drew of the leather helmets football players had worn back in the 1950s, except that it was a much lighter material and was decorated with stars and crescent moons. His face darker than Drew's, the monk had a beard of black wool that looked like it could defeat a wire brush.

He had to be hot under all that.

"Welcome to Deir Anba Bishoi, the Monastery of Saint Bishoi. I am Brother Yusuf. This way." The monk led them along a passage between buildings nestled against the outer wall on the left and what were probably the monks' quarters on their right. Brother Yusuf stopped and spread his arms.

"Here is the resting place of our beloved saint whose body remains uncorrupted after all these centuries. It is a miracle! Here also is the Well of the Martyrs. So called because during a Bedouin attack, forty-nine monks were killed, and the brigands washed the blood off their swords in the well." His rehearsed English was heavily accented but perfectly clear.

"A donation for the monastery." Zafer handed him fifty Egyptian pounds. "We're interested in someone who lived here as a boy. He left about twenty-five years ago."

"A boy who lived here?"

"His name was Tariq Soufanati."

"We would have to check the records …"

"If there's a fee, we'll be happy to pay it."

The monk shook his head. "I don't think that will be necessary, but we must see Father Al-Masri.

A girl, being chased by her sister or a friend bumped into Drew, her forehead colliding with his waist. She glanced up at him and then ran off, screaming happily.

Brother Yusuf led them to a courtyard taken up mostly by a lush garden that had been planted with a variety of palm trees, tropical flowers, and cactuses.

They found Father Al-Masri in an office that looked more like a storage room, the walls lined with bookshelves that held rows of faded ledgers. A small man with gray woven through his coarse beard, he sat at a large desk. A single window opened onto the courtyard behind him.

Brother Yusuf spoke in what Drew assumed was Coptic—it wasn't Arabic. The older monk looked at the two visitors, nodded gravely, and rose from his chair. He pulled down several ledgers from a shelf. One by one he opened them and followed his index finger up and down the pages. He shook his head after he had closed the last one and spoke briefly to Brother Yusuf, who translated into English: "No one by that name lived here."

Zafer thanked Father Al-Masri in Arabic.

"Scratch that one," Drew said as they headed back toward the parking lot.

Deir el-Sourian, Monastery of the Syrians, was next on their list. It was only about half a kilometer away. Architecturally, it was nearly identical to the first monastery although the walls were even higher. According to a sign written in English, the church had been built around a cave once inhabited by Saint Bishoi. The monk who came out to greet them wore the same long robes and odd cap with stars and moons on it, but also had a silent partner whom he glanced at from time to time.

Zafer spent another fifty pounds, and they were guided to another dingy office—this one without windows—and the same record-keeping system. One of the monks turned on a standing fan. The mechanical breeze felt good against Drew's sweaty face, but didn't do much to deter the flies.

"Please, if you will wait here. I will return in a moment."

They were left with the silent monk. Drew wondered why he was the only monk who didn't have a real beard, just three or four days' growth. Maybe he just joined up.

The monk smiled at Zafer, showing poorly cared for yellow teeth.

Zafer smiled back.

The Turk moved so fast Drew wasn't quite sure what hit the monk—probably a palm heel. The Egyptian fell against the bookshelves and sagged to the floor. Zafer caught him across the temple with a knee, and the Egyptian collapsed.

"What the fuck—?"

"Stand in front of the door. About two meters back—there, in front of the desk. Put your pistol in the waistband of your shorts, in the back." Zafer pulled up the robes of the monk, searched around and came up with an automatic pistol.

"How did you know?"

Zafer dragged the monk, who was starting to wake up, to the other side of the room and cuffed his wrists with Kevlar. "Look at his shoes."

They were black loafers.

"So?"

"He's the only 'monk' I've seen today who isn't wearing sandals."

"You attacked this guy because he's not wearing sandals?"

"He's the only 'monk' with trouser legs sticking out under his robes."

Drew hadn't noticed that, either.

"And he's the only monk without a beard. We walked in on somebody snooping for information just like us. Somehow, they made us, stripped a couple of monks, and had plans to interrogate us."

"They?"

"There's at least one more. Maybe two or three. Don't worry. They all have to go through the same door." Zafer grinned. "It'll be like Thermopylae."

Bait … again.

"When the door opens, expect a gun to be pointed at your chest. Just put your hands up. I'll do the rest."

Zafer positioned himself on the hinged side so that as the door swung open it would hide him. A few seconds later, two monks entered, one of whom, despite his coffee-brown complexion, looked a bit ashen. When he was pushed out of the way by the monk behind him, Drew saw why: the gun Zafer had warned him about was pointed at his face. For about a millisecond.

Zafer shot out from behind the door, grabbed the monk's wrist with one hand, the pistol with the other, and twisted violently. The gun came away in one hand; with the other hand, Zafer turned the monk's palm to the ceiling, which meant the elbow was also facing up. Zafer brought his armpit down on the Egyptian's upper arm. Arms, Drew was well aware, did not bend that way. With pressure exerted up on the wrist, but down on the upper arm and the elbow forced in the wrong direction, the Egyptian fell to his knees with a groan. Zafer let go of the wrist and cracked the monk in the forehead with an elbow. It was a light blow, just enough to leave him dazed. When the Egyptian looked up again, his own pistol was pointed at his nose.

Zafer smirked. "Shall we talk?"

9: 3

SLEEPING WITH A BLIND MAN

To HIS AMAZEMENT, Drew recognized the Egyptian Zafer was cuffing with Kevlar. "That's the guy who clubbed Kadir in Cairo."

Zafer nodded. "Now we know who sent them and how they made us."

"I can call the police now, yes?" asked the real monk.

"Please don't, Brother…?" Zafer waited for the monk to offer his name.

"Haddad."

Zafer took out his wallet and flashed his MIT identification. "I'm with the Turkish government. Would you let me handle this?"

Brother Haddad looked impressed as he scrutinized the ID held out to him. The fact that it was written in Turkish didn't seem to bother him. "Yes … yes, of course."

"What did they want?" Zafer tucked his wallet in the back pocket of his shorts.

"They asked about a …" He made a circular motion with his two index fingers as if he were rolling something up.

"A scroll?"

"Yes. They wanted to know are there any ancient scrolls in our library. Not written in Coptic, but Aramaic."

"Do you?"

"No."

Zafer walked over to Nabil's men. "Why are you looking for the scroll here?" he asked in Arabic.

Neither of them answered.

Zafer squatted down in front of the one who had attacked Kadir. "Do you want to walk out of here, or would you prefer to be carried?" He snatched one of the man's ankles. Placing one hand on the ankle and another higher on the leg, he twisted.

The Egyptian flipped his body back and forth like a hooked fish. "Nabil!" he shrieked.

Zafer relaxed his grip.

"Nabil found out Tariq lived in a monastery as a boy. He thinks the monks have the scroll."

"Much better." Zafer turned to Brother Haddad. "Is there, uh ... somewhere I can put these two for a little while? While you and I talk?"

The Copt looked down.

The men were both sitting on the floor, gazing up like dogs imploring their master.

"Well ... yes ..."

After Nabil's men were padlocked in a storage closet, Zafer, Drew, and Brother Haddad returned to the windowless office.

"They're just guessing where the scroll is," Zafer said to Drew.

"So are we."

Zafer turned to Brother Haddad. "Was Tariq Soufanati here? Maybe twenty or thirty years ago?"

The monk went through a set of peeling ledgers but failed to turn up any record of Tariq.

"Could I ask you a very important favor?" Zafer said. "Please forget Tariq's name. Even if the police want to know. Just tell them we were looking for a scroll."

The monk nodded. "*Aiwa.*" *Yes.*

"Could we ask one more favor of you? Could you wait three or four hours before calling the police? This is an extremely urgent and confidential matter involving Egyptian antiquities and Turkish nationals. It's best if our investigations remain separate."

"I see." He smiled weakly. "It seems a small favor to ask of me in return for a very great favor from you."

Zafer thanked him profusely in Arabic before he and Drew left.

The black asphalt of the parking lot looked like it was on the verge of melting. *How the hell do they live in this dustbin with all these flies?*

Drew wondered. He opened the door of the Renault, and a blast of hot air rose up to meet him.

"You know what this means, don't you, Drew?" Zafer started the engine and hit the air conditioner.

"If Nabil can get this close, so can the Sicarii."

"Right. I think you should go back to Alexandria."

"What?"

"If the Sicarii find that scroll before we do ..." Zafer shook his head. "No more insurance policy. It'll just be head shot from a rooftop. If they even *think* they can find it without us, we're dead. Even if we actually somehow manage to pull this off, you're probably going to have to get into a witness protection program ... or spend the rest of your life looking over your shoulder."

"I've been thinking about that."

"You've got almost a million dollars. Go back to Istanbul, buy all the books you want, sit in your *jumba*, smoke your *narghile*, and watch the sun set on the Golden Horn."

"What about you?"

Zafer shrugged. "The worse the odds are, the more interested I am. I can't help it. And I've got training. You don't."

Drew shook his head. "I don't have any illusions that this scroll is going to change all that much, but it's another piece in a huge puzzle. It's a little more of the truth. I want to know. Scholars should know. I'm in."

Zafer smirked. "*Körle yatan, shashi kalkar.*" *Sleep with a blind man, wake up cross-eyed.*

Drew nodded. "Yeah, I guess."

"There's one other thing."

"What's that?"

"Maybe Nabil's man recognized me, maybe he didn't. But with that long hair, he definitely fingered *you*. And by tonight the Egyptian police will have a description of us."

"What're you trying to say?"

"The hair, Drew ... it's gotta go."

9: 4

EZEKIEL'S *EXODUS*

THE MONASTERY OF THE VIRGIN of El Baramouse looked like an oasis. The extensive grounds were irrigated and green, and two tour buses were baking in the parking lot. In the surrounding fields, a monk rode a tractor.

Drew jerked his thumb in the direction of a bookstore on the edge of the parking lot. "Just let me poke my head in there for a minute."

Zafer frowned. "A *minute*."

It wasn't much of a walk, nor was it much of a bookstore. A few kitschy icons, some thin books about local history in poorly rendered English, some cheap crosses. But the back of the store seemed too small for the building housing it, and, nosing around, Drew discovered a second shop, hardly a third the size of the first. It wasn't manned by a Coptic monk. At least he wasn't dressed like the rest of them. Which meant any minute now, Zafer might break the guy's nose with a palm heel.

"Welcome." The old man dipped his shaggy head. He had a beard worthy of an Old Testament patriarch and an abundance of wiry gray hair. His eyes were set under crags of bone overgrown by snowy eyebrows. Wearing a white *jalabiya* and sandals, he couldn't have been more than five feet tall.

"You're not a monk?"

"The monks are very kind to let me keep my shop here. I am Jewish. My name is Shimon."

Drew remembered the synagogue near their first hotel in Cairo; the Egyptian police kept it under twenty-four-hour guard.

Shimon had a wide assortment of items for sale, everything from the usual tourist trinkets to what looked like genuine antiques. The ceiling was hung with an array of lamps. The ones dangling from the eaves clinked and ting-tinged when the hot breeze stirred them.

"You know who that is?"

Drew was looking over a mosaic depicting a bearded god. "Serapis?"

"Very good. What do you know about Serapis?"

"A man-made god."

"They're all man-made."

"Touche." The beginnings of a smile put a curve in Drew's lips. "I thought you said you're Jewish."

"We'll get to that. Tell me about Serapis."

It had taken Drew all of two or three minutes last night on the web to get a bio on the god. "Let's see ... when Ptolemy took over after Alexander the Great died, he put together a composite of Osiris and a couple of Greek gods. Serapis was the husband of Isis, just as Osiris had been, and his animal was the bull, like Osiris, but whenever he was depicted—"Drew pointed at the mosaic—"the likeness was clearly Zeus ... bearded, curly-haired, Greek. The idea was to unite Egyptians and Greeks in worship."

It was now obvious why the professor had led Drew to Serapis: it illustrated how, in the first-century Levant, it was entirely acceptable to found a new religion. It was *routine*. The Mystery religions, of which the cult of Serapis was one, were all classic examples. The Pythagorean Mysteries had taken the Mysteries of Osiris and replaced the Egyptian deity with a Greek one—Dionysus. It even worked on a local level: the Eleusian Mysteries near Athens venerated not Dionysus but Demeter and her daughter Persephone, while Artemis was at the center of the Mysteries in Ephesus. Using a familiar god as the front man—or woman—was a simple but effective way of adopting an alien religion or creating a new one.

Virtually unthinkable in the twenty-first century, Ptolemy's strategy had *worked*. Serapis became enormously popular and his cult spread well beyond Egypt, yielding some of the most astonishing temples in the ancient world.

"Well done." Shimon nodded. "I see you are not merely a tourist."

Zafer, after a cursory glance at the wares, lifted an impatient eyebrow at Drew.

"Alexandria was the greatest city of the ancient world—not Rome, not even Jerusalem," Shimon said as though he were offering the city itself for sale. "The Mysteries were practiced here but without secrecy. Judaism flourished beside Hellenism. Serapis was accepted by both Egyptians and Greeks. Here, the heart was open. The greatest of all the Alexandrian theosophers, Philo, wrote here. Perhaps you would like to see some of his books?"

Drew raised a hand and shook his head. "I have Philo."

"Ah, a rare customer. Then you must know that here in Alexandria Yaweh was not a vengeful, jealous god, but a symbol of the forces of the universe. Yahweh belonged to all."

Drew was nodding, looking for a way to leave without being rude.

"You ready, Drew?" Zafer asked in Turkish.

"*Evet.*"

"You are Turkish?"

Zafer answered: "Yes. *Türkche biliyormusunuz?*"

"I know only a few words. But my Hebrew, Arabic, and English are quite good. I also have some knowledge of Aramaic and ancient Greek. Here in the desert, there is plenty of time for learning languages."

"Impressive." Drew pretended to look over the wares as he drifted toward the parking lot.

"Here, you know, is where wisdom literature was born."

Drew held up a finger to Zafer. *"Bir dakika." One minute.* Q1 was a form of wisdom literature, and Q1 was what they had come for. "In Alexandria?"

"But of course. One god melded into another in Alexandria. People looked for similarities—not differences—and the old barriers between nations disappeared. What was important was the distinction between the wise and the foolish. Here they took great pleasure in uniting humanity, rather than dividing it. Would you like to see for yourself?"

Shimon waved a hand at the back of the store, which was lined with shelves crammed with books in various stages of decomposition. Some looked healthy enough, but others had moth-eaten covers and pages falling out of bindings—something like the prayer books in Kadir's stall in Istanbul.

Ah, here comes the pitch. "No, I don't think—"

"Did you know the story of the Jewish exodus from Egypt was made into a Greek tragedy?"

"By a Greek?"

"No. A Jew named Ezekiel."

Ezekiel's *Exodus*. The one keyword that hadn't shown up in any of his web searches.

"Here …" Shuffling over to a shelf, Shimon extracted a large volume with a rough cloth cover. "This is the book you want." The old man lifted a worn cover and began to read. *"All Wisdom cometh from the Lord, and is with Him forever. Who can number the sand of the sea, and the drops of rain, and the days of eternity? Who can find out the height of heaven, and the breadth of the Earth, and the deep, and Wisdom?"*

A breeze turned the brass lamps hanging from their chains into chimes.

"That's from Ezekiel's *Exodus*?"

Shimon shook his white head. "Jesus ben Sirach. Unfortunately, the Book of Sirach is often considered apocryphal, almost heretical. Do you know why?"

"No idea."

"Listen: *Wisdom hath been created before all things, and the understanding of prudence from everlasting. The word of God most high is the fountain of Wisdom; and Her ways are everlasting commandments. To whom hath the root of Wisdom been revealed? or who hath known Her wise counsels?"*

It was the Gospel of John again, except for *her*. "Wisdom was personified as a woman?"

"Wisdom, *hochmah*, is feminine in Hebrew."

And in Greek: *sophia*.

"According to Proverbs 8:22, She was indeed God's first creation." He held the book out to Drew. "This is why Sirach was not included in the Bible. The Church fathers could not accept Wisdom as a woman. Nor, for that matter, the Holy Spirit. Spirit is also feminine in Hebrew."

Drew took the weighty volume from the old man. *The Jewish Wisdom of Ancient Alexandria* had been scripted in gold, much of which had flaked away, across the black cover.

"The Jews living in Alexandria held wisdom up as a universal ideal.

Through Wisdom, one attained spiritual and moral perfection. This is more important than Ezekiel's *Exodus,* although that is this book, too."

Drew waffled the book in one hand. "How much?"

"One hundred, twenty-five Egyptian pounds."

Drew didn't think he would even need to open the book. Intuitively he was sure he already knew exactly why Ezekiel's *Exodus* was among Stephen's keywords—it was one of those clues there to define another clue: *The Bacchae. The Bacchae* was a play written by Euripides in the fifth century BC. By mentioning Ezekiel's *Exodus,* a play written in the style of Euripides, Stephen was pointing out that Jews had taken up writing Greek-style tragedies—a measure of the depth of the interpenetration between Greek and Jewish cultures.

"You don't happen to have any Euripides do you?"

Shimon stepped back and made a sweeping motion with his arm. "Euripides, Sophocles, Aeschylus, Aristophanes ..."

"The Bacchae?"

Shimon produced a battered paperback, small enough to fit in Drew's back pocket. "One hundred, thirty Egyptian pounds for both."

"How about a hundred and fifty?" It was less than $30.

Shimon slapped Drew's hand as though swatting a fly on the taller man's palm, but held on and shook his hand vigorously. "You are very generous, my friend."

Drew waved as he and Zafer crossed the parking lot.

On the other side of the impressive sand-colored walls, a monk in an information booth used a walkie-talkie to call one of the other monks to guide them around the monastery.

A burly man named Father Adwan greeted them in a courtyard. Although he had a beard of graying tumbleweed, he looked like he could bear hug a novice to the floor. He spoke clear English in a baritone voice.

Zafer listened politely, but he cut off the priest's next sentence with an explanation of why they had come.

Father Adwan shook his heavy head. "I have been here all my life. I remember no Tariq Soufanati."

"Is it possible that you ... forgot? It was a long time ago after all."

"I know all of the monks, and I know the names of all the children and novices we've taken in in the last fifty years."

"Father, this is the largest monastery we've seen. Are you sure you haven't forgotten a boy who lived here but never became a monk?"

"One hundred and twelve may seem a large number of monks to you, but when you have lived here among these people all your life, I assure you, it is quite small. And those who never became monks stand out for that very fact."

"Could we just … check the records? Just in case?"

"May I ask why?"

Zafer took out his MIT credentials. "Tariq is dead. His death involved certain … antiquities. Although he later converted to Islam, he spent some years in a Coptic monastery. We were hoping we could talk to someone who knew him."

Father Adwan shook his head. "No. We had no one like that."

"Could we look over the monastery records? Just to be sure?"

The monk shrugged his broad shoulders. "This way."

The records were kept, not in a windowless office buzzing with flies, but in a fluorescent-lit library humming with air-conditioning. A spindly librarian sat behind a desk with a computer on it. Father Adwan issued an order in Arabic, and the willowy monk got up and disappeared into a back room.

Drew noticed a portrait of Jesus hung on one of the walls. Even here, in North Africa, Jesus was depicted with blue eyes and fair hair.

The librarian returned after a few minutes. He shook his head.

Father Adwan shrugged. "It's just as I said."

Zafer nodded. "Thank you for your time."

"One more to go," Drew said when they were back in the sweltering parking lot.

Zafer opened the door of the Renault but didn't get in. "We'll check, but I don't think we'll find anything."

"Why not?"

"Because Father Adwan is lying."

9: 5

BROTHER PARAMOS

Zafer was at least half right: Deir Makarios, twenty-five or so kilometers away, had no record of Tariq either.

"Well," Drew asked, "what now?"

They were driving north.

"I'm going to have to make Father Adwan an offer he can't refuse."

Drew shook his head. "You're forgetting whom we're dealing with. Men like these you could starve to death, torture, burn at the stake, and they still wouldn't break."

"You have a better idea?"

It occurred to Drew that he did. "If you were a monk in Father Adwan's monastery and you had a scroll written in something that looked like Hebrew, whom would you take it to?"

Zafer looked confused. Then his face split open in a big grin. "The old-timer. Shimon."

"Right. Even if they didn't show it to Shimon, Shimon speaks Hebrew, and he reads Aramaic. He'll know which of the other monks know Hebrew. Or Aramaic."

Zafer's right hand flew from the steering wheel, and the broad palm thumped against Drew's chest. "*That's* our man."

Drew felt like a gong that had just been rung.

Zafer hit the accelerator, and the desert road disappeared under their wheels.

Shimon's bushy white eyebrows lifted when he saw the two foreigners in his shop again. "There is something else you would like to buy?"

Drew smirked. "You have any copies of the Q document?'

The surprise on Shimon's face was genuine, but even Drew saw the recognition in Shimon's eyes. He *knew*.

"A copy in Aramaic, not Greek."

Shimon looked from Drew to Zafer and back again.

"Tariq is dead."

Lifting his hands, Shimon tilted his face skyward and muttered in Hebrew. After lowering his hands, he shook his head. "I didn't know."

"It was an accident, but it was because of the scroll, and now there are men looking for it, people who would have no problem killing you or the monks. Has anyone else been asking about Q?"

Shimon shook his head.

"Then why did Father Adwan lie to us? He said he'd never heard of Tariq Soufanati."

Shimon sighed. "He never forgave Tariq for converting to Islam. As far as he is concerned, Tariq Soufanati never existed."

"Have you seen it? The scroll?"

Shimon didn't answer, which, in itself, was answer.

Church bells rang, signaling some service or other. They sounded plaintive, as though calling monks not to prayer, but to a funeral.

"Look, Shimon, we're trying to keep this scroll out of the hands of the Vatican. If you've seen it, if you know what it is, you know it'll just about pull the rug out from under Christianity."

Shimon nodded slowly. He could express his thoughts in five different languages, and his head held who knew how much accumulated knowledge, but Shimon was suddenly an old man fearing for his life.

"Believe me," Drew said, "we're not the ones you have to be afraid of. But they're not far."

Shimon's dark eyes shifted nervously under his craggy brow. "Brother Paramos," he blurted out. "You must find Brother Paramos."

"Is he in the monastery?"

"No. The desert. Until last year, the road to the monastery was not paved. We had solitude. I sold only books then. And very few. After the new road was built, Brother Paramos became angry. A monastery, he fumed, is not for tourists."

"Where in the desert?"

Shimon peeked warily out of his shop. "I don't want Father Adwan to see you talking to me. Come, this way." He led them to the side of his shop hidden from the monastery compound.

"You see those hills?" He pointed in a northwesterly direction.

"Those flat dunes?" Drew asked.

"They're stone, not sand. And there are caves. Brother Paramos lives in a cave well beyond those hills, but that's the direction you must take."

Drew grinned at Zafer. *"Bir mah'ara." A cave.*

Zafer nodded.

"When you reach those hills, look west. You will see three more such formations. The one due west—that is where Brother Paramos is now. It will take you perhaps an hour and a half on foot. Which, unless you steal our tractor, is the way you must go."

Drew stepped out of the shop. A hot gust made him squint. There was something carried by this wind. Not so much the grit, which was just earth with no place to settle, but something of the mummies he'd seen in Cairo's museum. You could marvel over how old they were, but you'd wind up the same way—bits flaking off and dusting away—if you stood in this wind too long. *Indifference.* That's what it carried. An awful indifference to you and what mattered to you.

"Wait!" Shimon pulled a folder of papers from a shelf and handed it to Drew. "I've translated the scroll into English."

Drew lifted the cover and glanced at the first page, marveling at the tiny, incredibly neat letters. He couldn't believe he was holding a copy of Q1.

Zafer's phone rang. He frowned, black eyebrows crinkling, as he checked the number. "Kadir," he said to Drew as he answered.

"Hello, Zafer."

The accent was French.

"Raymond," Zafer growled.

9: 6

IMMACULATE MIRRORS

"THERE IS SOMEONE who would like to speak to you."

"*Özür dilerim,* Zafer." *I'm sorry.*

Kadir's voice.

"I don't know how they found me."

"Where are you?"

Kadir didn't get a chance to answer.

"I recommend that you find the scroll before we do. When you find it, we'll be happy to return your little friend to you. If you don't find it ... only God knows what will happen to him. *Au revoir.*"

The signal died.

"*Lanet olsun!*" Zafer clenched the phone in his fist. "If we don't find the scroll before they do, Kadir's dead." Zafer looked at his cell phone. "And how long have they known this number?" He turned to Drew. "C'mon."

Zafer found a taxi driver in the parking lot and paid him a hundred Egyptian pounds to drive his cell phone to Cairo. He made the driver swear in the names of the Prophet and Allah that the phone would stay in Cairo. "I don't care what you do with it, as long as it doesn't leave Cairo for a week."

"What about mine?" Drew asked.

"For now just keep it off. We might need it later."

From the trunk of the Renault, Zafer grabbed a canvas bag containing canteens, flashlights, compact binoculars, a first aid kit, a narrow wooden box identical to the one that had held the Habakkuk Scroll, and an army spade with a folding blade.

"I don't know why I didn't tell Ashraf to get us an SUV." He shook his head. "Piss-poor planning."

Drew hoped it wasn't an omen.

Zafer slipped the strap of the bag over his head, and then wrapped his head in a white *keffiyeh*. "You, too." He held up another *keffiyeh*. "Can't go into the desert without covering your head."

Nodding, Drew doubled his ponytail so that it wouldn't stick out. He was about to drop the folder Shimon had given him on the front seat, but then thought better of it and put it in the trunk. Glimpsing himself in the reflection of the car's window—T-shirt, *keffiyeh*, sun-glasses—he realized what a ridiculous figure he cut.

"Let's go."

Shimon was standing just inside his shop. He looked as light as a bird under the white *jalabiya*, whose hem was being tugged by a breeze.

"There is a gate in the fence, there." He pointed.

It was a good time of day. The sun was still hot, but not quite as merciless as it had been a few hours earlier.

A monk waved them back as they walked through a cultivated field, but they ignored him.

In minutes the fields were behind them.

The earth under their sneakers became dry, but it was hard-packed. Tinted red. It seemed to get drier as they approached the first set of hills, and the land itself turned a uniform tawny.

Except for the wind humming in their ears as though through the chambers of a seashell, the scrape of their sneakers on the sand, their own breathing, and the rustling of their clothes, there was nothing to hear. No bird twitters, no insect hums.

They reached the hills—more like lumps of stone tortured by the wind—after about twenty minutes, their exposed forearms glistening with sweat. Drew saw a couple of black holes that looked like the entrances to burrows for some enormous breed of animal. Had Saint Bishoi inhabited one of those caves? Did his ghost hover nearby after sunset like a pale flame? Did it matter?

After skirting the southern end of the formation, they stopped and Zafer took out the binoculars. He panned back and forth for what seemed a long time. Even without binoculars, Drew could see their goal—a tiny lump on the horizon.

"Looks like we're alone, but I don't like this. We're too visible."

"Why don't we wait until night?"

Zafer shook his head. "If they know where we are, even the general area, then our best chance is to get in and get out before they show up. We're playing for keeps now." He put the binoculars back in the canvas bag. "You can still turn back, you know."

Drew used a middle finger to push his sunglasses higher on the bridge of his nose, but sweat made them slip right back down. "Not a fucking chance."

Zafer thumped him in the chest with the back of a hand. *"Hadi."* C'mon.

They disturbed a surface of fine sand as they walked, but it didn't hold the shape of their feet. Someone with a desert eye, maybe Raymond, could probably figure out that someone had come this way, but Drew saw no trace of their passage.

Zafer stopped frequently to scan the horizon, all 360 degrees of it.

Nothing. No sign of Brother Paramos or anyone else.

Sweat stung Drew's eyes. Although the *keffiyeh* absorbed most of it, he still had to use the back of a thumb from time to time to squeegee his eyebrows.

They were now close enough to see stony humps rising against a cloudless blue sky dusted with orange. The formation, more extensive than the previous one, was more or less split into two by a winding pass about fifty yards wide. They walked slowly through the rock-strewn gap.

"There." Drew pointed.

Off to their right, shaped more or less like a diamond, was a ragged tear in the stone. They clambered up the slope on their hands and knees. The bag Zafer carried swung just above the rough stone. As the Turk stood up in the opening, a yard ahead of Drew, a monk in robes and an embroidered cap appeared.

"What do you want here?" He spoke in English.

The austere landscape seemed reflected in the thin face pitted with dark acne scars. Even the monk's mustache and goatee were sparse, as though hair had difficulty taking root in that sharp-angled face. He was about Zafer's height, but looked bony beneath his midnight robes.

Zafer put a leg up on the slope and rested an elbow on his thigh. His face was about level with the monk's feet. "Tariq is dead."

The monk nodded. "I knew. I wasn't sure, but I knew. I hear his voice sometimes in dreams, but I am never able to see his face."

"We're here for the scroll."

"Why should I give it to you?" The monk turned and retreated into the cave.

Zafer and Drew scrambled after him.

The cave wasn't large, but it had a high ceiling. The rough walls were burnt orange.

Drew was thankful for the shade. Without the *keffiyeh*, he probably would have collapsed already.

"Sooner or later the people who killed Tariq are going to find you," Zafer said. "You're not safe here anymore."

There was a thin mattress on the cave floor and, against a wall, a stack of books, food in cans and boxes, large bottles of water, candles melted to varying heights, a rectangular mirror that looked like it had come off a truck, and a broom. The broom, Drew guessed, was Brother Paramos's chief weapon in fighting off the desert.

The only other sign the cave was inhabited was a circle of rocks with ashes in the center.

Where the hell does he get the wood? Drew wondered.

"It is not vanity," the monk said.

He must have assumed Drew was looking at the mirror.

"I am not the only monk in the desert. Sometimes, mirrors are our only means of communication."

Drew took off his sunglasses.

"Why should monks be tour guides?" The monk's voice rose in irritation. "For a few Egyptian pounds? If we had been able to sell the scroll, there would be no need of tourists. We need solitude. How else can we speak with God? We need silence. We need to free ourselves of the distractions that prevent God from communicating with us. Only when we are wholly cleansed, wholly pure, can we hear God's voice. Only when we have made ourselves into immaculate mirrors can He see His reflection."

"But why would you sell a scroll that could change the meaning of Christianity?"

Brother Paramos snorted like a horse. "What should I do? Keep it at the monastery? To draw more tourists? Besides, the four Gospels have been written. There are no more Gospels. There can be no new understanding of the Gospels."

"Will you show us where it is?"

"No."

His refusal wasn't loud, but it seemed to echo in the small cave.

"Brother Paramos, if we don't take it, the men who killed Tariq will turn this desert inside out until they find it," Zafer said. "Most likely they'll kill you as well. If you lead us to the scroll, we'll make sure you receive money for it."

Brother Paramos had stopped talking.

"Wasn't that the idea?" Zafer went on. "Tariq was going to sell it, you were going to split the money, and you were going to donate your half to the monastery provided they close it off to visitors?"

The monk said nothing.

In the pause there was the sound of something scraping against stone.

Zafer cocked his head.

Drew heard it again.

Someone was climbing toward them.

9: 7

HAND TO HAND

THE SOUND WAS COMING from the back of the cave, which disappeared in darkness.

Zafer lifted his chin. "Is there another entrance?"

Brother Paramos broke his silence. "Yes."

Zafer took the pistol out of the satchel. Cuffing the back of Drew's neck, he pulled his ear close to his lips and spoke in a harsh whisper: "Don't fire unless I'm about to be waxed—and I *mean* it. These are close quarters. Even if you don't hit me, a ricochet might. Just back me up."

Tipping his head to indicate that Drew should follow, he led the way.

The narrow passage branched to the left of the cave's back and became pitch black. Drew felt panic rise in him like something dead floating up from the bottom of a lake. For about a meter they had to feel their way along a rough wall. Gradually, light seeped in from what must have been the second opening.

They could hear voices now; there were two of them at least.

Zafer gestured to Drew to slow down and then put a finger over his lips. Crouching, he crept forward until he reached the edge of a precipice, but as he straightened up, the stone under his foot gave way. Zafer fell. He twisted hard, trying to right himself, but his Glock struck the stone lip and clattered somewhere below.

Drew was at the edge a second later, pistol drawn. The drop, to what was little more than a shelf, was only about five feet. Drew was just in time to see a man he assumed was Francis Collins dive to the cave floor for Zafer's pistol. Drew trained his pistol on Collins, but Zafer gained his balance and caught Collins full in the face with a sweeping kick. The Sicarii flew back, and a khaki desert cap flipped off his head.

Zafer's pistol bounced on stone again.

The second man, dressed in Army-issue shorts camouflaged for the desert and the same khaki cap with a neck flap, looked like an Arab legionnaire. Before Collins hit the floor, he swung a submachine in Zafer's direction.

Afraid to fire, Drew called out. "DROP IT!"

Drew pulled back from the stone lip as a staccato explosion of gunfire overlapped with the whines of ricochets and the hard rain of stone splinters against the walls.

Zafer, in a dim nether-realm of instinct, was still able to catch the distant echo of a last conscious fear: *Did Drew get hit?* He caught the legionnaire's weapon from underneath and pushed up. Another burst of fire drilled the cave roof. Zafer let go with a hammer-blow intended for the solar plexus, but he struck too low. The Arab grunted but held onto the submachine gun with one hand and brought an elbow down on Zafer's ear.

That *hurt.*

Head ringing, Zafer pushed the weapon higher and stepped into the legionnaire with an elbow to the throat. The tug of war for the weapon ended with the submachine gun flying and landing with a clatter a few feet away.

The Arab underhooked Zafer at the armpit and tried to swing him off balance. Zafer tightened his overhook, straightened his opponent up by pulling back—exposing one side—and landed two hard blows to the ribs. Reversing torque and pulling down now on the overhook, Zafer got the legionnaire off balance and landed three palm heels to the face in rapid succession. The commando's cap tumbled down his back. Pulling up again on the overhook, Zafer added a heel trip, and the Arab hit the stone floor hard. Driving all his weight down, Zafer landed three more strikes, smashing the man's nose to a bloody pulp.

He glanced up just in time to see Collins raising a pistol.

Some division of a second—a tenth? A hundredth? A thousandth?

before Drew understood what it would take to shoot another man, and the threat that if he didn't, someone close to him would lose his life. Just as Zafer drew the unconscious commando's sidearm from a shoulder holster and fired, Drew squeezed off two shots. His head reverberated with the concussive blows to his ears.

Francis collapsed.

"Did I …" The stink of gunpowder singed Drew's nostrils. "Did I hit him?"

"Forget about him." He pointed at the unconscious Arab. "You see what's happening here?"

"Raymond's calling up his old pals."

Zafer nodded. "Ex-legionnaires. They're throwing everything they've got at us." He waved a hand. "Go make sure the monk didn't go anywhere."

Reluctantly, Drew disappeared into the dark passage.

Zafer put Kevlar restraints on the legionnaire's wrists and ankles (he was too groggy to resist) and made sure Collins was dead. He'd been hit three times, so at least one of Drew's shots had been accurate. Zafer gathered up the weapons and tossed them up on the ledge from which he'd fallen. Taking a running lead and vaulting like a gymnast, he hauled himself over the stone lip.

As he approached the cave's other chamber, he saw Brother Paramos struggling to get past Drew, who was blocking off the passage to the rear entrance.

Zafer dropped the weapons he'd collected. "One of them's dead—you can't help him. The other will be fine, okay?"

Falling to his knees, the priest began to pray in Coptic.

"Francis is dead?"

Zafer nodded.

"Did I hit him?"

Zafer faked a smirk. "You missed." He whacked Drew's shoulder. "But you did all right."

Drew hadn't realized until that moment how close he'd gotten to Zafer —probably closer than he was to his own brother.

"You saved my ass, you know." Zafer shook his head. "Over-fucking-confident back there.

Before Drew could think up a cocky reply, Brother Paramos jumped to his feet and sprinted for the entrance of the cave.

"Wait!" Zafer leapt after him, catching him just at the entrance. Not a second later, Drew heard the crack of a rifle shot, and a cloud of red exploded behind Zafer.

9: 8

THE HAND OF GOD

HOHENZOLLERN COULD NOT BELIEVE his luck. *No,* he told himself, *it was not luck, it was God.* His team—Francis, himself, and an Algerian legionnaire named Abdullah—had been scouring the hills and caves. Seeing a small opening, Abdullah and Francis had investigated, but Hohenzollern had wanted to see if there was anything more promising. Indeed, he'd found a much larger opening. Using the scope of his sniper's rifle, he glimpsed the monk inside the cave, and his heart began to pound.

Then he'd heard an automatic weapon fire and pistol shots.

A few minutes later the hand of God interceded.

He'd wanted to go to the smaller entrance to support Abdullah and Francis, but something told him to stay close to the monk. He decided to take cover and train his scope on the larger cave mouth.

And then the monk had run out pursued—imagine!—by the Turk who had beaten Jan unconscious and had nearly broken his rib with a kick. *Next time will be different,* Hohenzollern had said. *See you in Egypt,* he'd replied. Overconfident idiot. Hohenzollern *had* seen him in Egypt. In the crosshairs of his scope as he tried to haul the monk back into the cave. Oh he recognized him—even with that Egyptian headdress on. It hadn't been a headshot, but it had been a clean hit. He would certainly bleed to death before help could arrive.

Neither Abdullah nor Francis answered his phone calls. They were probably dead. Which meant the cave entrances had to be connected. The Turk, he realized, might try to escape the back way. Hohenzollern decided to move to a position where he could cover both openings. Before he did, he called the other teams for back-up.

9: 9

AN ORANGE GLINT

ZAFER SAT WITH HIS BACK against a stone wall. He tried to slow his breathing, to keep his heart rate down, to bleed less. He'd been hit above and to the left of his heart. He wasn't coughing up blood so his lung had also been missed. The bullet had gone clean through, and the wound had soaked his T-shirt with blood. The pain—*Allah*! It hurt to move. It hurt to sit still. It hurt to do nothing but breathe. No pain he'd ever felt was anything like this.

Drew knelt in front of Zafer and reached out with a hand but he didn't touch him. Shaking, it hovered a few inches from his body. "There's so much blood …" His voice quavered. "How bad … is it?"

Zafer tried to smile, but it turned into a grimace. "You can't imagine." He winced. "How much it hurts." His left arm had gone mostly numb.

"We have to get you out of here. Fuck the scroll."

Zafer shook his head. "He's calling for back-up. Right now. If they get the scroll …" He shook his head. Even talking hurt. "They'll kill Kadir. Probably you, too. Even if it takes a couple of years. We have to hope … there's only one sniper. Take him out. There's no other way."

Drew threw his phone at the startled monk. Brother Paramos bobbled it but managed to hang onto it.

"Call those brothers of yours! Get an ambulance here!"

Zafer looked at the cave entrance. "Hohenzollern or Raymond. Could be both. Could be another legionnaire."

"*Hohenzollern?* The police arrested him in Istanbul."

"The Ecole probably bailed him out. Gave him a new passport. Hustled him out of the country."

Drew dug through the canvas bag. "We have to stop the bleeding."

"If there's only one shooter, he'll move to a spot where he has a shot no matter which end we come out."

Drew opened the first aid kit and tore open a package of cotton.

Brother Paramos was on the phone speaking rapidly in Arabic.

"We have to get your shirt off first."

Zafer couldn't bear even the thought of lifting his arm. "Just cut it."

Drew rummaged around the first aid kit until he found the scissors. When he cut away the shirt and actually saw the wound—a hole so dark at its core it was the wet black of overripe cherry flesh—he almost vomited. Blood didn't sicken him; seeing this hole in Zafer sickened him.

"Lean forward." Drew had known the exit wound would be worse, but he was close to shock when he saw how much flesh had been blown away and the steady flow of blood out of the hole. He saw ragged meat and the bone of Zafer's shoulder blade—a piece of it missing—like something hanging in a butcher's shop.

He's going to die.

"Christ," Drew breathed, and prayed that was one of the names to which God answered. As gently as he could, he stuffed the exit wound with cotton.

Zafer's moan was bone chilling.

"I'm sorry." The cotton turned red immediately—almost like some horrible magician's trick—and shrank as it absorbed blood. Drew pushed more into the wound and, again, Zafer moaned. Wiping away blood with the dry part of Zafer's T-shirt, Drew made a white asterisk of medical tape over the cotton.

He plugged the entrance wound the same way.

Zafer was pouring sweat. "I need a drink, Drew."

Drew brought the canteen to his mouth and held it for him.

He drained half of it.

"Okay ... now, break the ... the head off that broom. Keep as much handle as you can."

Using the side of his foot, Drew snapped it against a wall.

"Now ... that mirror ... use the medical tape ..."

Drew taped the mirror to the end of the broom handle, losing only a strip of reflective surface where the tape crossed the middle. He made a thick band of tape to make sure the mirror was secure.

"I'm counting on one shooter. We know he shot from across the pass. But he must have moved. Probably west. I'm going to the back entrance. Keep your phone handy. When I call you ... you're going to use the mirror. And stay *back*, Drew. Stick the damn thing *out*. As far as it will go. Don't give him a shot. See if you can spot him with the mirror. Look for his scope. For the rifle barrel. They might catch sun's rays. When you find him ... tell me where he is."

"How are you going to call me? Your cell phone is in Cairo."

"Dumb-ass. I always have two. Only Gökhan has the number to this one." He managed a weak smile. "Now you'll have it, too." He put out his right arm. "Help me up."

Drew pulled him to his feet. "Are you sure you're up to this?"

"You know how hard it's going to be? To hit him at fifty or sixty meters with a pistol? You can't make the shot. It has to be me."

"Then we'll wait. Till the monks get here. And the police. They have to be on their way now."

Zafer shook his head. "This isn't America. There probably isn't a police station for fifty miles. Even if the monks show up first, Raymond or Hohenzollern will put a bullet in one of them, and the other's will turn around. Let's go."

Shirtless and bleeding through the cotton wadding, Zafer wobbled down the dark passageway to the back entrance. Drew followed him As gently as he could, he lowered Zafer by his good arm over the stone lip.

Zafer had to stifle a scream when his feet hit the cave floor, jarring his body.

"You all right?" Drew called.

"Yeah. Get out of here."

The legionnaire was sitting up, his wrists and ankles bound together. Jagged streaks of blood ran from his nose.

"You're on the wrong side, brother," Zafer said in Arabic.

"Looks like you're in worse shape than I am."

Zafer held up his pistol. "Wouldn't take much to change that. Now, who else is out there? If you lie, I'll shoot both your knee caps before I ask you again."

"Just one."

"Who?"

"Hohenzollern."

"Good." Zafer glanced out the back entrance, which was just big enough for a man to squeeze through and opened to the north. He called Drew. "We got lucky. Just Hohenzollern. Find him."

Drew put his phone on speaker. He stuck the mirror out on shaky arms. If for some reason Hohenzollern had moved east instead of west, he'd have a shot at Drew. The mirror wobbled as he held it out. Drew couldn't see anything but rocks.

Where the fuck was he? *Look for the scope*, he told himself. *Find the barrel* ...

The sun was low.

A glassy glint. *Yes!* Drew saw the German sweeping east to west, then west to east—looking for them.

"I *got* him!" Drew tried not to shout. "He's at a point about midway, just like you said. Right above a rock shaped like a ... it's like a big tooth. A front bottom tooth sort of."

"Tell me when the rifle is aimed at your entrance," Zafer answered.

A ridge blocked Zafer's view. It also kept him invisible to the sniper.

It was going to be like a turn-around jump-shot in basketball: he'd have to pop up from behind the ridge, aim instinctively where he thought the sniper would be while trying to match that up with Drew's description of a tooth-shaped rock, and hope he had a clear shot before Hohenzollern did.

"He's coming back this way ..." Drew's voice was near panic.

One ... two ...

"He's facing east now."

Zafer dropped the phone and sprang up from behind his cover, but he didn't see the sniper or the tooth-shaped rock. He used the stone as a rest for his right forearm, but he didn't see the target.

"What are you waiting for?" he heard Drew's harsh whisper. "He's looking right at you ... *now*."

Zafer caught the dull glimmer of the black barrel. It was pointed at him. He aimed just above it. He was only going to get one shot.

The barrel had stopped moving, and Zafer realized Hohenzollern had spotted him. He aimed slightly high to adjust for the distance—about fifty meters—and the descent of the bullet's arc. He squeezed.

Drew heard two shots almost simultaneously. The head and scope suddenly disappeared from the rectangle of mirror.

"You got him!" Drew shouted. "You *got* him!" Dropping the mirror, he ran to the back of the cave and leapt down.

The bloodied legionnaire shook his head.

Drew's stomach felt as though it had been sucked into a vacuum. "Fuck do you know?" he snarled and squeezed through the opening.

Zafer lay on his back, head-down, on a slope a few feet away. In his rush to get to him, Drew lost his balance and fell. He crab-walked the rest of the way, refusing to believe Zafer had been hit—again.

The bullet had caught him at the base of his throat, had probably severed his spine.

"No." Drew shook his head. "*No no no no no no no.*" He kept shaking his head. "This isn't happening." He slammed stone with the heels of his fists. Again and again. "This *can't* be happening." He started to cry. "Bring him back," he whispered. "Please, God, bring him back." Drew grabbed Zafer's shoulders and sank his fingers into the muscles. He put a hand on his chest, feeling for a heartbeat where he knew there couldn't be one. "I don't give a *fuck* about the scroll! *Please!*"

Cradling the Turk's head, he pressed his cheek against Zafer's. He heard blood drip. The sound made him furious. He eased Zafer's head onto a bed of loose rock and clambered down the slope. Crossing the pass, he hiked up to where he'd last seen Hohenzollern.

The German lay on his back. Most of the top of his head was gone. The brown eyes had become dull stones, and the mouth was open a fraction of an inch.

Aiming his pistol at Hohenzollern's chest, he unloaded the clip. Red blossoms burst open all over the khaki shirt. After the deafening reports of gunfire in the cave, it was eerie how the sound of the shots was swallowed by the desert.

The slide had locked in an open position, and a wispy cloud of smoke drifted away from Drew. He looked at the gun as if it had betrayed him. He flung it away. He turned to find Brother Paramos standing behind him. He almost grabbed by the monk by his robe.

"I'm not asking anymore," he snapped. "Show me where that goddamn scroll is. If you don't, all this death will be for nothing. Absolutely nothing. Do you understand?"

Brother Paramos nodded gravely. "I'll take you."

9: 10

THE BIRTHPLACE OF CHRISTIANITY

AFTER RETRIEVING THE CANVAS bag from Brother Paramos's cave, Drew stripped the bodies of the two Sicarii first—wallets, keys, cell phones—and gathered up the weapons. The legionnaire, hands tied behind his back and legs double-bound at the ankles with Kevlar, hadn't moved.

Drew thought about asking Brother Paramos to clear out Zafer's pockets, but that, he decided would be the easy way out. Crying without sobs or racked breathing, he went silently about his task. Before abandoning him, he squeezed Zafer's hand half in farewell, half in the impossible hope that he would find a sign of life there.

There was none.

He left the body where it lay, as though there were something sacred or at least meaningful about the last position in which it had come to rest. Glancing over his shoulder—again that ridiculous hope there would be something to contradict what he knew was the truth—Drew stood and watched the legs of Zafer's shorts flap weakly in the breeze.

He turned away.

The legionnaire and the Sicarii had come in a jeep, which had been visible from where Hohenzollern lay although it had been parked about three-hundred yards away. The keys had been in Collins's pocket.

Drew and Brother Paramos drove south to another set of hills where the monk led Drew on foot to a crevice—probably an ancient crack that had widened over the centuries. Squeezing through sideways, Drew had to hold the canvas bag over his head. He looked up and saw a jagged strip of sky.

Back and chest abraded by rock, the two men sidestepped, twenty-five or thirty yards, until the gap finally widened, and they could walk comfortably.

"Here …" In the sheer wall there was a narrow gash whose pointed peak came up to Drew's waist. Brother Paramos got down on all fours and crawled in. Drew followed, his bare knees bitten by grit.

They were in a natural tunnel that, at ground level, had inhaled desert; sand and small stones covered the floor. Brother Paramos led the way while Drew held a flashlight. Just as his claustrophobic urge to turn back became nearly intolerable, the tunnel opened up. He stood up in a small chamber. Something about it looked familiar. "This is where you photographed it, isn't it?"

"Yes."

Drew swept the beam of his flashlight over the rough walls, the high ceiling, the floor strewn with rocks. He didn't see the slightest trace of anything artificial. "It's here?"

"This is why they could, as your friend said, turn this desert inside out and never find anything."

The beam of the flashlight leapt from one part of the cavern to another as Drew sought a niche in the walls, a hidden door in the ceiling, something in the floor. He saw nothing. "They would have tortured you, you know."

"Christians have been martyred before. If your soul is prepared to meet God, you can endure any pain."

"Why are you giving it to me?"

"When you threw your weapon away, I believed your reasons for finding the scroll could be trusted. I do not want Tariq and your friend to be dead in vain."

Brother Paramos bent down beside a large stone and began sweeping away sand and gravel with the edge of his hand. "After I found this hole, I made sure no one else would be able to discover it."

Drew could see now that the floor was a slightly different color where the monk was kneeling. The texture … well, some of the grit couldn't be swept away; it was embedded in the floor.

The monk ran a hand over the patch of floor. "This is what we use to repair the walls of the monastery." He tapped what looked like sandstone-colored cement with a finger. Picking up a large rock with two hands, he brought it down in a swift arc. The floor cracked. He struck it again, and chunks of mortar fell away; Drew heard them hit bottom a few feet down. Brother Paramos kept hammering until all that was left was the wire mesh he had used as backing.

Drew bent down and peered inside. Dust swarmed in the beam of his flashlight. The circle of light had fallen on a shrunken human face baring its remaining teeth in a ghoulish grin. The skin was as black as old leather, and where it had rotted away, bone was exposed. The lips were gone, which accounted for the permanent smile. Wisps of hair still clung to the scalp just as tatters of the shroud in which the body had once been wrapped clung to the bones. Beside the body was what appeared to be a limestone box. Fragments of the adobe-colored seal had landed on its cover.

"The scroll is in the box. In past centuries, important books were sometimes buried with a man. Perhaps so that he could draw on this wisdom in the afterlife. I believe this man was a monk."

"One of the Therapeutae?"

Brother Paramos smiled weakly. "Maybe."

It made more and more sense. Alexandria was the birthplace of Wisdom literature—that fusion of the Sophia of the Greeks and the genius of Jewish scripture. The Gospels themselves were an amalgam of Jewish belief and the Greek Mysteries. And here, in a limestone box beside the corpse of an ancient monk, another monk had hidden the sayings of the composite savior figure who had given Christianity its name.

The floor of the second chamber was no more than five feet below.

"There used to be another entrance," the monk said, "but it was long ago buried by sand."

Drew barely heard him. "Hold that light on me, would you?" He slipped into the hole, his feet landing somewhere behind the box. Bending at the knees, he ducked into a natural tomb that, until recently, had been undisturbed for something like two millennia. Drew glanced down at the mummified face. *So this is what discovery is like.*

He lifted the lid off the limestone box, and mortar chunks fell to the floor. White powder covered the bottom of the box. Natron. And there, sheathed in leather, was a papyrus scroll. He lifted it up to the beam of Brother Paramos's flashlight.

"*Hurry,*" Brother Paramos hissed.

9: 11

LOGIA IESOU

TWILIGHT HAD DESCENDED by the time Drew approached the monastery. The sky to the east, behind the walls and domes of the monastery, was a deep blue with an underbelly of purple. Behind him, it glowed a fading orange. Through the chain-link fencing, Drew saw two police cars, their lights off. "Shit."

He also saw Shimon. He was crossing the cultivated field Drew and Zafer had crossed this afternoon. He was like a diminutive scarecrow leached of color—hair, beard, and *jalabiya* all white. Except that he was walking toward the jeep.

Shimon reached the jeep and grasped the top of a door with his wizened hands. "I've been waiting for you. So are the police. You have the scroll?"

Drew nodded.

Shimon reached out and put a hand on Drew's wrist. "Your friend…?"

Drew shook his head.

"I'm sorry." He squeezed Drew's wrist and let go.

"The dead man in the cave …" Drew motioned Shimon back so that he could step out of the jeep. "Was he one of the Therapeutae?"

Shimon shrugged his slight shoulders. With his shaggy white head and the purple-blue sky behind him, he could have been Blake's Ancient of Days. "It is possible. The Therapeutae lived throughout this area."

"Why did they vanish from history after Philo wrote about them?"

Shimon smiled and shook his head. "They didn't. Nor did they call themselves Therapeutae. That was Philo's name for them because he considered them healers of the soul."

"Then who...?"

"They were the first Christians, of course. Just as the Church Father Eusebius thought."

"Christians before Christ?"

Shimon nodded. "That's where Eusebius was wrong."

"There were ... what? Sixty Coptic monasteries in this area at one time?"

"At one time, yes. Maybe more."

"The Therapeutae ... became Coptic Christians?"

Shimon swept an arm to take in the western horizon. "Egypt is where monastic Christianity began. As the name of Christ made its way west, the Therapeutae adopted the new god. Just as centuries earlier, they had adopted Serapis and the rites of the Mysteries."

"The Therapeutae worshipped ... Serapis?"

"It's not so simple. Gods were not so separate then. Of course they believed in Yahweh. Serapis was merely His Egyptian face."

Drew had been overconfident when he'd researched Serapis. He should have known it had been too easy, that everything was connected, on multiple levels, from first keyword to last.

If the Therapeutae had accepted Serapis, performing the Pythagorean as well as Jewish rites, what was one more composite god to them, this one named Yeshua? Mark had not been deceiving the world when he had written his gospel; he had been following a tradition of syncretism that pervaded all cultures. After the Babylonian captivity, the Jews had taken from Zoroastrianism the concepts of Hell, the Devil, and a Last Judgment. The Romans had adopted the Greek gods, laying them over their own pantheon while giving them Latin names—Zeus became Jupiter; Hermes was known as Mercury; Aphrodite—Venus . Pythagoras himself had borrowed the Mysteries of Osiris and turned them into the Mysteries of Dionysus.

"Why do you think there were already well-established churches when Paul began his ministry?" Shimon asked. "Just a few years after the Christ of the Gospels was said to have been crucified? Why do you think there is a legend that Peter sent Mark to Alexandria in 43 AD and that this is where he wrote his gospel? Why do you think that Mark is the patron saint and founder of the Coptic Church? How else could the Church explain all these early Christians who had never been anywhere near Palestine?"

Drew nodded vaguely, but he was struggling to recalibrate his understanding of Mark—both the author and the gospel.

"Mark was always here in Alexandria. He never lived in Palestine, so he was never 'sent' by Peter."

"How could you know that?"

"Haven't you ever noticed the geographical errors in his Gospel?"

"There's a small one ... when Jesus and the disciples are traveling from Jericho to Jerusalem ... I think Mark gets the order of the towns wrong."

"Yes, Matthew corrected the error in his own gospel." Shimon said. "But there are larger errors. Mark places Geras on the eastern shore of the Sea of Galilee, but it is more than forty-five kilometers southeast of the sea. Again, Matthew tried to correct him by renaming the city Gadara, but even Gadara is ten kilometers distant, and there is no slope that goes down to the water as Mark describes. There is also the journey in chapter seven from Tyre to the Sea of Galilee—by passing through Sidon. But Sidon is more than thirty kilometers *north* of Tyre while the Sea of Galilee, of course, is far to the southeast of Tyre."

Shimon shook his head. "Mark was a Gentile whose gospel was written for Gentile converts to Christianity. He had to read the Old Testament in Greek to write about Judaism. He read Josephus to find the names of Pontius Pilate, John the Baptist, and Herod. Why do you think Matthew has the flight to Egypt in his gospel? Matthew knew the true birthplace of Christianity is Egypt. Even Saint Epiphanius was dimly aware of this ... he believed that *Jesus* meant *healer* or *physician* in Hebrew. He was wrong, but—"

"But he wouldn't have made a mistake like that unless he had confused Christ with a Therapeut." The realization suddenly hit Drew. "Jesus Panthera...?"

Shimon nodded. "Jewish tradition invariably asserts that Jesus learned magic in Egypt. But it was Jesus ben Panthera, not Jesus of Nazareth."

"Luke." Drew looked at Shimon as if the old man had put the name in his mouth by some form of sorcery. "Luke has always been known as the physician, but Therapeut—*healer*—is almost the same word."

Shimon glanced at Drew's bag. "Do you know the title of the scroll you have?"

The beginning of the manuscript had been missing when the professor looked over the photographs. Drew shook his head.

"Sayings of the Savior. In Hebrew or Aramaic, that would be almost indistinguishable from Sayings of Jesus."

A definite article separated them. "Wisdom literature," Drew said softly.

"Yes."

"Modeled on The Wisdom of Jesus ben Sirach?"

"Probably"

"The Book of Sirach was included in the Septuagint, wasn't it?"

"Yes."

Drew no longer saw the darkening western sky or the diminutive Ancient of Days, the domes of the monastery, or the shadowy walls they capped. He'd gone back two thousand years. To a shore of the Dead Sea. Blinking his way back to the present, he said, "A friend of mine, a professor of religion, said this scroll was signed. By whom?"

"El'azar ben Ya'akov ben Yeshua."

"Eleazar? The grandson of Jesus ben Sirach? He's the one ... he translated his grandfather's manuscript for the Septuagint?"

Shimon nodded. "In the Greek translation of his grandfather's work, Eleazar also provided an introduction in which he claims these sayings were written in Hebrew in Judea and brought to Alexandria."

"When? When was he writing?"

"Maybe ..." Shimon waffled a hand. "One-ninety ... perhaps 200 BC."

"So his grandson would have compiled Sayings of the Savior ... right about the time Jesus Panthera was in exile in Alexandria."

Shimon shook his head. "Earlier. One-thirty BC or so. But it's entirely possible Panthera had studied it."

Drew recognized, once again, the theme of reconciling the Greek worldview with the Jewish.

"Can you drive, Shimon?"

"Yes."

Lifting himself off the seat, Drew dug a set of keys out his pocket. "Take the Renault about two kilometers down the road. I'll meet you there."

As Shimon hurried off toward the monastery, Drew pulled out. Making a circle around the fields, he came out to the newly paved road. Pulling the jeep onto a sandy shoulder, he got out and waited.

He saw the white Renault approaching about five minutes later at a pace consistent with an old man who'd lost his confidence behind the wheel. Shimon pulled off the road at an oblique angle. Riding the unpaved shoulder for the last fifty yards or so, he trailed a cloud of dust as he pulled up behind the jeep.

Drew opened the driver's side door to help him out of the car. "Should I drive you—?"

"I'll walk back. I'll enjoy the stars and the desert. Maybe they'll enjoy my company as well." He smiled, his crooked teeth mostly intact.

Drew kissed the old man on both cheeks, as he would have in Turkey. When they embraced, he felt the old man's light bones beneath his *jalabiya*.

Drew pulled away and watched Shimon recede in the rearview mirror. He hoped he wouldn't run into any roadblocks on his way back to Alexandria—and that Ashraf could get him out of Egypt.

9: 12

SAYID THE ONE-EYED

"DEAD?" ASHRAF GRABBED TWO FISTFULS of Drew's shirt and yanked him forward so hard, the cotton ripped. "He *cannot* be dead!" His left eyebrow was like a white-hot sickle.

Ashraf was taller, bulkier, and stronger. Only now could Drew appreciate how easily Zafer had handled the big Egyptian when they were fooling around earlier in the day.

Ashraf relaxed his grip. "How?"

"Sniper."

They were in the Egyptian's flat with its high ceilings and tall windows, its ceiling fans turning like soft propellers.

"Sniper?" The Egyptian began pacing the room like a caged bear. "He has always hated snipers." Ashraf stopped in front of a closed door and hurled his fist. The door was old and solid; Drew wasn't sure if the crack he heard was bone or wood. "Where is the body?"

Since Ashraf didn't fall to his knees in pain, Drew assumed the wood had given.

"The monks have it. The Monastery of the Virgin of El Baramouse." They had room for the body of one more saint.

"Do they know who he is?"

"They think he's from MIT, but I cleaned out his pockets. I didn't leave ID on anybody."

"What about cell phones?"

"I took out the SIM cards and dumped them in the desert."

Ashraf buried his face in his hands. The knuckle of the middle finger was bleeding.

Ashraf let his hands fall. "I can't believe he is dead. You are sure?" The veins were showing in the yellowish whites of his eyes like tiny red cracks, as though pure crimson rage lay underneath.

"I'm sure." He almost choked on the words.

"All right. You will need to get out from Egypt. And you have something you do not want the officials of customs to inspect."

"Yes." In spite of what he'd told Jesse, the original plan had been to get the scroll to the Egyptian authorities. It belonged to the Egyptian government after all. Kadir's kidnapping, however, had changed that.

"I don't know what is in that box you are carrying, but Zafer died for it. Do you understand what that means?"

Drew nodded, although he wasn't sure at all.

"It means that if it is necessary, you must die also for this box."

Drew nodded again, but the truth was that Zafer had died for Kadir, not the scroll.

"We will go by boat. They will be watching the airports. I am sorry for tearing your shirt. You should put on a new one. We have business with Sayid the One-Eyed."

After Drew had changed into a collared shirt with buttons, Ashraf led the way down a stairway that creaked under his thumping feet. The streets were crowded with Egyptians and tourists. The air smelled mildly of sea. Juice shops that encouraged customers to concoct their own blends were heaped with crates of fruit—strawberries, bananas, oranges. Souvenir shops overflowed with cheap replicas of statues and ceramics; Alexandria was another Egyptian city trying to cash in on the dusty gold shadow of its past.

A few minutes' walk brought them to Saad Zaghloul Street, one of the main thoroughfares. Tables from a café with the usual open front cluttered the sidewalk. Men drinking Turkish coffee or Egyptian tea, smoking *sheeshas* or playing backgammon crowded the tables. Steam from a huge urn behind a counter crawled along a ceiling of pressed tin and smeared the yellow light of a hanging lamp.

"Wait here."

Ashraf threaded his way among the round tables, nodding or offering a few words of greeting. He spoke briefly to a man who pointed at the tin ceiling. Ashraf walked back to Drew and beckoned with a hand. "Follow me." The Egyptian took only a few steps along the sidewalk before stopping in front of a door and ringing a buzzer.

Drew looked up and saw there was office space over the café. Light had turned a pair of windows incandescent. North Africans tended to be nocturnal, but it was still strange to see what appeared to be a business office open at this hour.

After a brief exchange in Arabic through the intercom, a solid clack followed a loud buzz.

Ashraf led the way up a dim stairway, his hand following a wrought-iron railing. The door he knocked on when they got to the third floor was beautifully worked but old and warped. Grain grayed by exposure to the sea air showed through where paint had worn away.

A voice shouted in Arabic through the door. Ashraf replied curtly. The antique door opened a crack. Ashraf made a gesture of impatience backed up with a few terse words, and the door swung inward.

The room, lit by a single overhead fixture and a battered, art deco desk lamp, was cramped and filthy, as though mechanics with greasy hands had touched everything in it. A modern air conditioner, narrow and long, hummed over the door. On a desk backed against a wall were stacks of money—euros, dollars, Egyptian pounds. Behind the desk was a light-skinned Egyptian in a white turban. One of his eyes was clouded over by a milky film. The other was a disconcertingly pale green.

A pair of bodyguards held submachine guns with long silencers on the muzzles as though the weapons were as much a part of an office as a fax machine. They each grabbed one of Drew's arms and frisked him thoroughly with their free hands.

Ashraf complained in Arabic.

The man with an eye that peered through a veil of jellyfish flesh came around from behind the desk and greeted Ashraf warmly. "These days," he said in English, "you can't be too careful, my friend."

Finding nothing on Drew, the bodyguards retreated to opposite sides of the desk.

"We need a boat." Ashraf continued in English. "Tonight."

"To where?"

"Turkey. Kash is probably best."

Kash was a resort town on the coast, almost due north of Alexandria.

Sayid nodded. "You'll need two boats. Mustafa can't take you into Turkish waters." A black phone with a dial instead of buttons sat on the desk, a squat relic of another era, but Sayid made the call from a cell phone. At the end of a brief conversation, he nodded, and Drew picked out the word "*Shukran.*" *Thank you.*

Closing the mobile, Sayid looked up at Ashraf. "Twelve thousand US."

Ashraf glanced at Drew. Drew nodded.

"Mustafa will be ready to take you in one hour. Do you know where his boat is?"

Ashraf nodded.

"Then there is only the matter of payment and our business is concluded. Half to me. Half to Mustafa."

Drew pulled a stack of dollars out of the money belt concealed under his shirt and counted out six thousand. He and Zafer had brought $25,000 of what the Turk called Bat money.

"*Bat money?*" Drew had asked.

"You know … to get us out of a fucked-up situation," Zafer had answered. "We keep it in our Bat money belts."

Drew would have burned all of it—the Bat money and every dollar they'd gotten for the Habakkuk Scroll—if it would bring Zafer back.

Out in the street again, Drew looked enviously at tourists who had no idea what lay above a coffee shop in this city. How, he wondered, was he going to get out of this underworld with an Egyptian he barely knew as his Virgil?

He glanced at Ashraf. "There's one other thing we have to do before we leave tonight."

9: 13

KILLING AN ARAB

NOT THREE QUARTERS OF AN HOUR after Ashraf and his Turkish-American friend with long hair had left, Sayid's buzzer rang again. His bodyguard Jihan answered the intercom.

"Buraq sent us."

Buraq was the owner of the coffeehouse downstairs. Sayid noted the Arabic had been spoken with an accent he could not place. Not Egyptian. Sayid nodded.

Jihan hit the buzzer to unlock the door downstairs, and a few minutes later, the knock came at the warped office door.

Jihan opened the door enough to see a foreigner with fair hair cut to stubble and strange blue eyes that could have belonged to a ghost or a *djinn*. The foreigner's face seemed to be nothing but the hard lines of bone underneath. "What are you looking for?"

"I need a boat out of Alexandria. The price is not important." His Arabic was clear and fluent, and now Sayid could make out the accent: French.

He nodded.

Omar, the other bodyguard, raised his machine pistol warily since Sayid had never done business with this man before.

"Hands up," Jihan commanded.

The foreigner complied.

Jihan let his submachine gun hang by the strap while he reached under the foreigner's arms to frisk him. The foreigner struck with frightening speed, and Sayid watched Jihan reel from the blow. The Frenchman guided him into Omar. Omar stepped to the side so that the wall could stop Jihan, but before he could fire, he caught two bullets in the chest. Less than a second later, so did Jihan.

The silenced barrel then swung toward Sayid, who had opened the desk drawer but hadn't had time to pull out the Beretta 9mm he kept there.

Another foreigner—huge, black-haired, grim-faced—stepped into the office, pistol drawn. "Close the drawer and stand up." He gestured with his pistol. "Now step away from the desk. Don't worry. We need you alive."

The Frenchman put one more slug into each of the fallen bodyguards—at the base of the skull.

"Now then … I am looking for an American. Dark skin, long hair."

"No. No one like that today."

"Alexandria is not a big city, Sayid. There are only a few men who could arrange a boat on an hour or two's notice."

Sayid shrugged. "Maybe he's coming, but he hasn't been here yet. If you wait a day or two, he might."

The Frenchman with eerily pale eyes aimed his pistol at Sayid's knee. "Do you want to be a cripple for the rest of your life?"

Sayid looked to the other foreigner as if he could get a better offer from him.

"I don't speak Arabic, but you ought to tell him what he wants to know."

Sayid knew if he told the foreigners what they wanted to know, they'd kill him. Why leave him behind and take the chance he might alert the American? If he didn't tell them, they would shoot him in both knees and perhaps a few other places. If he still refused to speak, they'd shrug and believe him. By that time, he might bleed to death, and he would undoubtedly be a cripple.

"I will take you," he said in English. He thought he might gain a modicum of sympathy; it was easier to kill a dirty Arab than a friendly Arab who spoke English. "The boathouse is hard to find. You will need a guide."

"What do you think, Gary?"

The big one shrugged. "He hasn't had time to set us up."

"Let's go," the Frenchman said. He had switched to English. "If you take us into an ambush, I'll make sure you're the first one to die."

9: 14

THE WESTERN HARBOR

PORT OF ALEXANDRIA was written in both English and Arabic atop a massive gateway that housed three floors of offices. Its surface mostly glass, it was crowned with either stone or a good imitation that had been artfully etched with scenes from the days of the pharaohs. Fluted columns with Egyptian capitals rounded the corners, replacing seams where the eye expected sheets of glass to meet. Beyond the gate loomed the silhouette of an ocean liner. The whole area was swarming with officials and police.

"How the hell do we get past all that?" Drew watched the gateway slide past through the windows of Ashraf's Range Rover.

Ashraf glanced over at him and smiled. "Alexandria is one big port."

Drew's hand kept returning to the stubble on his head in a kind of fascination. The back of his neck vulnerable to the breeze was an unfamiliar sensation. The barber Ashraf had taken him to had shaved most of his hair down to the scalp, but had left a couple of inches on top. Drew was consistently startled when he caught his reflection in a car or a shop window.

Ashraf, relieved that the haircut was their last task before leaving, had laughed as Drew's tresses fell to the floor. "I am sorry Zafer is not here to see this."

For at least a mile past the port gate, the waterfront was hemmed in by a cement wall studded with iron bars tipped like pikes. When this barrier ran out, it was replaced by low tin fencing that Drew could have hopped with a running start. The dilapidated buildings beyond looked like garages. In the spaces between these oversized shacks, Drew could see water glinting in the moonlight.

Ashraf turned off the coast road onto a side street of crumbling tenements. The cars parked here had dents, spotty paint jobs, fenders rotted by salt air. One had two flat tires. After finding a space for his Rover, Ashraf cut the engine. Although he'd gone to Sayid's unarmed, Ashraf had since strapped on a waist holster that held an automatic pistol and slipped a huge knife into a boot sheath, which he covered with a pant leg. A canvas satchel, no doubt holding more weaponry, was slung over his shoulder. Grabbing the handle of what could have been an instrument case, maybe about four and a half feet long, Ashraf pulled it out of the back seat. "Let's go."

A battered tram rumbled by, and the two men crossed the coast road as its last car disappeared around a bend.

The sidewalk was old and cracked, its edges lost in loose, black soil.

About two hundred yards from where they'd parked, a young Egyptian stood outside a tin fence that looked like a good push would knock it over. The boy opened a squeaking gate and motioned them in. He closed the gate behind them and snapped a padlock in place—a wasted gesture it seemed to Drew.

Dressed in pants with rolled cuffs, a T-shirt and sandals, he patted his chest. "Walid." He smiled at Drew. His light-complexioned face showed the kind of excitement you might expect from someone next in line for a roller coaster.

Drew didn't know what was in the rectangular case Ashraf was carrying, but he had a feeling it was lot scarier than a roller coaster.

Walid spoke to Ashraf in Arabic and opened a side door to the boathouse.

An older man, his jaw rough with razor stubble, held both arms open and welcomed them in English. He and Ashraf embraced warmly.

"This is Mustafa."

Mustafa and Drew shook hands.

The ex-commando handed Mustafa $6,000 of Drew's money, which went into a trouser pocket.

Mustafa grinned at Drew. "We are ready." He barked at Walid and jerked his thumb in the direction of open water. "Go with Walid. I will be there in a moment." He shooed Ashraf and Drew with a hand.

The boat was forty-five or fifty feet long, its hull a blue that might once have been turquoise, its bow an upswept curve. *SADAT* had been painted in white across the stern. Probably a trawler though Drew couldn't be sure. His boating experience was limited to the ferries in Istanbul and his annual diving expeditions in the Mediterranean.

Not ten meters from the *Sadat*, a wreck lay on its side. Its bow, facing the shore, reminiscent of an upturned nose sticking out of the water. Waves slapped gently against the wooden hulk.

Walid gestured toward the gangplank of the *Sadat*.

Glancing up, Drew saw someone through the windows of the wheelhouse. Someone else screamed for Mustafa.

9:15

THE LAST TO DIE

FIVE MEN STOPPED at the padlocked gate outside of Mustafa's boathouse. Two of the men, whose names Sayid now knew, held Sayid by his arms. His wrists bound, he was considering what would happen if he shouted as loudly as he could. There was a good possibility they would shoot him. But since he might still be of some use, it was possible they would club him with the butt of a pistol.

"MU-STAH-FAHHHHHHHHHH!"

Raymond elbowed Sayid viciously in the gut.

The Egyptian sank to his knees.

Shouting in French to the ex-legionnaires he'd brought with him, Raymond ordered them over the fence. "If the boat is gone, bring me prisoners. If it is still there, kill whomever you find. Remember it is God's work you do."

Submachine guns slung around their necks, they vaulted the wobbly sheet of tin and disappeared on either side of the boathouse.

Gary and Raymond hoisted Sayid by his shoulders and legs and tossed him over the rusting fence. Hitting the ground slammed the residual air out of his lungs, and he struggled to breathe.

Raymond pointed his pistol at Sayid's forehead.

The Egyptian, still preoccupied with breathing, had pulled himself to his knees.

Gary held up a restraining hand. "What if this is the wrong boathouse?"

Raymond pulled Sayid to a sitting position. "Kevlar his ankles."

Sayid glanced up and saw, arcing toward him, the pistol butt he had anticipated.

Drew heard the *Sadat's* engines rumble awake as Mustafa came bounding out of the boathouse.

Ashraf stuck a huge hand into his satchel and held out a submachine gun. "This is an HK MP5. Do you know how to use it?"

"Zafer taught me," he lied. He didn't want to be left unarmed.

"Remember, it will jump in your hands. You will shoot high and pull to one side if you hold the trigger more than half a second. You have thirty rounds to a magazine, but you will shoot nearly twelve rounds every second."

Ashraf had taped the magazines together so that one was upside down. When the first ran out, the unit could be ejected, flipped over, and the second rammed home. He gave Drew three pairs. The extra weight of long silencer on the gun's muzzle would not only hush the weapon, the extra weight would dampen its tendency to rise when fired.

Tightening his grip on the MP5 to steady his hands, Drew kneeled down behind the starboard gunwale. It barely came to his hip, and it was wood—not enough to stop a 9 mm.

Two shadows stepped out from either side of the boathouse.

Suppressed, automatic-weapons fire erupted in bursts. Walid stumbled backwards and fell into the water. He'd only untied one rope.

Mustafa, leaping off the concrete quay, splashed into the sea.

Drew returned fire, and a stream of brass shells clattered onto the deck. With only a feeble bulb over the boathouse door for light and the shadow he was aiming at a good thirty yards away, all he managed to do was stitch a side of the boathouse with holes. Drew fired two more bursts, practicing his aim and keeping the man pinned, while Mustafa climbed the aluminum ladder.

Glancing to his right, Drew saw a man in Ashraf's line of fire sprawled face-down in the boatyard. *How many more were there?*

Peripherally, Drew caught movement on his left. He aimed the MP5 and pulled the trigger. Nothing happened. The gun's breech was open, the slide caught by the lip of the empty magazine.

"Change clips!" Ashraf hissed.

Drew heard the staccato belch of the Egyptian's weapon; Ashraf was covering for him.

Drew hit the magazine release and caught the clip as it fell. He flipped it over and jammed it in.

By the time he'd reloaded, Mustafa had hauled himself over the gunwale.

The sinister popping of automatic-weapons started up again. Bullets raked the wheelhouse, shattering the windows and raining glass on the deck. Rounds struck so close to Drew that splinters peppered his chest. As he ducked down and rolled a few feet, he recognized the insistent tingle in his groin as the urge to pee.

The shots had come from an adjacent boathouse. Ashraf had returned fire in the direction of the muzzle flashes and maybe saved Drew's life.

"Move!" The Egyptian gestured frantically at Drew.

Of course, Drew thought, change position.

Mustafa, wielding a machete, whacked the rope securing them to an iron stump on the quay. The sliced end disappeared over the side like a beheaded snake.

Mustafa shouted for Ihab, the man in the wheelhouse.

The Sadat, its engines idling, began to drift, exposing the starboard side to the shore. A little farther and it would bump into the half-sunk wreck.

Mustafa kneeled behind a steel drum on deck and shouted into his phone.

Ashraf emptied two magazines, let them clatter to the deck, and slammed home another.

Drew fired where he'd last seen Sicarii, flipped his clip, and risked a glance at Mustafa. Mustafa had given up on the phone and was swearing in Arabic.

Ashraf scrambled on all fours to Drew. "We must protect Mustafa. He will have to steer the boat." He handed Drew three more magazines. Shoot at the second boathouse, then you must move."

Shots raked the gunwale; Drew and Ashraf flattened out against the deck.

The wheelhouse was hit again, metallic whines and twangs ringing in the air.

As soon as the Sicarii's guns had gone silent, Drew and Ashraf straightened up, took a knee, and began firing.

Drew swept a field of about ninety degrees, probably hitting nothing but rotting wood and rusting iron. When his trigger clicked uselessly, he reloaded and belly-crawled as rapidly as he could toward the bow of the ship.

A second later, bullets chewed up the gunwale where he'd been. Ashraf popped up again and fired in enviably controlled bursts.

Suddenly, the boat pulled forward and began to straighten out.

The Sicarii targeted the wheelhouse a third time.

Drew saw Ashraf spray the area around a muzzle flash. It blinked out. Ashraf dropped down and rolled away from the gunwale. Return fire sent chips of wood flying.

Drew jumped up and took the offensive. Braced for the jump of the weapon, he aimed low and fired in rapid bursts until the magazine was empty. Then he rolled all the way to starboard.

The trawler continued to pull away from shore.

The hull of the ship took a few dozen more rounds, but the shots tapered off and then ceased altogether.

Drew lay on his back, breathing hard, sweat trickling down the sides of his face. He wiped it away and looked at his hand. Blood. Wiping again, he jerked his head back when his finger encountered something sticking out of his face. A splinter.

"Mustafa!" Ashraf called.

Mustafa answered in English: "Ihab is dead!"

Drew closed his eyes wondering how long the respite would last.

Sayid had recovered from the blow he'd taken to the head in time to hear the firefight. It sounded as though Mustafa's boat had rumbled away. He smiled, although he was tied up like a sheep on the holy day of Eid Al-Adha.

He heard the engine of another boat turn over into a rough idle. The Frenchman must be stealing the one docked next to the Sadat. He also heard—oh, happiest sound of all—sirens. Never did he think he would be elated to hear the approach of the Egyptian police.

Suddenly he was grinning into the silenced muzzle of a pistol.

"I broke my promise, Sayid. You're the last to die." Raymond squeezed the trigger.

9: 16

IN THE SPOTLIGHT

MUSTAFA AND ASHRAF had taken Ihab's bullet-ridden body out of the wheelhouse and covered it with an oily blanket.

"How will I tell his wife?" Mustafa stood over the lumpy shape. "And Walid! He was my nephew! How will I tell his mother?" He shook his turbaned head. "Peace be upon them." He returned to the wheelhouse.

Drew had pulled three splinters out of his face and sponged off with water from a bucket that Mustafa had dipped into the sea. The salt's sting was perversely refreshing. "How did they find us?"

"They found Sayid," Ashraf said. "It was he who warned us."

The *Sadat* had holes everywhere—in the deck, what was left of the wheelhouse, the gunwales. Brass casings rolled and clattered as the boat rode swells. Chipped wood scattered at their feet made it look as though some sort of construction were going on.

"Bad news," Mustafa called from the wheelhouse. "We're being followed."

Ashraf cursed in Arabic.

"Can we outrun them?" Drew asked.

"We have a leak, and we are losing oil pressure. I cannot run the engine at full speed."

"Turn off our lights!" Ashraf snapped. "And keep me informed of their position!"

Drew pulled his cell phone out of a pocket and turned it on. It beeped to let him know there was a message. Yasemin. Now?

Drewjuh'um, I have been overbearing, too critical, narrow-minded, too proud to admit it. Enough flaws? I've made up my mind. Let's talk, but *only* when you are ready. I am a fool, but I am a fool for you, too.

If there was anyone he wanted to see right now it was Yasemin. She was the only one who could do something about stoppering the vacuum Zafer's death had left.

Tucking the phone under his chin, he dug through his wallet. He slipped out the card Zafer had gotten from Nabil in Cairo and punched in the numbers with his thumb.

"*Alo?*"

"Raymond…?"

"*Oui.*"

"Back off or I'll sink the scroll in the Mediterranean."

"I'll keel Kadir."

"You're going to kill him anyway."

"As God is my witness, eef you give up the scroll, we won't harm him or you or your Egyptian friends. Zafer is dead. How long do you think you can last without him?"

Drew felt his face flush with rage. Stephen was dead. Zafer was dead. Tariq, Ihab, Walid.

"Long enough to make sure you don't get that fucking scroll," he hissed.

"We will catch you, *mon ami.* We will kill you. We will take the scroll. We will kill Kadir."

"Whatever happens, I'll make sure I destroy the scroll before you get it."

There was a pause—a telephoned shrug. "Then you will be safeguarding the Church and doing our work for us. But I doubt very much that you will. You want the scroll to stay intact much more than we do. Eef you want to save Kadir as well as the scroll, then you have one choice."

"Kadir was *Zafer's* friend, not mine. The little bastard is as greedy as Serafis. He deserves whatever he gets."

"I see Zafer has taught you how to bloof."

"Bluff my ass. You made a big mistake, Raymie. You should have killed me, not Zafer. He would have given you the scroll without a second thought. Kadir was like a brother to him. Do you hear me, Raymond?" He spoke slowly, emphasizing each word. *"You ... killed ... the wrong ... man."*

Let him wonder, Drew thought. Thumbing a button, he ended the call and cocked an arm as though he were about make a throw from the outfield to third base. Stopping himself, he retracted his arm and tapped a name in his contact list.

"Drew? You didn't have to call right away ..."

"Yazz, listen, I only have a minute."

"I'm listening ..."

"I want to try, too. Nothing has changed since I tried to back out of the divorce before the papers were signed."

"I've been a stubborn eshek all these years. A proud, stubborn donkey. I guess I always understood, I just couldn't admit it."

Drew laughed. "Look, I'm not in Istanbul, but we'll talk when I get back, okay?"

"Drew ... *please* be careful. I love you so much—"

"It'll kill you if I die, huh?" He was looking down at glimmers of moonlit water through the holes in the gunwale.

"Allah korusun! Don't even say that. Where *are* you?"

"Alexandria. Off the coast. I love you, too, but I have to go now."

"Drew! What're you doing in Egypt? Why can't you tell me?"

"Yazz, please, just wait for me."

"How long, Drew?"

"I'll call soon, I promise. But not on this phone. You won't be able to reach me again at this number, okay?"

"Drew I can't take this—"

"We don't have a choice."

"Seni chok seviyorum, Drew."

"I love you very much, too. I'll call soon. I promise ..."

He ended the call and hurled the phone into the water. He barely heard the plunk over the sound of the wind and the boat's engine.

"Ashraf!" Mustafa pointed.

The other boat was visible, a silhouette gliding over the moon-tinted sea.

"How is our oil pressure?" Ashraf spoke in English, probably so he didn't have to repeat everything.

"I have only slowed the leak. We cannot run the engine at top speed."

"Then we will fight."

Sweeping away brass shells with an angry foot, Ashraf walked across the deck and opened up the "instrument" case.

"Holy shit, is that a bazooka?"

"RPG."

Sporadic gunfire started up, and Drew fell to the deck. He couldn't believe it was happening again. Not submachine guns this time, automatic pistols. More accurate. The wheelhouse took most of the lead.

Ashraf was on one knee at the back of the squared-off stern, the long tube resting on his shoulder. The business end of the launcher was capped by a mini missile—a sleek grenade. He glanced at Drew. "Stay down and stay back."

Drew hardly saw Ashraf's face except for the white of an eyebrow, like a curving scar on a shadow.

Ignoring the bullets zipping past, the big Egyptian took his time, but the way the ship was bouncing on the swells, aiming the RPG couldn't be easy.

"Zafer says hello … and good-bye."

Drew wasn't ready for the explosion—the back end of the launcher erupted in fire—and he thought Ashraf had somehow pointed the weapon the wrong way. No, he realized, that was blowback.

Risking a bullet to peer over the gunwale, Drew saw a thin trail of white smoke as the projectile hissed over the sea—and disappeared.

Ashraf swore, dropped to the deck, and crawled away.

The gunfire became more frantic, like a hard rain suddenly picking up.

"I can't aim this thing when we are going up and down like we are riding on the back of a fucking fish!" Ashraf turned and shouted instructions to Mustafa in Arabic.

The Sadat came about, exposing its port side to the Sicarii boat.

Reloading while flat on his back, Ashraf waited for the gunfire to subside. He got up on a knee, aimed over the gunwale, and fired again. The grenade exploded in the water three or four yards in front of the pursuing boat.

Another hail of bullets drove him face-first into the deck.

"Why do they not run out of fucking ammunition?"

Drew's cheek, like Ashraf's, was pressed against the deck. "If their automatic weapons and pistols are both 9mm, they're probably emptying their submachine gun clips and reloading their pistols."

"I had not thought of that."

"What about us? How many more grenades?"

"Two."

"I have an idea." Drew had seen spotlights on either side of the bow. He would have to point them by hand, then get away before Mustafa turned them on. Without waiting for Ashraf's approval, Drew bellied toward the bow.

"Where are you going?"

"The spotlights!"

A bullet whined past Drew's head. Shit! He'd felt it cut the air. Glancing up, he was relieved to see the port spotlight still intact.

Drew glared over the gunwale. The shadowy boat, lit by muzzle flashes as though it had attracted fireflies, was gaining on them. He swiveled the light to where he estimated its beam would hit the Sicarii wheelhouse. Ducking back down, he scrambled toward the starboard lamp. It had been shattered by gunfire.

Ashraf shouted to Mustafa.

A shaft of light instantaneously joined the bow of the trawler to the bow of the Sicarii boat. As expected, the small-arms fire intensified.

"Keep the light on them, Mustafa!"

Ashraf aimed. The beam had slid from the bow of the pursuing boat to the starboard side—the Sicarii were maneuvering away. Drew intuited— or imagined—Ashraf timing the rise and fall of the boat underneath him. "C'mon ..."

Ashraf fired.

The spotlight exploded and went dark, but the rocket was already a tracer scorching the salt air. Fire erupted and thunder cracked as their pursuers' wheelhouse exploded.

"They are dead! Dead in the water!"

Gunfire from the damaged boat ceased.

Ashraf reloaded and went down on one knee again. He used the burning wheelhouse to guide his last shot, but the boat bucked just as he pulled the trigger, and the grenade disappeared into the sky.

Ashraf shrugged. "We didn't sink them, but they can no longer follow us."

Drew looked back at the burning ship, which was now veering away from them. Had they killed Raymond? And what about Kadir? Had Drew just signed his death warrant?

BOOK 10: 1 - 13

KONSTANTINOUPOLIS

Is your faith based on the 'fact' that your Jesus said that he would rise again after his death? On his predictions of triumphing over the grave? Very well, let it be so. Let us assume for the moment that he foretold his resurrection. Are you ignorant of the many who have invented similar tales to lead the simple-minded astray? Zamolix, Pythagoras's servant, convinced the Scythians that he had risen from the dead though in fact he had hidden himself in a cave for several years. What about Pythagoras himself in Italy—and Phampsinitus in Egypt? Now let's see, who else? What about Orpheus among the Odrysians, Protesilaus in Thessaly and most of all Herakles and Theseus? But quite separately from all these risings from the grave, we must look carefully at the question of the resurrection of the body as a possibility for mortals. Undoubtedly you will admit that these other stories are legends, just as they appear to me, but you will insist that your resurrection story, this climax to your tragedy, is true and noble.

— Celsus, circa 170 AD

10: 1

GÜRSEL'S RULE

BOATS STINK. OF OLD OIL. OF DIESEL FUEL. Of rotting wood soaked in seawater. Of rot in general. A sulfurous, oily, briny reek. The head stinks most of all. And it's not just because that's where the piss and shit get dumped. In Drew's experience, limited mainly to diving boats, the head was always a nauseating compilation of every foul smell on the boat.

Another thing about boats: they were noisy. The smaller the boat, the noisier it was. In some places on the *Sadat*, it felt like the engines were rattling the ship apart. The smells or the noise—maybe both—had given Drew a headache with the tenacity of a barnacle. Sleeping on a fishing boat wasn't much fun either. Two consecutive nights.

He leaned over the gunwale at the stern, where the bounce of the waves was minimal, and the open blue had a pacifying effect. Hanging out on the bow was like being on a carnival ride; his stomach dropped each time the boat fell into the trough of a wave. His bristly hair no longer whipped across his face in the wind.

On a day like this, with sun sparkling on the water, it was hard to believe that Zafer had been killed not forty-eight hours earlier. It was hard for Drew to believe he was now connected with as many as a dozen killings, that yesterday he had been shooting at human beings. That he might have killed one. If not more.

Christ, how had his life gotten here?

Well, yes, that was exactly how: *Christ*.

Mustafa came out of the wheelhouse. "The boat that will take you to Turkey is very close." He pointed.

Drew crossed to starboard and saw it maybe half mile away. Another fishing boat.

"Where are we now?"

"Measuring by longitude, we are between Kash and Antalya."

They had agreed to go farther east since, from Alexandria, Kash was the obvious Turkish port to make for. They also wanted to avoid Bodrum, which would have been the natural choice for someone going on to Istanbul.

Ashraf came up from below decks wiping his hands on a rag. Barefoot, wearing rolled-up trousers and a white T-shirt that accentuated his albino eyebrow, he looked like a character out of a Hemingway novel—aligned with the currents, on a first-name basis with the variant winds that blew from Africa across the Mediterranean, a fisherman who knew nothing of hi-tech weaponry or black market dealings.

The Egyptian laid a hand of intimidating heft on Drew's shoulder and squeezed. "I will see that Zafer's body is returned to Turkey."

Drew nodded.

"Are you sure you do not want me to come with you to Istanbul?"

Again, Drew nodded. For reasons he couldn't explain, he felt he had to go back alone. He didn't imagine he could outfight or even outwit Raymond—if Ashraf hadn't killed him last night. He was operating on instinct now, and his instinct was telling him that he was best off on his own.

The Turkish boat, a good deal smaller than their own, pulled alongside the *Sadat*, and crew members tossed lines to one another. Grabbing hold of a line each, Ashraf and Mustafa pulled the boats—engines at idle—together. Bumpers that looked like huge rubber bottles hung from the sides of both boats and kept the hulls from battering each other.

"Captain Mustafa," the Turk said, "now that I see the condition of your boat, I am thinking I must raise my price."

Mustafa looked at Drew. "Gürsel makes a joke. Do not worry, my friend. He is a man of his word."

Wearing the cap Greek fishermen had made famous, Gürsel stood with his hands on his hips. A tank top with black and white stripes drooped over baggy shorts that hung just below his knees. His bare feet in touch with his boat, with the grain of the wood, Drew imagined he felt the sea through his toes.

Drew kissed Ashraf on both cheeks. The two men embraced as though last night had been an initiation rite, and they were now brothers. Maybe it had been. Maybe they were.

"Ma'salama."

Drew was pretty sure that was *good-bye* in Arabic. He replied in Turkish. *"Allah korusun." May God protect.* The verb wouldn't mean anything to Ashraf, but he'd get the Allah part.

He traded kisses with Mustafa as well, but there was no embrace, only a handshake.

Hefting his leather satchel, which held the scroll, the books he'd bought from Shimon, and very little else, Drew swung it to Gürsel by the strap. Minding the grinding sides of the boats, Drew jumped onto the deck and sprawled forward on hands and knees.

"Good-bye, my friend!" Ashraf untied one of the lines joining the boats together. "We will see each other again one day, *inshallah.*"

"Inshallah," Drew repeated. *God willing.* He waved.

The boats drew apart, and the engines kicked into gear. Drew waved to Ashraf, who smiled and waved back.

"Türkche biliyorsun, deh'ilmi?" You know Turkish, right?

Drew turned to Gürsel whose tanned face was as like a sweep of desert landscape. *"Iyi biliyorum." I know it well.*

"What you carry must be very valuable."

"It is."

Gürsel lifted his hat by the stubby visor and settled it back on his head. "There is one rule on my boat: if the Turkish coast guard approaches, all contraband goes overboard."

"What?" Drew shook his head. "I'm not throwing my case into the sea."

"I'm not going to prison. Not for a million dollars."

"Wait a minute." Drew looked in the direction of the *Sadat,* but it was already too far away to signal. Why the fuck hadn't he taken Ashraf up on his offer? "Nobody said anything about losing the cargo. You're a smuggler. That's a risk you take."

Gürsel shrugged. "I agreed to take *you* to Turkey, nothing else."

"If the case goes into the water, I go with it."

Gürsel nodded. *"Olsun." Let it be so.*

10: 2

DIVINITY UNJUSTLY ACCUSED

D REW IMAGINED EVERY SHIFT in shine on the waves, every speck on the horizon to be the Turkish coast guard. Well, the Turks were either coming or they weren't. No use staring at the water until he began to hallucinate.

He pulled the worn copy of *The Bacchae* he had bought from Shimon out of the messenger bag and leaned against the gunwale. Fortunately, the water was unusually smooth. Unfortunately, he had all goddamn day on this boat.

The play's introduction reminded him that Dionysus, the god of wine and fertility, was also the patron god of the theater. Drew knew well enough that Greek drama had *begun* with the Dionysian Mysteries, and that, coincidentally enough, the original chorus had consisted of twelve men who stood behind a single actor—the twelve apostles and Jesus.

The play itself, written more than four hundred years before Christianity was founded, was fairly simple. Dionysus is furious that his human family doesn't recognize him as the son of Zeus. They believe that his mother, Semele, simply gave birth to an illegitimate child. Semele, who died before the child was born, is branded a liar and a blasphemer for insisting that Zeus was the father.

Disguising himself as a blond youth, Dionysus returns to Thebes to prove he is the son of God. Cadmus, Dionysus's uncle, has passed the throne on to his grandson Pentheus, Dionysus's cousin. Pentheus immediately bans the Dionysian Mysteries in Thebes. He also has the blond stranger, arrested but is persuaded by his prisoner to spy on the rituals being performed in Dionysus's name. The god prevents the celebrants from recognizing Pentheus, and, in a divinely inspired frenzy, they tear him to pieces. Indeed, the name Pentheus—"Man of Sorrows"—was a kind of foreshadowing.

The parallels between Dionysus and the Christ of the Gospels were obvious enough: a long-haired, young man promulgates a new religion; the ruling authorities refuse to acknowledge him as the son of God; bread and wine are praised as the two supreme blessings given to man; and, after taking on human form to reveal himself to humankind, the son of God is arrested on false charges. In the Gospels Jesus' Jewish accusers claim that his teachings are leading the people astray; in *The Bacchae*, King Pentheus is portrayed as a tyrant who refers to the Dionysian Mysteries as *this new disease which fouls the land*. Divinity is unjustly accused, arrested, and tried.

Drew came across other points of correspondences, including one that almost made him laugh. Cadmus, advising Pentheus, says, "Even if this Dionysus is no god, as you assert, persuade yourself that he is. The fiction is a noble one." What Drew found most striking was that when Pentheus orders Dionysus to be chained, the god says, "*You do not know what you do. You do not know who you are.*" Euripides's Dionysus sounded nearly identical to Jesus on the cross and James in the Temple.

The Bacchae was the tragedy of Dionysus bringing the Mysteries to Thebes; the Gospels were the tragedy of Jesus bringing Christianity, a variant of the Mysteries, to Jerusalem. The most important element, Drew realized, was not any of the similarities between Dionysus and Jesus, or between the Mysteries and Christianity, but the drama itself. The Gospel authors wanted to frame Christ in the context of a tragedy. What better way to deliver their message to the masses? What better way to popularize the themes of a fledgling religion?

Drew was so absorbed in the play, he didn't realize Gürsel was standing over him with an automatic pistol in his hand.

"Sorry, my friend ... a Turkish patrol boat."

10: 3

INTO YOUR HANDS
I COMMEND MY SPIRIT

Hᴵˢ HEAD BUZZED with ricocheting thoughts. He voiced one: "Do you have diving equipment?"

Gürsel looked perplexed. "Below deck. Why?"

"Let me go overboard with my case. I'll keep my depth about twenty-five meters. I'll stay directly under the boat. They won't see any bubbles. When they're gone, I'll surface."

Gürsel glanced over his shoulder, then tucked his pistol in the waistband of his pants. "*Chabuk ol.*" *Hurry up.*

Drew grabbed his satchel, pulled out *The Jewish Wisdom of Ancient Alexandria*, and tucked it under a bench against the gunwale. No one would care about a decrepit book written in English. The same couldn't be said for a new messenger bag, which would have to go with him. The scroll, still in its box, was sealed in a durable plastic bag, the kind amphibious commandos used. His passport and wallet were Saran-wrapped with it, but his Bat money was still belted to him. Ashraf had waterproofed the scroll just before their rendezvous at Mustafa's boathouse—"Just in case," he'd said. But it wasn't a random precaution. As far as Ashraf was concerned, Zafer had died for the scroll.

Silently thanking the big Egyptian, Drew scrambled below deck. He picked up a wetsuit and looked at the tag. Medium. He grabbed the other one. Medium. *Shit.* Choosing the one that looked less ragged (they both had holes in them), he stretched the rubber to its limits as he writhed into it. When he finally zipped it up, the suit resisted his joints at every movement. Bending an arm was a struggle. He could have gone down without one, but body heat dissipated something like thirty-two times faster in water.

Mustafa stuck his head below deck. *Chabuk! Chabuk! Quick! Quick!*

Drew grabbed a mask and a pair of flippers, strapped on a weight-belt with about five kilos of lead on it, and with one hand yanked himself up the ladder. He felt like he had grown an exoskeleton.

Mustafa secured a tank to the BCD, a buoyancy control device, and connected the hoses while Drew struggled into the flippers—they were too goddamn small, too. Drew turned on the air and checked the gauge to make sure he had a full tank. Mustafa helped him on with the BCD and glanced over his shoulder.

The police boat was getting closer.

"Go! Go! Over the side!"

Drew sat on the gunwale, but before he could lean back, Gürsel planted a palm on his chest and shoved him. He fell into the water holding his mask in place with one hand, latching onto the messenger bag with the other.

The tank broke the surface of the sea like a wedge. A cloud of bubbles obscured his vision, cold water flooded his suit and, as always, there was that first panicked breath—he bit down on the regulator and sucked hard, half expecting to take in a couple lungfuls of water.

The second breath brought more trust.

With his BCD deflated and most of the excess air squeezed out of the sealed bag inside the leather satchel, he sank. Stiff-limbed in his overstretched suit, he went down like a dead crab while his regulator released huge pearls of air.

Swallowing relieved the pressure on his eardrums.

He put a little air into the BCD to slow his descent. Just below him, a fish flashed silver and disappeared.

He swallowed again to equalize the pressure in his ears. Down here, a pocket of air anywhere in the body could be a serious problem, even in a tooth that hadn't been filled properly.

Above him, the hull of Gürsel's boat was a long shadow on the water. And now he saw the coast guard ship spearing toward the much smaller vessel.

At twenty-five meters he adjusted his BCD so that he was more or less weightless. As long as he kept his breathing even, he would just bob in the current, neither rising nor descending.

All he could do now was wait. And pray the coast guard didn't figure out he was right underneath them.

Drew tried to slow his breathing, to burn less oxygen, but it wasn't easy with the prospect of a Turkish prison literally hanging over his head. He was using up air fast.

He closed his eyes and tried to imagine he was completely alone.

Fish that had scattered after his splashdown now became curious. One, neither big nor particularly colorful, moved to within a foot of Drew's mask. It looked as him as if it knew he was a harmless alien, and there was nothing he—ill-adapted land creature—could do about being gawked at.

Drew looked up at the two long shadows in the water. *When the fuck are they going to leave?*

After what seemed hours, but was only about twenty-five minutes judging from the oxygen he'd consumed, the patrol boat's engines revved.

Drew breathed a bubbly sigh of relief.

Until Gürsel's boat began to pull away, too.

Panic bubbled up inside him.

He had seconds in which to make a decision: surface and hail the coast guard or try to make his way back to land without knowing where the hell in the sea he was. Go up and be arrested or risk drowning. By the time he'd made up his mind, it was too late.

Breaking the surface, he saw that the coast guard boat was too far away to signal unless someone was looking directly at him. No one was even on deck.

While he watched, both boats disappeared from sight.

Nothing had ever paralyzed Drew like the sight of open sea in every direction.

He wasn't cold, but his teeth began to chatter. Even if he hadn't been wearing his rubber straightjacket, he wouldn't have been able to so much as kick a leg. This was the meaning of *I commend myself to God's hands*. He was going to die in a blue sea, under a blue sky, with a scroll that could rewrite Christian history sealed in plastic like a message in a bottle.

10: 4

DUE NORTH

ALL PRAYERS, HIS FATHER LIKED TO SAY, are answered, and sometimes, the answer is *no*.

Drew had lost faith in Jesus of Nazareth, but he hadn't lost faith.

Please, God, if I'm doing the right thing with this scroll, send a boat back for me.

What if Stephen had been *half* right? What if God existed, but there had never been a Jesus? Wouldn't God be kind of ticked off that a fictional character in a faux tragedy had been raised up alongside Him? Maybe God *wanted* this scroll to come to light. To correct a two-millennia-old error.

Drew took stock of his situation. There was a compass on the back of the depth meter/air gauge. Turkey had to be due north of where he was. If he could float that way and sooner or later he would to run into the Turkish mainland. Or a boat. He *had* to. As long as he kept the compass needle pointing toward north.

The problem was, if it took too long, he would die of thirst.

Water water everywhere, nor any drop to drink. With that line from a Coleridge poem looping in his head, he began kicking.

How far was he? How often did patrols cruise by? How long before he died of thirst? Two days? Three?

Without Zafer or Ashraf to hold his hand, he was a fuck-up. What had he been thinking when he decided to go back to Turkey alone?

What the hell had made him think he could take on an elite mercenary like Raymond? He remembered how Hohenzollern had handled that wicked-looking knife in Serafis's house and realized he'd be *lucky* if he only caught a bullet.

Drew stopped kicking and listened. He thought he heard a kind of thrum behind him. He let his feet sink until they were under him again. Paddling with a hand, he turned and lifted his mask, jeweled with seawater, to his forehead.

Fucking Gürsel. He'd circled around.

Drew watched the boat close in on him.

"*Merhaba,* Drew *Bey!*" Gürsel, shorts and sloppy shirt, captain's hat and stupid smile, was waving.

Drew lifted an arm. He could have cried hysterically, but he kept the expression on his face impassive. Silently, he thanked God a dozen times. That was how Zafer had moved through the world—giving away nothing.

A chain ladder spilled over the side of the fishing boat with a clatter. To negotiate it, Drew first had to yank off the ill-fitting flippers and toss them on the deck. Slipping the strap of the water-soaked case over a shoulder, he grasped one rung with his hands and caught another with his bare foot as the boat rose on a swell. Without water buoying him up, the tank on his back felt like solid lead, and he almost fell backwards. He climbed a rung at a time. Near the top, Gürsel and one of his crew pulled him aboard.

"Sorry about leaving you there, but we had to make it look good. I knew if you had any sense you would go north, and ... here we are."

Drew wanted to throw him off the boat. What if he hadn't surfaced? What if they were off by a few hundred meters in either direction? It would have been easy—very easy—to miss him. What if he hadn't gone due north? If he hadn't used the compass properly? "You could have missed me."

Gürsel shrugged. "A few more miles and you would see the coast. Someone would have picked you up."

Drew nodded, keeping his face as blank as a rivet head.

Wet, the diving suit seemed even less pliable. Gürsel had to alternately yank and peel to get it off him. Drew collapsed on a bench. The weather was warm this far south, but the breeze sent shivers through him. Sitting in the sun, dripping dry, he ran a hand through the remnants of his hair; salt had made it sticky and spiky.

What was he supposed to think now? That his prayer to God without Jesus as intermediary had worked? That the hand of God was helping him toward his goal? He didn't want to make the mistake human beings, particularly the ignorant and desperate ones, had been making for centuries—interpreting favorable events as "signs" of God's will.

He sighed and stared out at the sea. He could just make out the hazy lump that must be Turkey.

An hour later, they were gliding past cliffs ranging in color from tawny to burnt honey. Antalya's harbor was a small oval gouged out of the shoreline. It was crowned by well-preserved fortifications—crenellated walls and towers—built by the Romans and rebuilt by Seljuk Turks. Plants had taken root in the interstices between stone blocks and hung down like green beards.

Gürsel's boat cruised into the harbor, where dozens of boats were already moored.

Drew exchanged polite farewells with Gürsel and his crew but nothing more. He went ashore by simply stepping off the boat when it pulled up to a quayside gas station. Harbors, he noticed as he walked along a quay, stank almost as much as boats. On this one, the overpowering smell of diesel mingled with the reek of rotting fish.

Because Zafer had had the foresight to bring the stamps used by passport officials in Egypt and Turkey, Drew had already stamped his own exit from Egypt. Now, adjusting the date, he used the Turkish entry stamp.

From a public phone, he called Yasemin's landline and left a message telling her he would be back in Istanbul in a couple of days.

He took a cab to Antalya's bus station. It was a typical terminal with enormous sheet-glass windows, a web-work of steel supporting a distant ceiling, and departure announcements echoing in the cavernous space. The ride would be ten hours, but traveling by bus was a lot safer than flying into an airport.

Fortunately, Turkish buses were comfortable and modern. The one he boarded was a Mercedes-Benz.

As the driver pulled out of the row of slanted buses, Drew opened the sun-dried messenger bag and took out *The Jewish Wisdom of Ancient*

Alexandria. Once tar-black, the rough cloth cover was now worn at the edges, revealing a terra cotta-colored material that made a handsome if uneven border. This book had been carried by ship or plane—maybe by horse or camel—until it had found its way to an unlikely shop in the Egyptian desert. Between its aging covers was perhaps the last piece in the Christ mosaic: the wisdom literature compiled by Jesus ben Sirach, the grandfather of the man who had written Sayings of the Savior—an Aramaic version of Q1.

According to the bow-tied, bespectacled scholar whom Drew imagined had written the introduction to the book, some time during the first or second century BC, Alexandrian Jews, looking for common ground between Greek religious thought and Judaism, had identified the Jewish personification of Wisdom with the Greek concept of the Logos.

The Logos was originally thought of as the mind of God *and* the laws by which the universe operated. However, under the Platonists, who insisted that God was not part of the material universe but lay somewhere *outside* it, it was necessary to have some sort of intermediary between humans and God. Hence, the Logos. Similarly, Wisdom in the Jewish tradition acted as a go-between for humans and God.

But that was not all wisdom was good for. The introduction quoted Proverbs 3:19:

The Lord founded the Earth through Wisdom, and by understanding He established the heavens.

The author also singled out Proverbs 3:22:

I am Wisdom. The Lord created me in the beginning of his words, before his works of old. I have been established from everlasting, before there was ever an Earth. When He prepared the heavens, I was there. When He marked out the foundations of the Earth, then I was beside Him, as a master craftsman.

No one familiar with the New Testament could fail to see the parallel to the Gospel of John:

In the beginning was the Logos, and the Logos was with God, and the Logos was God. He was in the beginning with God. All things were made through Him, and without him nothing was made that was made.

But as Drew was well aware, Philo had already had this idea with his heavenly Adam. Writing a century or so before the author of John, Philo cast the heavenly Adam as the model of an ideal man who inhabited a heaven consisting of God's thoughts—a heaven corresponding to Plato's dimension of perfect forms. Sure enough, Philo called this celestial being Logos, "the first-born of God." Adam, the mortal husband of Eve, was merely a copy of the heavenly Adam, once again corresponding to Plato's concept that all material objects are vastly inferior copies of their flawless, eternal counterparts.

John's idea of Jesus as the Son of God and the Logos was a perfect match. Borrowing from Philo, John had created a *heavenly* Jesus—through whom the material universe was created—who would be followed by the human one who suffered and died on the cross.

Whereas Philo had equated Jewish Wisdom with the Greek Logos, John had identified *Jesus* with the Logos and, by association, with Wisdom. Wisdom lost Her identity as a feminine emanation of God and became, instead, the *Son* of God. This killed two birds with one stone: it excluded the feminine from Creation, and it joined Greek thought with Jewish theology.

John was the only one of the four Gospels to mention the Logos. Not surprisingly, scholars had shown John did not come from the same milieu as the other Gospels. What was interesting to Drew, however, was that the Logos—the heavenly Jesus—had *replaced* Wisdom as she appeared in the Old Testament. What was Q1, bagged and boxed on the seat next to him, but a collection of *wisdom* sayings—Wisdom when she was still the Thought of God? The connection couldn't be clearer.

Since Q had been written in Greek, Drew suspected that his scroll formed the original, Aramaic core, undoubtedly compiled in Alexandria and later translated into Greek. Just as Wisdom evolved into the Logos in Philo, the Logos had evolved into Jesus in John.

Simply put, Jesus of Nazareth was a later superimposition upon an already well-established tradition—nothing more than the latest incarnation of Wisdom.

If Drew was right, God was probably furious.

10: 5

TWIN TWIN

DREW CLIMBED THE MARBLE STEPS in the unlit stairwell and unlocked the steel door to the Office with Zafer's keys. The alarm began to beep ominously. Locating the keypad on the wall, he punched in the numerical sequence Zafer had made him memorize.

The silence was eerie.

The huge front room with its exposed rafters seemed to have taken on another coat of dust since they'd left. Zafer's worktables and their swan-necked architect's lamps as well. The gunmetal gray filing cabinets, the shelves, the desk. The oversized map of Turkey and the map, on another wall, of Istanbul's streets. This was his home now, a grimy industrial space where information was stored, documents counterfeited, identities forged.

Ironic that Zafer had been killed over a document. The irony would double if the scroll turned out to be a forgery—the joke would be on all of them—but Drew no longer thought that likely. Although he was neither a scholar nor a paleographer, he had an idea about how he might be able to verify the manuscript's authenticity.

He sat down at the steel desk and turned on the computer.

Logging onto the Internet, he tuned in a radio station that played Western pop from the '70s. He'd been a child in the '80s, but songs from the previous decade were still surrounded by the nostalgia of a time when the neighborhood bar his father disappeared into after work and what he did there were a complete mystery.

While Steely Dan told Jack to go back and do it again, Drew pulled up a webpage featuring a table that showed the sayings common to Q, Mark, Matthew, Luke, and the Gospel of Thomas.

He took a deep breath. "Either this scroll is a forgery and Stephen is wrong," he said aloud, "or this scroll is genuine and Jesus of Nazareth never lived."

He pulled out Shimon's translation.

The Q1 sayings were decidedly Greek and reflected the philosophy of the Cynics, who were already well-established in Alexandria by the third century BC. The school rejected not only material wealth but even the most meager possessions.

The first Q1 saying listed, which also appeared in Luke, was *Think of the ravens: they neither sow nor reap; they have no storehouse or barn, yet God feeds them.* This was lifted right out the life of Diogenes, the archetypal Cynic, admired even by Alexander the Great. Observing a mouse, Diogenes realized that mice don't put any effort into building a dwelling, they eat whatever they happen to find. They don't bother about the past or the future, and yet they got along well enough.

Q1 also included *I say to you, love your enemies. Bless those who curse you. Pray for those who mistreat you.* This saying was put into practice by the famous Cynic Epictetus, who had written: *A rather nice part of being a Cynic comes when you have to be flogged like an ass and throughout the beating you have to love those who are beating you as though you were father or brother to them.* When asked how he would defend himself against an enemy, Epictetus answered, "By being good and kind toward him."

Another oft-quoted saying in Q1 was *Judge not, lest you too be judged. For you will be judged by the same standard you apply,* another saying that could be traced directly back to Diogenes. When a disciple asked him how he could master himself, Diogenes replied, "By rigorously criticizing yourself according to the standard you use to criticize others."

The list went on.

The point was not that the author or authors of Q1 had plagiarized the Cynics; rather, the Jewish community that had compiled Q1 shared the same *values* as the Cynics. In Luke, Jesus commands the apostles "*Behold, I send you out as lambs in the midst of wolves. Carry no purse, no sack, no sandals.*" This was a precise description of the Cynics, who wandered about as beggars preaching their philosophy.

Scholars had puzzled for decades over which Hellenized Jewish community could have produced the Q1 sayings. The answer had become astonishingly clear: the Therapeutae. The Cynical values—praise of poverty, disdain of property, asceticism, a life harmonized with the rhythms of nature—were all embodied by those austere, monasterial communities near Alexandria. As Philo himself had observed firsthand, the Therapeutae *abandon their property* and *desert their brethren, their children, their wives, their parents*. A commandment in both Q1 and Luke expressed the same philosophy: "*If any one comes to me and does not hate his own father and mother and wife and children and brothers and sisters, yes, and even his own life, he cannot be my disciple.*"

If the earliest layer of Q belonged to the Therapeutae, Sayings of the Savior must have been among their scriptures.

Whatever city you enter, Luke had written, *and they receive you, eat such things as are set before you. And heal the sick who are there, and say to them, the kingdom of God has come near to you. Therapeut* meant *healer.* How much of Jesus' ministry had been healing? The blind, the barren, even the dead?

Drew put his head in his hands. His skull was ringing as though something electronic had been built into it. How had the obvious been overlooked for so long? He raked his face with his fingers. Even the Last Supper, in which the apostles are commanded to eat bread and drink wine in remembrance of Jesus, Drew now saw as a coded element. On the one hand, the use of bread and wine had clearly been inspired by the rites of Dionysus and Mithras; on the other, it alluded to the communal meals of the Therapeutae.

Drew looked over Q2, the second layer of Q, on the webpage.

None of the sayings in Q2 showed up in Shimon's translation. Distinctly Jewish, they were mostly apocalyptical warnings:

"*Woe to you Chorazin! Woe to you Bethsaida! And you, Capernaum, who are exalted to heaven, you shall be brought down to hell!*"

"*This is a wicked generation. It demands a sign, and the only sign that will be given it is the sign of Jonah.*"

"*There will be wailing and gnashing of teeth when you see Abraham, Isaac, and Jacob and all the prophets in the kingdom of God and yourself thrown out.*"

"*I came to cast fire on the earth, and would that it were already kindled! Do you think that I have come to give peace on earth? No, I tell you, but rather division.*"

How could the gentle sayings of Jesus the Cynic—or rather, Jesus the Therapeut—have come from the same man?

They hadn't. Once again, in the first two layers of Q, Drew found the familiar division between the Greek worldview and the Jewish. Their reconciliation wouldn't begin until Q3, and wouldn't be complete until the Gospels had been written.

Some of the Q2 sayings, even in the Gospels, were already attributed to John the Baptist, but *all* of them were worded in John's fire-and-brimstone style. Q2 *was* John. It was simple as that. While a few sayings had remained John's, most had been put into Jesus' mouth. It now made perfect sense. *There is one to come who is mightier than I. His winnowing fan is in his hand to purify his threshing floor and gather the wheat into his granary, but he will burn the chaff with a fire that can never go out.*

The Baptist never names *anyone*. Who was to say he was referring to Jesus? Only Mark. The Baptist's prediction had given Mark a perfect set-up—and where did Mark begin his Gospel? Not with a virgin birth or tales of a childhood Jesus, but with John's proclamation. It was a seamless fit.

The Gospel of Thomas, unearthed in Nag Hammadi, contained none of the drama of the canonical gospels. Jesus doesn't perform any miracles, he's not crucified, there's no resurrection. The same is true of Q on all three levels. Both Q and Thomas were simply collections of sayings. The authors of these documents had constructed a Jesus to be revered not for his willingness to die but for his wisdom—precisely the opposite of Paul's Jesus.

After the Church banned texts like Thomas, monks who held forbidden texts began to Christianize them. And that, Drew realized, was the Nag Hammadi Library connection Stephen had been pointing to. Almost exclusively Gnostic, the library contained a number of works that weren't remotely Christian—except for the fact that Christ's name had been used in them.

In Thomas, sayings had been attributed to Jesus to give the gospel the veneer of orthodox Christianity. But the strategy had failed. The sole surviving copy of Thomas had come to light only because it had been buried in the sand for a millennium and a half and discovered by an Egyptian peasant.

Originally, instead of *Jesus said*, or *the Savior said*, many of the sayings must have been ascribed to Wisdom. The evidence had been sitting in front of scholars for centuries.

With a compilation of proverbs, aphorisms, adages and the like in one hand—a compilation now known as Q—and the Gospel of Mark in the other, Matthew and Luke had composed their own gospels. What made it clear that neither had recorded the words of an eyewitness to the "events" about which they had written, was that whenever they shared a quote from Jesus, the words were spoken under entirely different circumstances. Not even the lines that led into the quote were the same.

In Matthew, for example, Jesus sits down by the sea and tells a gathered multitude a long series of parables, including the parable of the mustard seed. In Luke, however, Jesus tells the parable of the mustard seed after defending himself for exorcising a woman in a synagogue on the Sabbath.

Matthew's Sermon on the Mount is paralleled by Luke's Sermon on the Plain, delivered *in a level place*. Not surprisingly, the contents of the sermons were completely different. What had happened, clearly enough, was that Matthew and Luke had the sayings and the frame story but had had to create specific incidents around the sayings.

Philip Bailey, the front man for Earth, Wind & Fire, was hitting notes—in a falsetto that seemed to be a trademark of black male singers in the '70s—that would have cracked Drew's voice in three or four places. With the ethereal sound of "Fantasy" in the background, Drew re-read the opening line of the Gospel of Thomas: *These are the words that the living Jesus spoke and which Didymus Judas Thomas wrote down ...*"

Didymus was *twin* in Greek. Similarly, *Thomas* signified *twin* in Aramaic. Why this man had been called Twin Twin had puzzled scholars for decades. Drew thought he might have an answer. The author of the Gospel of Thomas was alluding to two strata: the Greek layer (the sayings of the Cynics) and its Jewish layer (the apocalyptic admonitions of Q2). The theme of the twin was now clear as well: Jesus was an *overlay*, a stand-in for Wisdom. The message was identical, but the messenger had been renamed. Jesus and Wisdom were one and the same—twins.

Drew sat back in his chair, Earth, Wind, & Fire's hit fading.

How many martyrs had died for a man who never existed? How many Jews tortured, imprisoned, executed as "Christ-killers"? How many wars had been fought in Christ's name? Because we had taken something meant for first-century Palestine and tried to apply it literally, the world over, in every succeeding century.

Wheels squeaked as he pushed the chair back and stood. It was time to find out if Kadir was still alive.

10: 6

VORGA

T HE AUTUMNAL CADENCES of Al Stewart's *Time Passages* followed Drew out a door that could have sealed a bank vault.

It was a short walk to Tünel Square, where steel rails formed a circle in the cobblestones and allowed the tram to turn around. Cables and wires criss-crossed overhead.

Four pay phones clustered just outside the entrance to a funicular that took passengers up the hill from Karaköy or down from Tünel. Directly in front of him was the entrance, marked by wrought-iron bars, to the courtyard where he'd surprised Yasemin drinking with her colleagues. Years ago it seemed. Drew inserted a calling card into a slot, the gold of its exposed electronic chip the only flash of optimism in the gray evening.

The phone rang several times.

Come on Kadir, pick up ...

"Alo?"

"Kadir...?"

"Vorga."

"What?"

"Vorga," Kadir said again. "*Iyiyim.*" *I'm fine.* "When you are going to get me out of here?"

"Soon. Very soon."

Drew could hear the phone changing hands.

"We want the scroll."

Drew recognized the voice. "You'll get it when I decide to give it to you."

"You're not being very cooperative."

"Why should I? You killed Professor Cutherton and Zafer. You tried to kill me. And you've kidnapped Kadir."

"Regrettable, but necessary."

"Yeah? Well don't call me, got it? I'll call you." He hung up the blue receiver.

When Drew turned around, he saw someone glancing at him from across the square. Dark-skinned but not Turkish-looking, the man was pretending to browse postcards on a rack outside the frame shop next to Kaffeehaus.

A Sicarii? One of the men they'd hired? Maybe just a Turk who didn't strike Drew as Turkish? He headed back to the Office, reversing direction twice.

The three cable-suspended lamps on Zafer's street were already lit, tiny moons burning over the slick cobblestones. In the fall twilight the building looked as though it had built out of blocks carved from sooty October sky.

Just as the heavy steel wing of the outside door swung closed, Drew thought he saw a man across the street watching him. "Fuck it," he said as he went up the steps of the dark stairwell. "If Raymond wants this scroll so bad, let him come and get it."

10: 7

THE LETTERS

VORGA WASN'T TURKISH; it was the name of a spaceship from one of Kadir's favorite science fiction novels. The ship had abandoned Gulliver Foyle to die on a derelict spacecraft. Foyle's sole reason to live from that point on was to take revenge on the captain of the Vorga. Since the Sicarii no doubt had hired an interpreter to listen in on the conversation, Kadir had used *Vorga* to send a message to Drew—he didn't care about the money. He didn't care about the scroll. All he wanted was revenge.

Drew glanced at the clock. He was playing a waiting game with Raymond. Well, time was one thing Drew had right now.

For the last few weeks he'd been adrift in the centuries. For thousands of years people had read or heard the stories of Osiris, Adonis, Attis, Dionysus, Mithras, eventually dismissing them as nothing more than the anthropomorphic poetry of defunct religions—as myth. Why then, when we came across the same tale set in a Jewish milieu, did we decide it described a particular carpenter from Nazareth?

A number of scholars believed that Paul had perverted the original message of Christianity by taking a man and making him into a God. Drew now understood that just the opposite had happened: Paul's Christ Jesus had never been a human being. Paul had been a species of Platonist. Perfection, he'd believed, belonged to a heavenly realm of pure spirit. He'd devalued the physical and emphasized the spiritual. *Flesh and blood,* he'd insisted, *cannot inherit the Kingdom of God.*

After the synoptic Gospels turned Paul's heavenly Jesus into an actual man, John had made the final synthesis, taking the Greek idea of the Logos and combining eternal god with suffering man.

These two schools of thought—Jesus as God, Jesus as mere man—had existed for centuries side by side until the Church settled the question once and for all with the Council of Nicaea and the resulting Nicene Creed, which had made Jesus into God.

Paul's complaint in Corinthians, that the Corinthians had received revelation through Wisdom, now made perfect sense: there could hardly be a clearer indication that a collection of wisdom sayings had preceded the Gospels.

Half a dozen scholars had pointed out that Paul's use of the language of wisdom sayings was not coincidental. And that meant that Paul must have been aware of a pre-Gospel collection of wisdom sayings. He then derailed the Savior he found in wisdom literature, changing Christ from a figure who offers spiritual salvation through *wisdom* to one who offers salvation through his own death, a concept borrowed from the Mystery cults. This was the core of Paul's teaching: faith replaced knowledge— and Mosaic Law—as the way to salvation.

What Drew hadn't realized when he'd re-read Paul's letters on the plane back from Cairo was that although Paul was thoroughly familiar with a tradition of wisdom sayings, Paul knew very well Jesus had not said them. Only later, in the Gospels, were they attributed to Jesus. Ironically, Paul's letters were the best evidence that before the Gospels had been written, these sayings had not been regarded as quotes belonging to Jesus.

There were at least twelve passages in Paul's letters that Paul attributes either to scripture or to God Himself but are attributed to Jesus in the Gospels. Paul never uses the preamble *As Christ Jesus said* but instead *As it is written*, a well-known formulaic introduction for anything taken from scripture. The conclusion was inescapable: the sayings had preceded the one who'd supposedly said them.

Perhaps most damning of all, 1 Corinthians 2:9 cites a famous wisdom saying: *Eye has not seen and ear has not heard nor has it risen in the human heart what God has prepared for those who love him.* Paul calls this a quote from scripture. The Gospel of Thomas, however, attributes it to

Christ. This saying also shows up in various forms in both Matthew and Luke—as direct quotes from Jesus.

Here was a wisdom saying older than both Paul's letters and Thomas. If Jesus had said it, Paul would surely have given him the credit. The fact that Thomas had attributed it to Jesus was clear evidence of the process of taking sayings originally anonymous or attributed to Wisdom and putting them into Jesus' mouth.

In Romans 13:9 Paul says *You shall love your neighbor as yourself* but never attributes this to Christ. Similarly, James 2:8 tells the Christians *You shall love neighbor as yourself* and claims this as Scripture, not as anything Jesus—his supposed brother—said.

This was how a Savior had been constructed. From scripture, wisdom literature, from sayings of religious leaders such as John the Baptist and James the Just, from the exploits of Jews rebelling against the Romans, from rituals practiced in the Mystery religions centuries before—all of it framed in the form of a Greek tragedy. And for two millennia it had succeeded brilliantly.

The downstairs buzzer sounded.

Drew flinched and shot a glance at the steel door. He waited.

"Drew? It's me." The muffled voice came from the other side of the door.

Jesse.

He got out of the swivel chair and sent it rolling back a couple feet. Unlocking the door, he found himself looking at the muzzle of an automatic pistol. Again.

10: 8

CON JOB

COINS LOST CENTURIES AGO and later unearthed by archaeologists showed Dionysus on one side and on the reverse, the god Mithras. Two different gods on a single coin was more or less unthinkable in the modern world, but the ancient Mysteries adherents hadn't tried to wipe each other out or brand each other confederates of the Devil. Nor did they hesitate to incorporate elements of different myths into their own worship. They burned incense and offered prayers in the temple of whichever god they happened to find themselves because there was always a possibility the god or goddess would appreciate the gesture.

Drew couldn't expect any such tolerance from a Sicarii. Backing up, he waved Jesse in. Pistol notwithstanding, she had put together an outdoorsy look: jeans, a white turtleneck, sneakers. "Put that thing away, will you?"

"Drew, I'm not alone."

"Raymond with you?"

"He's downstairs. I talked him into letting me come up alone." Jesse dropped the pistol in her purse. "You don't look surprised."

Drew lifted an indolent shoulder. "I had my suspicions. Starting with your fundamentalist mother, who named you Jesse. I couldn't help thinking of *Jessean*, an early name for a Christian. True, you didn't have to follow in your mom's footsteps, but the chase in Antakya finally made sense. Zafer knew right away the Sicarii weren't trying to kill us, but why bother scaring us when we were in the process of selling the scroll? The whole thing was an elaborate way for you to infiltrate our threesome.

The day we sold the Habakkuk Scroll to Serafis, I did a little web search. I found articles with your name—your married name—in the *Revue Biblique*, the Ecole Biblique's mouthpiece. You *claimed* a moderate, rational approach, but underneath the message was the same as your mother's: the Gospels are basically history. Although you applauded questioning the divinity of Jesus, you always lined up with the Church in the end. That's when we cut you out of the loop."

"That's why you wouldn't take me with you to Alexandria."

"X gets the square."

"Do you know how we found you?"

"Zafer said if you put enough people on it, you'd track us down eventually."

"He was right. We isolated the neighborhood you kept disappearing into, and just this evening someone finally picked you up. He missed you once because of the haircut." She shook her head. "It's not you."

He looked at her purse and lifted his chin. "The pistol isn't really you, either."

"Drew," she looked genuinely remorseful. "Maybe if … maybe if I'd realized I was with the wrong person. Back in college …"

Drew smirked. "Isn't it pretty to think so?"

The angles of her face sharpened, an incipient snarl. "Always the literature major. Are you going to come down with me? Or are Raymond and Jean going to have to come up after you?"

"I'll come along peaceably. *Marshal.* But first—" He squinted an eye and see-sawed a hand. "A couple of things I want to get straight."

"I thought you might have a few questions."

Drew held out a hand toward the couch. "Cushion for your ass?" He plopped down in the squeaky-wheeled chair. "You knew there was no Jesus of Nazareth, didn't you?"

She put her handbag down on the coffee table and perched on the edge of the couch. "We knew."

"So let me see if I've got the mosaic straight …"

She blinked slowly and nodded, her mouth almost as slot-like as Hohenzollern's had been. "Shoot."

"Jesus started out as an idea. He was the Logos of the Greeks. He was

Wisdom as personified in the Old Testament. So even before he was supposedly born, Christian communities existed—like the Therapeutae in Alexandria."

She nodded.

"Guys like Jesus Ben Sirach began to compile wisdom sayings. That was ....what? Around 170 BC? Other compilations followed. Then along comes Jesus Panthera. He's dazzled by the Therapeutae. He converts. He tries to bring the new teachings to Jerusalem, but he's accused of blasphemy and hung from a tree. And there's the seed for the drama of the crucified messiah—only it's around 90 BC, more than a century before Pontius Pilate shows up on the scene."

Unconsciously almost, Drew recognized the delicate opening bars of "Strawberry Letter 23", an ethereal funk hit that added to the unreality of the moment.

"Paul begins his ministry around 40 AD. He grafts the Mystery cults onto Judaism. What better way to reach gentiles? The Persians had Mithras, the Greeks had Dionysus, the Egyptians had Osiris, so now the Jews had Jesus—a Savior who is crucified and resurrected. But Paul doesn't mention when Christ was crucified or by whom. To Paul, he was still a mythical figure, like Dionysus or Osiris.

"As it turns out, the Jews aren't particularly interested in Christianity. By the time Paul is expelled from Antioch, he's failed to convert a single one. Even Barnabas, his apprentice, deserts him. So Paul goes to the gentiles instead—Corinth, Philippi, Thessalonika—where he promulgates his new god.

"His letters, supposedly the earliest Christian writings, don't mention any of Christ's sayings or miracles. You have to admit, that's a little odd."

Jesse said nothing, so Drew continued. "Decades later, recognizing the success Paul has had with the Greeks, as well as the miserable failure of the Jerusalem Church to convert Jews to their new sect, Mark, like any good Alexandrian looking to reconcile Greek wisdom with Jewish monotheism, not only adopts Paul's resurrected Christ, he adds miracles to entice the Jews. Matthew and Luke add a virgin birth, and the miracles pile up until John has Jesus raising Lazarus from the dead. But I'm getting ahead of myself."

Jesse smirked. "You have a tendency to do that."

"Still, the Jews aren't particularly interested in Christianity, even with all the miracles. After the death of John the Baptist, Jewish hopes shift to a new savior. The Qumran community believes it's James—the Teacher of Righteousness, the Zadokite who is hereditary heir to the high priesthood, the Nazarite holy from the womb. Unfortunately, James, like John the Baptist, dies without delivering the Jews from the Romans.

"The revolt of 66 AD follows four years after James's stoning, and Josephus mentions something like a dozen men who crowned themselves king or claimed to be the Messiah during the war. Jewish hopes are pinned on a military leader, a Zealot. But after the destruction of the Temple in 70 AD and the reestablishment of Roman hegemony, Mark sees the futility of a military messiah and cobbles together a *spiritual* redeemer ... from pieces of other religious leaders, pagan magicians, messianic figures, and Paul's letters. Why else does Christ talk sometimes like a Cynic, sometimes like John the Baptist, sometimes like a Zealot, sometimes like James the Just?

"Mark's gospel was not a deliberate deception. It was part of a tradition. It was midrash—religious fiction. Allegory. Entirely acceptable at the time. Wasn't Serapis a composite god? Weren't the rites of Mithras grafted onto the Saturnalia? Even the Qumran community did the same thing in its own way: past scriptures were interpreted as though they applied to the first century AD."

Jesse looked like she was going to yawn. If she knew all this, how could she be aligned with the Sicarii?

"The part of Christ's ministry where he addresses crowds is basically John the Baptist, the charismatic speaker. The same with his apocalyptic messages. This is all Q2. When we read about Jesus' holiness and perfection ... that's James the Just. His cry of *"He who does not have a sword, let him sell his garments and buy one"* in Luke belongs to Judas of Galilee. His sagely qualities, his praise of poverty and humility ... that was Jesus the Cynic and was meant to appeal to Greeks and Hellenized Jews like Philo."

Jesse's gaze wandered.

"Luke the Therapeut and Matthew follow in Mark's footsteps. They correct Mark's errors—Luke more than Matthew—and continue harmonizing Hellenic and Judaic concepts.

"The Christ mosaic was perfect except for one thing: the Messiah hadn't rid Palestine of the Romans, nor had the kingdom arrived. So expectations of the Kingdom to Come were indefinitely forestalled by the rumor of a Second Coming. Two thousand years later, people are still waiting. You gotta hand it to Mark—the greatest con job in history."

She shifted her position on the couch. "Anything else?"

"Not really. The Gospel authors completed the tragedy, literally, by pulling elements from *The Bacchae*. What better way to present the new god-man to the broadest audience? The best part is that this is all built into the Gospels. A blind man is named after one of Plato's dialogues. Brothers of Jesus are named after the messianic figures on whom his portrait was based. The Mysteries are encoded. I mean, even the incident in Gethsemane. If we re-examine the night Jesus was supposedly *delivered up*—that, as you know, is the actual Greek, not *betrayed* as it's translated—we find the same phrase was used for the Greek *pharmakos*, the sacrificial victim who also meets his death to atone for the 'sins of the world.' It's perfect. It combines the fulfilling of earlier Jewish scriptures with a concept right out of the Greek Mysteries.

"The problem here, Jess, is that Gospels weren't written for the twenty-first century—and especially not for twenty-first century *Americans*. They were written for Hellenized Jews and Greeks living in the first and second century. In Palestine, Greece, Egypt. That's why we *can't* read them anymore. We're too distant from that worldview. English isn't the right language. And the Mystery cults the Gospel writers borrowed so much from have long been extinct, obliterated by Christians themselves."

"Look ..." Jesse smirked. "It's trying to think."

The remark, coupled with her venomous smile, startled him more than opening the door and seeing her with a gun pointed at his chest.

10: 9

MERE MAN

"**Y**OU'RE JUST AS GODDAMN smug as you were in college." Jesse's lips were twisted in disgust. "The Ebionites have always known that the Gospel Jesus was a transparency laid over James the Just and that James was the Teacher of Righteousness among the Essenes.

"They also knew that James wasn't a Christian. Oh, James believed the so-called Son of Man was coming on Clouds of Glory, but his Messiah had nothing to do with a Jew crucified under Pilate, much less his own *brother*. He wasn't arrogant enough to believe he was the Savior, either."

Drew had known that the Ebionites sided with James over Paul, but he did not know that, like the Essenes, they believed James was the Messiah. Unlike the Essenes, however, they disguised their faith in the Teacher of Righteousness.

"When the Ebionites insist on Christ as mere man, it's because *James* was mere man. And yet he lived a morally pure life. The Ebionites found this encouraging. The life of James was something we could all aspire to whereas none of us is a god or the son of God. What's the big deal if the son of God is perfect? Why *wouldn't* he be? He's the son of *God*.

"Of course, by the time the Gospels were written, it was impossible to go on worshiping James. A man who'd been stoned to death by the Sanhedrin, who hadn't performed a panoply of miracles, who hadn't walked out of his own tomb or freed the Jews of Roman rule couldn't very well compete with the Son of God, now could he? But to this day, every time an Ebionite praises Jesus the Christ out loud, inwardly he's praising James the Christ."

Drew sat up a little straighter. "So that's why they were persecuted almost out of existence."

"Well, of *course*. Today, only their leaders accept these views. They understand that turning a man, whether James or some other messiah, into a god is a perversion. It takes responsibility for salvation off *you* and puts it on someone else.

"The real miracle was James himself. That mere flesh and blood could come so near perfection. But as the centuries passed, Christian writers consistently devalued him in favor of Jesus. Ask your average Christian, and she'll say, 'What? Jesus had a brother?' James has almost been wiped out of existence. But, like the Ebionites, not quite."

Drew mustered half a smile. "It seems obvious enough now. I mean ... all of it. Cosmic myth turned into earthly legend ... legend turned into history ..."

"More obvious than you think. Go back and re-read the hymn in Philippians ... *And being found in human appearance, he humbled himself and became obedient unto death, even death on the cross. Therefore God has exalted him and given him the name which is above every name, that at the name of Jesus every knee should bow, of those in heaven and of those on Earth.*"

"Okay...?" Drew's tone was a shrug.

Jesse shook her head with a mixture of disgust and disapproval. "*Think.* What does the hymn tell you?"

Drew had read Philippians, had re-read it on the way back from Cairo and missed the significance of the hymn. He'd missed it even after hearing Jesse recite it, but now it was absurdly clear. "Jesus had no *name*." Drew shook his head. "He had no name until *after* the Crucifixion."

"Exactly." Jesse's lips pulled back in a genuine smile. "Just as Jacob isn't called Israel until after he wrestles God in Genesis 32. It's typical tribal practice, a birth name and an earned name. Jesus' earned name, after he proves himself on the cross, is Yeshua—Savior. There's no birth name because, of course, he was never born. The whole crucifixion drama took place on some heavenly plane. The Gospels, as you just pointed out, took a cosmic myth and historicized it, using incidents and details taken from the lives of men like Jesus Panthera, James the Just, Judas of Galilee, and John the Baptist."

Drew was confused. "If you … if you already know all this—?"

Jesse rolled her eyes. "You can really be dense for a semi-bright guy. Of *course* we know the truth. We're protecting the rest of you."

"Protecting us? Seems to me you're dedicating your life to a—"

"A lie?

"A fiction "

"Go back to that little paper of yours that set my mother off in class … what's the difference between fiction and religion?"

A spring squealed as he leaned back in the chair. "Religions are fictions societies agree to believe in."

"Do you know what percentage of the world's population is college educated?"

"Five? Six?"

"One." She held up a finger.

The nail, he noticed, had been polished white to match her turtleneck.

"Now, what percentage of college grads do you think have read Philo of Alexandria? Plato's dialogues? Josephus? Do you think the guy getting his MBA keeps a copy of Augustine's *Confessions* in his briefcase? And what about your average peasant or blue collar worker?"

"I get the point."

"The point is people need something black and white, Drew, something easy to grasp. They don't want Philo's allegories. They want someone they can talk to in their most hopeless moments. Always with them. Always listening. Ever compassionate. Thy rod and thy staff comfort me.

"Don't you see? We can't inspire the hopeless with a mere man or woman, however extraordinary. Gandhi, Marie Curie, Martin Luther King—they're not enough. But … we *can* help the most despairing human being on Earth with a divine Jesus, with an all-powerful Savior who loves each and every one of us *unconditionally*—the poor, the sick, the maimed, the deformed, the ugly, the diseased—*all* of us without exception. No soul is too hideous to love. No crime is so great that it cannot be repented and forgiven. It is the hope of nations. It is the wealth of human spirit we're adding to. We can do that with a man who, by returning from the grave, has proved that death is not final. With a man through whom all things are possible. *All*, Drew. Jesus is hope itself."

"But …" Drew shook his head. "How can you do it with a straight face, knowing what you know?"

"I don't know *anything*, Drew, not for certain. And neither do you. Every day, somewhere in the world, there are miraculous incidents. Darwin's theory of evolution is only half right. And there are still more things under the sun than are explained in your philosophy. Horatio."

Horatio. A belated attempt to return to the innocence of their college days.

"You don't have to do it with deception, Jess. I mean, look at Dickens, *A Christmas Carol.* Does anyone believe that three ghosts—"

"Four," she corrected. "Jacob Marley's ghost shows up first."

"Okay, four. Does anyone believe that? It's a great book because it's so beautifully human. Redemption by itself is just a vague abstraction. But dramatized in Victorian London, it becomes as real as the cobblestones. The most jaded reader feels good at the end of that novel. That was Dickens's magic … we believe in his stories without believing they really happened." Precisely the reason Jesus, who's a vaguely drawn dying-and-rising god in Paul's letters, was historicized: to make him *real*, to arouse passion and compassion."

"Sounds good, Drew, but is someone dying of cancer really going to pick up a Dickens novel and feel better?" She shook her head. "A clever high school kid can figure out Genesis is a fairytale. I mean … Noah's *Ark*? Dickens's ghost story is more believable. And yet a poll last year showed that more than *half* of all of Americans believe the Bible is literally true. *Fifty-five* percent! You think Christianity will unravel because a few more people know the truth?"

He sighed. "The Church will just go on denying everything."

"It's worked for us for more than a millennium and a half."

"People believe what they want to believe."

That ugly smirk again.

"Cutherton said something like that before he died."

"What?"

A phone clipped onto her belt made the same chirp as the walkie-talkies Turkish police officers carried. When she answered it, he could hear a male voice on the other end, but couldn't make out the words.

"Everything's fine," Jesse replied. We're coming down now."

10: 10

KIND REGARDS

"You were there? When Stephen died?"

"Now's not the time to get emotional, Drew. Let's go ... out the door. You first."

"Fine." He stood up so suddenly the chair bounced off the backs of his thighs and squeaked across five or six feet of floor. "Why don't you talk while we're heading out?"

"Later. Once we have the scroll. Once we have Sayings of the Savior."

Raymond was at the bottom of the stairwell. Drew recognized him even though the left side of his face was bandaged. Half the hair on his head was gone. The rest was golden stubble. Ashraf had given him a third-degree burn or two to remember him by.

The Sicarii's blue eyes glittered in what little light there was.

Drew wasn't prepared, as he reached the last step, for the vicious backhand across his face. He his head snapped to the side and his vision blurred.

"Raymond! That wasn't necessary."

"No, but eet felt good."

Rough hands turned him around and shoved him against a wall. Raymond frisked him.

"I don't play with guns anymore," Drew said.

"That was a merry little chase you led us on across the Mediterranean, wasn't it?"

Drew figured no matter what he said, he'd get cracked again.

"Where ees the manuscript?"

"I'll take you."

"You've decided to cooperate, eh? I hope you don't mind if we take a look around upstairs first."

Drew shrugged. "Be my guest."

"The door's open," Jesse said.

Raymond spoke into a phone that doubled as a walkie-talkie. "Jean, Naim, get in here."

"Let's go." Raymond opened the door and shoved Drew in front of him.

The night was cold and damp. Drew was glad he'd grabbed his jean jacket on the way down.

Jean Saint-Savoy, shooting him a glance of vindictive triumph—and someone Drew didn't recognize—another ex-legionnaire from North Africa probably—pushed past.

Raymond held out a hand. "The keys to the flat."

Drew took them out of his pocket and dropped them in Raymond's palm.

The Sicarii looked up at the third floor. "Eef they find it up there, I will keel you on the spot." Raymond smiled. "I very much hope they do."

Saint-Savoy stopped at the doorway to the safe house and looked down. Although he knew Jesse and Drew had just walked out of the flat, he couldn't help looking for an electronic beam that would trip an alarm. Of course there was nothing. Stepping inside, he saw the alarm keypad and nodded to himself. "Disarmed, *bien sur.*"

Saint-Savoy and Naim split up. The Frenchman went to one of Zafer's work tables; the Moroccan to the other. Saint-Savoy saw something—a note perhaps?—in the center of the table. He felt the transition from wood to carpet through the soles of his shoes. But there was something else. Something … had shifted. A loose bit of parquet?

He snatched the note off the table.

Take a good look around. It's the last thing you'll ever see.
Kind Regards,
Zafer

"Merde alors!"

Naim's head snapped around.

Raymond was still looking up when the third-floor windows blew out with a muffled explosion—the magnified *whoomf!* of a gasoline slick igniting. There were no flames, only a flash of hot orange, and no concussive blast, although shards of glass pelted the buildings across the street and fell in a tinkling rain on the sidewalk and parked cars.

Jesse ducked and covered her head with her arms.

Drew tucked his head as though he had a shell into which he could retreat.

Raymond's knees bent as he dropped into a crouch, but he kept his head up and protected his eyes with a forearm.

Drew didn't even see where the knife came from. He heard the blade whisper against leather and then felt the point under his jaw. Raymond had simultaneously underhooked Drew's right arm to keep him from pulling back.

Drew spoke through his teeth. It minimized the discomfort of talking with a blade under his jaw. "Incendiary bombs."

"Yes," Raymond hissed. "I recognize the sound."

"How could—?" Jesse looked up at the blown-out windows with a blank expression. "We were just up there."

"Booby-trapped his work table. Pressure mats under the parquet. Carpet on top. Five-second delay. We didn't go near the table. Sucks the oxygen out of the air. Didn't want the neighbors to go up with the fireworks." Drew couldn't keep back a smirk. "Even dead, Zafer's pretty dangerous."

"If there are any more surprises waiting for us, I will make sure you and Kadir join him."

10: 11

BENEATH THE CITY OF CONSTANTINE

It HAD OCCURRED TO THE OWNER of the Asia Minor Carpet Shop, Mehmet Bey, that a courtyard trimmed with shrubs and flowers would look much better than the parking lot behind his establishment. While workers set about breaking up asphalt and overturning chunks of earth, they discovered a large chamber with the look of antiquity about it. Curious, Mehmet Bey undertook the excavation at his own expense and uncovered a series of vaulted chambers that turned out to be a section of basement directly beneath the former throne room of Constantine the Great's palace. What was left of the complex of buildings collectively referred to as the Great Palace now took up some thirty subterranean blocks in the Sultanahmet quarter of Istanbul.

After Enrico Dandolo's Crusaders had pillaged the city, they filled the basement of the throne room with their spoils. Later, when the city fell to the Ottomans, the dank rooms were converted into a dungeon.

Drew, sitting in the backseat of a Renault next to Raymond, gave Jesse occasional directions to the Asia Minor Carpet Shop. Turning to Raymond, he asked, "So ... who's left?"

Raymond whipped an elbow into Drew's gut.

Air came out of him in a soft explosion.

Drew waited for his breathing to even out. "Let's see ... Hohenzollern's dead. Collins. Saint-Savoy. Miskovicz is in prison—couldn't afford his bail, huh Raymie?"

An elbow hammered Drew again.

"Don't call me that. Jan was too old to be of much use in the first place."

"That leaves you, Jesse, and ... is Gary still in the game? Or did that RPG sideline him?"

"You'll find out soon enough."

"Left at the light, Jesse, " he said it as if she were giving him a ride home.

Raymond's walkie-talkie phone chirped. "Taxi dropped us off. We're here."

American accent: Strahan.

"Wait behind the building. We will be there in a few minutes."

Driving past the Hagia Sophia, they entered a cobbled street lined by a haphazard assortment of picturesque buildings from another century and more modern, fairly nondescript edifices.

The Asia Minor Carpet Shop was closed for the night. The only pedestrian was an elderly Turk. Bent either by age or the bag he was carrying.

Bumping the car over the curb, Jesse parked it on a tilt, half in the street and half on the sidewalk—a decidedly Turkish move.

Strahan, whom Drew recognized from his photograph, stood in the courtyard with Kadir and a man Drew assumed to be an interpreter.

"N'aber, Kadir?" Drew asked. *What's going on?*

"Hershey harika." *Everything's wonderful.* He looked up at the American. "This donkey Ferhat takes care of me well. You?"

"Couldn't be better."

"Where now, Monsieur Korchula?" Raymond shoved Drew.

Drew, reestablishing his balance, lifted his chin to indicate the railing around the rectangular mouth of a stairwell.

"Here?" Raymond looked mistrustful. "There are no gates, no locks?"

Drew shook his head. "The government hasn't paid any attention, and Mehmet Bey doesn't seem to be interested in turning the site into a tourist attraction." Drew's hands were almost numb, and his mouth felt as though it were full of sawdust.

"Remember what I told you—any surprises and I'll keel you both. Then we'll just have to find the scroll without your help."

Drew could feel his pulse in his temples. "We have to go down."

"Why didn't you tell us we would need flashlights?"

"We don't."

Mehmet Bey, with whom Drew had conversed over several glasses of tea on more than one occasions had not only provided a staircase with an iron frame and carpentered, plywood steps, but also installed an electrical system equipped with floodlights. With Raymond a step behind, Drew flicked a switch. The darkness retreated to a few niches and corners below them.

They descended the stairway into a vaulted chamber. A bulb glowing against flat Roman brick showed marble blocks supporting an arch. Exposed roots dangled from one of the brick domes like a sparse beard. Plywood and planks did a half-assed job of covering holes in the rough floor. The chamber was large and more or less square. In the center was a massive brick pylon supporting the vaulted ceiling. Floodlights had been set up in two different places, but neither was lit. Wires wound up the walls like leafless, gray vines.

With his ghostly eyes and half of his face bandaged, Raymond looked like a resurrected corpse. Drew watched him profile the room, counting exits, estimating distances, memorizing the general layout. Zafer had tried to get Drew into the habit.

"Where's the scroll?"

Drew looked at his feet. There was a barely perceptible circle scratched into the stone flooring. "Pull away those loose stones." He pointed to a stack against the chambers south wall. "It's underneath."

Kadir started forward, but Raymond stopped him.

"No! Not you." He glanced at Jesse and tipped his head toward the wall. "You do eet." He waved Kadir away from the wall with a pistol elongated by a silencer.

Raymond positioned himself about a yard behind Drew, while Strahan, maybe ten feet away, was directly in front of him—just about blocking one of two gaping doorways that led to the rest of the palace ruins.

Kadir was next to Drew, but so was Ferhat. His weapon, also bearing a silencer, was inches from the top of Kadir's head.

Raymond let the aim of his pistol wander around the chamber. He stopped the gun when it was pointed at Kadir. "Eef the scroll is not there, the dwarf is dead."

"It's there."

The stones, neatly piled, were a few feet to one side of an unlit floodlight. A circuit-breaker box and a set of light switches were directly beneath it.

Jesse began pulling the stones away. They fell and cracked against the floor.

Drew's entire body now seemed to shudder with each heartbeat—so loud in his own ears he could barely hear anything else.

"I found it!" Jesse's voice was almost a squeal.

Drew flinched, his legs now as unsteady as his hands. He saw the same long box with snap latches that had been used for the Habakkuk Scroll.

Bending down, she grasped the box at either end and straightened up.

The force of the explosion left Jesse on her hands and knees.

After a final spurt of sparks from the destroyed circuit-breaker box, the darkness was complete. It was not the darkness of a cloudy night; this was the pure black of blindness.

Drew leapt to his right as though making a flying tackle. Tucking his shoulder, he rolled, a drill he'd done a thousand times on the wrestling mat. He bounced to his feet and put his hand out. Brick. He'd come up exactly where he'd hoped—within arm's length of the massive pylon in the center of the chamber. A stone in the patchwork floor had slammed against his tailbone, and it had gone numb with pain. He'd practiced this escape with his eyes closed dozens of times, but had always landed on the plywood.

Raymond began firing almost immediately, estimating where Kadir had been.

A scream laid itself over the sound of someone collapsing to the floor.

The silencer on Raymond's pistol cut down on the muzzle flash, but for a fraction of a second, Drew saw a phantasm of Raymond's face.

A few sentences of mangled English and Drew realized Raymond had shot Ferhat.

Someone scrambled along the western wall—Kadir.

Raymond fired again, but the bullet struck brick and ricocheted. Changing strategy, he jackhammered the bottom of the chamber's west wall with bullets. Shadows leaped and vanished in a strobe-light effect.

"*Kahretsin!*" *Damn it!*

Kadir's voice. Not a second later there was a muffled explosion—Kadir had hit a tripwire. A peculiar, burning odor overpowered the stink of gunpowder. Now, even with the muzzle flashes from Raymond's pistol, only coils of thick white smoke were visible.

The chamber became silent except for Ferhat's whimpering and Jesse crying. Between sobs she muttered, "My ears ... my ears." For a second Drew felt sorry for her.

"Shut up, Ferhat!" Raymond snarled. "I can't hear him!"

Drew knew exactly where he was in the chamber. What he didn't know was where Strahan had positioned himself. He was fairly certain Strahan wouldn't shoot; only Raymond was fanatical enough to fire with next-to-zero visibility. And if Strahan thought about it at all, he'd realize they might still need Drew alive. But there was nothing to stop him from clubbing Drew like a baby seal with the butt of his pistol—if he could see Drew.

Strahan's gun went off.

Shit! Drew had misjudged. By the yellowish flash of the discharged weapon, Drew saw that Strahan had aimed at the ceiling, for the illumination. But the silencer had reduced the burst of light to a candle being blown out as soon as it was lit. All it had really done was show Drew where Strahan was: still blocking the doorway but looking in the wrong direction. He didn't know where Kadir was.

Jesse continued crying, now about five feet in front of him.

Drew had to move, but Strahan had planted himself in front of the only doorway Drew felt confident he could find in the smoke and dark. He waited until Strahan fired his weapon again. The whine of a ricochet was followed by the sound of shattered brick hitting the floor. This time, Drew saw, Strahan had his back to the doorway and had taken a couple of steps east—Drew's left.

Taking two long strides, Drew dove, rolled, and let the momentum carry him to his feet. Taking a breath and forcing himself to believe he wouldn't run into a wall in the dark, he darted forward. He knew he'd crossed the threshold when his ankle caught the trip wire he'd set and pulled the pin on another smoke grenade.

Strahan's fired again, but Drew could see only billowing smoke briefly stained yellow. The muzzle flash looked as though it had been wrapped in gauze. But Strahan, who must have heard him flit past, had started in his direction.

"It's not here!" Jesse screamed. "There's just some kind of ... *book*!"

Drew smiled.

"Raymond!" It was Strahan's voice. "We need Korchula alive!"

"Then keel the fucking dwarf!" Raymond called back.

Drew hoped Kadir had disappeared into the maze of the ruined palace. With one hand on the wall just inside the doorway, Drew listened to Strahan's footsteps. His nose burned and he had to fight the urge to cough. Estimating that the larger man was nearly on top of him, Drew lowered his shoulder and launched himself. His shoulder rammed into Strahan's midriff, knocking the breath out of him with a loud *whuff!* Instead of grappling for his gun, Drew whirled and slipped deeper into Constantine's palace.

A wall now separated him from Raymond, who had just snapped a new clip into place. Drew shoved a hand into his pocket and pulled out the lighter he'd used in Antakya. He flicked it on for a second. The thin beam made a bright spot on the wall next to a doorway. Memorizing the position of the arched opening, he dashed through it.

He flicked the penlight on again and saw that he was in a small chamber with a doorway so low he had to double over to get through it.

He heard Raymond fire a single shot—probably for light. Drew stopped. Raymond was on the other side of the chamber's northern wall. Sweat broke out on Drew's forehead. If he kept moving forward and Raymond did the same, one or two turns later they would converge on the same corridor. But he couldn't turn around either. Strahan was behind him, slowly making his way forward. Drew could hear him choosing his steps carefully. The floor was uneven, boards and plywood sheets didn't entirely cover holes, and dropping into an uncovered cistern was a distinct possibility.

Drew waited. He tried to breathe without breathing. He was sure Raymond could hear the air rasping in his lungs, the heart thumping his chest, the acid percolating in his stomach.

"Gary!" Raymond's voice was as shrill as metal tearing under stress.

Blades of ice sliced through him; the Sicarii was directly opposite him on the other side of the wall.

Padding softly across boards, dirt, and exposed stone, Drew negotiated a zigzag of passages that finally brought him to a spacious chamber.

"*Buradayim.*" *I'm here.* Kadir's voice was a harsh whisper.

"We have to keep going west …"

"How we are knowing which fucking way is the west?" Kadir hissed.

"Follow me."

There was a half circle of an opening just large enough for them to crawl through. It was protected by an iron grate.

"Push! Hurry!"

The rusty grate squeaked open and Kadir crawled through. Dropping down on his stomach, Drew waddled elbow to elbow, his body imitating a lizard. He closed the tiny gate from the other side and shoved an iron rod through a set of iron loops. "That's it."

"But there is no lock."

"It ought to slow them down just enough." Drew flashed a circle of light on a box in a corner of the room. "Go get yourself a flashlight."

"*Cok akilli!*" Very clever! Digging through the box, Kadir's glee suddenly soured. "*Salak! Hich silah yok!*" Idiot! No weapons!

"I'm sorry, Kadir. No more guns."

"But they will kill to us!"

"No they won't." He had packed a pair of small flashlights, flares, two cell phones, and two cans of pepper spray. "I've got one more surprise for them."

"Already they are here." Kadir's voice was a barely audible whisper.

Drew heard the Sicarii in the adjacent chamber. He clicked off his penlight.

A cigarette lighter cast elongated shadows of the bars on the stone floor.

Crouching down, Drew approached the opening from an oblique angle.

Strahan looked up just in time to get hit by a jet of pepper spray. He fell back with a cry, and Drew sprinted out of the chamber.

Kadir was waiting for him in a corridor.

"This way!" Drew didn't slow.

The beams of their flashlights shuddered and jerked as they ran through the brick-and-marble undergirding of Constantine's city. Drew stopped to consult the floor where he'd left a barely perceptible arrow scratched in the floor. Drops of sweat splattered at his feet.

Kadir pointed. "Look … there is light."

Flickering crimson turned a small doorway into an infernal mouth.

"There's a stairway just ahead that leads up to the street."

The low arch was composed of flat bricks, edge-on and arrayed to suggest short, thick rays of light. Ducking down, Drew followed Kadir through what might have been a forgotten gate to hell.

They entered an enormous chamber lit by sizzling flares. Drew recognized a row of arched openings, each large enough to allow a chariot through, as entrances to the stalls where vendors had once sold to the crowds that had thronged Constantinople's hippodrome.

"You made it!" Nathan was grinning. "Both of you." Nathan's skin seemed a variety of stone in the ruddy light of the flares.

Josh was a few feet behind him, his face flushed crimson.

Both men were dressed in commando black.

The victory grin on Drew's face melted as Josh raised an automatic pistol, pulled the slide, and aimed it at the back of Nathan's head.

10: 12

TRIAL BY COMBAT

"DON'T TURN AROUND. Don't even inhale."

Zafer's warning rang in Drew's head: *How hard can it be to infiltrate a church?*

"I'm sorry, Nathan, but I don't have any choice. This scroll is more important than you ... me ... all of us."

Kadir hurled his flashlight. Even from about fifteen feet away, his aim was good enough to make Josh duck. The shot went astray.

Nathan whirled around with a back-fist.

Josh blocked it with his right arm, but the gun was also in his right hand.

Nathan's hand slid up toward Josh's wrist and locked on. Stepping around him, Nathan hammered his ribs. Still gripping his wrist, he pivoted and brought his left armpit down over Josh's right arm, trapping it. Twisting Josh's wrist and pressuring down on the elbow with his weight, he forced Josh to his knees with a cry. Twisting again, this time at the trunk, he extracted another groan of pain.

The pistol clattered to the floor.

Without releasing his hold, Nathan kicked the pistol away. "It's over, Josh."

"Not yet." Josh struggled to free himself, but Nathan cranked the hold tighter, and Josh's cheek smacked the floor.

"I'll break your elbow if I have to."

Josh's left hand came up with a can of pepper spray, but Nathan made good on his threat, bringing all of his weight to bear on the elbow.

Josh shrieked, and the can of pepper spray did a brief, end-to-end tap dance on the stone. Joshed writhed in pain.

"Drew! Kadir!"

Drew grabbed Josh below the knees and held down his legs. Kadir concentrated on the uninjured arm. Nathan, patting Josh down, came up with a wicked-looking knife and a tiny pistol.

Drew and Kadir let him go.

Josh lay on his back, his breathing racked, his ruined arm curled against his chest. "Too bad ... Nathan," he wheezed, his face half grimace, half maniacal grin. "You've got my weapons ..." His breathing was rapid and shallow. "But you can't ... use them."

"I can." Kadir, his short legs planted wide and his arms straight out, held the pistol Josh had dropped. He fired four times.

One of the bullets caught Josh under the jaw and destroyed the top of his skull.

"That is for Zafer."

Two more shots rang out. Kadir fell. Josh's pistol hit the floor with a metallic echo.

For the second time, Nathan did the unexpected. He fired twice with Josh's .25 automatic, hitting stone both times but forcing the shadowy assassin back into in the archway from which he had emerged.

"I see you have given up your Ebionite oath." The English was accented by French.

"I see you've never known the meaning of the word Christian," Nathan answered.

Drew sprinted to Kadir. A bullet had entered through his back and come out the chest. Drew stripped off his jacket and shirt. He covered the wound with his shirt and pressed down.

"Go ahead, Raymond ..." Drew called. "Shoot me! In two days the scroll will go to the Turkish Antiquities Police by courier, and a group e-mail will be sent out to every contact Professor Cutherton had. This city will look like it's holding another ecclesiastical council."

"Drew, you *can't*." Jesse's voice was a melancholy echo.

"Go ahead, kill us, and see what happens."

"You are bloofing."

"You think I'm bluffing?" Drew stood up, his bare torso unnaturally red in the light of the flare. "Go ahead, Raymie, *shoot*."

"*Drew!*"

Drew ignored Nathan, his eyes on the low doorway from which Raymond had shot Kadir. He thumped his chest with a fist. "Go ahead and shoot!"

"Dreeeeew! Get down!"

"Zafer's dead. Kadir's dying. I don't care anymore. As long as you lose, Raymond, I don't give a *fuck*." He hammered his chest again. "*C'mon!*" he snarled. "If there's a God, I have nothing to worry about. But *you*! You're going straight to hell!"

"Goddammit, Drew, get *down*!"

"*Un moment, mon ami*. Kadir can still be saved."

"You're right. I'm calling an ambulance." Drew reached into his pocket and dialed 112.

"Yes, call them," Raymond said soothingly. "They will never find us down here. You will have to bring him up. Call … and then we will settle this." He came out of the doorway with his hands up, his pistol pointed at the ceiling.

Drew finished with the Turkish dispatcher and put away the cell phone.

Raymond knelt down and put the pistol on the floor. He took out his knife and put it down next to the gun. He began to unbutton his shirt. He looked at Nathan. "I know you won't shoot an unarmed man."

"Kill him," Kadir whispered. "Kill him, Nathan."

"You and I, Ebionite, we will settle this. Trial by combat. We will let God decide. Eef I win, the scroll is ours. All of you go free. As God is my witness, I swear this. Eef you win, the scroll is yours, and still all of you go free. Either way, there is no more loss of life. Agreed?"

Drew shook his head. "I don't believe him."

"Why does no one shoot him?" Kadir moaned.

"Look." Raymond held his arms out, and pulled up the legs of his pants to show he had nothing hidden in his socks. "I am at your mercy. Nathan can kill me now if he chooses. Or you. You can pick up the pistol Kadir dropped eef the Ebionite doesn't have the nerve for killing. By my Lord and Savior, Jesus Christ, I swear, eef Nathan defeats me, we will let you go. It ees the old way. The honorable way. The champion of one army fights the champion of another. Slaughter is averted. The will of God is revealed."

"It is stupid way," Kadir coughed out.

Nathan worked his way out of the flak jacket he was wearing and peeled off a black pull-over.

The two men, stripped to the waist, approached each other warily, each in more or less a boxer's stance. Raymond's upper arm was bandaged, and ugly splotches defaced his left side.

They circled each other patiently, each trying to read something in the other's face or in the position of his body.

The Frenchman was taller by several inches, his muscles wire-taut, his pale torso without any visible fat. A long scar marred one pectoral.

Nathan was stockier, his muscles less defined, but his body equally trim.

Drew tore the cap off another flare and tossed it onto the floor.

Strahan, rubbing his swollen eyes and blinking rapidly, emerged from the arched doorway.

Drew grabbed Josh's pistol and aimed it at the Sicarii. "HANDS!"

Strahan complied. "I can't even see." He turned to Jesse. "Throw him your purse."

She tossed the leather bag over to him.

Drew opened it up and took out her Walther; it was right next to *Bastard Prince of T'orrh*. He reached around and tucked the weapon in the waistband of his pants.

"Okay?" Strahan asked. "Feel better? Now we're perfectly matched. You have a pistol, I have a pistol. Only mine is in its holster and yours is in your hand. And I can't see."

Drew nodded. "Losing side gives up its weapons. Agreed?"

Strahan rubbed an eye. "Agreed."

Drew kicked his shirt toward Jesse. "Would you mind using that to slow the bleeding?" He tipped his head toward Kadir.

Jesse picked up the shirt and knelt beside Kadir.

"*Gyavur*," he growled.

"I don't know that that means, but I know it isn't good." She folded Drew's shirt into a rough square and pressed down on the wound.

Raymond stepped in with a jab. Nathan slipped to the side and let go with a kick at Raymond's ribs. Raymond brought an elbow across his flank and blocked it.

A long leg whipped out so fast Drew almost missed it. Nathan stepped back and parried. Raymond pressed the attack and somehow one of his lashing kicks caught Nathan in the temple.

Drew had never seen anyone break through Nathan's defenses before.

Nathan rolled with the blow as Raymond followed up with an overhand right. Nathan evaded the punch, and countered with a hook that landed flush on Raymond's jaw. At close quarters now, Nathan followed with a palm heel. Raymond blocked the palm heel and launched his own. Nathan took it on a shoulder.

Then began a graceful choreography of short blows—palm heels, elbows, forearm chops, knee strikes—all of which were expertly blocked or slipped by both men. In the space of perhaps thirty seconds, Drew lost count.

It was a head-butt that split open the flesh just over Nathan's right eye.

Nathan was actually *bleeding*. Drew had come to think of him as invincible, but fear opened a vacuum that sucked at his stomach. Would he honor an oath made to murderers? To Zafer's killers? To fanatics who were going to bury the greatest biblical find in history? Was saving their three lives worth it?

Deal with the Devil and you become one yourself. Where had he heard that?

A rivulet of blood poured into Nathan's right eye, broke jaggedly, and streaked the side of his face.

Raymond took advantage of the handicap. Circling to that side, he threw most of his strikes with his singed left arm and left leg. A punch landed over Nathan's eye and droplets of blood lit by the flare flew like ruby chips.

Drew stared in disbelief. *I'm not giving up the scroll!* he swore silently. He wasn't handing over anything to Zafer's murderers. *You have to find a way to win, Nathan.* He tried to reach the ex-cop telepathically. *You have to.*

The two men were grappling now. They went down hard on the stone floor, but Raymond seemed to have taken the brunt of the fall. It was hard to see in the crimson light exactly what was happening, but Raymond had writhed out from underneath Nathan and was gaining leverage.

Nathan caught Raymond's ankle in the crook of a bent elbow, jammed a forearm into the knee, and torqued the leg violently.

Something snapped.

Raymond's shriek was chilling.

Nathan whipped an elbow into the Sicarii's face. The wet crunch Drew heard might have been Raymond's nose breaking.

Raymond rolled away in agony.

"It's over, Raymond."

Moaning piteously, Raymond flopped end over end, his eyes squeezed shut.

Drew breathed a sigh of relief. It wasn't until Raymond flipped over twice more—slowly, almost as if for dramatic effect—that Drew realized how close the Sicarii was to his pistol.

"*NATHAN!*" Drew raised the Glock.

Raymond sat up, pistol in his hand.

A series of shots rang out, and Raymond's chest exploded in four different places. He fell back with his arms wide.

Strahan stepped forward, his automatic still trained on Raymond. He kicked Raymond's 9 mm away and then, dropping to his knees, put his pistol on the floor and slid it over to Nathan. "Gary Strahan, ex-FBI." He laced the fingers of both hands behind his head. "I'm on your side."

"What the hell are you talking about?" Drew didn't lower the Glock.

"The Bureau has been keeping tabs on fanatical religious groups of all kinds since 9/11, but field work in Rome and Jerusalem is a little out of our jurisdiction. Especially if you try infiltrating churches instead of mosques. I resigned from the agency. I guess I'm what you'd call a free agent. The Knights of Malta hired me."

"Well you waited till the last fuckin' minute, didn't you?"

"Sorry, Drew. That's just how it worked out. Now if you don't mind, I'm outta here ... I'm not real big on the idea of being arrested in Turkey. Keep the Glock."

Drew motioned with the muzzle of the pistol for Strahan to get up. "You know the way out?"

"I'll manage."

Jesse was sobbing into her hands. "I'm so sorry ..." She was looking at Raymond's body. "I never meant ..." She looked up at Drew, her face bloodied by the flare. She coughed into another fit of crying.

"You're an accomplice, but you didn't shoot anybody."

"Yes I did." She nodded frantically. "I'm the one. I killed Cutherton."

10: 13

CONFESSIONS

"**N**O." DREW SHOOK HIS HEAD. "You couldn't have." His face felt as though it had been injected with Novocain.

"I shot him, Drew. *Me.*"

"I don't want to hear it." His mind was a tar pit, everything hopelessly mired in it. "I can't handle it right now. I *can't.*" He led the way up a flight of stone steps. "We're going to wait for the ambulance." He wore his jean jacket, but had no shirt on underneath.

"You're not so innocent either, Drew." Jesse followed him up the stairs. "You helped kill my mother. You and Cutherton."

"Not now, Jess." Drew kept climbing.

"Your smugness. That's why she was so unprofessional that day. You were so sure of yourself, she couldn't stand it. It should have been over when you graduated, but it wasn't. Do you remember a student in our class named Lisa? Lisa Dent?"

Drew didn't answer. At the top of the stairs was a modern door. Drew ran his fingers along the top of the lintel until he felt a key. He unlocked the door, pushed it open, and flipped a light switch. Fluorescent tubes overhead flickered sleepily in a corridor.

"The quiet type? Methodical, diligent?" Jesse was right behind him. "You inspired her."

Drew was surprised he had inspired anyone, but his face was still numb, expressionless.

"She spent the next two years digging up the lies of the saints, the deceptions of the Popes, the contradictions in the Bible, the flaws in my mother's books. It led to a much more serious incident. The university forced my mother into retirement."

"Lisa's at Stanford now."

"You knew?"

"I saw her byline once or twice. I didn't know about what happened with your mother."

Their footsteps echoed softly.

"Where the hell are we?"

"In the basement of a high school." Drew pointed to a window in a door. Desks in a state of disarray were visible through the glass.

Drew took Jesse's hand and led them up another staircase. They let go of each other's hand at the same time.

Drew leaned into the cross-bar of a steel door.

The night air carried a dry chill. They were in a square just west of the Blue Mosque. Drew strode briskly toward it. He didn't want to look at Jesse.

She trotted to keep up. "After my mother was forced into retirement, she spent most of her time finishing the book she'd been working on for nearly twenty years. Cutherton, I'm sure you know, ripped it apart in a review that amounted to a personal attack."

Drew whirled on her. "So you shot him?"

"No. The plan was just to get information out of him, but he was so … *smug*. Just like you. Raymond and Jean were holding guns on him, but he told them he was an old man, ready to die. He promised us there was already enough research being done to dispel the myth of a historical Christ. He was gloating. I have to admit, when Raymond backhanded him, I enjoyed it."

Drew wanted to backhand *her*.

"Cutherton staggered a few steps, and his mouth was bleeding, but he laughed. 'And your mother,' he said to me … 'what a silly, old cow'.

"I warned him not to talk about my mother. He wouldn't stop. 'Mediocre is being generous,' he said. 'A disgrace to the profession, really.' Then he wanted to know how a woman of my intelligence could have fallen for her pathetically contrived arguments."

They could hear the wail of the ambulance's siren.

"I told him to shut up. He sat there, calm as could be, wiping blood from his mouth and chuckling to himself. 'Treating the Gospels as history,' he said. 'But then, people believe exactly what they want to believe, don't they?' He shook his head and muttered, 'Silly old cow.'

"I couldn't stop myself. I took the Walther out of my purse and shot him. Once I pulled the trigger, it wasn't hard to squeeze it again. It was only after, when I looked at him on the floor, when he made those awful last noises—air came out of the *wounds*—that's when I realized what I'd actually done."

Drew closed his eyes so he didn't have to look at her. He tried to focus on his breathing.

"Drew ..."

He didn't open his eyes.

"I'm so sorry."

She murdered him for being *right* and then stole the last thing he'd written.

"I am truly ... deeply ... *sorry*."

Drew finally looked at her.

Jesse's eyes crinkled at the corners, and she began to cry.

The siren was close now, a block or two away.

She put her arms around him.

Drew's arms lay dead at his sides as though the nerves had been cut. He thought of Epictetus. Socrates. Jesus.

Love the man flogging you like a donkey as though he were your father or brother.

If an enemy strikes you, turn the other cheek.

It is never just to repay injury with injury.

It didn't matter who had said what. He put his arms around Jesse and hugged her back.

She pressed her face into his shoulder. "They're going to put me in a prison now, aren't they?"

"What good would that do?"

She lifted her face to him.

"The best thing about Christianity is you get a chance to redeem yourself."

She shook her head. "How could I possibly...?"

"Stephen's manuscript. Finish it. See it through to publication."

Her face flushed luminous crimson; the ambulance had arrived.

"But I ... I *can't*. It goes against everything I believe." Her features were submerged in shadow again as the light rotated away from them.

Drew pushed her away gently. Kadir's life might depend on a few extra seconds. "Did someone tell you redemption was going to be easy?"

He took off at a sprint.

BOOK II: 1

ISTANBUL

To see a world in a grain of sand,
And a heaven in a wild flower,
Hold infinity in the palm of your hand,
And eternity in an hour.
— William Blake

ll: 1

WITHOUT AMBASSADOR

GARY STRAHAN SIPPED Turkish coffee. "It's not over yet."
The waiter had already cleared their dinner plates.
Drew squeezed Yasemin's hand. "We've been talking about that."
"What you have been talking about?"
It had been nearly a year since Kadir had been rushed to the hospital,
and the scroll, Sayings of the Savior, had been turned over to the Turkish
authorities, who, with much ceremony, presented it to a joint Egyptian-
Israeli delegation. Legally the scroll belonged to Egypt, but the Egyptians
were more than willing to allow Israeli scholars to study it.
Kadir was now sitting across from Drew in a restaurant near the top
of Galata Tower. Nathan sat next to him. A window set in a curving wall
nearly a yard thick afforded a spectacular view of the Bosporous, the Sea
of Marmara, and the Golden Horn. Dark mirrors, the waters reflected
the city's glow and the moving lights of the boats gliding over them.
Sayings of the Savior had been pronounced genuine by a consensus
of scholars, and its age had been estimated by radiocarbon dating, which
fixed the year the papyrus and its leather sheath had been sealed away
in a limestone box at 65 BC, plus or minus about half a century. The
remaining contents of the tomb in which the two artifacts had been
found corroborated that date. The margin for error, however, meant that
the scroll *could* have been written as early as 115 BC or as late as 15
AD—or, if the dating was just a shade off, 25 or 30 AD. But it was

highly improbable that this was the earliest copy; the compilation was almost certainly much older. Nonetheless, standing on this precarious ledge of possibility, traditionalists insisted "the Savior" mentioned in the scroll was none other than Jesus of Nazareth. They hypothesized that the scroll author had deliberately chosen not to identify the Savior by name and had—equally inexplicably—merely *claimed* to be Eleazar, grandson of Jesus ben Sirach. Pseudepigrapha, after all, were common enough in that era.

A number of scholars vociferously objected. What was astonishing, however, was how many scholars either supported the pseudepigraph theory or advanced others, just as unlikely, that protected the integrity of the Gospels. One PhD pointed out that radiocarbon labs only fixed the date at which the papyrus plants and the goat (whose hide had furnished the leather) had died. It was possible, he argued, that a scribe had used materials nearly a century old to compile the sayings. While several scholars had ridiculed this explanation, others had written articles upholding its plausibility.

Interviews conducted with the guy or gal on the street followed the same pattern. As Stephen could have predicted, most people—a few gloating atheists aside—went on believing what they wanted to believe.

Six months ago, Kadir had been the best man at Drew and Yasemin's second wedding. Nathan, dressed in a tuxedo, had also been among the guests. At Drew's insistence, a set of wedding pictures was taken while Kadir or he held a framed photograph of Zafer.

Yasemin had been off Paxil since the wedding, and no border clashes had ensued, but Drew had taken up counseling for his rage issues. He still sometimes got the urge to hang up on his father and occasionally looked around the room for something to break when things were tense, but so far had managed to get out the door without throwing a furniture-breaking tantrum. Yasemin couldn't accuse him of refusing to confront their problems since his therapist said "cooling down," by removing himself from the situation, was a singularly effective strategy for preventing destructive behavior. Besides, he still had to confront them when he got back.

A month or so before the wedding, Drew had seen Stephen's book off to a publisher in London. He was surprised, despite having used the professor's keywords as points of departure, at how radically some of his conclusions differed from Stephen's. Stephen had made extensive use of the Old Testament, meticulously demonstrating how earlier scripture had inspired the vast majority of incidents in the Gospels. On the other hand, although Stephen had noted similarities between Jesus, John the Baptist, and James the Just, he had not proposed a composite Christ.

Turkey, reaching an agreement with the Brits, had handed Jesse over to them for her role in Stephen's death. Thanks to Gary, who, pressured by Drew, had pinned the shooting on Jean Saint-Savoy, she had been cleared of murder charges but, as part of an agreement with the prosecution, had pleaded guilty to lesser charges. Ordered to serve at least two years of a five-year sentence, she had written an introduction to Stephen's book in her cell and, drawing on Sayings of the Savior, composed extensive footnotes throughout the text that substantially reinforced his thesis. Drew had sent a copy to Stanford University along with a letter addressed to Lisa Dent. Lisa, as terse on paper as she was in person, had written a few sentences back and eventually put together an eloquent review for *The Los Angeles Times*.

Gary had narrowly escaped jail time himself. While no one doubted he had not intended to perpetrate any of the crimes that had been committed in pursuit of the two scrolls, he had not been affiliated with any police enforcement agency and had technically been an accomplice. Only the intervention of his former employer, the FBI, which negotiated a closed-doors deal with the Turks and the Brits, had kept him out of prison. Part of the deal barred him from entering the UK for five years.

Since the scrolls had been returned to the Egyptians and Israelis, government prosecutors hadn't locked up Drew or Kadir on smuggling charges, but Drew had spent thousands on a lawyer who had petitioned the Turkish courts to allow him to stay in the country.

Kadir looked at Gary. "What is not being over?"

"Right now everything's calm ... the director of the Ecole Biblique took responsibility for Raymond and his crew—Jan was the only one who actually worked there—but he's a fall guy. The Sicarii are supposedly dissolved, but you might as well expect the Pope to change his mind about contraception and start handing out free condoms. What if they decide to sink that boat you keep down in Kash? With you on it?" He glanced at Drew and Yasemin. "What if they decide those two will have a little car accident? Maybe a year from now, maybe ten years from now."

"We've thought about that," Drew said.

"I can get you into the witness protection program ..."

Drew shook his head. "She'd never be able to see her family again, and we don't want to spend the rest of our lives in hiding."

"What about you?" Yasemin asked. "Aren't you a target?"

"I'm going back to the Bureau. I'll be pretty well protected." He looked over at Kadir. "Ever think about relocating to the US?"

Kadir shook his head. "My home is the Turkey. Here I will die."

"A little sooner than you think if you're not careful."

"Don't worry for me. I am be careful."

Gary grinned at Nathan. "I guess I don't even have to ask you."

"It wouldn't look good for the Ebionite Church if I just disappeared. Between the money Kadir gave us, and the donations we attracted because of the publicity, all of the sudden we're not so poor. I'd like to have a say in how the money is spent. For the first time in our history, we might be the most credible church Christians have."

No one at the table but Drew was aware of the irony: Nathan was an atheist.

Gary aimed a thick finger at the ex-cop. "Now you've touched on *my* problem. I'm not ready to let go of Jesus. I mean, I was raised Catholic, and maybe I didn't swallow everything the Church was spooning out, but Jesus was my savior. What the hell am I supposed to do now?"

"Why don't you become a Muslim?" Yasemin reached across the table and squeezed his hand.

"My wife would love that."

"Look, Gary," Drew said, "even before Plato, philosophers poked fun at worshipers who took stories about the gods literally."

"I got that part ... but how am I supposed to *live* with it?"

Drew glanced out the window and saw an enormous freighter—a tiny island dotted with light—headed for the open space of the Sea of Marmara. He turned back to Gary. "By realizing the message is more important than the messenger. It doesn't matter who said turn the other cheek—Socrates, a Cynic, a wandering Jewish preacher. That was half of Christianity's mistake ... the Church deified the messenger and mostly ignored the message."

"What was the other half?"

"Mistaking the symbolic for the historical."

Gary, letting out air between his teeth, sounded like a tire going flat. "That's it? That's all you got for me?"

Drew shrugged.

"What about you?" He lifted his chin toward Drew. "You used to be a Christian. How you handling it?"

Drew thought for a second. "Plato actually hated the idea of books because they always say the same thing in the exact same way. And they don't answer questions. He wasn't entirely off. I mean, any particular book is open to all kinds of spin. That's a huge drawback for revealed religions. Who decides which one is right? We're still fighting wars over that sort of thing."

"So what's the alternative?"

Drew sipped his coffee. "Dump the books."

Yasemin glared at him. "Did you really just say that?"

"They're a map maybe," Drew said, "but not the territory. Remember the Transcendentalists? Theodore Parker? Emerson? *It is by yourself, without ambassador, that God speaks to you.* That was the original function of Jesus, of the Logos—to be an intermediary. Emerson scrapped the idea. *Dare to love God without mediator or veil,* he said. You find God in yourself, in your relationship to the world, not in a sacred book or even in a religious leader. *It is God in you that responds to God without.*"

Gary waffled a hand. "I don't know. Sounds a little New Agey."

"You're clinging to an authority figure. Parker said—and this is weird, because I must have read this years ago, but I totally forgot it—he said even if Jesus had never lived, Christianity would be as solid as ever."

"How does he figure that?"

"He insisted the truths of Christianity shouldn't rest on the personal authority of Jesus any more than the axioms of geometry should rest on the personal authority of Euclid."

Kadir screeched—no, that was his laugh.

Yasemin told him in Turkish he was being rude.

"The man's having a crisis of faith here," Drew chided.

"I *am.*" Gary looked around the table. "I admit, I never read much of the Bible. I just listened to what they told me in church. Now, I don't know what to think."

"How many Christians actually *have* read the Bible? Or even the New

Testament? And how many of those who've read it have understood it? I mean ... *two thousand pigs?* Who knew a simple exorcism was so loaded down with meaning? What's worse, without being immersed in the Levant of the first century, which is pretty much impossible, we *can't* understand it. Not completely. That world is gone."

Gary turned his palms up. "So we're right back where we started ..."

Drew nodded. "Sort of. It really is hard without the mediator. We *want* a face. We *want* a name. We *want* something cut down to human size—not a booming voice from the clouds. We want Jesus of Nazareth."

"Or James the Just," Nathan said.

"Or Muhammad," Kadir added.

"Or Buddha," Yasemin agreed.

Gary pushed his coffee cup toward the center of the table. "So are you a Transcendentalist or an Ebionite or a Buddhist or what?"

Drew lifted an eyebrow, tilted his head, and gave a little shrug. "Maybe I've gotten past labels."

"Oh yeah?" Gary smirked. "So where does God fit into the world according to Drew?"

Drew drained his coffee to the silt at the bottom of the tiny cup. "I like the idea of the Mystery cults. I like the idea of bringing worshipers face to face with ... I'm afraid to say God because I don't think God is any more recognizable than an electron cloud. And I think it's time we admitted our ignorance. We barely understand *this* world, how are we supposed to know anything about what's beyond it?"

Gary leaned back and sighed. "Got a point there."

"As far as I'm concerned, it's about personal enlightenment, personal revelation. Not something you're going to impose on everyone else. Except maybe as a poem or a painting, a blog post, or whatever. If you plug into the Oversoul as Emerson called it, you can find divinity just about anywhere—a stone, a weed, a landscape. Maybe that's *how* you plug into the Oversoul, by recognizing that every atom belonging to you is part of everything else. It's not New Age, it's an older age. The Lascaux artists saw the world this way. So did the Native Americans. When's the last time something brought you nose to nose with the Creator? I bet it wasn't a sermon."

"I get where you're coming from," Gary said, "but that's still a little fuzzy for me."

Looking out the window, Drew watched the freighter, a receding glow on the inky sea, continue toward a horizon invisible in the dark distance. It *was* fuzzy, indistinct. We didn't get certainties—no matter how much we wanted them—we got possibilities. Probabilities. The kind that mystified philosophers and stumped quantum physicists.

Of all the televised street interviews Drew had seen, he kept coming back to one with a middle-aged woman—a lawyer or maybe an executive. Her face serious, her movements clipped, confident. A reporter asked her what she thought about the possibility Jesus of Nazareth had never existed and pushed a microphone in her face. "I don't care if Jesus was a real person or not." She whirled around, long hair whipping past the reporter's face, and stalked off. Unexpectedly, she turned to add, "He'll always live in my heart."

Where he's been, Drew thought, *from the beginning.*

HISTORICAL TIMELINE BC

198 Judea comes under the control of the Seleucids, the Greek dynasty established in Syria after the death of Alexander the Great.

167-164 Judas the Maccabee (Judas the Hammer) leads a successful revolt against the Seleucid King, Antiochus IV. The Temple is rededicated (an event commemorated by Hanukkah) and the Hasmonean Dynasty is established.

Late 2nd Century The Essene community at Khirbet Qumran is established as a protest against the Hasmoneans, who took over the office of High Priest, which the Essenes demanded go to a Zadokite, that is, a descendent of Zadok, grandson of Aaron and grandnephew of Moses. Zadok served as the first High Priest in the First Temple built by Solomon.

67-63 Civil war breaks out with two Hasmonean brothers vying for power. King Hyrcanus II and Aristobulus II, the High Priest, lead the opposing sides. Each brother appeals to foreign powers, such as the Greeks and Parthians, to intervene on his behalf. Both eventually turn to the Roman general Pompey, who has just conquered Seleucid Syria, and while he ends the war and settles the dispute, Jewish independence is gradually lost to Rome.

40 The Roman senate proclaims Herod king of Judea, effectively ending the Hasmonean struggle to regain power.

6 Extrapolating from Matthew, Jesus of Nazareth is born about two years before the death of Herod in 4 BC.

4 King Herod dies and Judas of Galilee initiates a local revolt.

AD

6	Judea is placed under a Roman prefect and, at the order of Rome, Quirinius conducts a census for tax purposes, which Luke later mentions as coinciding with the birth of Jesus of Nazareth. Judas of Galilee re-emerges and leads a revolt to protest the new Roman taxes.
26-36	Pontius Pilate rules Judea as prefect.
30	Most scholars think the Crucifixion took place in 30 AD.
48-60	The Apostle Paul composes his letters.
66-74	The Jews rise up as a nation and revolt against Rome.
68	The Essene community at Qumran is destroyed, and the Essenes are likely annihilated in the battles against Rome.
70	The Romans capture Jerusalem, and the Roman general Titus orders the destruction of the Second Temple.
75-85	The Gospel of Mark is composed by an unknown author and circulates unsigned.
85-95	The Gospel of Matthew is composed by an unknown author and circulates unsigned.
90-110	The Gospel of Luke and Acts of the Apostles are composed by the same unknown author and circulate unsigned.
95-120	The Gospel of John is composed by an unknown author and circulates unsigned.

HISTORICAL FIGURES

Pythagoras of Samos (c. 570–495 BC) — A mathematician and philosopher, he was also founder of a Mysteries cult and was commonly held to be the son of Apollo and a mortal virgin. According to Iamblichus, he spent twenty-two years in Egypt as a student of the Osiran Mysteries and performed any number of miracles, including calming the waves of rivers and seas in order that his disciples might the more easily pass over them.

King Jannai, Alexander Jannaeus — a Hasmonean king who ruled Judea from about 104 to 78 BC. The Pharisees, furious that the Hasmoneans had usurped the office of high priest, rebelled against him in 94 BC. After six years of civil war, Jannai won decisively and exacted revenge by crucifying eight hundred Pharisees. Part of their torture was to watch soldiers slash the throats of their wives and children.

Jesus Panthera, Yeshu Pandera or Pantera — Put to death during the reign of King Jannai, Yeshu ben Panthera was allegedly the best student of Yehoshua ben Perachiah, with whom he had fled to Egypt to escape Jannai's persecution of the Pharisees. He is mentioned only in the Talmud, and there is great confusion and disagreement as to exactly which passages refer to him and what is actually said about him. It is generally believed that he learned magic in Egypt, became a religious teacher, and attracted five disciples. He was stoned to death as a sorcerer on the eve of Passover.

Judas of Galilee, Judas the Galilean — In 4 BC, after the death of Herod the Great, a Zealot named Judas attacked Sepphoris, a wealthy, cosmopolitan city in Galilee. He and his followers broke into the armory and began a revolt against the Roman-backed rule of Herod's descendants.

Some scholars (with whom I agree) believe this was the first time Judas of Galilee rebelled against Roman rule. His better-known regional uprising against Roman rule took place in 6 AD. He also founded Josephus's fourth sect, the Zealots, as well as the Sicarii—Zealots who functioned as assassins. They are named after the small daggers, or sicae, they kept concealed under their clothing. Judas, mentioned in Acts 5:37, is thought to have died at Roman hands although Josephus never says how he was killed.

Philo of Alexandria, Philo Judaeus (25BC – 50 AD) — A Hellenized Jew who interpreted Jewish scripture allegorically and attempted to harmonize Greek philosophy with Jewish philosophy. He believed that a literal reading of the Old Testament would severely limit humanity's understanding of God. His concept of the Logos as the personification of God's wisdom had a clear influence on Christian thought. He also believed that Moses (as well as the prophet Jeremiah) was a hierophant (a high priest of the Mysteries) and that Judaism was a Mystery religion. A prolific writer, he was a well-known commentator on Judaism and other religions.

Seneca (4 BC – AD 65) — An exact contemporary of Jesus, he was a Roman statesman, Stoic philosopher, and tragedian. He was also advisor to the emperor Nero. His elder brother, Gallio, is mentioned in Acts.

Josephus (38–107 AD)—Born Joseph ben Matityahu, Josephus authored *Antiquities of the Jews* and *The Jewish War*, two books that remain scholars' greatest source of information about 1st century Palestine. Originally a Zealot who fought the Romans, he later embraced the Roman general (Flavius) Vespasian as the Messiah and is now known by his Roman name, (Flavius) Josephus.

Simon Bar Giora — Although he was of peasant stock, Simon's skill with a sword and natural gift for leadership eventually brought an army of 40,000 under his command. According to Josephus, Simon entered Jerusalem in 69 AD as a savior and a preserver. He reigned as king, had coins struck with the motto Redemption of Zion, and was thought by many to be the Messiah. When Jerusalem fell to the Romans, however, he was captured, sent to Rome, publicly tortured, and executed.

Ananus — A Sadducee, he held the office of high priest for only three months, but in that time committed his most memorable act and brought James the Just before the Sanhedrin; James was subsequently stoned to death. In 68 AD, during the First Jewish Uprising against Rome, Ananus sided with the Romans and was killed by Edomites, with whom the Zealots had allied themselves.

Ebionites — Their name is derived from the Hebrew word *ebyonim* or *ebionim*, meaning "the poor" or "the poor ones." They were early Christians who observed Jewish law. Although they considered Jesus to be the Messiah, they did not believe he was the son of God. Of the four Gospels, they considered only Matthew to be valid. They revered James the Just, and rejected Paul as an apostate in violation of the Law. According to Gibbon, "Although some traces of that obsolete sect may be discovered as late as the fourth century, they insensibly melted away either into the church or the synagogue."

Papias (c. 70–140) — Bishop of Hieropolis in Asia Minor (Pamukkale in modern-day Turkey), Papias claimed that Matthew's Gospel was originally written in "Hebraic dialect" (probably Aramaic). Very little is known about him although he is said to have compiled *Expositions of the Sayings of the Lord* in five books, all of which have been lost. Only fragments survive.

Saint Justin Martyr (100–165) — A Christian apologist born of pagan parents, he considered himself a Platonist until a conversation with an elderly man convinced him to convert. He eventually founded a school in Rome, where he was denounced as a Christian and, after refusing to sacrifice to the gods, beheaded according to Roman law. Most of his writings are now lost, but two apologies and his most famous work, *Dialogue With Trypho*, have survived.

Saint Hegesippus (c. 110–180) — A Christian convert from Judaism, he was a historian of the Church who wrote prolifically. His entire body of work, however, has been lost with the exception of eight passages recounting Church history as quoted by Eusebius.

Clement of Alexandria (c. 150–215) — Born in Athens to pagan parents, he converted to Christianity and, after travelling the world, settled in Alexandria, Egypt, where in 190 he became head of the Catechetical School of Alexandria.

Saint Origen (184–254 AD) — Born in Alexandria, Egypt, he became a pupil of Clement of Alexandria. He later founded a school in Caesarea and in his numerous commentaries on the Bible advocated for symbolic and allegorical readings of scripture rather than literal readings.

Eusebius of Caesarea (260 – 340 AD) — Often referred to as the Father of Church History, he studied in the school established by Origen in Caesarea and in 314 became bishop of Caesarea. While his most important book is *The History of the Church*, Eusebius is known to have been a fanatical defender of Christianity and is often unreliable.

Muhammad the Wolf (Muhammad adh-Dhib) – Bedouin shepherd who accidentally discovered the Dead Sea Scrolls in caves along the shore of the Dead Sea in 1947.

John Allegro – Born in London, England in 1923, John Allegro was the only scholar on Father de Vaux's international team who was not a Catholic. He was often at odds with other team members studying the Dead Sea Scrolls.

Father Roland de Vaux - Director of the Ecole Biblique et Archeologique, a Dominican school based in Jerusalem. Deeply conservative, both religiously and politically as well as reputedly anti-Semitic, he grew up in France and ultimately led the international team that studied a trove of Dead Sea Scroll fragments found in Cave 4 in 1952.

A NOTE ON THE PRONUNCIATION
OF TURKISH WORDS

A note on the Turkish words in this novel: I chose to use phonetic spellings (and the English alphabet) rather than to spell the words according to the Turkish alphabet because I wanted to make the words easier for readers to pronounce. The Turks use a Latinized alphabet, but there are significant differences. The Turkish "c," for example, is pronounced like the English "j." I could have put in a pronunciation key, but in my experience, readers rarely refer to such keys and simply pronounce the words according to the spelling they see. So "uncle" in Turkish, which is spelled "amca," is actually pronounced "omm-jah," but without referring to a phonetic key, most readers would simply read it as "omm-kah." Purists made not agree with my decision, but I think the vast majority of readers will.

AFTERWORD:

MYTHICISTS AND HISTORICISTS

You shall no longer take things at second or third hand,
nor look through the eyes of the dead,
nor feed on the spectres in books,
You shall not look through my eyes either,
nor take things from me,
You shall listen to all sides and filter them from your self.
— Walt Whitman

In 1596 a cobbler was brought before a tribunal in Amsterdam on charges of heresy. In spite of his blue-collar background, the shoemaker had taught himself Latin and Hebrew in order to bypass the Dutch clergy and make his own study of the Bible. The incident is recounted in *Still Life With a Bridle*, Zbigniew Herbert's lyrical and brilliantly observed essay collection. (Do buy the book to see how it all turned out.)

Our ambitious shoemaker was a Historicist; that is, he believed in a flesh-and-blood Jesus of Nazareth, albeit one thoroughly demoted from his status as the Son of God.

Thomas Paine, on the other hand, the most famous pen-wielder of the American Revolution, was a Mythicist. In part III, section 4 of The Age of Reason, he wrote:

These repeated forgeries and falsifications create a well-founded suspicion, that all the cases spoken of concerning the person called Jesus Christ are made cases, on purpose to lug in, and that very clumsily, some

broken sentences from the Old Testament, and apply them as prophecies
of those cases; and that so far from his being the Son of God, he did not
exist even as a man — that he is merely an imaginary or allegorical
character, as Apollo, Hercules, Jupiter, and all the deities of antiquity
were. There is no history written at the time Jesus Christ is said to have
lived that speaks of the existence of such a person, even as a man.

In other words, Paine believed Jesus of Nazareth was entirely a fiction.
(*The Age of Reason*, incidentally, published in three parts between 1794
and 1807, became a bestseller.)

Clearly the idea that Jesus never existed isn't new. What is new is
that the idea is gaining currency. So much so that renowned biblical
scholar Bart Ehrman felt the need to pen, or rather key (who writes
without a keyboard anymore?), a book called *Did Jesus Exist?*, which (no
doubt deliberately) shares the title of a book by GA Wells, a scholar
among the contemporary Mythicists Ehrman attempts to refute. (Wells,
it should be noted, has somewhat modified his position since presenting
his original thesis.)

If you read Ehrman's book without the benefit of having made
some sort of in-depth study—formal or otherwise—of the Bible, or if
you fail to give equal attention to the counterarguments of those who
have, Ehrman's case seems persuasive. It is rather convincingly refuted,
however, in *Bart Ehrman and the Quest of the Historical Jesus* (another play
on titles; this time the allusion is to Albert Schweitzer's *The Quest of the
Historical Jesus*, first published in 1906 in German). In this collection of
essays, Frank Zindler, Richard Carrier, and Earl Doherty, among others,
take Ehrman thoroughly to task, highlighting some rather unscholarly
mistakes and some that are downright embarrassing.

My own awakening to the possibility that Jesus of Nazareth probably
never walked the Earth began with Timothy Freke and Peter Gandy's
book *The Jesus Mysteries*. I knew virtually nothing about the Mystery
religions before Garrett Gilmore, an American ex-pat living in Istanbul,
loaned me his copy. I read it with great interest although even as I did so,
I saw numerous signs that Gandy and Freke were fudging the evidence
... skewing translations, lumping Mysteries gods together to make it
easier on the reader, adding too much paint-thinner to their pigments.
Nonetheless, there was plenty of material in the book to raise serious
doubts in my mind about whether Jesus had been an actual man.

I went on to read Samuel Angus's 1925 classic, *The Mystery-Religions, A Study in the Religious Background of Early Christianity* and Walter Burkert's *Greek Religion*. Having already read *The Golden Bough* (a reprint of the two-volume, 1890 edition), Joseph Campbell's *Occidental Mythology*, as well as other books dealing with the evolution of mythologies and religions, it became obvious that the dying-rising aspects of Jesus had been borrowed from much older Mystery cults.

Despite the fact that my father, the late Robert E. Czyz, Sr., was an atheist and had raised his children as atheists, I was firmly in the camp of the Historicists—until reading *The Jesus Mysteries*. I wasn't, however, quite convinced. The two scholars whose works led me to defect to the Mythicist camp are Robert Price and Earl Doherty (Doherty is a classicist, and while he does not have a PhD, his cogent arguments and command of logic more than make up for the absence of post-surname letter clusters). Price's *Deconstructing Jesus* and *The Incredible Shrinking Son of Man* were nothing short of revelatory, as was Doherty's *The Jesus Puzzle*.

Around 2006, while living in Istanbul, I was browsing the Internet for books about the Dead Sea Scrolls (I knew even less about them than I had about the Mysteries) and came across a number of provocative observations made by John Allegro, several of which found their way into the novel. Like my protagonist, I made frequent trips to Istanbul's Market of Second-Hand Booksellers, and on one of these trips I came across Robert Eisenman's *James, the Brother of Jesus*. I found Eisenman's interpretation of the Qumran legacy persuasive although I'm well aware many scholars (Ehrman among them) disagree with Eisenman's conclusions. I'm also indebted to Mr. Eisenman for his interpretation of the written material, biblical and otherwise, relating to James the Just.

Another book that shaped my view of Christianity and early Christian history is Helmut Koester's *Ancient Christian Gospels*. While Koester is a Historicist, he is an objective observer, and his book perforce contains material that seriously challenges the Gospel portrayals of Jesus. I should also mention Frank Zindler's four-volume collection *Through Atheist Eyes*, which, though I came upon it only recently and have read very incompletely, has confirmed much of what I have come to believe and furnished a number of compelling details that add a little more resolution to the overall mosaic.

For those who cling to Ehrman's thesis that there was a historical figure known as Jesus of Nazareth, Ehrman himself has rather disturbing news: Jesus of Nazareth was neither divine nor "the suffering Messiah." In *Jesus Interrupted*, he points out that both of these concepts are Christian inventions. In other words, the most ardent defender of the historical Jesus categorically denies both Jesus' divinity and a literal reading of the Gospels. Robert Price, an avowed Mythicist, sometimes avers that maybe, possibly, there is some shadowy likeness of Jesus to be found in the first century, but once we strip away the falsehoods and deliberate fictions, there is so little left, nothing definitive can be said about him.

A novel such as *The Christos Mosaic* necessarily depends on the work of scholars whose works, in turn, depend on the work of still other scholars. While I've acknowledged my intellectual debt to scholars and authors who have scrutinized scripture (above), there are two other writers whose books were vital to my research: Peter Watson, author of *The Medici Conspiracy*, and Roger Atwood, author of *Stealing the Past*. Both books discuss in disturbing detail the unmitigated cultural disaster known as the black market for antiquities and both are engrossing if dismaying reads.

Frank Zindler, a polymath and tireless researcher no matter the field, mentions somewhere among his numerous essays that he has seen one paradigm shift (continental drift was a radical idea when first introduced), and he would like to see another in his lifetime: the recognition that Jesus of Nazareth is as much a mythical figure as Osiris or Dionysus.

I'm somewhat less ambitious. I hope this novel will lead readers to do their own research (like our cobbler) and perhaps heed Emerson's exhortation to establish "an original relation to the universe." It's time to admit that Jesus—in the absolute best-case scenario—was merely a man, and a man of his time at that—not the Son of God (a rather odd concept to begin with, as if God would need to procreate, an act that would belie His perfection since He should be able to accomplish whatever He wills without a son, a holy spirit, or any other helpmeet), not a prophet (Jesus didn't even predict the discovery of the two continents where he'd eventually have more followers than anywhere else), not even terribly original. It is time to stop looking outside ourselves for a savior and start doing the work on our own. We don't need superpowers or magic despite the films breaking box-office records by pandering to this savior complex. Whatever your perspective happens to be—Historicist, Mythicist, agnostic, Muslim, Jew, atheist, or something else—I think Professor Cutherton's dictum applies: the unexamined faith is not worth believing.

ACKNOWLEDGEMENTS

I would like to thank a number of people who helped me over a period of years with this novel. Garrett Gilmore, Barry Leach, Bernadette Wroblak, and Jeffrey Kahrs read the manuscript in its earliest incarnation. Among this group I'd like to single out Bernadette for her extensive commentary and Jeff, in addition to his commentary, for introducing me to the antiquities black market in Istanbul. I would also like to thank Perry Jones for his motorcycle expertise. The most thorough reader of the novel in its early phase was Anne Marie Monzione, and I am indebted to her for her incisive critique as well as her editorial suggestions.

The person who most helped shape the final version of this manuscript is my editor, Kristy Makansi. She made meticulous cuts, excellent word choices, and critical suggestions, particularly in terms of character development. I would also like to express gratitude to my agent, Carolyn Jenks, for her patience, persistence, and wisdom in guiding this book to publication. Finally, I'd like to acknowledge my wife, Neslihan, who was on hand when I conceived this novel, accompanied me to many of the sites I researched, and supported me through to its completion.

ABOUT THE AUTHOR

VINCENT CZYZ received an MA in comparative literature from Columbia University, and an MFA in creative writing from Rutgers University. He is the author of the collection *Adrift in a Vanishing City*, and is the recipient of the 1994 Faulkner-Wisdom Prize for Short Fiction and two fellowships from the NJ Council on the Arts. The 2011 Truman Capote Fellow at Rutgers University, his short stories and essays have appeared in *Shenandoah*, *AGNI*, *The Massachusetts Review*, *Tampa Review*, *Quiddity*, *Louisiana Literature*, *Logos Journal*, *New England Review*, *Boston Review*, *Sports Illustrated*, *Poets & Writers*, and many other publications. Although he has traveled the world and spent some ten years in Istanbul, Turkey, he now lives and works in New Jersey, where he was born.

CPSIA information can be obtained
at www.ICGtesting.com
Printed in the USA
LVOW12s0842181016

509173LV00005B/7/P